A NEW HISTORY OF THE FUTURE IN 100 OBJECTS

A NEW HISTORY OF THE FUTURE IN 100 OBJECTS

A Fiction

Adrian Hon

The MIT Press
Cambridge, Massachusetts
London, England

This is a work of fiction. All of the characters, organizations, and events portrayed in this novel are either products of the author's imagination or are used fictitiously.

This book was set in Stone Serif by Westchester Publishing Services. Printed and bound in the United States of America.

Library of Congress Cataloging-in-Publication Data

Names: Hon, Adrian, author.
Title: A new history of the future in 100 objects : a fiction / Adrian Hon.
Other titles: A new history of the future in one hundred objects
Description: Cambridge, Massachusetts : The MIT Press, [2020]
Identifiers: LCCN 2019059150 | ISBN 9780262539371 (paperback)
Subjects: LCSH: Speculative fiction.
Classification: LCC PR6108.O535 N49 2020 | DDC 823/.92—dc23
LC record available at https://lccn.loc.gov/2019059150

10 9 8 7 6 5 4 3 2 1

CONTENTS

ACKNOWLEDGMENTS

When we think of the future, we are really thinking about our past and present. It's therefore fitting that *A New History of the Future in 100 Objects* was prompted by the excellent work of the British Museum and the BBC on *A History of the World in 100 Objects*. There are few explorations of history that surpass it in imagination and vividness, and as soon as I finished listening to the hundredth episode, I immediately began thinking of what the next hundred objects might be.

More broadly, I owe a debt of gratitude to the writers who have inspired me: Vernor Vinge, Iain Banks, Neal Stephenson, Kim Stanley Robinson, Lewis Hyde, Ted Chiang, George Orwell, Stanislaw Lem, and many more. Without their stories and ideas, the future would be a darker place.

Thanks to my editor at MIT Press, Susan Buckley, for her invaluable advice, and the editors of the first edition, Richard Dennis and Andrea Phillips. And thanks to my agent, Veronique Baxter.

Thanks to my family, especially to my parents, Metis and Bernard Hon, and my partner, Margaret Maitland, for their support and encouragement.

Thanks to my friends, Naomi Alderman, Andrea Phillips, and Alexandre Mathy, for their advice and humor. And thank you to all of those who backed the first edition of this book on Kickstarter. Without you, this book wouldn't exist.

INTRODUCTION

Why write a history of the twenty-first century?

Now that we've reached the end of the century, it may seem foolhardy for a mere human to attempt to analyze the data at our disposal. After all, we're awash with information from every corner of the world, covering every second of the century. A thousand detailed histories of individuals and systems can be generated at the snap of a finger. And yet I believe that our century, as it draws to a close, demands not that we look at just the big picture but at the small details on the scale at which human lives are lived. This has been an extraordinary epoch in the story of humanity.

Every century is extraordinary, of course. Some may be the bloodiest or the darkest; others encompass momentous social revolutions, or scientific advances, or religious and philosophical movements. The twenty-first century is different. It represents the first time in our history that we have truly had to question what it means to be human. It is the stories of our collective humanity that I hope to tell through the hundred objects in this book.

I tell the story of how we became more connected than ever before, with objects like Babel, silent messaging, the Nautilus-1, and the brain bubble—and how we became fragmented both physically and culturally with the Fourth Great Awakening and the biomes.

With the Braid collective, the Loop, the Steward medal, and the re-chartered cities, we made tremendous steps forward on our long pursuit of greater equality and enlightenment—but the locked simulation interrogations, the Sudan–Shanghai Letter, the Collingwood meteor, and the downvoted all showed how easy it was for us to lapse back into horror and atrocity.

We automated our economy with the UCS Deliverbots, the mimic scripts, the negotiation agents, and the old drones, destroying the entire notion of work and employment in the process. And we transformed our politics with Jorge Alvarez's presidential campaign and the constitutional blueprints.

Not satisfied with the trifling benefits of smart drugs and Glyphish, we transformed ourselves even further and faster. The amplified teams, Miriam Xu's lace, the javelin, and the posthumans demonstrate how *Homo sapiens* became something very different—and not always in the way we intended.

With our new-found abilities, we left our mark in streets and buildings and oceans and mountains all over Earth, as well as on the moon, Mars, a thousand asteroids, all over the system, and even further beyond. We did what humans do: we transformed the world. And in what will surely be our most memorable feat, we created new forms of life.

Not all of the hundred objects are physical. Some stories were best captured through the software and data that began to govern our lives or through memories and impressions. Where appropriate, I have collected and transcribed those objects for this book.

The future remains as murky as it ever has. Yet we can be certain of one thing: the next century will not be ours. It will belong to our creations, and only if they understand our achievements and our tragedies in this most swift of centuries can we hope that they will improve the next.

This book is not the history of the twenty-first century; it is only a history, and a hundred objects can only tell a fraction of our stories. Some we can be proud of. Others we might prefer to forget. My goal is that this book will give our successors some useful knowledge, some insights, or at least some amusement.

Perhaps, I hope, it might even share some guidance.

—London, 2082

1 ANKLE SURVEILLANCE MONITORS

San Jose, US, 2020

"Six months doesn't sound so bad. I mean, compared to the guys I've met who were in for five years or 15 years, I had it good. But it's still plenty long enough to lose your job. Lose your family. Even lose your friends, people you thought you could rely on. Seemed like more than enough punishment for carrying some weed."

In 2020, Ralph Turner, a 25-year-old truck driver and father of two, was arrested in San Jose on suspicion of possessing an illegal quantity of marijuana. After a short trial, Turner was convicted and given a mandatory sentence of six months in prison.

California's prisons were full to bursting, and with the state in the midst of a severe and extended budget crisis, it couldn't afford to build any more. Faced with no alternative, the court enrolled Turner in a pilot probation program aimed at low-risk offenders.

Turner was taken to an induction center and shown a short video. His mobile phone number was entered into a computer. A technician looped a measuring tape around Turner's ankle and, after a short wait, snapped a light plastic ring into place. He was free to go, albeit with certain restrictions, and inadvertently Ralph Turner became one of the first people to benefit from America's slow turn away from its ruinously expensive and ineffective penal system.

The object I'm holding right now, an "ankle surveillance monitor," is a thin ring of plastic, maybe half a centimeter thick if you count the inner padding. Inside the plastic is a simple computer, a radio, and a far-field microphone array.

Like earlier monitors, it can locate the wearer by satellite positioning and send a warning if the wearer leaves or approaches a restricted area. But Turner's monitor is a little different. Its microphone array constantly records and streams every nearby sound to a remote server, so if the wearer is suspected of violating their probation, the relevant audio section can be decrypted by court order. More controversially, in a concession to public fears, the monitor doesn't just relay its position to the police and judicial system. It also informs a wide range of "concerned parties" including schools, hospitals, and airports.

The theory was that this new generation of ankle monitors could be used for nonviolent low-risk offenders, such as those convicted of drug possession, petty theft, or vandalism. Not only would they save tens of thousands of dollars per person, they'd also allow the wearers to continue their jobs and live with their families. Coupled with mandatory community service, the monitors seemed to be the best—and only—alternative to a penal system that was too expensive and barely appeared to reduce crime at all. Expert Amira Goss elaborates:

> More than ten million people worldwide were imprisoned in 2020, and nearly a quarter of them lived in America, a country with only five percent of the world's population. Incredibly, most Americans gave little thought to their system of incarceration. If anything, many felt it was too lenient. The fact that prisons only became commonplace as a means of punishment in the nineteenth century was completely overlooked.
>
> From a historical perspective, America's penal system was little different from the old debtors' prisons, with many inmates made to work at below minimum wage to pay their way. Not only was it incredibly wasteful, but, worse still, it didn't really work. Recidivism rates were stubbornly high, and even long sentences didn't seem to deter criminals who had few other options in life. They became more about retribution and the very literal removal of criminals from sight—an understandable impulse for severe crimes like murder, but not for petty theft.

Between 1970 and 2020, US incarceration rates increased five-fold thanks to mandatory sentencing laws, privatization of the prison system, and much stricter attitudes toward crime and punishment compared to other rich countries. The human cost of putting close to one in a hundred adults in jail was horrific and certainly not worth the relatively modest decrease in crime rates, even assuming that there was any causal link.

Prison had become a place that destroyed families and jobs and bred a virulent criminal culture. As befitting the time though, it wasn't the human cost of imprisonment that led to our ankle monitor; it was the economic cost. By the early twenty-first century, the price of keeping someone in jail was almost as much as the average US income.

The new ankle monitors encountered fierce resistance in California from all points across the political spectrum. The ACLU argued that the ankle tags violated human rights on an unprecedented scale, while state

Republicans claimed that "freeing" tens of thousands of prisoners would create a wave of violent crime. As revealed by data miners taking advantage of transparency laws enacted in the 2050s, much of the opposition was funded by donations from corporations profiting from private prisons, and their warnings were accepted by a frightened and receptive public.

The US government had little choice, though. It simply couldn't afford the expense of housing so many prisoners. Thanks to a powerful speech from Reverend James Malone, a charismatic religious leader, the public was eventually convinced that it was better to try and reintegrate prisoners into society rather than spend a fortune on them.

The problems began almost immediately. Whether or not they were wearing an ankle monitor, many wearers still committed crimes, even though they were swiftly apprehended. Dozens more simply vanished, and hundreds of wearers were unfairly punished for simple malfunctions on their monitors.

As predicted by security experts, monitors were reverse-engineered in order to spoof and intercept the tracking signals. A firmware update eventually addressed these issues six months later, but for a while it was possible for anyone with the right equipment to track the wearers. Most damningly, the audio recordings were often too poor in quality to be useful as evidence, at least until new hardware was released in 2022 and integrated with the wearers' other sensors.

Yet the US government forged on. Too much had been invested to give up now, and the promise of massive savings dazzled their judgement. Three years on, the pilot program was expanded to all low-risk offenders and taken up by several other cash-strapped states convinced that it was an easy way to save money. In New York and Pennsylvania, the monitors were linked into a flexible community service system that allowed a much wider set of institutions—churches, charities, libraries, businesses—to bypass the prison system entirely and work with offenders directly, helping them find work and stability in their personal and family lives through mentoring and education programs.

In the vanguard states, sentences became shorter, swifter, and surer. By 2036, the prison population in the US had been cut by a third, saving tens of billions a year—and more importantly, helping millions of offenders stay in work and keep their families intact.

What fascinates us today about ankle monitors is how they represent the dilemmas and compromises that were typical of the early twenty-first century. It would be a mistake to attribute the sweeping changes in the US penal system to a mere piece of technology rather than its human backers and designers, but they still remain a powerful symbol. Social historian Julie Yao observes:

> The monitors were important because they helped to break a spiral of alienation and failure among prisoners. It's easy for us to think that the Americans of 2020 were somehow heartless, but the truth is that most genuinely believed that prison was the only thing that stopped people from committing crimes, thanks to the sensationalist media of the time.
>
> Monitors brought punishment and rehabilitation back into the open—but at the cost of normalizing ubiquitous surveillance, a decision that had serious consequences later in the century.

We can't know what Turner was thinking during his six months of monitored probation with his ankle monitor, but inspection of his nascent casters including Facebook, IMs, and text messages shows that he seemed to fare well enough. In an interview years later, Turner remarked, "I didn't enjoy being a guinea pig, and I sure as hell didn't appreciate someone being able to listen in on every damn thing that I did. But if you gave me the choice between prison and the monitor, I'd have strapped that thing on with my own bare hands."

2 SPEEKY

Cambridge, US, 2020

It was hysteria, pure and simple. They'd line up for hours, even days. They'd bid ten times or even a hundred times its price just to get their hands on one. Rich or poor, if you had a child, you had to have one. The voracious demand led to sales of twenty million units in just two months, making it the most popular new toy of the decade.

I'm talking about a small, furry, and frankly rather cute toy called the Speeky. Behind this deceptively simple object lies a complex combination of crowdfunding, outsourced manufacturing, international politics, and five million freelance actors.

A Speeky looks very much like a teddy bear of old—about 20 centimeters tall, covered in bright fur, with beautifully expressive eyes. While pleasant enough to look at, looks alone don't warrant millions of sales. To understand, you have to turn the Speeky on.

Now, if I place this Speeky on top of its charger unit (a miniature bed, of course), it'll start to wake up—stretching its legs, rubbing its eyes, that sort of thing. And once it's fully awake, it will start talking to me.

It's not really the Speeky that's talking. Conversational-level AI was over a decade off in 2020. It's not reading from a script either, because I can ask it quite a wide range of questions, like whether I should go to the park or the beach today, and it'll give me appropriately personalized responses that take into account previous conversations I've had with it. You see, the Speeky isn't a toy so much as a puppet controlled by an operator who might be anywhere from next door to the other side of the planet.

Invented in early 2020 by a team of MIT students, the Speeky took advantage of the rapidly falling prices of components such as elastic Omni-Skin actuators, motors, cameras, and wireless chips—the "smartphone war" dividend, if you will. Robotics historian Stan Malhotra relates the students' path to success:

The students drew up the first plans for the Speeky more as a thought experiment than a business venture, and when they sent them to a factory in Guangdong, they weren't expecting to make anything other than mementos. But like many breakthroughs, it was a chance encounter between one of the team, Alice Stephenson, and a group of amateur performers from Boston University that gave them the idea to create online tools that would allow actors to easily 'puppet' the Speeky. One Kickstarter project later, and they had more than $20 million in pre-orders.

It wasn't the first internet-connected toy to be sold, but it was the first that combined cheap but well-designed robotics components with a puppet interface. Crucially, that interface was simple to use for anyone who'd ever played an action or role-playing video game—in other words, several hundred million people across the globe. Puppeteering the Speeky's movements, however, while amusing for some younger children, was far from enough to satisfy most users, who wanted voice interaction.

This turned out to be surprisingly easy, even for puppeteers who weren't native English speakers. The Speeky platform automatically altered voices into a range of suitably saccharine tones, rendering accents moot. Indeed, some fast typists just used text-to-speech software during their puppeteering. What really mattered was that a human was controlling the Speeky, someone who could provide genuine affection and empathy.

None of this came for free. Speekys were bundled with ten hours of free voice interaction, but after that parents had to purchase extra puppeteer time via either subscription or microtransaction. A market rapidly developed, with novice puppeteers offering their time for free in return for good reviews at one end, and highly skilled and highly paid entertainers at the other. Parents could pay extra for vetted puppeteers, but most trusted the market's real-time peer-review systems that saw puppeteers monitor one another.

But who were the puppeteers? Stan Malhotra explains their origins:

> If you asked the average person in North America or Europe where the best puppeteers were, they'd have said the patriotic thing and picked their own countries. But in practice, a huge number of highly skilled puppeteers came from all over the world—from inland China, Indonesia, India, South America—all these places that had fantastic actors who finally had access to rich, paying audiences.

Wherever they were based, puppeteers usually had access to vast quantities of Western content online, from games to TV to movies, and they had little problem learning how to (illegally) mimic characters from popular franchises such as Disney, Harry Potter, and Nintendo. Outsourcing had finally enveloped the performance industry.

In 2021, new Speeky models with different skins (dragons, monsters, woolly mammoths, etc.), and capabilities were developed for teenagers and adults. However, the design and technology platform had already been thoroughly reverse-engineered and cloned, and a glut of cheap competitors offering better profit splits with the puppeteers ensured that the MIT students were quickly brought back down to earth.

While Speekys and their clones were eventually superseded by wearable devices that displayed ever more fantastic and interactive creatures, and the role of puppeteers was replaced by effectively free AI performers, Speekys never quite went away. Instead, the attraction of retro physical products and vintage robotics ensured the Speeky's immortality as a classic toy, alongside the rocking horse and the doll's house.

Sitting here with a Speeky that's being puppeted by a colleague from the museum, I can just about imagine how a child from the '20s might have felt as they unwrapped this colorful bear and watched it wake up, talk, dance, and play for the very first time. I can also imagine the amazement of the puppeteer sitting halfway across the world as they watched their account being credited by the minute for as long as they could keep a smile on a child's face.

3 THE GUIDE

Seattle, US, 2021

What is the good life? Philosophers, wise men, preachers, televangelists, self-help gurus—all have tried to answer the question of how we should live and thrive. Some have been driven by a sense of moral duty and religious zeal, others by a quest for power and money, but for millennia they have never lacked a wide and willing audience of those eager to better themselves and the world around them.

Unlike those who came before her, the guru who created one of the early twenty-first century's most influential moral instructions wasn't an eloquent writer or a charismatic performer. She was a programmer, and she made an application called "The Guide to Greatness." Most knew it simply as "The Guide."

Sophia Moreno was the only child of Ernesto and Claudia Moreno. Ernesto was a union representative at a chemical engineering plant in their home town of Santo Andre, while Claudia taught psychology at Universidade Federal do ABC. Sophia had a quiet childhood playing games and studying hard. It wasn't until she studied computer science in Rio de Janeiro that she stepped onto a path where her actions would change the world.

On arriving in Rio, Sophia struggled with depression as she tried to fit in with her new surroundings. She flirted with religion, falling in with an evangelical Christian student society for a few months, then, just as quickly, leaving and burying herself in work. Over the next two years, she excelled in her studies, regularly scoring in the top five percent of her class and earning a placement in Seattle at Amazon.

But according to her friends, Sophia often complained about her unfulfilling job at Amazon that saw her "shaving milliseconds off the shopping experience." Soon, she left to pursue her own projects. Her first independently made app was a comparison-shopping utility and was downloaded fifteen thousand times. Her second app, an exam study helper, had a mere seven thousand downloads.

Sophia's third app was the Guide, launched in 2021 after a year of development. Within twelve days, it had been downloaded ten thousand times. In six weeks, it reached a million; in twelve months, twenty million; and after two years, three hundred million downloads.

> The Guide is about connection. Look around you. At the clothes on your body, the chair you're sitting on, the walls beside you, and the phone in front of you. Everything we touch, eat, watch, and play is created by other people in this world.

That is the message that greets users when they first launch the Guide. It continues:

> Every one of us wants to become happy and successful and strong, but we can't do that if we just focus on ourselves and ignore those whose lives touch us. Everything and everyone is connected every second of every day. The Guide will show you how to see those connections, how to harness them, and how to help yourself and everyone around you gain strength.

It's not very original. But as a smartphone and smartwatch app that users kept at their side day and night, the Guide was in a unique position to directly interact and intervene in its followers' lives. It helped them set and achieve goals, and it guided their behavior in more subtle ways—from special greetings when they woke up, to inspirational messages before important meetings marked in their calendars. Naturally, being integrated with the online social networks and casters of the day, the Guide had a wide network of supporters right from its launch, meaning that users could find like-minded souls instantly.

The Guide launched with one hundred audio lessons, such as "How to Live in the Moment" and "Why We Must Forgive," along with twenty-five interactive exercises ranging from emotion journals to games that helped users identify things in their surroundings that gave them joy. Naturally, the Guide took full advantage of the "gamification" craze of the early twenty-first century, hooking unwitting users with the lure of experience points and leveling up. Sociologist and app historian Professor Colin Leigh explains its sensational success:

> The Guide directly addressed the lack of community and purpose felt by many in rich countries experiencing the "speed-up." Traditional religious groups were too conservative to take full advantage of new technology, and those organizations that did have the expertise simply couldn't comprehend or weren't interested in more spiritual matters. It's true that mindfulness and meditation apps were also popular at the time, but their appeal was waning due to their peculiarly individualistic focus. Moreno's background as a hybrid developer-guru marked a genuine turning point.

Not all of the hundreds of millions who downloaded the Guide were active participants. Most tried it out of curiosity and quickly abandoned it. Others used it more as a positive-psychology productivity app. Even so, many millions used the app every day and took part in the community rituals that became so crucial to the app's success.

These rituals included everything from dinners and parties to exercise clubs, celebrations, and protests, and helped cement the bonds between followers in the real world. The fact that they were expected to actually turn up somewhere and meet with strangers in order to progress in the Guide set a punishingly high bar, a bar that was later recognized as real insight on Moreno's part. Moreno had correctly understood that the retreat of organized religion and comparable social structures had left a vacuum that people desperately wanted to fill, something she felt the Guide could do.

For a while, it seemed as if the Guide itself was becoming a kind of religion. However, despite Moreno continuing to provide updates to the app for the next three years, it became increasingly clear that she was deeply ambivalent about the success of the Guide. In her few public statements, she questioned whether her followers understood the meaning of her app and wondered if she had led some people astray. Most scholars speculate that the weight of responsibility she felt toward her followers was more than she wanted to bear.

Four years after its launch, Sophia Moreno sent out one final update. In it, she explained that she was delighted and proud of what her followers had accomplished, but now it was time for them to pursue their own "paths to strength" independently.

The Guide's user base fractured overnight. Some larger groups began developing their own open-source versions of the app, while competing apps made a landgrab for users, offering to transfer the achievements and experience points they had earned in the Guide to their own apps. As quickly as the Guide rose, it vanished.

Sophia Moreno retreated from public life, living off her revenues from the Guide and occasionally releasing obscure interactive artistic experiments. Yet her app, short-lived as it was, proved there was a desire for a philosophy of life that complemented a market-based mindset with one rooted in communities and gifts. As for established religions, it was a reminder that their strength was not to be taken for granted.

4 THE BRAID COLLECTIVE

Flanders, Belgium, 2021

This small circular digital watermark, about two centimeters square, contains three interlinked rings. Known as the Braid, the symbol could be found on thousands of books, artworks, songs, games, and apps, and it represented a new kind of financial support for artists, writers, and designers—distinct from the market or patronage. Scholar Lewis Hoult explains its significance:

> The Braid symbol meant two things: firstly, that the work was created by members of a cooperative in which profits were reinvested; and secondly, that works were at least partly crowdfunded by individuals through pre-sales and donations. It was a genuinely supportive community that led toward a fairer, more open, and more diverse creative world.

There used to be a well-worn route for aspiring writers to become "published"—that is, for their words to be distributed for sale in a large market. You'd go to university and then take on a job with enough spare time to write. Eventually, you'd send a manuscript to a publisher, who, if they liked it, would advance you money so you could quit your job and devote yourself to writing full-time. It wasn't a perfect system due to the bottlenecks on the publishers' side, but thanks to high production and distribution costs, it was a necessary evil.

Until it wasn't. Publishers of all kinds—not just of books, but also music, games, and software—had long held an oligopoly on putting products in front of a large audience thanks to their scale and their relationships with physical retailers. But the advent of the internet saw companies such as Amazon, Apple, and Tencent loosen the publishers' grip on power, giving creators a much more direct and potentially lucrative route to customers. Organizational theorist Tim Oxford notes:

> Even though the big physical retailers had the money and the capacity to dominate digital retail, they consistently failed to keep up. A recent deep-meme study

proves that they suffered from classic failures of conservatism and shareholder-driven shortsightedness—failures that would subsequently haunt Amazon and Tencent themselves in the '20s and '30s.

The internet gave successful artists the means, motive, and opportunity to abandon their publishers and establish a more direct relationship with their audience. J. K. Rowling, Anil Vipulananthan, and Jorge Mathy were among the first wave, using their name recognition to draw fans to their own websites and distribution channels. Mathy went on to pioneer a real-time reader-engagement system that analyzed the reader's reaction to his stories, as well as his ancillary merchandising, games, and the shared story universe he operated.

Newer authors had more mixed fortunes. Publishers had less cash to subsidize unproven names, and a freer market also meant a more competitive one. Some made millions, but the vast majority earned very little. Some viewed this as a long-expected reversion to the historical norm, where writers would have a "day job" that would support their writing on evenings and weekends. The only problem was that day jobs were evaporating as well.

A partial solution lay in traditional crowdfunding websites such as Kickstarter, through which creators would announce their books, films, toys, utilities, and products, and ask for advance orders. If they raised enough money, the project would go ahead—and if they didn't, the money would be refunded, establishing a critically important signal of demand that was missing in more centrally controlled art schemes.

But since it was based around discrete, time-limited projects, crowdfunding wasn't a good way to get a reliable income. Variations like ongoing patronage-based websites like Patreon were more suitable but still lacked a way to spread financial success to newcomers, a duty that some publishers had seen as an important responsibility.

Jessamyn East, a librarian from Flanders, Belgium, understood that many successful artists realized they owed a debt to the greater creative community from which their ideas flowed. Given the right opportunity, East thought they would be happy to support that community financially. By combining crowdfunding with cooperatives, East formed the Braid.

Members of the Braid received a very modest stipend on joining, enough for them to dedicate at least a day a week to honing their craft. They were assigned mentors who encouraged them to regularly post projects on the Braid's crowdfunding platform. Nonprofits and successful members provided matched funding to novices' projects, and the reinvestment of profits from successful projects helped keep the community going. It grew slowly but steadily, and after a decade it had come to rival the ailing publishing industry in both size and influence.

Not everyone was happy with the Braid's model, though. Some authors felt that the practice of pre-funding projects made creators pander toward the public, with noted author Metis Hui saying, "You can't sell a poem before you've written it." Others were skeptical about whether the artists would stick with the cooperative and give up a portion of their profits after they became successful, and certainly there were more than a few who did leave (to very public shame, at least).

By and large though, members of the Braid recognized the value of a creative community that wasn't merely about maximizing profits, but instead about encouraging excellence and diversity. A community that was a gift to one another, and to the world.

5 SILENT MESSAGING

Earth, 2022

rebought carbon passes for special special someone
no no no no no yes maybe OK let's go
ughh polldown—no more primary debates for him now

Three mundane messages, lost amid a stream of 1.2 billion more, all sent on a single day in 2022. Like the emails, instant messages, and tweets that came before, the messages were purely electronic, totally invisible, and completely silent.

If you watched the participants in these conversations, though, you'd have been hard pressed to notice that they were talking to each other at all. They weren't typing at keyboards or even thumbing on a smartphone hidden in their pocket. People born a century or two earlier might have resorted to magic as an explanation, but a perceptive observer would have spotted the particular brand of glasses and necklaces the person was wearing, as well as the tell-tale twitches of their vocal cords. Those glasses and necklaces heralded a revolution in how humanity communicated with one another. A revolution that can still be felt today.

The glasses I'm holding right now don't seem particularly special. They have a thick black frame with boxy lenses—a typical style of the 2010s, and indeed they wouldn't have looked out of place in the 1960s. A closer examination, however, reveals that they contain holographic waveguide displays embedded into the frames, providing the wearer with a virtual 3-D image. The arms of the glasses hold a modest amount of computing power along with a short-range radio antenna to connect to a nearby smartphone.

On their own, the glasses aren't good for that much. The model I have here can't even tell where I'm looking, preventing any decent augmented reality applications. What's more, the image resolution is far too low for any real work to be done. They were cheap toys.

I also have a necklace here, although it's so short that some might call it a choker. It's very light, made of a silvery metal, and has an unusually wide clasp around the back. If I put it on and adjust it properly, I can feel it resting comfortably against my throat, which is really the point as that's how its embedded electrode array picks up the nervous impulses from my vocal cords and translates them into words. All I need to do is mouth a sentence without making a single noise, and it'll be instantly digitized. Like the glasses, this necklace had a limited market, aimed largely at people with speech disorders and the military.

But as Ivo Petrovic from the Museum of Rijeka explains, it was the combination of the glasses and the necklace that mattered:

> The pairing of these two objects—one that can "hear" your subvocalized words without you having to make a sound, another that can display those words on a floating screen—meant that people could communicate while doing more or less anything at all. They could be at dinner, in a meeting, a lecture, or even an exam, and they could talk to any number of people anywhere in the world without anyone nearby knowing. It was a new medium that rivaled the telegram and the radio in importance, and almost incidentally provided a near-perfect ubiquitous method of data capture.

As usual, it was the young who truly embraced the new technology. Children and teenagers have always struggled with their guardians for independence and privacy, especially during the recurrent moral panics in the twentieth and twenty-first centuries (and, to be fair, the rest of known history). Necklaces were simply the newest outlet for their desires, and certainly the most inconspicuous.

Several competing messaging networks sprung up within a few months of the first devices' launch, with Dees and Pype dividing up most of the pie.* Judging by the billions of messages being sent each day by 2022 and the trillions sent just a few years later, there was massive demand for silent messaging. SMSes enhanced and replaced a slew of older interfaces, and by eliminating the gap between intention and action to produce a crude form of "thought control" of devices, they were unrivaled until direct brain interfaces.

SMS users rapidly invented a new vocabulary to suit the technology. Since the subvocal impulses that necklaces detected couldn't convey the richness and nuance of normal speech, new words and repetition were

---

* With both networks being commercial entities, they most certainly did not interoperate, and it wasn't until 2023 that efforts by the Institute of Electrical and Electronics Engineers and grassroots organizations finally established a common protocol for the new "silent messaging service," allowing the technologies to flourish.

required to remedy the effects of the lowered bandwidth. Of course, the ungrammatical nature of this new vocabulary disturbed contemporary conservative commentators, but attempts to treat SMSes in the same way as phone calls or instant messages were sorely missing the potential of the new medium.

Soon enough, the euphoria of SMSes quickly gave way to renewed fears about privacy and dependence. Just as letters, phone calls, and early casters such as Facebook and Twitch gave teenagers new freedoms and parents new fears, glasses and necklaces linked friends together in a way that meant they never, ever had to be alone.

"Cognitive entanglement" was a term used to describe how young people used SMSes to share thoughts and moods in a way that seemed like telepathy. We use the term in a very different way today, but it's easy to see how startling this new mode of communication must have been to adults who had previously used laborious interfaces such as keyboards and screens to talk to one another. It must have been deeply unnerving for them to see groups of completely silent teenagers abruptly bursting into laughter or performing some other kind of coordinated behavior with no warning whatsoever.

As glasses and necklaces became even lighter and more invisible, they forced the reevaluation of many traditional practices including exams, interviews, and all other kinds of in-person assessments. Students in India, Taiwan, and Japan were such notorious users of SMSes during exams that some authorities suggested constructing Faraday cages around their premises, and employers struggled to deal with interviewees who seemed to have the perfect answer to every question.

Another unexpected side-effect of the explosion in SMSes was that conversations and thoughts that had previously gone unrecorded were now made permanent, if not necessarily public. Beyond the expanded surveillance and censorship that this enabled, they aggravated the problems faced by corporations, particularly financial firms, that tried to avoid recording any potentially illegal conversations. Some resorted to the obvious tactic of banning SMSes, but this usually slowed down their operations to an unacceptably uncompetitive level. If you wanted to work, you had to be proficient with SMSes.

It's easy for us historians to see SMSes as simply an archive of low-grade information about early twenty-first century culture, yet, in truth, they represented a massive transformation in that most fundamental of human behaviors—communication.

6 SMART DRUGS

Kigali, Rwanda, 2022

Can we change who we are? For millennia we eagerly bought potions and medicines that promised to make us smarter and wiser, and for just as long we were bitterly disappointed. Yet we kept coming back. There was something irresistible about improving ourselves without any effort.

And then the promises came true.

Today we might pity those who never had access to personality reconstruction, desire modification, and metacognitive mapping, but it's easy to forget that mind-altering substances have brought a cruder kind of relief and variety to our lives for a long time. From alcohol and caffeine to cannabis and amphetamines, we've never lacked ways to both stimulate and relax our minds.

It was much trickier, however, to create drugs that would increase elements of our intelligence, such as improved attention or linguistic abilities, without harmful side-effects. It wasn't until the '20s that we had the tools to produce the first truly effective cognitive enhancers, or "smart drugs." Unprecedented in history, they caused quite a stir.

I have a range of samples lined up here, provided generously by Professor Arienne Niyonshuti from the Kigali Museum of Medicine. All of them are from the first wave of consumer-grade smart drugs that hit the market in 2022. On the left here, we've got an orange pill called Mnemosyne, which improves memory formation and recall. Next to it, there's a square chocolate, Tricity, that helps with language translation. Then there's a green pill, Numony, that reduces fatigue and stress. And finally, on the right I have a pill of the most well-known smart drug: Ceretin, a broad-spectrum cognitive enhancer.

So, let's try one out! Here's a glass of water. ... And I think I'll take the Ceretin. Now, I've been told that we're not supposed to take these drugs any more since they get automatically expunged by our neural laces, which can give you a terrible headache, but I've had Professor Niyonshuti's team temporarily disable my lace's usual functions aside from recording. Professor Niyonshuti will explain exactly what's going on in my brain right now:

> We can see quite clearly that the active components of Ceretin are entering your bloodstream, crossing the blood–brain barrier, and altering the behavior of your synaptic neurotransmitter receptors in the frontal cortex and cerebellum, the effects of which will temporarily improve your attention and analytic abilities. It takes a few minutes for the drugs to take effect though, so we'll wait a little while before giving you the cognitive tests I've prepared.

What's extraordinary about these drugs is that their inventors actually had very little idea about how they operated. Scientists in 2022 could observe their effects and check for any harmful side-effects, and they had hypotheses about their method of action, but they would lack anything even approaching a complete model of the brain for at least another twenty years.

It feels like the Ceretin has taken effect, so I'm now going to perform a few old-fashioned tests to assess my memory skills, along with reasoning and attention. I won't bore you with the details, but they basically involve tasks such as predicting the next symbol in a series and distractor tests.

…And here are the results! Across the board, my cognitive performance has increased by 14 to 20 percent compared to the tests I took beforehand. These results don't prove anything in themselves, of course. I'm just one person, and this wasn't a double-blind experiment, but I definitely feel a fair bit sharper. I can only imagine how exciting it must have felt when they were invented, having your mind improved for an entire day after taking one pill.

Ceretin, Numony, Tricity—these weren't the first smart drugs on the market (Modafinil, an "alertness" drug, was released in the 2000s), but they were the first to gain widespread popularity, particularly in China, Japan, and Singapore, where they were heavily advertised on *Starcraft* and *ZRG* casts (the US and the EU lagged behind owing to safety concerns).

Smart drugs gave students an edge in the all-important university entrance exams, and they helped corporations eke out another percentage point of so-called productivity. However, their high cost prompted violent protests from those who argued that they should either be made freely available or banned, with mandatory drug testing before exams. In response, one South Korean chaebol, NSK, provided Mnemosyne for all of its thirty thousand employees.

Of course, it was impossible to stop smart drugs from being illegally imported from Asia and sold in Europe and the US at inflated prices. This caused further tensions in highly unequal countries like the US, where they became another symbol of the power the rich had to simply buy success. In 2026, President Alexander addressed the issue head-on by legalizing not just smart drugs but also recreational drugs, and allowing for the production of cheap generic smart drugs just five years later.

Smart drugs had their downsides. Though it was difficult to tell at the time, researchers later discovered the benefits conferred by any given first- or second-generation smart drug often came at the long-term expense of other cognitive functions like creativity, long-term memory formation, or empathy. The drugs also contributed to the damaging "speed-up" culture of the time, increasing the pressure on already frantic workers.

It's time to turn my lace back on now, and that means the Ceretin will be flushed out of my system within a few seconds. While that's happening, it's fascinating to look back on how smart drugs, however crude they were, paved the way for our laces. Not long after the first generation, researchers were testing ways of combining neuroplasticity-enhancing drugs with portable transcranial magnetic stimulation to truly enhance people's mental capacities and even personalities. But it all started here with these four pills.

7 THE TWELVE TECHNOLOGICAL VIRTUES

San Francisco, US, 2022

Toward the tail-end of the "speed-up," a period in the 2010s and early '20s that valorized scale above all and saw the enclosure of the internet by monolithic technology companies, glimmers of what might come next became apparent in San Francisco, the epicenter of so many cultural changes.

A curious new practice spread amongst programmers and designers and entrepreneurs in that city. As they imagined new ideas that might make money using computers–or re-clothed old ones–they had always performed a series of rituals, some of which survive today: marking out the sacred crosses of SWOT (strengths, weaknesses, opportunities, threats) analyses, reverently delivering "post-it" offerings onto business model canvasses, conjuring financial models from a dash of data and handfuls of hope. To these, a new ritual was added, subjecting their ideas to the ordeal of the twelve technological virtues.

This ordeal originated from philosopher Shannon Vallor's book from 2016, arguing that one of the only ways to promote human flourishing in an age of unpredictable, civilization-threatening technological change was to cultivate her twelve new virtues of honesty, self-control, humility, justice, courage, empathy, care, civility, flexibility, perspective, magnanimity, and wisdom–each derived from much older Aristotelian, Confucian, and Buddhist ethical traditions. This was not merely the precautionary principle by another name. Rather, Vallor sought a balance between thoughtless techno-utopianism and reactionary techno-pessimism.

Vallor's book was overlooked for several years due to Silicon Valley's noted suspicion of the humanities. It only found a wider audience when the engineers who had created the software that conquered the world became disillusioned with the superficial communalism of the Guide and the piecemeal solutions offered by the "Time Well Spent" movement. Vallor's virtues demanded more, yes, but they also promised more.

The ritual of the Twelve Technological Virtues, invented by one of Vallor's followers in San Francisco, was an "ethical premortem" consisting of a checklist of questions to consider before embarking on a risky new venture, demanding to measure your ideas against the twelve virtues.

Simple enough. Too simple, in fact. A normal questionnaire wouldn't have the specificity or interactivity to adequately interrogate the ideas of flighty Silicon Valley entrepreneurs, and the laughably primitive chatbots of the time certainly weren't capable of replacing human interlocutors. But knowledgeable humans were expensive, and, worse, they were untrustworthy. Few entrepreneurs were willing to discuss their secret new startup ideas with potential competitors.

But what if it were possible to take an idea and automatically fashion it into a different idea that retained all the essential ethical properties of the original? That way, you could share your misgivings about psychologically profiling children while they played videogames and be confident that the details would remain secret. This was the secret that lay behind the ritual, a real-time analogical remapping system, not unlike the multidimensional translation algorithms pioneered just a few years earlier by Google.

None of this technology was on show. To conduct the ritual, you merely opened an app that anonymously connected you to another person who ran through a series of probing ethical questions about the virtues, and as you spoke, your secrets and confessions would be instantly transformed into analogies, rendered harmless. "Training nurses in virtual reality" might become "teaching therapists using videoconferences." The remapping was performed on your own hardware rather than in the cloud, ensuring security. It was all free. You were only asked to help someone else in the same way.

As for the questions, they were designed to unsettle. A designer proposing yet another quantified self application would be challenged on the virtue of perspective. Might users who became fixated on tracking their calories and sleep patterns lose the time and ability to examine their own overall character? An engineer building a "carebot" to replace human caregivers would be asked if the genuine good it could provide might be outweighed by the gradual erosion of our virtue of caring, of being able to respond to and meet the needs of others—a virtue cultivated only by our repeated, intimate exposure to our mutual concern, dependence, vulnerability, and gratitude for one another.

The rituals often failed to change minds. People were stubborn, as they still are today. But the sincerity of the twelve virtues was shocking enough to jolt some out of their routines, to force them to consider their values, to make them realize they had a choice in how technology could be used to help or hinder the future of humanity. And it was only because they were able to talk about their real dilemmas, remapped onto analogous examples, that the conversations retained real force.

Although the twelve virtues faltered at reaching beyond Silicon Valley, let alone the United States (the virtues were not quite as universal as their authors hoped), we know from anonymous interviews conducted in the '30s and beyond that the twelve virtues genuinely changed the minds of people who would go on to become highly influential designers, engineers, and entrepreneurs, including the renowned inventor Kalli Jayanth.

It is still not known who funded the development of the real-time analogical remapping system, a quietly astonishing technological achievement for the time. Some suggested, only half-jokingly, that it was made by an ancestor of Narada, the trickster AI, leading humans on the first of its merry dances. Others pointed the finger at James Maitland, the billionaire founder of Schematic, atoning for past corporate misdeeds, although he never publicly admitted to it. Whatever their motives, they helped remap an ancient tradition of virtues into one that worked for the twenty-first century.

8 LOCKED SIMULATION INTERROGATION

Washington, DC, US, 2022

"Do not attempt to remove the goggles. Any attempts will be noted and punished. Do not attempt to remove the gloves. Any attempts will be noted and punished. Do not attempt to dislodge the headwear. Any attempts will be noted and punished. Prepare for Scenario 288 in 10 seconds. ... 5, 4, 3, 2, 1."

Being locked inside a hostile virtual reality simulation easily ranks among the worst nightmares invented in our century. Today we have strict laws regulating the use of locked sims, laws that are baked into hardware and enforced by severe punishments. Locked sims have very few legitimate uses outside of specialized therapy, but, unfortunately, they have plenty of illegitimate uses, interrogation being foremost among them.

Records from the United States Federal Bureau of Investigation (FBI) indicate that the first use of locked interrogation sims dates back to 2022. Following the fifth bombing in a series of domestic terrorism attacks in North Carolina, FBI agents detained a suspect who they believed had aided the bombers. This suspect was not responsive to the legal interrogation techniques of the time, and with physical techniques such as waterboarding prohibited by Congress in 2021, the FBI decided to test out a new, experimental procedure.

The suspect was fitted with a set of modified Oculus virtual reality goggles and gloves, along with a galvanic vestibular stimulator to artificially alter their sense of balance. This system was powered by the FBI's computing cloud to provide a highly immersive simulated environment.

So far, so mundane. Any rich person could afford the same setup.

However, the FBI also fitted the suspect with a portable brain scanner, allowing them to closely monitor the suspect's reactions to a simulation of their supposed meeting with the bombers. Any highly emotive reaction to a phrase or face would make the next iteration of the simulation focus and elaborate on those specific elements, quickly narrowing in on the "truth."

Uncooperative behavior was swiftly punished by fear-inducing simulations, which themselves were refined based on the suspect's reactions.

Over the course of 572 simulations lasting an average of eight minutes each, the FBI determined the likely locations and identities for three of the bombers. Using this information, they followed the suspected bombers and uncovered more members of their organization, allowing the FBI to apprehend them before their planned sixth bombing in Charlotte, NC. In a much-publicized press conference following the arrests, the FBI credited the use of new "noninvasive, zero-contact questioning techniques" with saving thousands of lives. Political analyst Katy Clarke describes what happened next:

> A major terrorist threat averted thanks to a seemingly magical, noninvasive inter-
> rogation device? It wasn't surprising that security services around the world were
> given carte blanche to use adaptive VR interrogation. Of course, they didn't real-
> ize that the system wasn't quite as reliable as it seemed. It turned out the North
> Carolina case was more of a happy accident than anything else. Too often in
> other cases, adaptive VR simply generated nonsense information.

Nevertheless, over the next fifteen years, adaptive VR interrogation became a standard part of law enforcement agencies' toolkits. At first it was used only to investigate major suspected terrorist attacks, but it ended up trickling down to much more routine and minor criminal cases. Successes were publicized and failures were covered up, resulting in an almost perfect public image.

But the severe and permanent psychological damage caused by adaptive VR interrogation also became clear over those fifteen years. Even with the best will in the world, security services were not able to prevent innocent suspects from being scarred by VR interrogation. Days of locked sim interrogation frequently resulted in mental trauma. Many suspects developed a lifelong aversion to any environment or person presented in adaptive interrogations, tearing apart friendships and families.

Ultimately, there were three major flaws with adaptive VR interrogation. The first was that the crude brain-scanning technology of the time frequently placed too much weight on subjects' innocent emotional responses toward completely irrelevant people or places within the simulations. Secondly, as the Mossad demonstrated on numerous occasions, trained subject-antagonists could withstand hundreds of simulations by conjuring up vivid and consistent imaginary worlds with which they could fool interrogators.

Thirdly, this mode of interrogation was only as good as the people and data that were fed into it, and there were more than enough personal and political biases in the anti-terror and criminal endeavors of the time to fool the people observing the simulation.

Following *Dickson v. United States*, a case that was brought before the US Supreme Court in 2033, the use of adaptive VR interrogation was ruled illegal as a violation of personal privacy, and, controversially, as a violation of the Eighth Amendment against the use of "cruel and unusual punishments." It was a landmark case defining the use of brain-scanning technologies for law enforcement—but it wasn't the last.

9 DISASTER KITS

Tehran, Iran, 2023

A magnitude 8.2 earthquake in Alaska in the summer of 2022, super-typhoon Mellar in the Philippines a week later, severe flooding of the Danube in 2023, and a landslide that killed 190 people in Darjeeling that same year—natural disasters are a way of life and death on our planet, deepened by our self-inflicted wound of climate change. Even today, there's little we can do to prevent them, and we've only recently been able to predict them with any certainty. What we can control, however, is how we prepare for them.

In the early twenty-first century, governments in disaster-prone areas such as Japan and California had long held regular disaster drills and encouraged citizens to prepare disaster supply kits. Unfortunately, this assumed that people would have the time, money, and inclination to buy and assemble a kit containing food, water, medicine, and tools, which was sadly proven wrong time and time again.

By 2022, the "solution" of asking people to make their own kits was deemed to be desperately inegalitarian given the human and economic costs of not being prepared. Consequently, the United Nations began to recommend that states supply disaster kits to citizens for free, with the UN giving poorer countries subsidies.

Among the first to adopt the practice were earthquake-prone countries such as Iran, Turkey, and those around the Pacific Ring of Fire, plus flood-prone areas along the Yellow River and Yangtze River in China, and in Louisiana and Florida in the United States, natural calamities amplified by climate chaos.

The curators from the National Museum of Iran have kindly lent me a splendidly preserved disaster kit from 2023. The kit sits inside a tough thirty-centimeter by twenty-centimeter plastic case. Five sides of the box are covered in solar panels that trickle-charge the modular transceiver embedded into the case, allowing it to be located even when buried below meters of rubble or earth. The sixth side holds a shatter-resistant mirror for signaling. Inside, there are high-energy food bars, a multifunction knife, a first aid kit, water, gloves, a whistle, a torch, a reflective blanket, and more—objects perfectly familiar to people from well over a century ago.

But there are a few new tricks here as well, not just objects such as water purification straws and a high-capacity battery to recharge wearables or phones, but also new ways to better distribute scarce supplies.

Take the first-aid kit, for example. These cases all include the standard items—penicillin, painkillers, bandages, and so on. However, there are many other medicines and drugs that any given person or family might need during a disaster that can't fit inside their own kit. The solution? Among the millions of disaster kits they made, the UN spread a wide variety of antivirals, antibiotics, analgesics, and electrolytes. On its own, these random medicines solved little. Hoping to stumble across someone with a kit that held exactly what you needed was hardly a smart strategy.

That's where the transceiver came in. It had two roles: firstly, as a high-powered emergency transponder; and secondly, as a mesh network router. Embedded in the carrying straps of the case are aerials that allow the kit to communicate with all other kits within five hundred meters. They didn't have a high bandwidth—only 20 mbps—but they were capable of temporarily restoring a basic data network in areas suffering total infrastructure failure. Simply opening the kit activated the transceiver, automatically registering its location and contents with the local network so that people could find and share medicine.

After the 2023 earthquake in Ardabil, Iran, the disaster kits helped survivors locate one another far faster than in previous cases and helped reestablish proper network functionality within hours, saving thousands of lives and substantial resources. These capabilities didn't go unnoticed, with other countries ordering or manufacturing tens of millions of kits over the next year and beyond.

It wasn't just nation states who paid attention. Activists also desperately needed a secure mode of communication that didn't rely on centrally controlled infrastructure. While the early twenty-first century is often depicted as a time of plenty—abundant hydrocarbons, favorable demographics, and a comparatively pristine environment—the truth is that most people lived extremely precarious lives, with low income security and little control over their future. Even the richest people in the richest countries, notably Western Europe and the US, were fearful and unhappy—their beliefs clouded by a media that told them that things could only get worse.

The unhappiest of all were those with the least to lose. Whether they were students with a decade and a half of full-time education but no job prospects or people in their forties and fifties on low-paid temporary work, they were united by a deep frustration in democratic politics. Elections held every four or five years, usually featuring the same small handful of professional politicians beholden to their parties and other interest groups, seemed to question the notion of "representative" democracy.

This dissatisfaction frequently erupted in the form of strikes or one-off rallies and protests, and just as frequently was dismissed by governments as illegitimate. After all, the government had been voted into power by the people themselves, and therefore held the ultimate mandate! And so, while the protests continued, many were skeptical of their effectiveness.

Over time, the protests became larger and lasted longer, taking over entire districts of cities, such as the SAZ Puerta del Sol in Madrid. While the protesters were resourceful enough to bring their own food and supplies, they were quickly isolated from the world as authorities cut landlines and jammed wireless and satellite transmissions. For movements that depended on a steady flow of information and support, the silence was fatal.

Disaster kits filled that gap. Modifying the mesh network firmware allowed protesters to encrypt their data, and careful use of the kits' solar panels kept them alive for weeks. Despite regular attacks on the network infrastructure—such as the highly destructive "Pinkerton" worm that exploited a flaw in the kits' baseband processors during the 2025 Jubilee Marches—the protesters usually managed to issue patches via USB.

The kits were only a small part of those activist movements, but they did their job well. What had been invented as a way to address purely physical suffering during natural disasters had been adapted to alleviate the suffering of the soul.

10 UCS DELIVERBOT

Wuhan, China, 2023

One morning in May 2023, Karen Collins spent an hour sorting vegetables from her garden into six plastic containers. When she was close to finishing, she messaged her local market, and it dispatched a Universal Courier Service courier to her house. Half an hour later, Karen left the containers with the courier and went for a jog in the park.

The only human involved in this process was Karen. The local market was online and fully automated, and the UCS courier was an unmanned "deliverbot"—one of the most unassuming yet disruptive technologies of the twenty-first century.

I'm at the Wuhan Museum of Transportation in China, where curator Henry Whittaker has kindly set up a UCS vehicle for me. It's a compact thing, about a cubic-meter in size and shape, made from lightweight carbon fiber, with four small wheels and a sliding door on the top. UCS picked yellow as its corporate color, supposedly to catch the eye and make sure any human drivers wouldn't miss it, and this courier is no different.

If I walk up to the vehicle, it should recognize the glasses I've been given and send an authorization code to check that I'm the right person. And yes, I now have permission to slide open the top and deposit this package I'm sending to Dr. Whittaker. Some couriers had individual lockable compartments that could be reconfigured depending on requirements, but this one just has a single large compartment. Of course, before it'll let me drop anything in, I have to peel off a tracking sticker and put it on the package so that I can track it.

With the package safely registered inside, the courier begins trundling away, navigating to its destination at a top speed of eighty kilometer hour using a combination of laser rangefinders, satellite positioning, and video cameras. If we were back in 2023 when millions of people were using UCS every day, then this courier might have picked up other items and made deliveries along the way, or perhaps stopped to recharge its batteries before arriving at Dr. Whittaker's. Its route was determined by traffic levels, congestion charges, fee levels, customer location, electricity costs, and so on.

Since we're the only two people on its list, I can see that this bot is heading off straight toward Dr. Whittaker, who's waiting on the opposite side of the museum. You might not think that such a simple robot would be so influential (it can't even make anything or talk to anyone, after all), but it turns out that moving things from A to B was an extraordinarily expensive and cumbersome business before UCS appeared.

This little vehicle changed entire industries. It created millions of jobs, and it destroyed tens of millions more. How did it get there? Dr. Whittaker says:

> If you look at the media from the 2010s, the thing everyone was most excited about was driverless cars. However, getting all the safety and insurance regulations in place for their use on public roads took years. It was deliverbots that paved the way. They faced less opposition from lobbyists, and, frankly, they seemed less likely to cause injuries or scare people.

In 2020, when UCS was founded in Toronto by Kevin Wing, it wasn't competitive with existing shipping companies such as FedEx, DHL, and UPS, as it simply didn't have the infrastructure. Instead, UCS focused on two specific types of market: underserved areas in UCS-friendly states such as Nevada and California, and high-density, high-volume cities such as New York and Singapore.

The high costs of installing charging garages and manufacturing their fleet of couriers almost crippled UCS before it got off the ground, but a series of timely contracts with city governments keen to reduce their wage and pension bills helped stave off the company's bankruptcy. UCS's success in fulfilling those contracts attracted more business, and before long they were offering subscription plans across North America and Europe. People were becoming positively affectionate toward the bright yellow vehicles.

But UCS's vehicles were only part of the picture. What UCS delivered wasn't merely goods but the disintermediation of supply. Before deliverbots, getting goods to customers was too costly for most producers. Instead, they had to work with middlemen such as distributors, shops, supermarkets, and warehouses, all of whom took fees that increased the sale price.

UCS changed that world completely by giving producers a direct route to their customers' front door, at a lower cost than ever. People came up with all sorts of novel applications. In New York, grassroots fast-food restaurants dispatched fresh dinners across the city every evening (eliminating food deserts in the process). In London, you could hire a UCS courier for free to take away unused perishables and unwanted clothes and send them to charities. In Helsinki, residents regularly borrowed appliances, power tools, kitchen utensils, suitcases, and gardening equipment from one another via UCS rather than buying them and letting them sit unused for months or years. In Berlin, lovers sent perishable mementos such as scented flowers to one another. And across the world, small-scale farmers delivered their produce directly to the door.

Since the couriers could work twenty-four hours a day and seven days a week without tiring or complaining, their services were priced dynamically. Some smart businesses took advantage of low off-peak prices by dispatching couriers with free samples of their products in order to gain new customers. It was hard to resist trying on a pair of perfectly sized shoes when they were delivered straight to your front door.

When UCS, with its share price sky-high, bought FedEx, it took over its network of warehouses and sorting hubs, allowing it to cheaply route goods on a global scale. UCS also went head-to-head with Walmart and the other giant retail chains. Just as phone and internet carriers from the previous decade had become "dumb pipes" with little to tell them apart, retailers had become "dumb warehouses," ripe for disruption.

These advances came with a massive human cost: millions of people working in the transportation industry lost their jobs to UCS and its competitors in the '20s and '30s. While deliverbots weren't as versatile as human workers, they were much cheaper and rapidly consumed the most profitable parts of incumbents' transportation and retail businesses. Looking back, it's clear that the social upheaval and increasing inequality resulting from the job losses contributed to the demand for basic minimum income that spread across the world in later years.

For a while UCS was the darling of the world, swiftly popularizing new courier systems such as the Silver Retriever, a six-legged "packbot" that could be deployed from larger couriers to carry goods across uneven ground or up and down stairs, and the Storks, copters that specialized in time-sensitive deliveries.

Yet less than two decades after it was founded, UCS itself had become obsolete. Deliverbot manufacturers began to directly rent their vehicles to customers using an open-delivery protocol, and then even the vehicle designs were open-sourced. Just as UCS had disintermediated shipping, open standards disintermediated UCS.

11 THE CONVERSATION BROKERS

Dhaka, Bangladesh, 2024

> I can't go outside without being streamed. I can't visit a shop without people downvoting me. At home I get all sorts of mail through the door, and now you're telling me I can't even have a private conversation in a restaurant? Don't we have any privacy anymore? Is this what our country has come to?

So said Dr. Rajib Ahmed, the Bangladeshi Minister of Law, in an interview in front of the High Court during his corruption trial. The previous year, the Minister had been accused of soliciting bribes from corporate executives in Dhaka in return for favorable legislation.

In itself, this was not an unusual incident in Bangladesh—or anywhere else in the world. Indeed, corruption is still with us today. What was unusual was how the evidence for the case was gathered not through emails or forensic analysis or a whistleblower, but from a necklace array recording sold through a conversation broker.

By 2023, necklaces had become an essential component of wearable computers, largely thanks to the rise of silent messaging. The first models had basic microphones to pick up their users' voices and sub-vocalizations, but later models soon included more advanced array microphones that could record and locate conversations with multiple participants in 3-D space. Social historian Andrea Galloway from the Long Now Foundation explains their unexpected effects:

> If you give people technology that lets them listen into conversations from dozens of meters away, and this technology is capable of recording all the time. ... Well, is it any surprise that all sorts of embarrassing and confidential conversations began appearing? The first recordings were supposedly made available by accident, but it wasn't long before the disruptive nature of the technology became fully apparent.

Dr. Ahmed was one of those who had been recorded. In the corner of an upscale restaurant in central Dhaka, a woman happened to notice Ahmed on his way out. She was no fan of the Minister, and at home she decided to see if she could isolate his conversation from her necklace array's buffered memory. When she discovered that she could, she uploaded her recording to an online leaks Dropbox and received several thousand dollars from a conversation broker. The next day, Ahmed was hauled in for questioning. He simply hadn't imagined that a quiet, private conversation in an exclusive restaurant could possibly be at risk of being recorded.

Excited by the secrecy-busting potential of necklaces, enterprising hackers worked on improving their capabilities. By repurposing acoustic software originally designed for tracking insects, they managed to create virtual, distributed microphone arrays by networking individual necklaces together with highly accurate centimeter-level positioning. Just a few people scattered across a conference room floor or a crowded party could record and isolate every word uttered and identify every speaker, even if there were hundreds of people in the room.

This level of surveillance technology was a chilling scenario for those concerned about privacy, and it got worse before it got better. Galloway explains:

> Most conversations people overheard weren't valuable to them or to anyone they personally knew. But some entrepreneurs understood the corollary: that all conversations are valuable to someone. They became "conversation brokers" and created a huge market that was constantly being supplied with new eavesdropped and streamed conversations. Unscrupulous journalists bought conversations of confidential chats and phone calls; blogs bought every word said by celebrities; corporate espionage firms bought the private conversations of important executives. Hundreds of thousands of people signed up with the brokers within days of their launch, salivating at the prospect of big payouts if they happened to record the right people.

Since it was already illegal in most countries to make unauthorized recordings of private conversations, the biggest conversation broker sites were quickly shut down. But they persisted underground—the technology was too powerful and the rewards too high. Indeed, conversation brokers saw plenty of semi-legal activity, particularly by law enforcement agencies and lawyers. A favorite tactic was to cause mistrials by catching jury members carelessly discussing trials in public.

Many people sought to defend themselves. One strategy involved "defensive recording," constantly streaming their own digitally-signed audio, marking it as their own and thus private so that any attempts to upload similar recordings could be matched and removed by court order. This saw some success but didn't prevent transcripts or altered recordings from being posted. A variation was to forensically examine unauthorized recordings and determine the necklace wearer's identity. Again, this worked for a little while, until virtual repositioning software was released.

A more extreme approach was to simply stop talking out loud. Silent messaging was by definition immune to necklace arrays for at least another two decades, and so the more security-conscious began to exclusively use SMSes to discuss anything remotely private. Contemporaries describe the deeply unnerving feeling of walking into a busy conference hall or a packed restaurant and not hearing a single word spoken out loud. Thankfully, this odd practice has mostly died out now, although for a while there were scary stories about people completely losing their ability to speak as a result of "SMS overuse."

Rajib Ahmed, reminiscing in India forty years after his conviction,* had this to say about the necklaces:

> I heard some say it was the death of privacy. Hah! When I was a child, they said exactly the same thing about CCTV and Google and drones. But being able to eavesdrop on anyone you want, well, it was a real leveler! I don't just mean that you could listen in on rich crorepati or politicians like myself. I mean, you could listen in to your neighbors and friends and enemies and parents. Yes, it caused the most enormous fights, and yes, it made us all a lot more careful about what we say. But maybe that was a good thing. You see, everyone learned that sometimes we say things we don't mean. Sometimes it's okay to be wrong, and to take things back. It's okay to be humble.

In the years after he was released from detention, Ahmed became a fierce anti-corruption activist. However, he maintained that the greatest gift of necklace arrays and conversation brokers was not their ability to catch criminals such as himself, but a more enlightened attitude toward the hypocrisy, weakness, and faults of others. When everything is being recorded and everything is being remembered, you have to be more forgiving of others and of yourself. You have to be kind.

---

* Ultimately based on grounds unrelated to the recording, since it was inadmissible in court.

12 46 CENTRAL GREEN

Santiago, Chile, 2024

Today, if you ask someone what an artificial person is, they would give you a dirty look. Go back a hundred years and they might have talked about robots or computers or neural networks. But if you asked a lawyer or an economist in that time, they'd have given a completely different answer: a company.

At its core, a company is an association of people or organizations who each provide some capital toward attaining a goal, typically "make more money." Centuries ago, companies were recognized as legal or artificial persons that could outlive their founders, persons that had unique abilities and restrictions.

The very first companies, such as the VOC and the British East India Company, were often formed to carry out difficult, risky, and expensive ventures. Accordingly, they were massive and ideally extremely long-lived. But over time, it became useful to set up companies for smaller and shorter endeavors, and by 1856, individuals in the UK could set up limited liability companies on their own.

Our "object" is the founding document for an organization that might once have seemed wholly pointless—a company that didn't last for decades or years or even months, but just two weeks. It was called 46 Central Green. 46 Central Green wasn't a shell company or a holding company, nor a convenient legal fiction for the shuttling around of assets or rights. It had real, human employees from Cordoba, Santiago, and Madrid. Like other "real" companies, it created a real product, sold it, made a profit, and then dissolved itself. It just did it much faster than normal.

Social historian Ernesto Morales of Universidad Nacional de Córdoba explains:

> The prolonged and, as it turned out, systemic unemployment that occurred in the
> early twenty-first century saw the UK, Ireland, Australia, Singapore, and various

US states attempt to stimulate job growth through a package of enterprise-friendly measures including cutting the time required to form a new company. Instead of taking a few days and a number of forms, anyone could set up companies within minutes at practically no cost. Throw in ready-made legal structures, smart contracts, voting systems, and banking that operated purely online, and you could create and run companies without the need for any physical meetings or papers to be shuffled around.

This acceleration didn't have the desired effect of reducing unemployment, which was never properly addressed, but it did open the door to instant enterprises. These companies could take advantage of new opportunities and get products and services to market far faster than larger incumbents.

One might have thought that large companies—some of which had thousands of people and billions in capital to spare—would be best placed to take risks on new products. A mere fraction of their capital could be spent to create new hydroponics kits or design more efficient ships, and their economies of scale—not to mention their established relationships with suppliers, regulators, and customers—would surely demolish any upstart companies.

There were two problems though. The first stemmed from Clayton Christensen's classic problem identified in *The Innovator's Dilemma*, in which successful incumbent companies become fixated on increasing their sales and short-term share price rather than developing risky but innovative new products. The second was the fact that economies of scale were beginning to vanish. While there would always be capital-intensive ventures such as space travel or geo-engineering, larger and larger swaths of the economy required less and less capital to enter.

When there's a 3-D printer on every street, when everyone owns a pair of powerful glasses, when gigabit connectivity is effectively free and ubiquitous, and when delivery can be bought through UCS-FedEx and any number of out-of-the-box fulfilment companies, it makes much less sense to speak of the advantages of large companies. Instead, it's more accurate to talk about their disadvantages—the groupthink, the aversion to disrupting existing business models, the "not-invented-here" syndrome, and the lack of motivation and reward among most employees.

The co-founders of 46 Central Green, Fernando Lopez and Michael Mullen, met at a gallery opening in Santiago in 2019, where they discovered a mutual interest for personalized sculptures. Both were in between projects, and within a few hours, they hit upon the idea of software that would design personalized, procedurally generated Celtic-styled chairs, desks, and dressers. They engaged the services of an HR expert to assemble a team for their requirements and quickly incorporated a company.

The motley group of students, artists, and one former lawyer that comprised 46 Central Green decided to adopt the North Portland model for their legal structure, voting system, and compensation scheme. Under this model, employees would get paid in proportion to the time and effort they put in, with multipliers for skill (based on reputation metrics and records of achievement) and capital injected, plus independent assessments of their results. Once enacted, the actual work of programming, writing, designing, and marketing could begin, conducted furiously over window conferencing and shared VR environments.

Two weeks later, it was all done—their furniture was on the market and selling well, and they'd just accepted an offer to have their designs and software bought out by another company in return for royalties. It was a little quicker than expected, but with the project completed, the company automatically dissolved, and the team went their separate ways. They saw no need in tying everyone together if there wasn't work that justified it. Still, many would work together again on future projects.

To outsiders, it seemed like a strange and mercenary exercise, lacking in the stability and community of companies of old. The truth was, those old companies didn't really exist anymore; they were mostly dead "artificial people" walking. Skipping between instant enterprises was often a stressful and risky way of life, particularly in the times before basic minimum income and before wider cooperatives emerged. But, it was fairer than freelancing; it was fast; and it was powerful—a taste of what was to come.

13 MIMIC SCRIPTS

Earth, 2024

Of all the things we covet—power, money, possessions—there is one that remains stubbornly elusive: attention. A finite resource that must be husbanded carefully, attention cannot be increased.*

Given the absolute limits of human attention, it was all the more galling for people in the early twenty-first century to have to "pay" attention for easily-automated jobs or social signaling. Think of the billions of hours they once wasted every year in dull meetings or sitting in front of desks pretending to work, unable to attend to more interesting matters. One wonders how anyone managed to survive the hierarchical corporate structures of the twentieth and early twenty-first centuries.

By the '20s, a significant minority of meetings were taking place over videoconferencing. Naturally, people were still expected to pay attention during these meetings, but attention had become easy to fake. Real-time video manipulation became affordable for the masses, and the sophistication of expert systems and the size of the databases available to them led to perhaps the most powerful attention-saving device yet—the mimic script.

AI historian Leo Kandel from University College London explains how mimic scripts worked:

> Imagine that you're sitting in your home, taking part in a videoconference with a dozen other people. You're not expected to say anything important apart from perhaps answering a few questions at the end, but you'd rather not spend an hour just staring into a screen and doing nothing else when you have plenty of other things to do, whether for work or pleasure. So, you turn on your personal mimic script.
>
> The mimic simulates your face and body and reacts according to the context of the meeting by, say, nodding along when everyone else is nodding. While this

---

* Except through drastic augmentation techniques.

is going on, you're free to get some real work done, make a sandwich, look after your kids, play a game, or whatever. And if you do get called upon, the mimic will immediately alert you while buying you some time with a 'That's a good question,' or some such.

It doesn't sound sophisticated, and it wasn't. Early mimics were little more than pattern matchers coupled with actual hand-scripting and 3-D engines, but they were good enough to be used by several hundred thousand people within a year. Subsequent investment from companies such as Leverage and Apple created mimics that could carry out simple conversations, first via text and audio, and then over video.

Many people, particularly those from highly structured societies and organizations, found the use of mimic scripts to be lazy as well as extremely rude. It was a common refrain to hear of workers being fired for supposedly "slacking off" at work with mimics even though, technically speaking, the work was still being done. But rudeness notwithstanding, opportunities abounded for these highly productive, extremely lazy pioneers. Skilled mimic script users could handle 20 sales video calls at once, dipping in and out as necessary and tweaking their scripts for each situation.

If that was all mimic scripting was used for—freeing up attention for busy or easily distracted service workers—it would hardly merit a footnote. When people started buying and selling mimics, however, a whole new host of applications opened up.

Mimic scripting, though useful as a labor-saving device, was far more valuable as a kind of emotional prosthetic or tutor for the affectively impaired. "Expert" mimic scripts were made for everyone from doctors with poor bedside manners to the neurodiverse who had problems with social situations. Coupled with wearables, the scripts could be used everywhere unobtrusively, using face recognition to detect who you were talking to and provide the appropriate lines.

Zoe Lem, an early user of mimic scripts, explains how important they were to her:

> When I was growing up, I was incredibly shy. I found it really difficult to talk to people, even friends and family. I just never knew what to say. When a relative died and I said some stupid things, I decided to put a general-purpose mimic script on my glasses. It didn't solve everything, but knowing that I'd always have a line, something to say, when I met people, it made me so much more confident. I kept on using it for several years until I got an agent.

Zoe's mimic was designed by Al-Qahirah, a worldwide collective of actors, data miners, and programmers, who created low-cost scripts for noncommercial purposes. For a fee, users could "borrow" assistance from specialized actors. These actors both finessed scripts for users and also provided real-time affective support (as it happens, many actors had previous experience as Speeky puppeteers). In other words, they'd listen through your ears, watch through your eyes, and tell you how to act and what to say.

If conservatives found general mimic scripts troubling, they thought borrowed-mimics were downright unnatural. How could you tell whether the person you were talking to or even the person you were in a relationship with was mimicking a script—or worse, mimicking another live person? What about the security implications? Asking people to remove their glasses wasn't practical, especially with active contacts starting to enter the market, and mimic detecting software was notoriously inaccurate.

Today, these assumptions of unitary and stable identity seem quaint, but they were fiercely argued at the time. You don't give up thousands of years of tradition and law on a whim. Questions of liability had to be thrashed out in courts around the world, and new applications had to be found before mimics could fully flourish. While most users initially hired instant expertise, in the long run, it was the sharing of expertise that mattered most, along with the construction of amalgamated expert mimics that were useful across a broad spectrum of situations.

Technologically speaking, mimics were a far cry from agents and true AIs, but their surface appearance to users was similar. The ultimately positive attitudes formed toward mimics would later shape the fate of the next technological revolution.

14 THE ALGAL BOOM

Guelph, Canada, 2025

It made the world go 'round. It powered cars and planes, sparked wars, made fortunes, and billions relied on its steady flow. For two centuries, oil—or, more broadly, petroleum—was the lifeblood of the world economy thanks to its high energy density and its ease of transportation through pipelines and on tankers. At its peak, more than one hundred million barrels of oil were transported and consumed per day, with the US, EU, China, and India accounting for much of the total.

By the twenty-first century, new extraction methods from shale rock, tar sands, and deep-sea drilling meant that peak oil was not considered to be a major problem. Even so, the grave political and environmental costs of an overdependence on oil led many countries to seek alternatives.

But what could replace it? The vast majority was used to fuel cars, planes, and other vehicles. While it was relatively straightforward to build electric cars that could travel short distances, high-capacity batteries remained expensive for years, and finding a good alternative to jet fuel was even trickier. Energy historian Dr. Elena Somaiya describes the challenge:

> There was just too much infrastructure and legacy technology that depended on petroleum. In the short and medium term, the best countries could do was to try and manage their addiction and combat its harmful effects wherever they could. In the early decades of the twenty-first century, the world was stuck with needing oil whether it liked it or not.

And inside this flask of greenish-looking water is the substance that turned out to be a brand-new source of oil.

If you look closely, you'll see that the water is swimming with particles of algae—genetically modified algae that could convert atmospheric carbon dioxide into "petroleum-replica fuel molecules." This algae seemed like the perfect solution to the world's needs, replacing fossil fuels without releasing any extra greenhouse gases, and superior to biofuels that required significant processing to work in most vehicles.

The scientific community, however, found it frustratingly difficult to work out how to keep the algae growing reliably and at scale. As with much of the science of the time, advances were made in a haphazard, trial-and-error manner. Researchers were faced with frequent die-offs, competing natural strains, inadequate computing resources, and viruses—not to mention considerable public opposition.

After all, these algae had to grow somewhere. With characteristic early twenty-first-century naïveté, most thought that high-tech energy production would be confined to glass and steel-walled facilities, out of sight and out of mind. Some specialized algae strains—the ones that were usually shown on TV—were indeed housed in bioreactors in advanced labs. The majority, however, were kept in thousands of square kilometers of ponds situated close to carbon dioxide sources like coal plants. Ponds full of increasingly expensive and scarce water.

At the same time, algal oil struggled to compete with more reliable sources of energy, such as natural gas. What ultimately saved it from obscurity was not a single person or company or government; it was a community. The cost of synthetic biology and biofabricators (biofabs) was plummeting, putting the ability to genetically engineer organisms into the hands of thousands of curious experimenters. Algal oil production held a strong appeal due to its real-world applications and the challenge of tailoring strains specific to particular environments around the globe.

The first breakthrough came from a collaboration in 2025 between a retired professor in Nairobi and a team of undergraduates at the University of Guelph in Canada. Their new adjusted strain used an ingenious cocktail of enzymes lifted from bacteria to increase their resistance to environmental shocks while also keeping growth and oil production high. It still wasn't quite hardy enough to be used outside, but subsequent tweaks to suit local conditions pushed its efficiency over the edge and into commercial viability. Biofab historian Kate Spader explains the consequences of this breakthrough:

> Adjusted algae became competitive with traditional modes of oil extraction surprisingly quickly. Yes, countries such as Saudi Arabia were still pumping out millions of barrels per day, but adjusted algae allowed companies and countries—and even cities and towns and households—to produce oil to their own specifications. Transportation costs and price instability were slashed, and the competition was fierce, favoring the water-rich global north in particular.

Along with the traditional oil extracting states, the "algal boom" also harmed the fortunes of global energy companies such as Shell and BP. While you might not have been able to tell from their PR campaigns, their profits still largely came from oil. A few farsighted energy companies rode the boom by investing in biofab startups and algal infrastructure, but adapting to the new world of decentralized research and power generation proved too much of a shock for most of the oil majors. The introduction of the global carbon tax in 2026 was the beginning of the end.

"The Stone Age did not end for lack of stone, and the Oil Age will end long before the world runs out of oil"—so said Sheikh Zaki Yamani of Saudi Arabia in the 1970s. With adjusted algae, the world will never run out of oil, but oil-producing countries did run out of money.

15 NAUTILUS-1

Deimos, Mars, 2025

For a brief time, Kevin Wing, CEO of UCS-FedEx, was the world's sixteenth richest person. His face was captured in countless photos, games, movies, and plays, but the most enduring image of Wing must be him clad in a spacesuit, giving a thumbs-up as the crescent curve of Mars drifts above him. When he landed on Earth two years later, casually sipping from a glass of water refined from Deimos, a Martian moon, he had returned from one of humanity's most extraordinary adventures in centuries.

The history of Wing's glass of water is a story of twenty-first-century exploration, with the forces of science, capitalism, nationalism, and solidarity propelling humanity four hundred million kilometers—all the way to Mars.

Since Schiaparelli and Lowell's early observations of the planet in the late nineteenth and early twentieth centuries, Mars has held a special fascination for humanity as a potential source of alien life. It wasn't until the Apollo moon missions that a human visit to Mars was seriously considered, but the sheer expense meant that for decades robotic missions were the only politically acceptable option. Early space exploration demanded a scale of resources available only to rich governments. Launching just a few expendable chemical rockets required thousands of highly skilled workers, and advances in propulsion technology were halting and slow, owing to short-term thinking and budgeting.

Governments were happy to pursue space exploration for reasons of propaganda, science, and industrial policy, but in the early twenty-first century they were forced to scale back their ambitions due to economic pressures. NASA and ESA turned their efforts toward Earth observation and robotic exploration, leaving the development of launch systems to private companies such as SpaceX, who built on NASA's previous work and moved aggressively to reduce costs.

This is where Kevin Wing stepped in. In 2020, Wing formed a consortium with two other billionaires, plus NASA and SpaceX, to build the Nautilus-1. The Nautilus-1 was a deep-space exploration craft, the first ever capable of traveling to Mars and back—although not able to land anyone on the planet's surface.

Wing's mission for the Nautilus-1 was ostensibly scientific: he wanted to retrieve samples from Phobos and Deimos, perform low-latency teleoperation of robots on the Martian surface, and to test long-duration space exploration technology. However, he wasn't shy in admitting his desire to become the "first person above Mars," nor was he against making a little money in the process by selling media and merchandising rights.

Wing was one of six American crewmembers on board Nautilus-1 when it departed from Earth orbit in 2025. Many scientists were skeptical about the crew's ability to remain psychologically healthy while cooped up in a vessel for two years, but their living conditions were without doubt far superior to those faced by explorers from previous centuries. They had fresh food provided by a hydroponic farm, a centrifuge so they could exercise and sleep under gravity (thus avoiding muscle atrophy and bone density loss), constant video communication with their loved ones on Earth, and effectively unlimited VR entertainment.

It was hardly a grueling ordeal, but it wasn't without mishap.

Six months into the voyage, the ship's controlled ecological life-support system, Plant-Lab, malfunctioned, requiring the crew to resort to mechanical carbon dioxide scrubbers to keep the cabin atmosphere clean. In an unlucky turn of events, the scrubbers contained defective seals that caused them to gradually lose efficiency over a period of months. The ship's 3-D printers weren't capable of replacing the seals, and even with a shortened stay in Mars orbit, they ran an even chance of running out of breathable atmosphere by the time they returned to Earth.

A frantic search for a fix began on Earth, with the Nautilus-1 consortium and its volunteers running tens of thousands of rescue-and-repair sims. Ultimately, the only guaranteed solution was to physically send replacement carbon dioxide scrubbers to the stricken ship—and the only ship capable of making it in time and performing the necessary docking maneuvers was Yinghuo-7, a Chinese spaceship built along the same framework as the Nautilus-1, the product of recent CNSA cooperation with SpaceX.

Yinghuo-7 was stationed in Earth orbit at L3 undergoing testing, but the Chinese government quickly agreed to mount a rescue mission, spurred on by a desire to cement their new position and responsibilities as "first among equals" in the world economy (and it was a good opportunity to distract its increasingly fractious middle-class). NASA and SpaceX launched extra supply and fuel modules for Yinghuo-7 and provided two astronauts who had been training in Jiuquan for a future Chinese/American Tiangong mission. After a single month of frantic preparation, they departed.

Meanwhile, Wing and the crew of the Nautilus-1 continued on to Mars, apparently unfazed by their potential doom. When Wing made his first spacewalk in Mars orbit, he was watched by 2.5 billion people. But the mission's most memorable moment—even more dramatic than Chawla and White's subsequent "moonwalk" on Deimos—was the rendezvous between the Nautilus-1 and Yinghuo-7, the first above a distant planet.

In an hour full of emotion, the Chinese taikonauts ceremoniously exchanged flags and handshakes with the crew of the Nautilus and handed over the replacement parts. People across the world held thousands of rendezvous parties in celebration. Even the taikonauts and astronauts joined in the festivities, with Wing managing to "accidentally" switch the cameras off for a few hours.

The Nautilus-1 returned to Earth first, while the Yinghuo-7 remained in Mars orbit to conduct more research. In the following years, the Nautilus-1 was sold off to a consortium of research universities in India and Europe, and both ships continued to cycle between cislunar space, Mars, and various asteroids.

While the two ships faded from public view, the ties between China and the US remained strong. The events aboard the Nautilus-1 and Yinghuo-7 bound these last two superpowers together more closely than ever before, to the relief of the world, with the samples from Deimos studied by an international consortium and joint US-China space-training missions increasing in number and complexity. This newly invigorated goodwill was never more important than during the Golden Week riots the following decade, during which relations were strained but not broken.

A billionaire's personal stunt had transformed into a symbol of genuine harmony. If that wasn't worth seeing Wing waste the most expensive glass of water in human history, what else was?

16 GLYPHISH

Earth, 2025

A dismissive shake of the head. An arched eyebrow. A warm, familiar smile. An indifferent, rolling shrug.

So much of how we communicate relies on nonverbal cues. Writing may be the most resilient and portable form of information in history, but it lacks the rich context of face-to-face communication. It wasn't until the advent of recorded audio and video that we could imagine conveying the subtleties of personal conversation at a distance.

But video is not perfect. As a passive, noninteractive medium, recorded video could be slow and boring, and videoconferencing was saddled with the expectation that participants would commit their full attention to a real-time conversation, whether or not it was required or justified. Even near-perfect telepresence failed to solve these fundamental problems.

One odd convention from the late twentieth century offered a way forward, though—emoticons. Try turning your head sideways to look at the following punctuation:

:)
;)
:O

Though undoubtedly clunky, it's easy to see what they represent, and in those input and bandwidth-restricted times, emoticons were a simple, cheap, and highly effective means of expressing nonverbal cues in text.

Through the early twenty-first century, emoticons remained popular online and were soon joined by a broader range of vernacular graphics known as "gifs," "animated gifs," and "emoji." From these roots came Glyphish, a new medium that would soon exert a startling dominance over long-distance communication.

Glyphish began as a very basic system to convert physical gestures into symbols by means of electromyograph sensors woven into active clothing.

These sensors, like the ones I'm wearing right now, detected the precise movements of wearers' fingers, hands, arms, shoulders, and facial expressions, and abstracted them into glyphs that would accompany silent text messages (SMSes). Let's turn it on. Ah, and there I've made the glyph for amused tolerance.

While the abstraction process was automatic, users always had the option to omit or alter the generated glyphs, placing them in total control of the message content—in other words, preventing their bodies from betraying their true emotions, as frequently happens in face-to-face conversations. This manual approval process tended to be used mostly by older or less-confident users who were worried about what their interlocutors might think of them, but "Glyphish native" users preferred to bypass it in order to accelerate their conversations. Indeed, many Glyphish natives would find it suspicious to be conversing with someone who took unusually long to reply, believing that it signaled dishonesty rather than a lack of confidence.

Glyphs evolved rapidly. Some originated from widely known symbols and images such as an upraised hand or the Mona Lisa, while others might draw on short videos of celebrities or cats.

At first, glyphs were displayed on recipients' glasses or lenses as simple line drawings, much like earlier emoticons (although obviously not sideways). Over time, they grew in sophistication as people customized their Glyphish systems to recognize a wider variety of gestures. Instead of performing a one-to-one mapping of gestures to glyphs, they could modify glyphs with the flick of a finger or the wrinkle of a nose to turn an angry human-faced glyph into a frustrated cat glyph—all in a fraction of a second. Skilled users could incorporate their glyphs into shared AR environments; a faux pas at a dinner might elicit a dust devil bouncing down the table, visible to all.

Unsurprisingly, these more advanced gestures proved easier for some to pick up than others, leading to a balkanization of communication—although many commentators argue that it was ever thus.

Glyphish blossomed in other ways. While it was initially designed for private conversations between individuals, it was also used in one-to-many and many-to-many conversations. This unnerved inexperienced users, who might receive thousands of glyphs in response to words they'd uttered only seconds ago, but they eventually learned to view them as useful feedback, or else simply ignore them. Likewise, glyphs could be broadcast to massive numbers of people, crossing language and cultural barriers.

Most profoundly, Glyphish became incredibly influential for nonhuman communication. Even as uplifted animals and AIs made significant strides in their Turing scores in the '40s and '50s, many people remained deeply uncomfortable with talking or writing to them. Glyphish helped provide an intermediate language that allowed machines to express instructions or even feelings in an intuitive manner. It's for this reason that many elderly people have a strong affection for "cleaning fairies," which were one of the first household drones to use glyphish as a primary mode of communication.

By the early '30s, Glyphish was in daily use by more than half the world's 8.5 billion population. As an open protocol, it was put to use in every way imaginable, including real world environments—with glyphs being "thrown" into the air at parties and mass gatherings—games, stories, schools, sims, and, of course, Shakespeare adaptations.

Inevitably, though, Glyphish's time in the sun came to an end. Advances in neural laces by the '40s made it possible to converse at even faster speeds, and in richer and more intimate ways, and the near-universal use of AI agents as intermediaries meant that visual glyphs came to be regarded as stiltedly formal.

Yet like all other media before it, Glyphish refused to die. Its combination of the written word and visual design led to a flourishing in new forms of illustration and graphic design, reminiscent of the beautiful flowing style of Islamic calligraphy. To this day, Glyphish continues to inspire new generations of artists—just as it was inspired by previous generations.

17 THE VALUE OF WORK

Earth, 2026

Fast-food chefs. Drivers. Supermarket checkout attendants. Bookshop managers. Street cleaners. Call center operators. Teaching assistants. Bookkeepers. Pilots. Soldiers. Lab technicians. Publishing executives. Warehouse fulfilment workers. Fishermen. Farmers. Copywriters. Couriers. Assembly-line workers. Actors. Bank tellers. Financial traders. Parking attendants. Personal trainers.

The value of a skill decays over time. Some skills have a half-life measured in decades, such as automobile repair or secretarial work. Others are highly unstable, such as the custodians of mayfly technologies such as Betamax. A few skills may last for centuries or millennia, such as politics or writing or hunting or acting, but even those are not immune. Time, chance, technology, and artificial intelligence affect all skills.

There is a limit to the speed at which normal humans can learn new abilities, and if what they choose has too brief a half-life, even the fastest learners can fall permanently behind.

That was the way of the twenty-first century. A wave of machine-powered creative destruction engulfed the human-powered economy—machines that didn't just magnify human productivity but replaced human thought. Entire tracts of society found their skills literally worthless within the space of a decade. The resulting reduction in costs saw individual productivity rocket—for those individuals who still had jobs.

Why should we continue to work so hard, Bertrand Russell asked, with such productivity? Why can't we spare time to luxuriate in our wealth? It was "only a foolish asceticism, usually vicarious, [that] makes us continue to insist on work in excess quantities now that the need no longer exists." He continued, "There is no reason to go on being foolish forever."

Unfortunately, a century was not quite long enough for us to grow out of our foolishness—or to put it a little more charitably, the virtues of hard work that made so much sense for so many millennia are not so easily abandoned. Idleness and relaxation were to be punished; only work could make you valuable.

This archaic view survived well into the twenty-first century, propped up by the resentment of the privileged who were forced to successively compete against women, ethnic minorities, LGBTQIA+ people, young, old, atheists, and countless others for the jobs and wealth that they had believed were their birthright. Even as the jobs dwindled and wealth was sucked past the event horizon of the plutocracy, those who preached the gospel of competition and the so-called free market couldn't imagine an alternative, so they taught us that we should have loyalty to no company, no city, no country, no community, no one. Only to the "brand of me."

A competition needs winners, and for every winner, there must be losers.

Few professions were immune, not even "creatives" or the highly technically educated, those anointed classes of the turn of the century. By the '20s and '30s, a massive oversupply in programmers, fed by shortsighted education policies in the 2010s, caused wages to plummet. And with the low-hanging fruit of the digital transition now thoroughly picked clean, profits had become shrunken and more concentrated.

Millions of computer-science graduates wondered what had happened to the promises of a safe career as they replicated and automated their way through the economy. Anything they produced that was remotely original was copied within weeks or months. It was hard to stay ahead of the curve, but a few individuals and corporations managed it, insulated by thick layers of capital and connections. Others, such as the amplified teams and the hive minds, were so fast they looked like they were cheating. These winners were unaccountable, transnational, transplanetary. Hard to understand. Hardly human.

But even they weren't invulnerable, their fear belied by their desperate grip on the last vestiges of an unfree market. They wielded patents, copyrights, monopolies, planned obsolescence, addiction, locked-in ecosystems, regulatory capture, political corruption, advertising, and lobbying. They guzzled social contributions, such as open-source software and crowdsourcing and incoming personal data, and gave nothing back other than free-if-you-don't-look-closely services. Anything to maintain their position in a vanishing capitalist system. It worked too well for too long.

The fall came from within. Median wages stagnated as automation took its toll and margins were squeezed tight. With fewer people earning money, who was left to buy what the machines were making? How many servants and entertainers could even a billionaire employ? And then there were the burgeoning nonprofit and mutualized services, organizations that made everything and required zero return to shareholders. They could operate leaner than the best, but they only benefitted a select group of the most organized. It was a slow fall, but it didn't stop for a century.

The basic minimum income, funded by a wealth tax, was first introduced in Northern European countries in the '20s, decoupling living standards, health, and wellbeing from the need to find an increasingly scarce job. In halts and starts, it spread through the rest of Europe, South America, and parts of Asia in the following decades. It was not a panacea. China still had to deal with its massive environmental damage, Japan walked farther down its path to becoming an empty, haunted fortress, Europe struggled with maintaining democracy.

Yet there was reason for optimism. The cost of labor had dropped, but so had the cost of capital. A billion companies bloomed. Desire modification, co-ops, free digital entertainment, open-sourced designs, reduced patent lengths, the coming Long Congress—they all reshaped the world, over and over again, faster and faster.

The march toward the basic minimum income seems inevitable. It was not. Political and economic power had become fragmented and chaotic, spiraling out of centralized control. The admirably and infuriatingly cautious grand old tradition of representative democracy was crashing straight into the newborn speed-of-thought digital democracy. Both challenged the other's legitimacy. Both were needed to enact change.

Yet they shared the same ideals: that we are all equal under the sun, and that, as humans, we all have rights.

That if jobs can't be found, we shouldn't go begging.

That there is virtue in working less and flourishing more—pursuing what makes us humans, not machines.

That productivity is a solved problem, but wellbeing is not.

The half-life of tradition is long. The half-life of empathy is even longer. A culture that values toil over all does not die overnight, even when faced with suffering. But it does change, atom by atom, person by person, through the hard work of campaigners who believe in a better world.

Utopia is not a place; it is a process of unending struggle, hard fought and hard earned, to make a more perfect world.

18 TWO TOWERS

Dubai, United Arab Emirates; Mumbai, India, 2026

This is a tale of two towers. One soared a kilometer and a half into the sky, a slender shard of metals and composites whose highest floors could see above the clouds. The other, a squat, functional building made from old-fashioned concrete and steel, barely reached a tenth of that height. Both remain today. One is empty and silent; the other is still filled with laughter and life.

The first building is the Burj Al Shams in Dubai, a small city on the Arabian Peninsula. The second is the NR Tower 14 in Mumbai, India's famous "Maximum City."

We normally look at single objects in this history, but sometimes we can get a better understanding by comparing two. I can't imagine two more similar yet different objects—both among the largest in this book—that symbolize the virtues and excesses of the world in the late '20s.

I'm in Dubai now, standing at the base of the Burj Al Shams, looking up. With the naked eye, I can barely see its summit 1.6 kilometers above me, atop 300 floors. The Burj Al Shams, the "Tower to the Sun," was the tallest structure in the world when it was completed in early 2026, coming amid a global skyscraper race. Newly rich countries such as China, Russia, Saudi Arabia, and India were all eager to overawe their citizens and neighbors with ostentatious displays of wealth, and few things are more ostentatious than skyscrapers.

Dubai had been a frontrunner for some time, flush with oil money and a desire to build an infrastructure that would attract high-value service industries before the money ran out. The Burj Al Shams was to be their jewel in the crown. It was a self-contained and self-sufficient structure with all the offices, apartments, pools, restaurants, concert halls, and even gardens that one might desire—an "arcology." The Burj Al Shams projected a gleaming high-tech and environmentally friendly image; it even contained its own wind turbines and power generators, with smart climate control systems.

There was just one problem: the Burj Al Shams sat in the middle of a desert with vast amounts of empty land nearby. No amount of on-board power generation and hydroponic farms could produce true self-sufficiency, meaning that the so-called arcology was still reliant on outside resources, which raised the question, why bother with a skyscraper when low or medium-rise buildings would have been cheaper? And for that matter, was a truly self-sufficient building with residents living, working, sleeping, and shopping all in the same space even a desirable thing?

One imagines that the builders of the Burj Al Shams knew it was a physical contradiction, but their patrons didn't mind. They wanted to copy the success of other cities such as New York, Hong Kong, and Tokyo by mimicking their external characteristics—high-tech public transport, shiny buildings, expensive hotels, sweeping concert halls—without having to make any societal changes toward egalitarianism.

On opening in 2026, the skyscraper did attract hundreds of the ultra-rich to buy apartments, and several large government-owned firms and multinationals were persuaded to lease office space, but more than a third of it remained empty for a decade, even after rates were cut significantly. The assumption of rising real estate prices proved to be false, and Dubai's luster was beginning to wear thin when compared to the other "re-competitive" countries such as Indonesia and India. Dubai still had money and their status as an increasingly important transport hub, but rising civil unrest made companies and individuals increasingly reluctant to make the Burj Al Shams their home.

Home is exactly what several thousand people called the NR Tower 14, a thirty-five-story skyscraper. Unlike the Burj Al Shams, this building is far from unique—from where I'm standing, I can see five identical towers. In fact, it has the same basic design and construction as buildings from decades earlier: a solid core to contain the vertical elevators with a light curtain wall surrounding it. There are no fancy adornments, no wind turbines, no gardens, and certainly no concert halls—just apartments and shops.

In the early '20s, Mumbai was one of the most densely populated cities in the world, with more than twenty million inhabitants crammed into only six hundred square kilometers. The living conditions were awful. Millions lived in slums, sanitation was poor, healthcare was poor, and quality of life was poor—yet more and more people flooded into the city, lured by the prospect of higher wages and more social freedom, just as occurred in industrial revolutions across Europe and North America centuries earlier.

After the planning laws that restricted tall buildings were modified in 2023, hundreds of medium and high-rise towers sprang up in response to the severe overcrowding. At first, these buildings were far from affordable for slum-dwellers. They arguably weren't much safer either, judging by the number that had serious structural faults due to the low-quality concrete and steel used. Worse, there was resentment among those who weren't fortunate enough to move into the new buildings, and raw anger and riots from those displaced to make way for the new developments.

Yet as the government enforced improved building standards in the late '30s and helped finance the construction of affordable housing, living conditions for many of the poorest in Mumbai began to rapidly improve. Compensation was provided for the displaced. Local governments insisted that these new buildings also incorporate mixed multi-use housing, with shops and offices next to apartments, in an effort to create more livable neighborhoods. Gradually, the towers provided stability and safety to millions and gave the city a basis for becoming the economic and cultural powerhouse of the '40s and '50s.

The NR Tower 14 was one of those "second generation" slum-replacements—solid and reliable, if not beautiful. What made it special was not its technology, but its lack of it. Over the years, the tower and its sisters were reconfigured and reused for a multitude of purposes, from offices to hotels to community centers, and new waves of technology were grafted on to the cheap frame. Its simplicity and versatility were a strength, not a weakness.

Today, the Burj Al Shams lies mostly empty, its tenants having abandoned it for more flexible or practical accommodation. Twenty years ago, it was given to a collective of artists under the agreement that they would take care of it. Now it stands mostly as an art project or a sculpture, depending on who you ask.

The NR Tower 14 in Mumbai, however, is still thriving as a newly renovated set of apartments and flexible community space, firmly embedded in the center of a vibrant city of millions. In this case, simpler was better.

19 THE SUDAN—SHANGHAI CONNECTION

Shanghai, China, 2026

"I can personally guarantee that our partnership with the Chinese Transnational Multi Fund to develop high-tech farms and infrastructure will usher in a new phase of prosperity for the Gambella region." —Elala Asfaw, Ethiopia, 2021

"After everything we did for them, this is how they pay us back? We should make them understand they can't do this to China and kill everyone in Africa who had a part in the bombings!" —Han Peng, Shanghai, 2026

Our object today is a letter—a letter that was written in ink and in blood, carrying a message that underscored the growing power and disparity between two very different countries.

It all begins with the price of food in China.

It wasn't China's billion-plus people that caused food prices to rise; it was their appetites. As China grew richer, it followed a well-trodden path that saw the country's demand for meat, fish, and specialty produce increase dramatically. While crop yields also increased thanks to genetic modification and new technology, the pressures on farmland from urban sprawl, topsoil degradation, and water scarcity made it impossible for domestic growers to keep up with demand. But if there was no space left at home, one option was to look abroad.

Like other nations in the Middle East and North America, many Chinese companies secured millions of acres of comparatively cheap farmland in countries such as Ethiopia, Kenya, Nigeria, and Sudan. The theory was that foreign investment could pay for better crops, improved fertilizers, and higher-quality management. The host countries would gain from the improved infrastructure, extra jobs, and new revenues, while the foreign companies would receive much needed food and profits. It didn't hurt that the companies' governments usually blessed these strategic investments in food security.

Unsurprisingly, the reality was rather different, as Dr. Anthony Liu from Tsinghua University describes:

> In contrast to the orthodox capitalist view which stated that these foreign 'food security' investments would benefit everyone in the host countries, the truth is that those benefits flowed principally to their elites. Land in Sudan, Ethiopia, Nigeria and other countries was often seized from those who had been living on it for generations, sold below market rates, and forcibly occupied. Plenty of kickbacks, bribes, and 'consultancy fees' went to local administrators, developers, government officials, and politicians—but little went to the general populace.

In a thousand villages and towns, the promised jobs didn't materialize, and the hospitals, roads, schools, clinics, and railways were second-rate and shoddily built. Despite the desperate unfairness of the situation, it seemed that any negative effects would be strictly limited to the host country— until the 2026 terrorist attack. Let's trace it back.

In 2020, the Multi Fund made a routine investment in fourteen million acres of farmland in Northern Sudan. While much of the land was developed immediately, a small and less fertile region in Al Jazirah was left alone until April 2021, when local police and contract security services finally moved in to clear the area. The inhabitants were given money for their land—a fraction of what it was worth—and just one month to move out. Most left, but a few locals resolved to fight.

During the first unsuccessful eviction attempt on May 24, 2021, seven locals were shot dead and thirty seriously injured; twelve policemen were also injured. Two days later, a larger police force supplemented by multifund-hired security forces cleared the area, killing a further thirteen locals and scattering the rest. Online media and TV pundits were outraged, but the resulting government investigation was toothless, with only three midranking police officers fired and the Multi Fund paying a few minutes' worth of profits in fines. Overseas reaction was even more muted due to a tsunami in India.

Yet we now know that relatives of those killed in Al Jazirah were planning a response. Many were desperately poor, but their fervent desire for retribution found willing ears in rich Kenyan religious fundamentalists eager to stoke anti-Chinese sentiment. Ironically, the China Transnational Multi Fund had little loyalty to China—its investors and staff were wholly international in nature—but it did have Chinese patrons and a Chinese face, and that's what the fundamentalists planned to strike at.

Three Sudanese men traveled to Shanghai under business visas, ostensibly to meet with electronics manufacturers. Instead, they checked into a hotel near the airport for two nights, then drove out to a flat near Dongtan owned by a Kenyan expat. There the men assembled components for a bomb and hid it inside a van (it was later discovered that many of the parts were stolen, with several Chinese policemen and security officials bribed to look the other way). For the next two weeks, the men from Sudan surveilled the financial district to determine precisely when and where they should attack. During that time, one of the men wrote our crucial letter.

On Thursday, November 6, 2026, the three men drove their van into Shanghai. Two men armed with assault rifles were dropped off in the busy tourist district of the Bund. Before they were shot and killed by policemen, they managed to kill 142 people. Five minutes later, the van rammed into the glass frontage of the Agricultural Bank of China skyscraper and exploded. Twenty-five people standing nearby were killed instantly, and during the resulting fire and structural damage to the building, 598 others died.

The Chinese government initially pointed the finger at Uighur separatists, but a blog post and video from the Sudan Resistance Front quickly clarified matters. The letter from Sadiq Naguib that I'm holding here explains that he was doing this in retribution for "China's occupation of our sacred homeland," and that with luck, this attack would cause them to think again. "I may die," he wrote, "but there are countless others who will take my place."

The bombing was a significant moment for China. The country wasn't a stranger to violent protests or even terrorist attacks, but most had come from regions in China's periphery such as Tibet or Xinjiang, not halfway across the world. The Chinese middle class, at the time dissatisfied with high levels of corruption and economic slowdown, were momentarily distracted by the prospect of an exciting retaliatory attack on the terrorists' "base" in Sudan, which ultimately accomplished little other than killing fifty people and radicalizing a hundred times more.

In an echo of the US's "wasted decades" following 9/11, China intensified its already ludicrous domestic security measures and alienated its former partners in Africa. China's own economy suffered excessively as a result, along with its social compact with its citizens. Unfortunately, it would take over a decade for the country to fully recover.

20 EMBODIMENT

Earth, 2026

The garment I'm inspecting now is hard to grasp. It has the shape of a long, loose shirt that falls to just above the knees, similar to a kurta. It's a one-of-a-kind, designed specifically for its wearer, patterned with scales that warp and bloom any light that falls upon it. No doubt the wearer would make an extraordinary impression at any gathering.

This kurta tells the story of how "blink avatars" consumed the fashion industry in '20s, and, as with all fashion, how they embodied deep divisions within society.

Originally a concept from Hinduism, an avatar was the material incarnation of a deity on earth. From the late twentieth century, the word was adopted for the graphical, digital representation of a user in a computer system, typically in communication software, social networks, and games. As people spent more and more of their lives in digital and virtual environments, the sophistication and value of avatars grew to the point where significant sums of money were spent on creating or acquiring avatars that would reflect the user's taste, or more often, their wealth.

With the advent of affordable, high quality virtual reality and augmented reality heads-up displays in the '20s (even before the creation of Glass), avatars were freed from their stiff, pre-set "emote" gestures like waving or dancing, triggered by tapping a button. Their movements were now mapped directly onto bodies, as graceful and subtle as their own users. The rapid adoption of VR and AR saw the balance tipped over such that millions of people began to spend more time in virtual or augmented environments than unenhanced "base" reality. For them, avatars became more significant than physical clothing. Especially for the poor and marginalized, it was a way to express themselves that did not and could not exist elsewhere.

Being wholly digital creations, the appearance of these avatars could be instantly and freely changed. At first, the choice of avatars was strictly limited by the strictures of the virtual environment you happened to inhabit, but as protocols and moderation technology matured, users could create and inhabit any imaginable avatar, from essentially humanoid figures to fantastical beasts and beyond.

This led, inevitably, to an arms race of sensational avatars. New avatars and clothes for those avatars arrived every week, every day, every hour. Thus, the term "blink avatars," such was the rapidity of change. Amongst more impressionable crowds, failure to keep up with the latest fashions risked ridicule and social banishment.

Like physical clothes, avatars came in all qualities. Modeling their bodies in 3-D and "rigging" their skeletons took skill and experience and time, and discerning users could easily distinguish between rush jobs and true craftsmanship. When attending a social function in VR or AR, such users preferred to wear high quality, well-made avatars. Better yet, one should have a personalized avatar—a one-of-a-kind. And for that, one required a tailor.

Visiting a tailor whether in base reality or in a virtual environment could be an intensely intimate experience. A good tailor wouldn't merely take your measurements; she would observe your posture and movements, and adjust the fit and congruence of your avatar accordingly. More importantly, she would help you design your avatar, often incorporating aspects of your work, personal values, relationships, and accomplishments into its patterns. Appointments were frequently social, with customers seeing their favorite tailors in groups, just as they did at hairdressers and salons. Once you left, the work of actually coding the 3-D avatar was typically, as ever, left to lower-paid artists who received only a fraction of your payment.

Labor relations notwithstanding, avatars became an affordable and environmentally-friendly alternative to the ugly habit of buying cheap, disposable clothing fueled by "fast fashion" trends. In the early twenty-first century, around three hundred liters of water was required to manufacture a single T-shirt. A pair of jeans would run to over a thousand liters of water, blowing past the limits of sustainability in a world that had to save every drop of clean water it had.

At this time, avatars remained largely anthropomorphic. Conservative tastes were only a partial explanation. There were technical limitations to avatars that didn't directly map onto human skeletons and movements, and besides, it was generally seen as being impolite to take up too much space by becoming a centaur or dragon, even in augmented reality. Yet there were still plenty of ways to attract attention with blink avatars, providing you picked up the latest fashions quickly enough.

But this kurta is not an avatar. It's not even a piece of clothing for an avatar. It is, in fact, a physical object. And that takes us to the next phase of this fashion's development.

In the '20s, augmented reality was delivered through heads-up display glasses, and the visual technology meant that the avatars displayed on top of their human wearers looked better or better and worse when combined with certain types of real clothing. Finely-patterned or striped clothes could induce interference in waveguide optics. The reflection of sunlight off shiny surfaces could result in linearly polarized light that produced unusual flares and blooms for viewers. These effects were not desirable from a purely technical perspective, but they certainly were dazzling. And so, our kurta was designed to deliberately induce dazzling effects that would enhance augmented reality avatars.

It was tailored specifically, not merely for the wearer, a jewelery magnate from Hyderabad, not merely for a specific avatar but for that avatar when viewed in a specific set of weather and light conditions. The wealthy might commission a hundred such garments each year, each costing a hundred times as much as a high-end digital avatar.

A trend created by the poor and marginalized and adventurous had been warped into an exclusive expression of wealth and power. It was, in a word, fashion.

21 INSURGENCY IN A BOX

Durban, South Africa, 2027

If you've played a popular costume drama role-playing game such as Star Trek, today's object might seem familiar. It's a replicator. In classic science fiction, replicators can instantly materialize more or less any object, exemplifying late twentieth-century utopian post-scarcity thought and inspiring countless scientists and engineers—including the people who made this box.

What I have in front of me isn't a real replicator, of course; they're still complete fantasy. But it is the first portable and high-quality scanner, a metal and plastic box a little over half a meter on each side with a door on the front. If I open it up and place a toaster inside—also from the late '20s—and subvoc an instruction to it, then it'll initiate a scan.

It takes a couple of minutes to do a coarse millimeter-level scan and a few hours for a more detailed micron-level scan (along with the necessary tomographic reconstruction from the scanning data), but the principle is simple: the scanner uses high-power X-rays to look through the object inside slice by slice and determine the external and internal structure.

Combined with other portable sensors and smart guesswork to figure out the identity of any unusual materials, a user could completely reverse-engineer any moderately complex device or machinery. But this scanner wasn't available for the average person; it was a much more restricted device. So, who used them, and who invented this particular scanner in the first place?

In the early '20s, the US Defense Advanced Research Projects Agency (DARPA) was investigating tools to destabilize unfriendly countries and organizations, from doctored smart drugs to sentiment-altering generative music and games. One project was informally titled "Insurgency in a Box." Successful insurgencies have always required, among other things, a reliable flow of material and money, but with governments becoming increasingly adept at aerial and online surveillance and interception, it was more difficult than ever to keep insurgents supplied. Better, DARPA thought, to make just a few deliveries and make them count.

The scanner, paired with a similarly advanced 3-D printer, was the solution. With enough feed stock for the printer, insurgents would be able to reverse-engineer and sabotage enemy equipment, fabricate bomb components, weapons, custom electronics, keys, tools, and complex machinery. Generous government funding funneled into the project under the guise of the 100 Year Starship Study ensured that a prototype was developed within four years.

Unfortunately, while the DARPA researchers managed to miniaturize the components required such that the scanner could be carried, they weren't able to sufficiently reduce the power requirements. Generating the x-rays required a lot of energy—enough to be noticed by authorities and more than could be supplied by fuel cells or other off-grid generators. The project was a dud, and its researchers moved on to more promising fields.

However, some ideas are like zombies: they never die. The 3-D printer eventually found its way into Union Orbital's factories via a NASA PPI program, but the advanced scanner only saw the light of day through plain carelessness.

During some routine data housekeeping, a DARPA manager wrongly assigned the scanner plans to a lower security level, allowing a junior researcher traveling to the Antarctic to transfer them onto a personal storage device. The researcher fell ill during the journey and had to return home, leaving his storage device behind on his seat, along with his encryption key. By the time he'd realized his mistake, the plans had already vanished.

A few hours later, the unencrypted scanner plans appeared on an anonymous file sharing site for eighteen minutes, at which point the site abruptly vanished, never to be seen again. In those minutes, two hundred people downloaded the plans, including Lerato Lenabe, a thirty-two-year-old entrepreneur in Durban with a background in rapid prototyping. Lenabe had performed well at university and received a number of job offers from Europe but decided to stay in South Africa to care for her parents.

Unemployment was rife in South Africa due to a real estate bubble and stock market crash, and Lenabe hadn't been able to raise capital for the custom medical prosthetics company she'd wanted to set up. Instead, she was forced to work in a series of short-contract 3-D modelling jobs—hardly a situation ripe for flourishing. When she downloaded the plans out of curiosity, she quickly realized the capabilities of the scanner and decided to try and build it using her contacts at the university.

This was no mean feat. While many of the scanner's components could be constructed from off-the-shelf parts, some of the x-ray detection components were still state of the art. Lenabe's story would have ended right there, if it weren't for the fact that the "Insurgency in a Box" (IIAB) had, unknown to DARPA, been deployed in nearby Zimbabwe by the CIA to aid Zimbabwe Liberation Army (ZLA) freedom fighters, preloaded with an enormous library of plans for bomb and weapons components.

For four months the IIAB was powered with energy covertly siphoned from the Batoka Gorge hydropower station, after which the ZLA decided that they would benefit more by selling it to China. It was packed up and sent to South Africa, whereupon the US called up a stealth drone strike on the transport convoy. The drone strike only partially succeeded, and the mostly intact scanner parts eventually made their way to Durban, where Lenabe bought them from a tech market. With some help from some moonlighting engineering colleagues from the University of California, she used the parts, along with the plans she had downloaded, to create a working prototype.

None of this came cheap. Lenabe financed the prototype with a loan from customers who expected to use it to rapidly reverse-engineer (i.e., pirate) toys, medical devices, glasses, and so on. True, there were plenty of other companies around the world doing exactly the same thing, but Lenabe gained a crucial edge with the advanced DARPA scanner. Even a day's head-start in reverse-engineering an expensive device could be worth a tremendous amount of money on the blueprint markets. Soon she was making more than a hundred times her former salary and attracting all sorts of unusual attention.

To throw investigators off the scent, Lenabe made it known that she had received financial support for her scanner from an anonymous wealthy benefactor interested in archaeology and proceeded to invite friends from local museums and galleries to scan items for free, pretending it had been made for that purpose alone. Lenabe scanned thousands of precious and fragile objects at the micron level, revealing microscopic details about their construction and provenance, from Ife sculptures to Bantu relics. More than a few papers were written, and more than a few fakes were discovered.

All good things come to an end. The DARPA scanner's edge over the competition didn't last forever, and three years later, more advanced and energy-efficient scanners were becoming available. Lenabe gave the scanner to a local charity and used her newfound wealth to set up an archaeological technology company, her imagination having being piqued by her museum work. The scanner now sits in the New Library of Malmö in Sweden.

22 TROPICAL RACE SIX

Earth, 2027

At the turn of the millennium, hundreds of billions of these objects were consumed every single year around the world. Yet, in 2026, they went from a daily snack to a dangerous, expensive luxury.

And now I'm going to eat one.

The unusual thing about this fruit is that it comes with its own wrapper—biodegradable, of course. I'm told there's a certain trick to twisting off the stem, but—oh, that didn't work so well. In any case, once you've unpeeled it, the soft fruit inside exudes such a tempting smell that you forget about all the hassle and take a bite.

Mushy, textured, soft, and completely unique. It's a banana, and this strain is one of the few still in existence today.

From the early twentieth century onwards, the Cavendish banana was the variety of choice for countries exporting mass quantities to consumers worldwide. The banana was sturdy, easily transportable, and offered a decent yield to farmers. By the beginning of the twenty-first century, the Cavendish was practically the only variety of banana being grown for export. The risks of monocultures were well known by that point, but the short-sighted nature of hyper-capitalists meant those risks were ignored.

In 2021, Tropical Race Four, a soil-borne fungus named Fusarium oxysporum threatened that business, decimating plantations across Taiwan, China, the Philippines, Indonesia, and Australia. The only thing that prevented the fungus from spreading to the real heartland of the banana business, Latin America, was the robust quarantine regulation set up in the 2010s, handily boosted by fears of international terrorism. Following the scare, stockpiles of methyl bromide chemical sterilizer were ordered in case TR4 ever did gain a foothold.

But nature abhors a monoculture. In 2024, only three years later, an unusual sickness was spotted in five different banana plantations in Colombia. Worried researchers identified it as Tropical Race Six, a fungus that had only been characterized earlier that year in China. Somehow it had slipped past the quarantine and evaded eleven separate Colombian fungal detection spot checks. Ten of the checks failed because the inspectors' detectors were fixed on TR4, and the eleventh didn't occur due to the inspector being distracted by a football match. By the end of the year, TR6 had spread across tens of thousands of acres—and by 2026, it had infected millions of acres.

The sheer scale of the problem made coordinating an effective response impossible, especially with regions across South America already struggling from the damage caused by three super cyclones in the space of five years. There was nothing to stop the banana blight from wiping out the entire industry in the space of three years, and nothing to stop the severe unemployment and social unrest that resulted, contributing to the wave of popular revolutions in Colombia and Honduras.

Earlier efforts to create a new banana variety resistant to TR4, "New Cavendish," had come to nothing. The Fundación Hondureña de Investigación Agrícola (FHIA) had managed to breed a resistant hybrid, but not one that the notoriously choosy North Americans enjoyed eating. At the same time, promising genetically modified strains designed by the Queensland University of Technology were mired in patent litigation and suffered from anti-GM opposition from the EU.

In 2026 and beyond, research into an NNC variety (New New Cavendish) resistant to both TR4 and TR6 proceeded much faster, fueled by hundreds of millions in agribusiness investments. But "fast" is a relative term, and the process took more than five years before arriving at a banana that ticked every safety and taste box. By that time, North American and European tastes had moved on, and heightened global warming was making the economics of banana plantations in Latin America look distinctly dicey. When the few NNC plantations that had been established in 2030 were threatened by a new Banana Restricted Ripening Virus in 2034, the major agribusiness investors chose to write off their losses and abandon the banana business entirely.

Life went on for domestic consumers in Asia and Africa who didn't have to worry about transporting their bananas long distances or storing them for weeks. They had never adopted the Cavendish monoculture, instead growing enough varieties that the occasional virus or fungus couldn't harm them too much.

Eventually in 2040, the banana industry re-emerged, thanks to the genetically modified NNNC variety and the use of sterile growing techniques borrowed from cloned-meat pioneers such as Tiersen. Yes, bananas returned to the market—at fifty times their former price.

The banana I have here right now is the Cavendish, not the New Cavendish, or the New New, or the New New New. No, it's very much the old Cavendish, exactly the same variety that millions ate back at the turn of the century, except grown in a sterile environment and guaranteed free of TR4, TR6, and any other fungi or viruses. I'm not going to tell you how much this cost, but I can say that I finally understand why people ate billions of them a century ago.

23 *DÉSIR*

New York, US, 2027

Our next object is a 2027 interview with Anna Kasell, a representative of the Sex Workers Union (SWU) and producer of *Désir*, the sensationally popular sex game.

Q: My first question has to be: why now?

A: We may be the world's oldest profession, but the past doesn't always predict the future. We've read *The Innovator's Dilemma*. We know what's coming next. So, we've decided to be on the right side of history and get ahead of the curve.

Q: Before we get onto *Désir*, I'd like to talk about the protests. Clearly not all sex workers agree with your organization's move.

A: People will always have differences of opinion. That's fine, and it's their right to disagree. Maybe they think that they can survive on their own for the next five or ten years, but I have a responsibility to take care of all of our members in the long term. And honestly, I think some people are underestimating the capabilities of this new technology.

Q: So, *Désir*. Does it seem—

A: Have you tried it?

Q: Well, this isn't about me, it's—

A: Because there's no point in us talking about it if you don't know what it's like.

Q: Okay, yes. I have tried it.

A: Wonderful! I'm sure many of your followers have as well, even if they might not be quite as brave as you to admit it.

Q: So. Désir. I understand that while the Sex Workers Union contributed a lot of time toward the design and training of the agents, most of the technology was handled by Moshii. Why did you choose to work with them instead of Oculus or Huawei or doing it yourself?

A: We've got an Oculus at home for games, but it's no good for genuinely sensual experiences. We chose Moshii because they're hands-down the best when it comes to epidermal stimulation, and their olfactory capabilities are industry-leading. As for doing it ourselves, that's very flattering, but we're not technologists. We're sex workers.

Q: Désir is far from being the first to market. Back in the early '20s, were you worried when sex games were becoming widespread?

A: Not at all. They looked awful! The AI was just terrible, and there was no galvanic nerve stimulation. But yes, I was worried about what they might become. The best real-world sex will always be superior to the even the best *Désir* agents, but let's face it, real world sex isn't as convenient; it isn't as accessible; and it costs a whole lot more. So, we know from history who wins and who loses in this kind of competition. I couldn't bear the idea of our profession being cannibalized by a bunch of outsiders, so I decided that if it was going to happen, it'd better be at our own hands.

Q: Désir has a lot of competition, particularly in Europe and China. They're cheaper and they're catching up quickly. Spice alone has a quarter of a million new users joining every single day.

A: Trust me, there's a point at which cost doesn't matter anymore. If they want to fight over the teenage market by providing cheap, mindless dolls, they can go right ahead. *Désir* is a premium product, and our clients choose us because they know every agent and every scenario has been tested to perfection. We've got the best tech, the best writers, the best artists, and all of that costs money. We're the Apple of sex games.

Q: Exactly what involvement does the SWU have in *Désir*? Did you just provide the capital and help design it, or do you have an ongoing role?

A: We're fully involved and fully committed. We just announced our API yesterday which allows *Désir* agents to create their own custom puppeteering interfaces and hardware, and we're looking at opening it up to the public soon. Our agent AI is pretty good as it is, but, like I said, nothing beats the intimate connection that only a real human can make. SWU members are experts, they know what to say, how to move, and how to act better than the best AI, so I think any of our members who choose to get involved in puppeteering will boost their income more than they think.

Q: What about the morality of *Désir*? Do you pay much attention to critics who say you're devaluing and destroying real relationships?

A: What we're doing is healthy. There's absolutely nothing wrong with a sexual appetite, and even in the best mono relationships it's common for partners to want something different. Normally that'd lead to a messy affair or a one-night stand—which is far worse than seeing a sex worker, if you ask me—but now they can just use *Désir*, and there's no harm done. Believe me, we've had messages from thousands of couples who thank us for saving their marriages!

Q: But not everyone agrees with that. Representative Spence just introduced a bill calling for regulation of sex games, saying that they're a danger to society and to young people's minds.

A: He's full of shit, if you'll pardon my French. Thirty years ago, he'd be trying to outlaw gay marriage and sixty years ago, he'd be saying television is the devil's work. He won't get the votes. I can guarantee that.

Q: What about the case in Florida, though, about the serial rapist who was found with a copy of Spice and the skins of his victims in the game?

A: Are you serious? That man was sick. He would've been dangerous with or without sex games, and I find it offensive that you'd even make the connection. I'm sure he's on Glass as well, and no one blames them.

Q: Still, you've got to—

A: No, I don't. We've got study after study showing the overall rate of sexual assaults has been declining in the US, both before and after the introduction of sex games. The Kinsey Institute at the University of Indiana just published figures that prove sex games help reduce sexual violence. People like Representative Spence should be directing federal tax dollars toward us, not threatening more regulation.

Q: The US wouldn't be the first country to establish regulations, though.

A: If a democratic country decides to regulate sex games after a reasoned, well-informed debate, that's their choice. But let me tell you, I've got access to our own stats, and we're still seeing plenty of demand from countries where we're banned. All it means is that they don't get to tax our revenues. If they really want to stop people using sex games, then they'll have to figure out a way to stop people wanting to have sex. Let's see how that goes down with the voters.

Q: So, can you comment on the allegations that you're assisting the illegal export of *Désir* to countries that regulate sex games?

A: Don't be absurd.

Q: And finally, what's next for *Désir*?

A: Our number one most-requested feature has been multiplayer, for obvious reasons. It's a tricky one to crack because we need to get the latency way down and launch a rock-solid matchmaking service for people with different fantasies, but we think we've figured it out.

Q: Player numbers still growing?

A: That's right. Our ambition is to have the majority of the world signed up to *Désir*. After all, we're fulfilling a very basic human need.

24 SAUDI SPRING

Riyadh, Saudi Arabia, 2028

This is how the revolution began: not out of the barrel of a drone but with a stone hurtling through the air. For all that life was moving online, it was the physical world that really mattered when it came to power and control in Saudi Arabia in the late '20s. A thrown brick, hefted by human muscle, was the rawest challenge to that power, just as it has been for thousands of years.

Some of these very first weapons used in the "Saudi Spring" are laid out on the floor in the National Museum in Riyadh. Rough, pitted stones prized from the ground or torn from smashed walls, they were used as projectiles to beat back the government's security forces. We know that these are the very same stones used by the revolutionaries thanks to the sheer quantity of documentary recordings made from literally millions of angles and viewpoints across the country—from glasses, necklaces, buildings, cars, bicycles, copters, drones, blimps, and satellites.

The Saudi Spring was not a peaceful revolution, nor was it particularly bloody, but it was watched by the whole world, peering in from every angle, second by second.

Saudi Arabia in the '20s was a national contradiction. It ranked amongst the region's most powerful economies, spending lavishly on military equipment and social welfare, but it was a precarious kind of power. The vast majority of the country's wealth and exports flowed from oil, and the resulting high youth unemployment bred a virulent dissatisfaction with the government.

None of this had been a problem for the previous few decades, but by the '20s, the situation had changed. One difference was oil. Developed countries were diversifying their energy sources with natural gas, adjusted algae, wind and solar power, and pebble-bed nuclear reactors. Saudi oil exports were still large, but oil prices were stagnating, and long-term projections for demand were resoundingly negative.

Lower oil revenues meant less money to distract from the vast differentials in wealth between the poorest and richest, less money to hide the wasteful profligacy of the monarchy. No longer was it possible to dole out massive amounts and create useless jobs whenever unrest flared up. Instead, the government chose to spend its dwindling reserves on the security services and faltering attempts to diversify the economy through cargo cult-like, high-tech cities, all of which ran straight into the country's stultified bureaucracy and long-standing opposition to entrepreneurial culture. The protracted Yemen civil war, inflamed by Saudi adventurism, resulted in millions of refugees at the borders, further heightening internal tensions.

Like many other countries in the Middle East, the majority of Saudis were under thirty. They had grown up with access to the internet—albeit censored and monitored—and satellite TV. While they were rightly skeptical about the wonders of the West, they were still attracted by notions of freedom of speech, rights of assembly, access to advanced technology, gender and sexual equality, cognitive enhancers, and free and fair elections. Norah Al-Asmari, a political historian from Riyadh University, says:

> We wanted what the rest of the world had. Living in Saudi Arabia at that time was like sitting in an online lobby waiting to join a game but always being passed over because you were too slow or too new. We were being overtaken by everyone—by Egypt, by Bahrain, even by Iraq! I wanted to smash my phone, I was so angry. And that's not even counting how bad us women had it. So what if we could drive? Who cared, when our net access was restricted, we couldn't get jobs, we couldn't hope to achieve or to dream or to discover. We saw what happened in 2011, and we thought it would happen here. But it didn't. Not until 2028.

The Spring revolution began in Riyadh on May 18, 2028. A crowd of three hundred gathered outside the Ministry of the Interior to demand justice for Muhammad Al-Farahan, a popular streamer who had been jailed, tortured, and killed for accusing the monarchy of destroying the country's youth.

The Ministry made no official response, and security forces kept their distance, hoping not to draw attention to the protesters. But when thousands took to the streets in Al-Awamiyah, Jeddah, and Qatif the following day, the government made the rash decision to temporarily shut down internet access across the country with the aim of destroying the protesters' ability to communicate.

The crackdown didn't work. In fact, it only drew attention to the protests. Three days later, a march of twenty thousand people in Riyadh, coordinated by repurposed mesh-network disaster kits, turned into a massacre. As the crowds approached the Ministry of the Interior, fearful ministers ordered troops to fire warning shots. Some went fatally astray. The crowd responded by tearing up the street and hurling stones, setting cars on fire, and barricading the road. Scenes from the march taken from a thousand cameras were spread over the mesh and across the country within minutes, spawning dozens of new protests across the country. More were killed, and even more came forward to fight.

Having anticipated protests for decades, the monarchy acted quickly, putting into place a contingency plan prepared years earlier. Deepfake videos and forged emails were released on government websites that "proved" the protests had been instigated by Shiite spies and provocateurs from Iran. A disinformation campaign about "pernicious Western involvement" followed soon after. Most people distrusted the official accounts enough to continue the fight, but those allied to the royal family understood that their interests lay in the status quo and so did nothing.

Other countries, including the US, declined to officially intervene. It was an internal matter, they said, and besides, they were too busy with their own domestic strife. And so deadly clashes raged across Saudi Arabia for the next two weeks, leaving thousands dead. At first, it seemed the trained troops and powerful military of the government forces would easily triumph. But the revolutionaries received considerable help in the form of weaponized drones smuggled in from Iraq and intelligence from sympathizers in the Saudi Arabian secret services.

Together, they provided the revolutionaries with their own means of communication and control, crucial to their survival. One of their leaders, Wajnat al-Sharif, told her followers to "tear out every wire, destroy every radio, smash every antenna, and block every frequency" in order to blind the monarchy and give the rebels a monopoly on communication.

For weeks, there was no knockout blow on either side. The monarchy was reluctant to make their crackdown too bloody in fear of inciting further anger from the families of the youths, and the revolutionaries didn't yet enjoy enough popular support to overcome the military. It wasn't until technicians at the King Abdulaziz City for Science & Technology—the hub through which all international internet traffic flowed into Saudi Arabia—released terabytes of damning evidence of corruption, graft, torture, and illegal orders that the monarchy realized their position was becoming untenable. Losing the trust of the people was one thing; losing their trust in the technology they depended upon was another.

A truce was declared. King Ahmed accepted strict limits on his power, and a new constitution was introduced. The military remained loyal to the monarchy, but the revolutionaries forced in their cameras and surveillance devices. There was little the military could do when almost literally every word they spoke and typed was being watched.

A year later, the first elections were held. A new chapter had begun in Saudi Arabia's history.

25 THE HALLS

Liverpool, England, 2028

There are few things more quintessentially human than eating together. We celebrate with food, we commiserate with food; we renew old ties and create new ones over breakfast, lunch and dinner. Having good company while eating is something we can all enjoy—even the word "company" originated from those who eat bread together.

The object I'm sitting in front of represents that tradition perfectly. It's a very simple, long wooden table, big enough for about eight or ten people sitting on either side. It doesn't come with any robots. It has no radio tags or resonance chargers or wireless antennas; in fact, it doesn't have any wires at all. It's just a table. Made out of wood.

This table sat in the Castle, a pub built in Liverpool, England, in 1948. The Castle changed hands a dozen times, gradually passing through ever larger corporations until the crash in the '20s, when it was bought and restored by a local family, the O'Reillys, at a fraction of its old price.

Rather than running a normal for-profit pub, however—a risky proposition, given that many locals had grown used to staying at home and buying cheaper drinks—the O'Reillys converted the Castle into a subscription-based canteen. Guests were encouraged to pay in advance for bundles of meals, and while there were few choices on their daily menus, the pub more than made up for that in affordability, healthiness, and variety over time.

With predictable cash flow, no rent to pay, and strong ties to the community, they were able to just about make ends meet, although they did have trouble finding enough subscribers for the first year. Over time, though, the Castle became a regular destination for many locals who might visit once or twice a week to catch up with neighbors, meet new people, or simply get some healthy food.

In 2028, a popular caster from France featured the Castle in a piece about communal restaurants—which she termed "halls" after classical monastic refectories and the collegiate system in Oxford and Cambridge—and triggered a mass movement that rippled across the world.

It's hard to pinpoint one particular reason why halls became so popular as a way of eating. One simple attraction was that the meals served at halls, being bought and planned in advance, could be freshly cooked from high-quality ingredients bought in bulk and delivered via UCS-FedEx. Another was that subscribers often helped with preparation and cooking. Many appreciated being able to learn how to cook in practice rather than through augmented reality (AR) or mimic-scripted tutorials, and it was common to see children getting involved as well.

Halls varied in size from dozens of subscribers to thousands, but the most successful tended to attract a few hundred reliable guests who would come a few times a week. This represented another of their strengths: the vibrant mixing of individuals and classes that occurred at mealtimes. While guests could, and frequently did, choose to sit with friends and acquaintances, smart hosts would gently encourage them to occasionally talk to new guests, something that they typically enjoyed and which helped to cement the community together.

Of course, not every hall could do this. Some were just too small to allow for proper mixing or had too homogeneous a group of guests. One popular way of tackling this problem was to offer discounted or free meals to travelers or by arranging "exchange" dinners. Another way favored by more adventurous halls involved consensual AR environments. These environments joined together multiple halls around the world to form a "virtually infinite" hall, where physically sundered guests could mix and talk. This usually worked best when the halls coordinated their menus and even furniture, leading to more than a few halls adopting the same style of tables and chairs that the Castle had.

Today, halls are commonplace, seemingly part of a continuous tradition extending thousands of years back to ancient Greece and Sparta. But we shouldn't forget how deeply alienated many people were from their neighbors during the twentieth and early twenty-first centuries. It was an uncomfortable, unusual period that began with the movement of millions from the countryside into cities, sundering whole communities, and ended with the development of new forms of local and virtual communities.

Halls speak to our strong need for social interaction and for the ages-old idea that people will always need to eat—and they'll enjoy doing it together.

26 AMPLIFIED TEAMS

Earth, 2028

In 2028, interest in amplified teams increased sharply, with many companies offering matchmaking and integration. I'll let one of the brochures of the day tell the story.

"SO, YOU WANT TO JOIN AN AMPLIFIED TEAM?" BY AMPLIFIED GREEN

Congratulations! Amplified teams are among the most valuable and productive members of our society. They perform challenging and intellectually stimulating work that others cannot, and they are highly compensated for their efforts.

Chances are that you've heard about amplified teams before. Maybe you've watched a stream or read a book or played a game that featured a team. Fiction is different from reality, of course, so before you make the decision to join, you should understand that reality.

> Being on an amplified team is like knowing the answer to a question before you ask it—or like wearing lenses and using scripts and speaking to agents after a lifetime without them. Everything in life becomes so much richer and more vibrant. Everything you see and feel becomes drenched in data and connection and meaning.
>
> —Deborah Deans, member of Amplified Green

The Basics

Amplified teams contain three to seven human members supported by software that allows them to communicate with one another and with AI support systems at an accelerated rate. Unlike traditional networked teams, most amplified teams work in close physical proximity in order to reduce lag and take advantage of nonverbal cues that can increase trust and bandwidth. This helps develop heightened levels of team reasoning and "limited collective utility" maximization.

These are just general principles. In practice, every amplified team operates in its own unique way. Larger teams of up to ten and even fifteen members aren't unheard of, although coordination instability can become a problem. Some translunar teams are capable of working at great distances and high latency, with members communicating with multiple light-second delays. It's safe to say these are true exceptions though.

The compact, personalized, stable, and tightly networked nature of amplified teams makes them ideal for tackling knotty or time-sensitive challenges that cannot be easily distributed to the usual problem solvers. Take the case of a globally simultaneous product launch or an important real-time political speech: an amplified team will be able to provide unified, coordinated, and instant responses to second-by-second changes from the market or the audience. Team members will communicate constantly with one another and with their AI support systems to work on the most critical parts of the challenge, resulting in a flawless product launch or a perfectly-pitched speech. But their strengths do not come easily.

Ultimately, amplified teams are consistent in their abilities rather than their features. They possess a complex network of similarities, a set of "family resemblances," that cuts across technologies and processes. What they share is the ability to outperform any individual human or any lesser-integrated team at any intellectual task.

What Makes a Good Team Member?

Since every amplified team is different, there's no single model for an ideal team member. Research shows that the people who integrate well and perform best with an amplified team have the following skills:

- Excellent empathy and communication skills
- Ability to speak multiple languages
- Advanced skills in at least one area (such as writing, programming, negotiation, kamilanning)
- Interactional expertise
- A high degree of adaptability

If you do have these skills, congratulations!

Some signs that you may be a good team member candidate include:

- A talent for conflict resolution
- Genuinely good listening skills
- The ability to let arguments drop

Do I Still Keep My Personality?
Of course! While some amplified teams choose to present a "united" face to the public, even the most integrated team members remain fully capable of an independent life. It is true that after leaving a team, some detached members may appear to have a substantially changed personality, but the same would be true of anyone undergoing a significant life event. At Amplified Green, we pride ourselves on our detachment expertise, with a 99.6 percent success rate as measured by the International Amplified Team Organization.

What Kind of Linking Technologies Do Amplified Teams Use?
Although magnetoencephalography and dermal tattoos are currently in favor, some teams have had success using extremely low-tech solutions such as necklaces and glasses, or even terminals. Others prefer to use experimental and even physically invasive techniques. Unless all of a team's members are experienced and confident in a particular linking technology, we usually recommend that they try out the full range before settling on a solution.

What Kind of Jobs Are Amplified Teams Good At?
There's no limit to the challenges that teams may take on. It's not all science and political problems. Last year's "Best Picture" at the Oscars was created largely by the Scarlet Heart team based in Los Angeles! Other notable occupations include:

- Games development (Corazon)
- Swarm teleoperation (BHA-ETH)
- Negotiation (The Stuarts)
- Hypothesis development (Chandra)
- Intelligence services (Banburismus/UCC)

Are Amplified Teams Good for Society?
Though they are still comparatively new, amplified teams have made countless positive contributions to society. They have made technical and scientific breakthroughs, improved the efficiency of companies, charities, and governments, and produced critically and popularly acclaimed works of art. While some claim that teams are displacing other workers, the truth is more complicated and cannot be measured purely in employment figures and inequality indices. Many advances made by teams have created new jobs and new forms of wealth, and many teams voluntarily fund retraining programs for anyone affected by their work.

Sounds Great! How Do I Sign Up?

It's easy—just complete the attached test and grant Amplified Green limited access rights to your social/medical/psych records. We keep all information in confidence, and we should have an answer about your suitability back to you within ten minutes.

Why Choose Amplified Green?

Amplified Green is a fully integrated agency approved by the IATO. We've recruited for many of the world's leading amplified teams, and we help introduce them to new jobs and clients. Our deal is simple: we perform testing, matchmaking, and training; we customize your hardware and software and offer use of our job market exchange; and we offer world-leading detachment therapy and fully comprehensive insurance.

All of this is in exchange for 12.5 percent commission on your earnings for the next five years, plus a negotiable share in royalties for any inventions or discoveries made. There are no advance fees or hidden costs, and we are confident that our services cannot be matched—just check our reviews!

27 MIDDLE EYE

Hilbre Island, England, 2029

At low tide, you can walk to Hilbre Island. It's only a kilometer and a half off the coast, but unless you're prepared to get your boots soaked, you'd be wise to circle in from West Kirby's newly-restored beach. As soon as the waters recede, you'll head straight west until you hit Little Eye, a flattened slice of red Bunter sandstone, the first of the two islands before the main attraction. Then it's northwest to the dagger-like Middle Eye with its wind-blasted plane of tough grass and scrub, and a final short stroll to barren grandeur of Hilbre Island itself. It's an hour's walk, and you'll have another hour to explore the ruins or join the birdwatchers looking out for oyster-catchers, shelducks—even a purple sandpiper, if you're lucky. No one has lived on the island for decades, so unless you fancy shivering in the cold for several hours, you'll want to set off before high tide.

The exiles had no such luxury. A group of fourteen who had been formally ostracized by their people, they were taken here and prohibited from leaving or communicating with the rest of the world for ten years. Even the drone surveillance was fully automated to prevent any chance of messages being read from the air. In a time of connection, they were one of most disconnected and intentionally and successfully hidden communities on the planet.

They arrived in 2029. They were permitted to leave in 2039.

The UCC, a quasinational Russian charitable organization, purchased Hilbre Island in 2025, the nadir of England's financial depression. Following its exit from the European Union, the United Kingdom effectively dissolved when Scotland and Northern Ireland voted for independence. Distracted by ongoing battles against Welsh separatists and desperate for hard currency, England sold off entire villages, towns, hills, and islands to the highest bidders.

In all, hundreds of square miles of territory were signed over with ninety-nine-year leases. The lease agreements prohibited the deployment of military assets or personnel, but otherwise leaseholders had unfettered control over their land and airspace. The English were inured to the dissolution of its borders. Few cared about a few more pieces of their map being scrubbed out.

Most of the "Leased Territories" built upon England's unique heritage and location, becoming tourist resorts, theme parks, spaceports, network operation centers, and data stores. A few were used for more unconventional purposes–such as an open-air prison.

The Universal Cause Collective was an independent Russian research organization originally dedicated to the improvement of amplified team technologies. Not long after its founding, however, it ventured into new fields including life extension, resurrection, and transhumanism under the direction of its charismatic lead scientist, Evgeny Pasternak. Its early breakthroughs in artificial intelligence attracted millions of customers eager to buy its services, fund its wildly ambitious goals, and pledge their allegiance to its cause.

In order to transform the soul, Pasternak believed that he must also transform society. Of course, he was more than willing to lead that society himself, and amid the second collapse of the Russian Federation, the UCC attained effective self-rule in a series of massive enclaves, buying independence from cash-strapped local authorities through block voting, judicious political donations, and outright bribery. Their towns and cities were reorganized around a real-time cybernetic economy planned by quantum-powered AIs, with their human population seemingly united in a drive for human transcendence.

But even when a society shares the same goals, the details of execution can be debatable, and what some societies would call the loyal opposition, others would call heretics. Treat them too leniently, and you risk their ideas spreading out of control, but punish them too harshly, and you create martyrs. The middle path is often the best.

Standing at the foot of the former Telegraph Station, you can take in the exiles' dwellings, repurposed from the existing buildings on Hilbre Island: the bungalows, the bird observatory, the central Telegraph House and Buoy Master's House, and for one unlucky couple, the Sea-watching Hide on the northernmost tip of the island. It was hardly Alcatraz–the exiles weren't flight risks and they never tried to escape–but there was little attempt to make the dwellings anything beyond safe and livable. Since the exiles had all necessarily supplies delivered each month however, they had plenty of time to engineer their own improvements. And it was as engineers that landed them on Hilbre Island in the first place.

To put it plainly, they were exiled due to a small, petty disagreement, not out of any grand philosophical principle. Pasternak's planned economy had directed their group to research a particular kind of molecular manipulator using a particular kind of superconducting material, and the exiles wanted to use a different material.

As the UCC saw it, their refusal to even consider the suggested research direction constituted a breach of trust in the leaders of the society they had voluntarily joined. Because they refused to leave the UCC and the UCC preferred not to eject or imprison them, exile was accepted as the least-worst option.

Due to the UCC's monopoly on surveillance, we have few contemporaneous records of the exiles' activity while on Hilbre Island, and since their return the exiles were strangely silent on their stay. Archaeological evidence however, sheds some light on how they occupied themselves: rebuilding the bird observatory, clearing a running loop around the perimeter of the island, retrofitting the Telegraph Station into a wind turbine, and—unexpectedly—building a new dwelling on Middle Eye.

It's unclear how the disagreement arose, but in the summer of 2033, three people were effectively exiled to Middle Eye. Forensic analysis of the environment on both islands is suggestive of a complete break between the two new groups other than the regular transfer of supplies every month.

Perhaps this time there was a meaningful philosophical difference between the Hilbre Islanders and the Middle Eye Three. Or perhaps they just couldn't stand each other any longer. They had already been separated from the rest of humanity. What more was another separation? Sometimes dialogue can only take you so far, and besides, their little world had enough space for a peaceful but disengaged co-existence.

Who knows, perhaps the Middle Eye Three had their own differences. But then Middle Eye was small enough as it was and Little Eye not fit for human habitation.

Only a year after the exiles returned to Russia in 2039, the UCC fell apart. Pasternak had died from a rare cancer in 2037, and absent his leadership, his collective disintegrated into competing companies and cults. Thanks to massive amounts of Chinese investment, the Russian government was once again exerting its centralizing power, absorbing the UCC's enclaves. What was once divided become integrated, and the exiles' crimes were soon forgotten.

28 *THYLACINUS CYNOCEPHALUS*

Minnesota, US, 2029
Rolling Stone, *June 2029*

The Queen of Clades, Natasha Frei, wakes up, grabs her glasses, and takes in a report. It's packed with data and interactives and all manner of sims from her staff, but there's really only one thing she cares about: the Number. The Number is how far the 500 Project has reached in its single-minded pursuit of reversing all the human-caused animal extinctions of the past half-millennia—and the reason it matters is that Natasha Frei is running out of time.

It's March 23, 2029, and the Number is nowhere near where Frei needs it to be. She had planned to reach 11 percent by now, but sequencing failures for the Labrador duck and endogenous retroviruses wreaking havoc have meant that right now she's only at 8.4 percent. Some think that she's blindly optimistic, that she's been driving the 500 team too hard for too long, that she's putting their funding at risk. That news would be bad enough, but there's worse: some whisper that she's a micromanager, just as bad as Musk. That they'd be well beyond 10 percent by now if it weren't for Frei.

But maybe that's not a bad thing. Like her wards, Frei's a throwback to the past, an avatar of old-school command and control that has somehow emerged unscathed in our Age of Fragmentation. Micromanagement might not win popularity contests, but it does give the Project the kind of laser-like focus that more distributed teams can only dream of.

Frei doesn't listen to the whispers. She just hates wasting resources and talent. If that means an authoritarian approach, so be it. One thing is clear, though: Frei is committed to the Project. "We're going to clean up our own mess," she says.

"Our mess" is the legacy of the past half-millennia of the Holocene epoch, where hunting and environmental change have caused an estimated ten thousand to one hundred thousand extinctions. You could make those numbers bigger or smaller by fiddling with the time window, but the

Project claims that going back only, say, a century is shirking our inherited responsibilities. And why five hundred years? That's the half-life of preserved DNA, which also explains why we shouldn't be expecting any dinosaurs. As they say, you can't clone from stone.

It started with *Thylacinus cynocephalus*. You'd know it as the Tasmanian wolf, a surprisingly large, striped, carnivorous marsupial—or at least, you would if you lived in the 1930s before it became extinct. We thought we'd never see it again, but less than a century later the thylacine was successfully revived and restored to the Tasmanian wilderness, and the researchers involved were covered in glory.

Frei was one of them. She quickly became a leading light in the de-extinction community, founding the 500 Project. She set up partnerships with the Beijing Genomics Institute, a wonder of the world capable of sequencing a megagenome per hour; the Frozen Zoo in San Diego; and the Svalbard and Sussex Seedbanks. When Frei went toe-to-toe against a US consortium intent on patenting the genomes of revived species, she firmly established herself in the public eye. She pursued them right up to the US Supreme Court and won, forever ensuring the genomes would remain in the public domain. To top it off, she managed to get double her funding from the National Science Foundation. She is a woman who gets things done.

The 500 Project has a budget in the tens of billions, fueled by a mix of government contributions and direct subscriptions. It's not the only de-extinction program out there—others have set their sights even further back in time, backcrossing extant genes in living animals to reach long-extinct species—but it's the biggest. And after the Siberian debacle, where amateurs released revived species back into the wild unprepared, Frei is also seen as the responsible choice. Relatively speaking.

She's taking a rare physical visit to the Project's facilities in Minnesota today. On the car over, she fires off responses to the cloud of journalists following her. For instance:

"Isn't the 500 Project taking money away from other conservation efforts? Won't people ignore endangered species if they think you'll just revive them once they're extinct?"

Frei sighs. "They always ask the same questions," she tells me.

She murmurs a quick reply: "Reviving a species is much more expensive than conserving it, so I've always said the world should spend more on conservation efforts. But you need a backstop, and that's the 500 Project. Oh, and the work we do highlights the importance and joy that revived species can bring and that helps everyone in the conservation community."

She doesn't mention the spin-offs. Maybe she's tired. Two years ago, the Project worked out how to reliably make induced pluripotent stem cells—reprogrammed adult cells that can differentiate into specialized cells—from fibroblast cell cultures. They use them to create germ cells for the de-extinction process, but the same technique can also help increase genetic variability among highly endangered species.

Sometimes the help travels the other way: cellular reprogramming and phenotypic simulation tools developed by the conservation community gave the Project a vital breakthrough in devising optimal surrogate chains. Likewise, improvements in the Project's captive breeding programs, taken from the conservation community, have reduced deaths in revived species when they're released into the environment. It's a tough world out there for newly de-extinct species without mothers to teach them how to behave.

As soon as her car arrives at the facility, Frei strides in, still murmuring answers to journalists. She already knows the scientists here are struggling with endogenous retroviruses that are hiding within the so-called noncoding regions of the genome. They're a knotty problem. They can pop out and become exogenous, becoming harmful to nearby genetic species. The risk of a pandemic has made governments jumpy enough to introduce new genetic safety regulations, slowing the Number's pace even further.

In the conference room, voices are raised. Professor Hwang says that more work needs to be done on identifying and neutering the viruses; Professor Church fires back, replying that they're an essential part of the genome and if they're removed, we don't know what might happen. Frei considers the arguments and tells Hwang that he has four weeks, after which she's going to pressure the WHO to provide support.

As soon as she's in, she's out, her eyes darting across her glasses. There's a big announcement coming soon: after many false starts, a live woolly mammoth is about to be revealed to the world—a notable exception to the "500 years" rule. It's hard to think of a more iconic species, and it's sure to provide a big boost to fundraising, but Frei has already accounted for the extra money and begun thinking ahead to the next problem: where to put the mammoths. Not every revived species is as fortunate as the thylacine, which had an ecosystem and community ready and waiting to accept it. The mammoths will need plenty of space to roam, and she's not sure the Canadians will give her enough.

She drums her fingers on the car window and looks at a sim of one of the proposed Ascension biomes again. It seems fantastical, a custom-made biosphere in a hollowed-out asteroid, not even remotely possible for the next thirty years, but then again, people felt the same way about de-extinction until the thylacine appeared. "We'll see if they can get the ecosystems right," she says, doubtfully. She fires a round of bullet-point questions to an expert at Centre National d'Études Spatiales and frowns at the reply. "I wouldn't put it past them to start messing about with the gravity because they think it'd be more fun for tourists or something."

Here's another problem. While the US has become more receptive to the Project, seeing how it might help repair the environment in the Great Plains, the EU has been distinctly chilly. Frei thinks that it's because the Europeans have forgotten what wilderness looks like. The whole continent has been domesticated for centuries. "They think the countryside is natural, so they can't imagine where they'd put any of our revived species."

It's a long drive back to the station. Before having a nap, Frei takes one last look through her glasses, leaping from country to country to see the research progress. In Arizona, she pauses and jumps in, scrutinizing a newborn auroch, the ancestor to the domestic cattle. It's unsteady on its feet, falling over once, twice. The scientists look on with concern, ready to rush in. The baby auroch clambers back up and takes another step. Frei smiles. Briefly. Then moves on.

29 THE CURVE OF BABEL

Forest of Dean, England, 2029

I've just traveled into Beechenhurst Lodge on a rather charming steam train that has a permit to burn actual coal. For once, it appears the rain has held off today, which I'm very grateful for as I'm here to walk along the sculpture trail and see one object in particular: the Curve of Babel.

The sculptor of the Curve is Alice Singh, and I'm delighted that she's agreed to come along with me to talk about it in her own words. It's words that make the Curve so special—the words engraved into its surface in hundreds of living and dead languages from across history.

In 2029, there were more than five thousand "living" languages in use around the world, with English, Mandarin, and Spanish serving as humanity's principal tongues. Even with China's rise, English remained the international language of trade, science, and politics. At the same time, the shift of every form of media from physical to digital was in full swing, with vast quantities of content indexed by search and semantic engines every day. This information became an ever-expanding corpus that was used to improve the performance of brute-force machine translation, where words and glyphs in unknown texts were correlated with those in human-translated text.

Only a minute fraction of the content coming online had been translated by humans, though—mostly political statements, legal texts, news, and popular books, movies, TV shows, and games. That fraction still counted for a lot, but it wasn't quite enough, leading companies such as Dragon and Babylon to partner with massively multiplayer online language education games to put players to work translating content in return for free access and virtual currency.

The process wasn't perfect, but, combined with smarter forms of translation and speech recognition, it improved machine-translated speech such that it achieved over 99.8 percent accuracy within a single second; just about fast enough to be used in conversation if you had a bit of patience. Here's what Alice Singh thinks:

> Babylon fascinated me. I remember being on holiday in Myanmar and just walking up to someone at a bus stop and talking to them. My words were translated through the Babylon program on my necklace into Burmese, and his words came back in reasonably good Malay. He was just as surprised as I was! Looking back, it does seem rather slow.... We're much better off now with simultaneous translation.

We're at the Curve of Babel now, a twisted ribbon of dull grey metal arcing over the ground just below head height, sitting inside a small clearing. From a distance, it looks as if the sculpture's surface is slightly mottled, but if you look more closely you can see it's completely covered in writing and symbols. The largest words are tens of centimeters tall, but they shrink down to just a few millimeters and even smaller still. You'd need very good optics to see the smallest words, only micrometers high. I'll let Alice explain what it means:

> Before these translation systems came along, there were an awful lot of people worried that the world would settle on just one or two or three universal languages, like Mandarin and English. It wouldn't have been the first time that languages had become extinct, like many Indonesian ones such as Bonerif or Usku have in recent centuries, but it looked like the rate of extinction might begin to drastically accelerate. A very 'Anthropocene' trend.
>
> When Babylon came along, it was the best thing that ever happened to the smaller, regional languages. It meant people could continue using them and teaching them to their children without being excluded from the world's culture. Automatic translation helped them to communicate with the rest of the world in their own voices.
>
> But there's always a balance, and it seemed to me that Babylon created a new problem, or at least a different problem. Automatic translation is a wonderful thing, but it isn't a substitute for the true mastery of a language. If anything, it encourages people to be lazy in how they write and communicate. You'd see people writing books and movies and games in their native languages with a style that they knew would be easily translatable into English, and I was very much saddened by that. They were limiting themselves.
>
> So, the Curve was a response to that. It has phrases from 539 different languages written on it, phrases designed to be as difficult as possible to translate, relying on idioms and unique cultural qualities of the language itself. Try translating the Finnish "kirjoitella" into English when English lacks the relevant grammatical category or finding a single-word translation for the Yiddish "makhatunim." You couldn't use Babylon on them—not the first version, anyway. I think even today a lot of AIs would have a hard time with the more obscure languages. Of course,

that made my life quite difficult. I speak six languages, but I still had to rely on native speakers to contribute phrases for the other 533 languages I've included so far.

Alice is right. Auto-translating the text on the Curve mostly reveals nonsense. If I want to try and understand it, I can bring up annotations, but like she says, it's only a shadow of what true understanding would be.

The Curve has become something of a pilgrimage for linguists, and it has inspired many other artworks that express the uniqueness of each and every language that has been developed.

"Some people think that the Curve is an argument against translation. It's certainly not intended in that way. On the whole, I'm glad we have automatic translators, such as Babylon and Dragon. Back when they launched there were a lot of ugly sentiments flying around after everyone's ears were suddenly unplugged, but a lot of new friendships as well. Better that people talk to each other directly than through an intermediary, I think."

Alice comes here every few years or so to update the sculpture with phrases from new contributors. Today, she's adding her 540th language. She hopes to keep coming as long as she can—and that there'll always be new languages to add.

30 *THE WORLD OF GLASS*

Earth, 2030

There's a moment in *The World of Glass* when you, as Erica Lin, CEO of Glass Networks, face the most important choice you'll make in the game. It comes just after you've reached half a billion users on the augmented reality (AR) system, a system that superimposes information and interfaces on top of the user's view of the world via glasses or contacts. And your choice has the potential to transform every single one of those users' lives. Let's start up an emulation—I have a game saved at just the right moment—and see what that choice is.

Open versus closed. Quality versus mediocrity. Wealth versus well-being. It's a deceptively simple choice about the design of Glass Networks's information ecosystem, but understanding it requires learning more about Glass Networks and its influential augmented reality protocol.

In the late '20s, as heads-up displays transformed from creepy and fragile gadgets into cheap and essential tools, it became common for people, organizations, and businesses to interact with each other via virtual or augmented reality interfaces. At first, these interfaces usually had some grounding in physical reality, such as a shop overlaying prices on its walls and windows simply because that was more familiar to users.

But not everyone who wanted to overlay AR interfaces onto the world owned the physical real estate in question, which meant they had to overlay them (or "ground" them) on top of spaces owned by others. Popular choices included billboards, posters, monuments, and public buildings—all these might be transformed into a student's art portfolio, a portal into a massively multiplayer game, or a live video from a political rally.

The problem was that any given physical space could have hundreds or even thousands of competing AR interfaces and media grounded on top of it. Navigating these interfaces was a frustrating process. Turn them all on at the same time, and you'd be confronted with a nightmarish mélange of colors, objects, and animations until your glasses crashed from the processor load.

There were two schools of thought regarding how to manage this. The first, favored by Open Augmented Reality (OAR) and Sopol (the largest AR technology conglomerates of the time), was to let anyone create and ground interfaces wherever they pleased. OAR would then recommend and display what they felt to be the most relevant interfaces based on the user's preferences.

This relatively open system was quickly outgunned by Erica Lin's Glass Networks. Lin's team had been pioneers in the market, developing an attractive and intuitive AR system—no mean feat for an entirely new method of interacting with computers. Under Glass Networks's "walled garden" ecosystem, interfaces had to be approved before being grounded and made visible to Glass Networks's users. The company favored high-quality interfaces over those made by amateurs, and they protected the interests of existing real-estate holders, advertisers, and brands. The end result was a cleaner and more consistent experience than OAR's and Sopol's, but one that was unmistakably closed.

For a while, it seemed that this battle would play out in a similar way to other open versus closed platform wars in the past, such as the titanic web vs. smartphone app wars in the 2010s. Most experts believed OAR's open approach would give them the lion's share of users, if not necessarily profit, but this time it was different. Whereas previous platform wars took place in what seemed like entirely new and purely digital spaces such as the internet, AR was intimately linked with the real, physical world and all the economic and political concerns that stemmed from it.

These concerns weren't high on any users' minds during the early years of AR when it was more of an expensive curiosity than a ubiquitous tool, but as time went on, many became concerned that AR was dominated by purely commercial concerns, submerging the medium's potential of reasserting old notions of public space. Social historian Andrea Galloway elaborates:

> It's hard to realize exactly how much of the public space—by which I mean the streets, marketplaces, squares, and mass transit links of the world—had effectively been ceded to the highest bidder back in the early twenty-first century. AR held out the promise of reclaiming that space without the expense of buying the physical real estate. As such, it was deeply threatening to the entrenched businesses and capital owners of the time. Glass supposedly stood on the side of big business, while OAR and Sopol took the side of the public.

This brings us back to the choice that you can make as Erica Lin in *The World of Glass*. In 2030, Glass was the world's dominant AR platform, the darling of venture capitalists and advertisers, but it was clear that Glass was facing a growing backlash from the public.

You can choose to keep Glass as a closed ecosystem that favors corporate interests—and make billions in the process—or adopt the same open protocols as OAR and Sopol. Riches and fame on the one hand or a gift to the common good on the other.

In the real world, Lin kept Glass as a closed system, a walled garden that continued to provide a slick, simple, and restricted experience to users for many years. Other AR systems including OAR tried to compete on the basis of the freedom of expression they gave to the public, but they struggled to make an impact, barely taking any market share away from Glass's polished world. It wasn't until the late '30s that Reservial leapfrogged Glass by developing AI-driven consensus environments that intelligently merged AR interfaces for everyone from individuals to crowds.

Every player makes a different decision, but if *The World of Glass* showed us anything, it's that the movement toward the consensus-based politics of the later twenty-first century was by no means a smooth path, and that the way an individual perceives the world and the choices they make has ripples that affect everyone.

31 STRUCTURED LIGHT

Earth, 2030

There are many kinds of light.

There is the light from our sun, a wash of waves and particles that ripples across a vacuum for 499 seconds. By the time it touches us, its black body radiation has become tarnished, ultraviolet absorbed by our atmosphere, blue scattered by the air. Its power remains enough to sustain and to burn, but it is moving static: confused and free of information.

There is the light from life—the light of fireflies and jellyfish and squid, a conflagration sparked by luciferin and luciferase. It camouflages, communicates, warns, illuminates. It's so powerful it has evolved over forty times in evolutionary history. It is not meant for us; our understanding is unnecessary.

There is the light we make for our own eyes, a million-year tale of ingenuity and commerce, of destruction and invention. Its uses are obvious, its patterns incidental or merely annoying—the vibration of a tungsten filament, the pulse width modulation of an LED.

And then there is the light we make for the eyes of others.

It's thrown from vehicles navigating through the world, straining to reach every surface in sight. To freeze this light would reveal an intricate continuous wave, modulated in frequency, bearing tidings of distance and velocity back to its emitter. The structure of this light reveals other structures, a kind of seeing needed only by a vehicle conveying precious cargo at tremendous speeds through deadly traffic. And though a thousand rays may intersect in the tumult, though the structure of this light is delicate, it is hardy enough to survive the confusion. It was crafted to safely return its own precious cargo of information—a unique wave, never quite the same.

It emanates from the sky, a curtain of light drifting across jungles and oceans and cities alike. It sinks through forest canopies, scattered by leaves once, twice, three times, before returning to its heavenly source, its time of flight unveiling the truth of the land. Not just the truth of the present but traces of the past betrayed through subtle dips and rises in the signal. Perhaps it is a relief for the land to give up its secrets after millennia.

It blasts as a grid of infrared before our unseeing eyes. Warped by the contours of our nose, cheeks, chin, smile, the light is scrutinized and compared to your younger self. Your moving face is your passphrase; it verifies you a thousand times a day.

We submerse the world in structured light because we wish to know it as it truly is so that we may control it. A single snapshot only tells us of the world at a frozen moment in time. It's not enough to navigate by or to build from or to verify. We want more. A picture every day, every hour, every heartbeat, every blink. Eternal illumination.

There is a chaotic beauty in this, a furious superimposition of patterns and frequencies and signals that somehow does not interfere. This beauty can never be seen by us or by any one of our creations. It can only be seen by the totality of them.

To know that beauty would be to know the whole world.

32 TIANXIA

Shanghai, China, 2030

How far back in time would you like to go? To the Ice Age 150,000 years ago to warm the world by just a few degrees and help the hominids out? Or perhaps sixty-five million years, to nudge an asteroid's path so it avoids Earth, preventing a mass extinction? How about 1.4 billion years, to fine-tune the balance of the planet's atmosphere? Or 3 billion years, to alter the magma flows under the surface and reshape the continents? Or even further back, to change the atoms scattered by supernovae that eventually coalesced into our world?

I'm holding a virtual world in my hands, and I can alter it any way I please. This was *Tianxia*.

From 2032 to 2034, *Tianxia*, or "all under heaven," was one of the most popular forms of entertainment in the world, attracting 400 million players and 2 billion viewers. For a while, it even consumed more than 6 percent of the world's total processing power. *Tianxia* was simultaneously hailed as a revolution in our understanding of planetary science, geology, and evolution, and condemned as a distracting, insidious pseudoscience.

Tianxia was originally conceived as an academic investigation, free from controversy. In 2030, an amplified team at Shanghai Tech consisting of Professor Ernest Han, three graduate students, and seven expert systems was analyzing data from the Zheng He Orbital Telescope. The team wanted to understand how a set of sixty-five Earth-like planets had formed and whether they might harbor any life. Their chosen strategy was simple: "rewind time" by a few billion years and then simulate the physical and chemical processes that the planets would have undergone. To reduce the near-infinite set of simulations required to a more manageable number, Professor Han's team planned to enlist amateurs on the Zooniverse network to manipulate the simulations as they progressed, regularly winnowing out obviously "lifeless" planets.

While Professor Han's team had created one of the most sophisticated and detailed simulations ever presented to the public, amateurs stayed away; the software was just too difficult to use. But when an enterprising fan forked the code, grafted on more explicit game mechanics and a dramatically upgraded graphics engine, and renamed it "Tianxia," interest exploded.

To understand the importance of *Tianxia*, I spoke to Estelle Egan, simulation historian:

> It may seem like a crude toy to us today, but in the '30s, *Tianxia* offered players the chance to create their own miniature worlds that could be rendered and examined in astonishing detail, all the way from orbit down to rivers, trees, and animals. It was perhaps the first game to fully deliver on the extravagant promise of earlier games such as *Spore* and *Worldcraft*, a promise of complete control over a living, breathing, and highly complex world.

Unlike those previous games, players usually didn't micromanage their creations in *Tianxia*. Most preferred to set the initial starting conditions of their world and then sit back and watch the simulation unfold, only occasionally interfering to guide the path of an errant asteroid or prevent an ice age from killing off a favorite species. The best *Tianxia* players attracted followers (and money) based on the "interestingness" of the worlds they nursed. For example, a barren, unchanging rock was far less popular than one with a functioning and stable ecosystem.

Successive patches to *Tianxia* saw extra detail added to the geological and environmental systems, with perhaps the most popular being the "agent" simulation introduced in 2033, allowing the creation of basic societies within the game. Run a *Tianxia* simulation long enough and your world might end up going to war with itself, or become so advanced they could run their own primitive simulations.

Other patches included unusual and fantastical styles of planets such as ringworlds, orbitals, Dyson spheres, and tweaks to the speed of light or gravity. However, most players tended to stay closer to Earth-like planets in their games, enthralled in the richness and complexity of the worlds created by themselves and their friends. Thousands of players made good money selling beautiful custom *Tianxia* worlds through branching and remixing. Needless to say, by this point *Tianxia* had strayed far from its original academic goals, and its original creator, Professor Han, refused to even acknowledge the existence of the game.

Why was *Tianxia* so popular and so engrossing, and how did it manage to stand out from the seemingly endless array of live-action role-playing games that had dominated entertainment for the previous few years? Egan provides some insight:

> *Tianxia* was the right game for the right time. Humanity was beginning to grasp the depth and meaning of its mastery over nature. We were on the cusp of world-changing geoengineering projects we thought would fix the oceans and atmosphere, and we gazed upon thousands of worlds across the galaxy, thinking we could capture their past and future. We felt we understood the world because we could simulate it and visualize it and model it.
>
> But in truth, those simulations didn't reflect reality, not at the scale they were reaching for. They only reflected our hubris. We realized that soon enough.

Yet for a brief moment before that calamity, the world relaxed. Four hundred million people recalled the words, "in the beginning," and they created their own heaven and earth.

33 NEGOTIATION AGENTS

Unified Korea, 2031

This simple interface may at first appear to be a mimic script, but it represented a step-change in humanity's use of external computing power for everyday decision-making.

Imagine a company—let's call it Alpha—that has invented a revolutionary type of computer chip. So revolutionary, it could stand to make some people very, very rich. But mere days after their chip is announced, another company—Beta—announces a similar chip.

To Alpha's eyes, it's not just similar, it's an outright copy based on proprietary confidential information. They believe that a senior employee who recently resigned from Alpha has stolen the information and sold it to Beta. Alpha sues Beta, and things unfold as they ever have in a lawsuit, with parties obtaining evidence from one another via the discovery process.

Now imagine that you are a lawyer representing Alpha. In response to your requests Beta have sent you:

- 523 megabytes of text
- 7,492 hours of audio recordings
- 4,830 hours of video
- 5.3 petabytes of miscellaneous data including 3-D reverse-engineered models, mimic scripting agents, company server logs, and biometric data.

How do you sift through that asteroid of information and find the nuggets of evidence that could constitute a coherent case? In the early twenty-first century, it would have taken dozens if not hundreds of skilled lawyers many months just to read everything, let alone understand its significance. Even then, it's likely that they would miss important details.

Luckily, it's not 2010. It's 2030. You have access to affordable AI agents that can automatically scan and meaningfully summarize content, and if you have the funds, you can employ an amplified team to analyze the results and generate some potential next steps.

And then what? You still need to argue the case. If you're tech-savvy, you could opt for a court system that allows lawyers to deploy mimic scripts and amplified teams. But if you want to save time and money, you might try a negotiation agent first—an AI system that can help opposing parties come to a mutually satisfying agreement.

At this point, it's useful to remember the origin of negotiation agents. During the '20s, the government of Unified Korea tasked its top scientists, lawyers, and engineers to fix the country's cripplingly slow and byzantine legal system, which reunification had only made worse. To simulate the outcome of any proposed solutions, they adapted a negotiation system used during the ASEAN (Association of Southeast Asian Nations) carbon-credit deadlock crisis, building it into the first recognizable negotiation agent. Many attribute the success of Unified Korea's legal reforms to the negotiation agents, which were soon adapted to work in any number of countries and scenarios.

More recently, negotiation agents have been improved so they can process and weigh vast quantities of data in a way that even an amplified team cannot. The reason you should use a negotiation agent in a dispute, however, isn't because they're faster or cheaper than humans—it's because you can trust them to be perfectly impartial precisely because they aren't human. When everyone concerned believes the agents are unbribable, implacable, and utterly fair, parties that can't agree on anything else can still agree to use an accredited open-source negotiation agent.

Now, naturally your client, Alpha, may not favor the use of a negotiation agent. They may be old-fashioned and worry that it cannot capture the subtleties of their position or that it might not fight hard enough on their behalf. They are wrong, of course. When they see the record of the negotiation agent you're recommending, they'll come around—especially when you point out the long-term savings.

Finally, this is where you come in! Amid all the talk of summarizing agents, mimic scripts, and amplified teams, we still need plain old humans. Alpha is old-fashioned. They're not comfortable talking with a negotiation agent—but you are. It's your job to act as a friendly, biological interface between the two. After all, that's what humans are best at: talking with other humans.

34 READING ROOMS

Melbourne, Australia, 2031

Understanding the changing role of books in spreading knowledge and ideas in the early twenty-first century requires us to examine the reading experience itself. Let's look at this contemporary account of Forster's Books in Melbourne, Australia, and its reading rooms.

By the '20s, Melbourne's out-of-town retail centers and malls had been hollowed out by the superior at-home shopping experience offered by deliverbots and online stores. Richard Forster, a moderately successful novelist, took advantage of the glut of retail space to buy a disused supermarket with several hundred collaborators and convert it into a bookshop.

Forster's Books offers the usual range of services one expects today, including rapid custom fabricators, author subscriptions, and remote talks. However, it is the unique paid memberships offered by the bookshop that have led to its recent success. Rather than attempting to compete with Amazon Book Club's all-you-can-read subscription service, Forster's has focused on providing members with higher-value physical services. These include extended printed book borrowing rights, priority access to librarians for research assistance and personalized recommendations, early reservations for author visits, book therapy treatments, and access to the shop's reading rooms.

Given the myriad distractions and media available today, many readers find it difficult to finish books of more than a hundred pages. The reading rooms are intended to put an end to those distractions.

The general reading room requires readers to silence all nonurgent alerts and notifications but is otherwise reasonably relaxed.

The quiet reading room not only enforces the no-alerts rule but also restricts a wide range of activities such as games, videos, and voice messaging by means of limited user-privilege grants. Readers may only enter and exit at thirty-minute intervals.

Finally, the high reading room absolutely prohibits all nonreading activities—even subvocal messaging—again by user-privilege grants. Readers may only enter and exit at hourly intervals.

Readers, particularly those who are younger and have less experience of reading books, are advised to gradually acclimatize to the rooms a few weeks at a time rather than heading straight for the high reading room. Those who ignore this advice can cause undue distress to themselves and to those nearby. However, a friendly and forgiving atmosphere among readers and librarians helps spread good habits.

Supposedly there exists an ultra-high reading room encased in a Faraday cage that blocks all electromagnetic transmissions. All media are prohibited save for printed books, and its doors are only unlocked once every three hours. The Ultra High Reading Room is generally believed to be apocryphal or at the very least not especially practical.

The Reading Rooms' popularity has led Forster's to institute a lottery for new registrations until they can open additional branches. The demand represents the yearning of Melbourne's inhabitants to carve out just a few hours of "thinking space" every week—a desire more generally embodied by the worldwide Secular Sabbath and Slow Tech movements.

At Forster's Books, that desire is focused directly on the dying, but not wholly forgotten, skill of sequestered deep reading.

35 PAN-PAN-CLIMATE SAGA FIVE-NINER HEAVY

Alice Springs, Australia, 2031

The boneyard at Alice Springs is a two-tone world, blue sky and red dirt bisected by a white horizon. Its dry heat is perfect for preserving aircrafts out in the open air. To my left, there are ranks of last-generation emergency rescue drone craft laid out in an uncannily precise grid; to my right, a forest of heavy lift cargo copters. All are ready to be called into service, should the need arise. This is a boneyard, not a graveyard, and each aircraft is diligently maintained and regularly inspected, especially the one in front of me.

Of course, you've seen this aircraft before. There's nothing quite like it—a long, slender wing, with boron fiber composite laminate for the wing box and a telescopic strut to alleviate wing loads. Its broad, hefty body is hunched down, as if embarrassed by the weight of its fame. Beyond it are 169 identical aircraft, all constructed by the Sixteen Nations Alliance. Together, they form the most illustrious fleet in human history.

In 2028, heatwaves across central and south Asia killed 171,000 people. Heatwave deaths were hardly new a phenomenon, but nothing close to this scale had ever been seen before, and scientists agreed that climate change had, at the very least, exacerbated this seasonal disaster.

The next year, 467,000 people died, a quarter of a million in India alone. The temperature was only slightly above the previous year's highs, but in a disastrous coincidence, the heatwave occurred at the same time as widespread power outages that knocked out air conditioning to millions. The majority of deaths were in dense, urban areas, where heat islands formed from asphalt and concrete. Almost all were aged over fifty, with chronic health conditions—those who were least able to help themselves. In a society like India's, this was a total moral outrage.

This particular plane, the Maselis, was constructed in 2031. Once you've looked past the wings, you can't help but notice the enormous engines, seemingly oversized for its otherwise modest fuselage. The four engines were designed to provide a high maximum takeoff weight of over two hundred tons and to reach much higher altitudes than typical passenger planes of the time. If you somehow hadn't seen this plane before, you might want to climb inside and take a look at what could possibly justify such an unusual design. Unfortunately, you'd be disappointed, because the Maselis is entirely unmanned, with no entrances designed for humans.

In the aftermath of the 2029 heatwaves, India's government almost collapsed. Millions of protestors demanded a solution, and of the many that were offered–subsidized air conditioning, weather modification, mass resettlement–geoengineering seemed the only one that confronted the enormity of the problem.

There had been plenty of studies examining how humans might engineer a reduction in the Earth's temperature, with most countries favoring a "slow response mitigation" strategy of removing carbon dioxide from the atmosphere. But this strategy was very slow indeed. It was projected to take decades to make a significant impact on the climate—far too long for those who had already lost their families and friends.

Faster geoengineering strategies existed, but they had all faltered due to disagreements about who should pay what and, more importantly, concerns about the deadly risks of a botched geoengineering project. The strategy India chose to revive was solar radiation management: increasing the amount of light from the sun that was reflected back into space, thereby cooling Earth. Global dimming, some called it.

The crash geoengineering program of 2029 was led by India and Australia. There wasn't time to deploy exotic concepts like a space mirror which, even if it was theoretically cheaper and safer, required brand new kinds of engineering. The two governments preferred a more down-to-earth solution that could be deployed immediately. In response, their scientists looked to nature. More specifically, they looked at volcanos.

In 1815, the eruption of Mount Tambora in Indonesia ejected sixty megatons of sulfur dioxide into the atmosphere, causing the "Year Without a Summer" in 1816. The sulfur dioxide combined with water vapor to form sulfuric acid, which in turn condensed into sulfate aerosols. The aerosols absorbed solar radiation, creating a short, sharp chill down on the Earth's surface. Despite the misery this inflected on the world, which included tens of thousands of deaths from harvest failures and famine, the injection of sulfur dioxide into the atmosphere was touted as a natural solution to climate change, unlike space mirrors. While the governments admitted possible detrimental effects such as ozone loss, they spun this as a positive. After all, at least they knew what the problems were! And at least the problems would be only temporary, since sulfate aerosols only remain aloft for a few years.

With the strategy decided, the specifics remained to be agreed on. Following some frantic backchannel diplomacy between India, Australia, and other interested parties (which quickly became the rest of the world), a reduction in solar energy of two watts per square meter, equating to a lowering of global surface temperature by two Celsius, was targeted. The Pratyush 8 network at the Indian Institute of Tropical Meteorology in Pune was tasked to determine how best to disperse the required sulfur dioxide into the atmosphere, and the funding effort began.

Surprisingly, the whole program cost less than ten billion US dollars per year—a pittance given the potential benefits. The financial burden was shouldered mostly by the founding partners of the Sixteen Nations Alliance, with India again taking the lead, albeit with massive donations from individuals from richer countries. Those countries were generally unhappy with the proposed aerosol release, worried about dangerous side-effects and their lack of control, but the Alliance made it clear they viewed their program as a matter of life and death. In fact, any attempt to halt it would be considered an act of war. In the face of such threats, even China was quiescent.

There's a smaller, separate fleet in the boneyard that also belongs to the Alliance, a motley assortment of twenty-seven re-engineered Gulfstream G650 and G750 business jets. These jets, starting with the Petter and the Kulik, were used for experimental flights to eject sulfur dioxide into the lower troposphere, accompanied by a swarm of research drones. In truth, these flights achieved little, but they were crucial for boosting morale. At the same time, work began on a new type of aircraft, designed specifically for high-lift and high-altitude operation. These aircraft would be powerful enough to perform in situ conversion of elemental sulfur into sulfate using a Brayton cycle combustor and a catalytic converter, an innovative process that cut payload requirements in half. Designated as the Stratospheric Aerosol Geoengineering Aircraft, they are better known as the SAGA series of jets.

The SAGA jets were workhorses. They incorporated only reliable technology and were built to last. Ultimately, a fleet of 170 SAGA jets would perform close to 300 flights per day. Every year, they would lift two megatons of elemental sulfur that became five megatons of sulfuric acid aerosol, dispersed nineteen kilometers high. Flying from India, Chile, Algeria, Kenya, Malaysia, and Australia, they covered a large chunk of the tropics, with the aerosols whipping around the world soon after being ejected.

From 2031 to 2039, the SAGA fleet released over forty megatons of sulfuric acid aerosol and offset almost one Celsius of surface temperature warming that would have otherwise occurred, doubtless saving millions of lives from future heatwaves—although many other millions still perished. The fleet, however, was meant to operate until at least 2041 in order to reach its intended ten-year lifespan. So why was it cut short?

If you crouch underneath the loading bay of the Maselis, you can still make out the scorch marks. The attack occurred in August 2039, while this craft was flying under the call sign Pan-Pan-Climate SAGA Five-Niner Heavy—a "heavy" aircraft, the fifty-ninth of the SAGA fleet, with the Pan-Pan prefix denoting its urgent life-saving status. The marks came from a drone laser strike intended to blind the scientific instruments and navigation optics of the Maselis. The strike succeeded. The Maselis was forced to perform an emergency landing in Algeria, and all further flights were temporarily suspended pending an investigation.

It soon emerged that a coalition of nations including the US and China had decided the Alliance's geoengineering program was starting to do more harm than good. Global dimming had been achieved in a way that had been helpful to most countries but at the expense of continued warming of the deep and polar oceans. These changes caused continued, albeit slower, melting at the icecaps and a corresponding global sea level rise. Together with ozone loss, it just wasn't worth it.

But neither was a third world war. The coalition, seeking to avoid unnecessary hostilities, informed the Alliance of the drone strike in advance, while promising to further accelerate their "slow response" carbon sequestration program, which at that point was achieving real results. And so, in 2040, the Sixteen Nations Alliance declared victory. The SAGA fleet embarked on a goodwill tour across the world, eventually landing for the final time in Alice Springs.

Out of all the SAGA fleet, the Maselis flew the furthest. It was the last plane to deliver its cargo into the troposphere, and for a while, it was feted by millions. But people were happy it didn't have to fly again.

This boneyard in Alice Springs isn't a museum. It isn't a historic site for tour groups and children to visit. It isn't a place of honor. It might be a symbol of humanity's ingenuity, but it's better viewed as a symbol of humanity's shame—that we had to come to this to save ourselves.

36 ACTIVE CLOTHING

Victoria and Albert Museum, England, 2032

According to Western culture in the late twentieth and early twenty-first centuries, the ideal person should strive to be slim, tanned, and unblemished. Such traits would signal their exceptional health, wealth, and freedom to spend time outdoors indulging in leisure and physical pursuits—opportunities that lower-status manual laborers and office workers lacked.

But the imperfect were not bereft of hope; they could still climb toward this pinnacle of beauty by spending their scant time and money on expensive gyms and diets, on sunbeds and cosmetics. These solutions were advertised and prescribed everywhere you turned—in magazines, newspapers, websites, games, TV, billboards, public transport—all showing doctored images of "perfect" bodies. They said, if you want to be happy and loved, you should be beautiful. Which meant thin.

It wasn't always so. The ideal body shape has varied throughout history. Just look at any painting or sculpture from before the twentieth century and you'll see that slim people were often perceived as unhealthy. In contrast, the powerful and rich were stouter and with lighter complexions because they could afford to stay and work indoors and eat more food, unlike the peasants who had to work out in the sun on farms.

During the early 2030s, many cultures remained obsessed with appearance. Anything that could help people become slim and toned—or at least, appear to be slim and toned—would sell well, especially if it was quick and required little effort. Something, perhaps, like this "active vest" I've borrowed from the Victoria and Albert Museum in London.

To someone from the '30s, it'd look like any other plain white cotton vest—thicker and bulkier and not very stylish, but nothing too unusual. But when I put it on, I can tell there's one very big difference: it can move! Right now, it's slowly contracting around my stomach and abdomen and shaping my torso into, well, what it thinks a proper man should look like.

All of this contracting and relaxing is accomplished through muscle-equivalent electro-active polymers woven into the fabric of the vest, along with thin, flexible batteries. Originally, the technology wasn't invented to make people look good; instead, it was a matter of life and death. Clothes that could apply pressure to an area meant they could slow down and stop bleeding, vital for the military and emergency services.

In such an image-conscious society, you can imagine how well the vests were received. Tens of millions were sold, and the technology soon found its way into dresses, trousers, T-shirts, jeans, and more. But to be fair, it wasn't all about beauty; active underwear also provided real health benefits to those with circulatory and muscular problems.

In 2034, "next-generation" active clothing went on sale, providing haptic "force" feedback to wearers. Active clothing expert Chi Ying from the V&A Museum explains:

> We all know about the supposed five senses: sight, smell, touch, hearing, and taste. For a long time, the notion of adding more senses was dismissed as foolishness, especially since we know that our brains are structured in a way that makes them highly efficient at processing those five sensory stimuli.
>
> But our brains are not set in stone—they have "plasticity," so areas can adapt their function over time. That means we can map new senses onto existing ones, like the ability to sense north or detect electromagnetic fields. In the case of haptics, we can map the position of north onto a vibrating belt around the waist, exploiting our high degree of sensitivity to physical stimuli.

Sensing the opportunity, active clothing manufacturers developed an open-source haptic software platform, and apps flooded the market. One popular virtual reality game of the time, *Désir*, developed an add-on that allowed partners to sense each other's emotional and physical states through subtle vibrations and contractions. A tense buzzing might indicate fear or anger, while a slow ebb and flow would signal happiness. Other apps propelled games to new heights of realism, replicating the sensation of being punched or hugged or shot.

Active clothing wasn't just a one-way proposition either, as Chi Ying explains:

> Once you've got someone wearing a garment with electro-active polymers, you can reverse the process to measure where and how the garment is being deformed—to see how people's bodies are moving in real time, how they're breathing in and out, how they're twisting and stretching. And if they're wearing absolute positioning sensors like rings or thimbles, then you can create a perfect record of their precise movements. Aside from the obvious medical and artistic

applications, it means that the whole body can be used as an input mechanism rather than just people's hands and voices.

It's quite astonishing to think of how crude interfaces were before active clothing. There's no doubt that our hands and voices are extraordinarily versatile tools, but they have their limitations and can't be used in every situation. Creating a real "body language" allowed for an entirely new and often subtle set of glyphish-type gestures to be used in combination with glasses, contacts, and necklaces.

Despite its utility, not everyone bought into active clothing.

"It was very difficult to learn body-glyph-language accurately. People who hadn't grown up with it found it tricky learning how to control their bodies and muscles in that kind of precise way, so there was a genuine 'clothing divide' with young or technically adept people on one side and others who were more used to subvoc and tablet input on the other," notes Chi Ying.

One group who positively loved body language was one that didn't have any other—babies! A simplified version of body language was derived from baby sign language, which allowed babies to signal whether they were hungry or tired or afraid. Active dungarees and tops made it easy to teach and translate baby language at the very earliest ages, helping to finally break one of humanity's most persistent communication barriers. Out of the arms of babes…

37 THE CONTRAPUNTAL HACK

Earth, 2032

Frank N'Doye was a talented pianist and composer. In 2032, he'd been hard at work on his Fourth Symphony, "Ceres," for the past six months, but he'd hit a creative block. Frank decided to take a break from composing and listen to some tracks he'd composed years earlier.

"As soon as I pressed play, I could tell that something wasn't right," said Frank N'Doye. "The track had a more impatient rhythm than I remembered, much hastier. At first, I thought I was just imagining it or maybe that I'd set up the mood reactivity wrong. But the more I listened to it, the more I was convinced that this was not the track that I had recorded. No one else believed me, but it turned out that I was right, and that wasn't the only thing that was wrong."

On listening to the two versions, it's possible to detect a difference at ten minutes and eighteen seconds into the track. It's a subtle difference, but in the altered version, the rhythm no longer precisely matches the melody.

Frank was the ideal person to discover the "Contrapuntal Hack." Not only did he have an exceptionally good ear and an eidetic memory, but he had a habit of keeping old pre-cloud physical backup media around his studio with which he could cross-check his suspicions. After confirming that his old tracks had indeed been altered by some kind of hack or viral attack, he contacted Tara Diop, a friend who worked as a security researcher. Diop recalls what happened next:

> It took a few hours of focused effort, but I determined that the subtle alterations to Frank's data—and it wasn't just his music that was altered, it was exabytes of other information—were made by a novel and unknown intrusive agent.

This agent, later named "Contrapuntal," had circumvented the strong security systems that Frank and billions of others relied on to store and protect their data in the cloud. While some experts had theorized that such an attack was possible by highly skilled state-backed actors, they were sure that such an attack would leave some kind of trace, but Contrapuntal's actions had been almost, yet not quite completely, invisible.

Here's how: Contrapuntal not only falsified user records when it altered their data, but also inserted eerily believable sham usage patterns. By using a Markovian Parallax Denigrate function, Contrapuntal edited digital memories to make it seem as though its intrusions were in fact the work of the data's owners. When Diop made her discovery public and developed a tool to detect Contrapuntal, billions more hosts were found to have been infected. It was a hack of epic proportions.

The next breakthrough came courtesy of Bruce Cabrera, a freelance security researcher from Venezuela:

> I needed to observe Contrapuntal up close, so I created a honeypot for Contrapuntal in a virtual network and ran it about ten million times. Sometimes Contrapuntal would hijack the user's delegated authority preferences to divert money and privileges to different individuals. Other times it would make strange edits to archived messages under the guise of obfuscram operations. On a couple of occasions, it even composed passably good poetry or issued blackmail demands via professional-grade AR. I found it baffling, to be frank. I couldn't tell what its goal was.

Whatever its ultimate purpose, Contrapuntal was wreaking genuine havoc. Its ability to rewrite history caused huge financial damage, and the world economy itself came under serious threat as people began to lose their faith in their information. Only a concerted effort by thousands of researchers and amplified teams sufficed to weed out Contrapuntal from every online host. The subsequent painstaking reconstruction of data took months, and the ultimate effects of the hack were estimated to consume more than 0.4 percent of global economic product that year.

To prevent Contrapuntal or a similar attack from occurring again, authorities mandated that all vulnerable hosts required patching; any unpatched devices would be marked as untrustworthy and their communications ignored. On June 14, 2032, in the most intensive computer-security operation of its kind in history, 1.4 trillion hosts were patched within a forty-eight-hour period—and it worked without a hitch. People let out a deep breath and carried on with their lives.

And that's where it would have ended, a mystifying act of data terrorism with no obvious target or goal and frustratingly few leads as to the perpetrator, were it not for a chance event nineteen years later.

In 2050, Tara Diop was examining logs from 8.1 million network sensors as part of a historical security exercise, unrelated to the events of 2032.

During her investigation, she noticed a strange spike in power usage across the sensors that had been almost perfectly concealed. Working backwards, she traced the spike's timing to the firmware patch that supposedly eliminated Contrapuntal. To her horror, Diop discovered that in making devices secure against the hack, the patch had in fact ended up exposing devices to another completely different intrusive agent, Contrapuntal-2.

Thankfully, further investigation revealed that compared to the original Contrapuntal hack, this Contrapuntal-2 was much more short-lived and apparently wholly benign. In a fraction of a second, the Contrapuntal-2 executed a short series of operations across 1.4 trillion devices and promptly erased itself. It remains impossible to reconstruct those operations or know for what purpose they were made, but it is safe to assume that it was some kind of distributed computing task that required intensive, concentrated, and widespread processing power.

Speculation continues to this day about this odd series of events. The most beguiling but sadly unprovable hypothesis is that the 2032 event, in its similarity to the emergence of Narada, the so-called trickster AI, also represented the birth of a new intelligence. Narada, of course, isn't talking—and neither is the intelligence behind Contrapuntal.

38 THE KILL SWITCH

Jalal-Abad, Kyrgyzstan, 2032

In the final days of the Kyrgyzstan civil war in 2032, General Askar's forces were routed in a rapid series of battles across Jalal-Abad Province. Most observers believed that the Transitional Authority had defeated Askar's insurgents through superior numbers and materiel. While that appeared to make sense, it was still puzzling how the insurgents had crumbled so quickly after putting up a strong resistance for more than two years.

It later emerged that in those closing battles, General Askar had been the target of forty-seven separate "kill switches." The kill switches, when activated, massively degraded his forces' communications and drone network. Plagued with constant crashes and, in the case of some glasses and drone recharging pods, physical explosions, Askar's army was left near-defenseless. The Transitional Authority took advantage of the confusion to decapitate the elite "Green Guard" with their special forces, take the General prisoner, and end the war.

I have a pair of sunglasses from the civil war in front of me, owned by one Colonel Erkebaev of Osh, an experienced officer in Askar's army. The glasses have thin silver rims and tough plastic lenses—not particularly fashionable, but very much military spec, manufactured by FPLS UK in Unified Korea. Its frame and legs contain a standard waveguide display, CPU, a high-capacity silicon alloy battery, and an array microphone. The entire unit is hardened against electromagnetic impulses.

Let's take a closer look at the glasses with academician Pieter Juica from the Aragon Institute of Technology:

> It's clear from the scorch marks that the batteries overheated, destroying the glasses within seconds. Luckily for Colonel Erkebaev, she wasn't wearing them, because they would've burned her quite badly. The cause of the overheating lies in a special hidden chip located at the tip of the right arm. If you look at the official schematics or manufacturing models, you won't be able to find the chip; only a painstaking forensic examination reveals its existence.

This chip does two things, and two things only—it waits for a signal, and when it receives it, it overrides all the safeties on the batteries and burns them out. It's a classic kill switch.

What's remarkable about this chip is that it doesn't use the glasses' in-built wireless system. If it did, there would be a risk, a tiny risk, that the kill signal might be detected and intercepted. Instead, it uses the glasses' frame as an antenna to receive ultra-low bit-rate messages out-of-band—a master-ful, deadly piece of engineering trickery.

At exactly the same time that Colonel Erkebaev's glasses exploded, twenty other glasses used by Askar's top leaders suffered catastrophic fail-ures. Within an hour, the Transitional Authority's forces were attacking—and they were met with little resistance.

Kill switches were hardly a new invention. They'd been introduced into weapons and computers by advanced security services since the twen-tieth century. Countries such as the US, the UK, Germany, Israel—and in the twenty-first century, China, Taiwan, Japan, and Unified Korea—all had the engineering expertise and facilities to subtly alter software and devices without notice.

As all devices became increasingly reliant on computer power, the threat of kill switches also grew. Unbeknownst to their citizens, governments around the world scrambled to cope with a flood of billions of potentially compromised electronic devices—devices used by almost everyone, includ-ing politicians and military officers. Of course, they did this while simulta-neously developing their own exploits.

The two leaders in this race were Unified Korea (aided by the United States' National Security Agency) and China. Both countries routinely inserted compromised chips and circuitry into consumer and military electronics that even most professionals would miss. Colonel Erkebaev's glasses, made by FLPS UK, are thought to have been part of a batch that were specially modified by the NSA. When the NSA discovered that General Askar had ordered glasses, they swapped in their modified batch in Turkey, while the devices were en route to Kyrgyzstan.

After informants confirmed the glasses had successfully made it to the insurgents, a series of low-power transmissions were made from local radio stations in Jalal-Abad. Over the course of a month, various backdoors were activated on the glasses that gave Unified Korea and the US access to the insurgents' networks. After they had gathered all the data they could, they activated the kill switch and ended the civil war in a stroke.

To provide cover for their actions, the US faked an intrusion into FPLS UK's systems that "revealed" emails proving that the glasses' malfunctions were the work of internal sabotage by an indignant, racist manager. This story held for a few days until researchers, concerned about exploding batteries, began investigating their own glasses. Inconsistencies began mounting, and when students at Second Copenhagen Free School published electron microscopy results with the insert chips clearly labeled, the ruse was discovered.

Naturally, none of the parties involved ever admitted culpability. Yet, as people worried that their own devices were at risk of exploding and started independently verifying the integrity of their hardware, it was clear that kill switches had finally become unacceptable. Nanoscale "fabs-in-a-box," which allowed small organizations to make their own "trusted" microchips, enjoyed a mini-boom until people found the chips were too unreliable and expensive, leading most to return to mass-produced electronics.

Government intrusion into people's lives had already been taken as a given in many authoritarian countries. In some places, it was even welcomed. But changing attitudes toward personal freedom and an increasing distrust of politicians (thanks to endemic corruption) altered that equation. Kill switches represented the worst intrusion imaginable, and the sheer arrogance of their creators became their downfall.

39 MICROMORT DETECTOR

Buenos Aires, Argentina, 2032

Every second of every day, we're confronted with choices that test our appetite for risk. Should you eat that tasty but calorific dessert? Should you walk to the shops or take the car? Do you really want to take that spacedive? Sure, it'll be fun. It might even, quite literally, be the trip of a lifetime.

Sometimes it's easy for us to make the calculation, especially with high-risk activities that are saddled with a known probability of death. Most of the time, though, we make decisions unconsciously, even though their cumulative impact may have more weight on our chances of living to old age than any single spacedive.

But what if you could measure and quantify those decisions immediately and directly? What if you could have a number that told you exactly how risky an action was going to be? That's what Mutual Assurance, an insurance cooperative based in Buenos Aires, set out to make with their Lifeline bracelet in 2032.

The bracelet I'm about to put on is a slender band of sensor-packed composites that tracks the usual things: blood pressure and oxygenation, heart rate, metabolic panel readings, galvanic skin response levels, and so on. The Lifeline also hooks into the wearer's glasses and other technology to determine, in short, what they are doing and how risky it is. All of this health and behavior data is then combined and converted into a single number—the micromort.

A micromort is a unit of risk representing a one-in-a-million chance of death. Drinking a couple of glasses of wine would accumulate a single micromort, whereas spending an hour canoeing would accumulate ten micromorts. As I take a bite of an Owen's Original burger, you can see my Lifeline here recording an extra 0.1 micromorts. I suppose it isn't happy with the salt. In theory, a Lifeline would detect the entire sum of its wearer's activities—every wash of their hands, every flight, every run, every drink, every human function—and calculate their associated risks in real time. Mutual Assurance's aim was to help individuals make more informed choices about the risks they took in everyday life and, of course, to better assess insurance premiums.

Initially, Mutual Assurance had planned to make the bracelets available solely to their own customers, but the tremendous demand encouraged them to ramp up production. No doubt much of the appeal of the Lifeline came from its novelty value. Plenty of people were intrigued to see their micromort count gradually ratchet up as they drank a coffee or went for a swim, but a great deal of interest came from how it played upon the fears of the aging baby boomers and gen-Xers of the time. In an interview a decade after the Lifeline's introduction, CEO Maria Mendoza admitted, "It didn't escape our notice there was an entire generation who were very, very anxious about their mortality and that we could help them address and manage that anxiety by quantifying their mortality in a way they understood."

The Lifeline didn't alleviate anxiety, though—it accentuated it. Many wearers obsessively checked their micromort readings every hour, worrying over statistically insignificant increases and becoming paralyzed with indecision. Sadly, their heightened anxiety usually increased blood pressure and cortisol levels, further increasing their micromorts for the day, which increased stress, and so on.

There were other problems with the Lifeline. One was the inaccuracy of the risk data it relied on for calculations. Most of the data had been calculated on an aggregate basis, and so their applicability to specific circumstances or individuals was comparatively low. Another was the inconvenient tendency for humans to be contrary. Some users deliberately tried to increase their micromorts as much as possible without harming their health, regularly embarking on risky sports activities and venturing into dangerous areas just to get a high score.

A few years on, attitudes had shifted. People were tiring of such simplified measures of their lives. Ian Kyd, a gamification historian, comments:

> The fashion of trying to precisely quantify everything in the universe, from health and happiness to intelligence and inspiration, had its roots in the turn of the century when the politics and economics of the time rewarded people for thinking in strictly numerical terms. Back then, they really did think that representing things like happiness with a number out of a hundred was not only a good idea, but the best idea. The ideals of the self-quantification and gamification movements reached as far as the '30s and then thankfully retreated as the Modern Romantic movement emerged.

Ultimately, the Lifeline was never particularly accurate nor useful as a tool for managing risk and improving health. It did, however, succeed in inspiring a new range of mostly ridiculous but occasionally thought-provoking knock-off bracelets that purported to measure tiny, incremental amounts of change, such as the "Microfun detector," the "Microsmarts detector," the "Micromorals detector," and so on.

And that's perhaps the most useful thing that the Lifeline did. Those trying to use its simple metrics to guide their behavior were frequently stymied, but that very effort often prompted a fleeting understanding of mortality and caused subtler, longer-lasting changes in outlook. It wasn't a magical device that made people wiser; it was a memento mori.

40 CHINESE TOURISM

China, 2033

In the '30s, China became the tourist destination of choice for the world's elite. The amenities and resorts were scarcely believable and usually inaccessible to the lower classes, but novelist and travel enthusiast Colin Priest managed to find his way in. Let's take a look at some of his reviews now.

THE FIVE WINDS, WENZHOU: 4/5

One of the most renowned resort destinations in China, The Five Winds owes its fame to its ever-changing array of attractions and monuments.

Scarcely a week goes by without a new hotel or ride or arena being fabricated according to the latest trend, whether it's a facsimile of an Ancient Wonder, a re-enactment of a historical event such as 9/11 or Zheng He's voyages, or a tie-in with a blockbuster Disney/Starling ARG. To support this continual cycle of construction and destruction, The Five Winds holds close to a million aerial and ground constructor drones—so many that it builds and sells its own drones.

The casual visitor will not notice this daily whirlwind of creation since it takes place at night and is hidden by aerial lenses and consensual augmented reality (AR). Instead, they'll most likely be enjoying the hundreds of betting venues, from traditional casinos and racetracks to brand new Crossball and Battlefield arenas, or they'll be on sightseeing excursions to Dongtou, the "County of One Hundred Islands," and Yandang Mountain.

The Five Winds has a dedicated carbon-neutral maglev to the local airport and contains on-site backup generation facilities. Visitors are advised to avoid the weeks of the high summer unless they are comfortable with active clothing.

HIGH DRAGON, LHASA, 5/5

High Dragon is regarded as the most exclusive holiday destination in the world. Anchored in the Nyenchen Tanglha Mountains, High Dragon is not a building but a conglomeration of aerostats that drift through the clean mountain sky, occasionally docking with each other and mooring at one of three peaks to take on new guests and supplies.

The High Dragon aerostats range in size from tens to hundreds of meters and can be configured with swimming pools, miniature parks, spas, and cutting-edge sim chambers. Some parties opt to hire groups of aerostats for parties, docking them to increase the space for their guests, but most guests prefer to spend their time alone, contemplating the white peaks.

The combination of a staggeringly high price tag, the near-complete physical isolation from civilization, and a rigorously enforced no-fly zone surrounding the area has resulted in High Dragon becoming the favored destination of the ultra-rich on Earth (but perhaps not off it). Of course, the fact that rising sea levels have placed the remaining desirable island resorts under UN stewardship hasn't harmed High Dragon's prospects.

Only the richest 0.05 percent in the world could reasonably afford to visit High Dragon. It is safe to assume that you are probably not among them.

MGM PARIS MACAU, 2/5

The MGM Paris Macau, a gleaming gold-shaded sixty-story building with almost two million square meters of floorspace, five thousand suites, six thousand slot machines, two thousand gaming tables, and a twenty-five-thousand-seat arena, opened its doors in 2021.

While the hotel and casino remain open and somewhat popular among less affluent visitors, it stands as a reminder of the ugly affair of its bankruptcy in 2027, which saw the deaths of six workers in a brutally suppressed labor strike and the eventual demise of its owner corporation in the US. Since then, the casino has changed hands four times, ending up with MGM last year.

The resort is hopelessly dated compared with the more modern and attractive offerings elsewhere in China, but when its plans were first drawn up, investors were convinced that it would enjoy the same success as the other Macau resorts that attracted millions of rich visitors from the mainland. Unfortunately for the investors, the economic slowdown in the mid '20s saw the central government finally succumb to increasingly desperate calls from regions starved of tax revenues for casino construction to be legalized.

Competition increased. Visitor numbers fell. Investment in facilities and upkeep plummeted. People moved on.

Today, the Paris Macau represents good value for money for the budget-conscious tourist, especially for those interested in period gambling. A car from Hong Kong will take only twenty minutes, with direct ferries and cruise ships also available. However, we advise checking up on net connectivity closer to your visit as Macau has recently suffered from sporadic outages, supposedly from student pranks.

41 OWEN'S ORIGINAL CLONED BURGER

Hamilton, Canada, 2033

In the mid-twentieth century, visions of the future often depicted people getting their nutrition from pills or possibly some kind of synthesized slurry. You can understand the reasoning. While we all need to eat to survive, taste, from a purely biological perspective, is mostly irrelevant. The only thing that matters is getting the right mix of nutrients into our bodies, and pills can be swallowed faster than potatoes. However, quite aside from the sheer impossibility of getting enough calories from such a small volume of matter, such a passionless approach completely ignored the pleasurable aspects of eating a good meal. Life is not simply about survival, and it would be a shame to ignore millennia of good food and communal meals in favor of saving a few minutes here and there.

Since the agricultural age, food has generally meant vegetables, but that changed in recent centuries with the advent of new farming techniques that allowed the production of cheap meat on an industrial scale. By 2033, more than sixty billion chickens were living in factory farms, with billions more cows, pigs, and other animals all slaughtered to feed the world's voracious appetite for animal protein.

Most of these animals were kept in cramped conditions with little to no access to the outside world, let alone space to walk around in. While there was some progress in improving farm animal welfare in the twentieth century, it was painfully slow since drastic changes would have harmed the profits of retailers, which in turn would have increased prices for consumers.

No, ethical considerations were not the sole reason for why the world moved away from factory farming in the twenty-first century. Environmental, economic, and scientific changes played just as large a role, and each of those is summed up in this object—an Owen's Original Beef Burger, first sold in Ontario, Canada.

I've managed to obtain this Owen's Original via the efforts of Mary Alderman, a chef at Fifth Column in Berlin. Thankfully, this burger is not actually from 2033. Instead, it's a rather sprightly ninety-seconds old, which is a good thing because I'm about to take a bite of it right now. And yes, it's just as delicious as they said it would be—a strong peppery taste, yet still surprisingly tender and flavorful. But the meat in this burger didn't come from a cow grazing outdoors or cramped indoors. It came from a bioreactor. Mary Alderman explains:

> I grew the cells in this burger inside a sterile test tube environment, seeded around a printed scaffold made from organic materials. Now, if I left it at that and provided only the necessary nutrient bath, your burger would basically be an unsightly blob of animal cells. I imagine that's not the sort of thing you'd enjoy eating, so I needed to encourage the formation of blood vessels and arteries so that the tissue would turn into muscles that are, well, tastier and look better. Those muscles were stimulated electrically, and I made sure that the stem cells worked right. Well, I could go on, but I won't.
>
> Anyway, if you know exactly how to do it and you have the right tools, it's easy enough to make cloned meat. But the pioneers had to work it all out from scratch and make their own tools. Compared to the usual way of obtaining meat by rearing and killing animals, it must have been incredibly frustrating!

Frustrating, but well worth the effort. There were two pressures driving the development of cloned meat. The first was that the traditional farming model had been built on the assumption that cheap land, cheap water, and cheap electricity would last forever. But climate change and increased competition for arable land proved those assumptions wrong. It was also becoming more difficult to keep livestock healthy due to new restrictions on the use of antibiotics, resulting from the global rise in dangerous antibiotic-resistant bacteria in the previous decade.

Even with traditional meat becoming more expensive in the '20s, cloned meat—still only being grown in labs at huge expense—didn't constitute a genuine alternative. It would take a second pressure to make cloned meat affordable: the demand of the mass elderly for clean and nutritious food, and a corresponding breakthrough in mass-produced bioreactors. Across the world were hundreds of millions of consumers who wanted to live healthily. Only cloned meat could be guaranteed to be germ-free, impeccably sourced from bioreactor to deliverbot to the dining table.

Not only that, but cloned meat could be tailored to different consumers so that it contained the perfect balances of nutrients. An early manufacturer, Tiersen, said that it was "more medicine than meat—except this medicine tastes good." The fact that Tiersen employees were anonymously stoking fears of traditional meat contamination on casters and scenario engineering sites didn't hurt their business either—at least, not until the company was forced to pay a (sadly modest) $1.2 billion fine in 2031.

As other companies joined the tailored meat bandwagon, the cost of bioreactors began dropping, and more scientists began engineering cell lines, some of which were open-sourced. Soon, it wasn't unusual to see bioreactors sitting beside sous vide machines and laser searers at high-end restaurants, and from there, it was a short trip to fast food outlets and community kitchens.

That's the origin of my Owen's Original here. Surprisingly, Peter Owen is actually a real person, not a corporate invention, and these days he's living in Hamilton, Ontario. He apparently arrived at the recipe for his burgers by experimenting for several months with a bioreactor setup he'd picked up from a fire sale at a bankrupt pharmaceutical company.

After many unsuccessful attempts, his friends finally gave him the thumbs up. Owen started selling subscriptions to his burger recipes to restaurants around the world, with a considerable discount if they kept his name on the menu. Owen's Originals proved to be a long-lived success, selling tens of millions of burgers over five years before Peter Owen decided to accept an open-source bounty for his recipe, release it into the public domain, and move on to new ideas.

All of this talk of "cloned meat" is, of course, rather baffling to us today since we usually just call it "meat." The prospect of actually eating an animal tends to equally divide people between those who find it distasteful and those who see it as a special treat. Whatever your own view, I think we can all agree that we'd rather not return to a world where tens of billions of animals are slaughtered every year.

42 THE USTC CRASH

Hefei, China, 2033

The last known words from Xu Yao at the University of Science and Technology of China in Hefei were, "stupid copter taking off outside going to check it out," sent via SMS to his sister. Xu's neighbor, Jennifer Liu, was finishing up a homework assignment, while across the hall, Tiffany Chen was cooking noodles before a dance class.

A few seconds later, at 6:37 p.m. on Friday April 1, 2033, a helicopter taking off from a nearby car park clipped an electricity pylon running beside their four-story dormitory. It tipped over and smashed directly into the building. Multiple gas lines immediately ignited, causing an explosion that incinerated the entire western wing, instantly killing nineteen students and staff. It wasn't until the next day that emergency workers and drones were able to clear the rubble and carry the last few survivors to hospital. In total, 148 people died and 201 were critically injured. This blackened rotor is all that remains of the helicopter today.

The explosion was covered in real time by more than a thousand separate cameras and audio sensors. While only two hundred had public feeds—mostly students' glasses plus some unauthorized drones nearby—there was enough data available to identify the helicopter and all of the people involved in the accident.

A cursory examination of the footage revealed that the helicopter was registered to Wuhan 57958 International, a shell company. Tracing the ownership trail back revealed that it was actually used by Dr. Alexander Yang, a billionaire investment manager from Shanghai. His son, Herbert Yang, studied at USTC. It emerged that Herbert Yang had been in the helicopter when it crashed. He had been intending to skip the traffic jams on the way to his home outside Hefei.

Civilian helicopter flights were strictly regulated within Anhui and, indeed, all of China. It was certainly illegal, not to mention extremely unsafe, for Herbert Yang to be taking off from a car park so close to a residential building. But corruption was common and few questions were asked of such people—especially of the son of a billionaire who counted several third and fourth generation "Immortals" among his close friends.

In the hours following the crash, more than seventeen million people signed an online petition for Dr. Yang to be prosecuted for manslaughter, along with civil aviation officials in Anhui. China's internet monitors had been tracking sentiment regarding the USTC crash almost immediately, and with the petition gaining traction, they ordered Weibo and other social networking casters to block the transmission of all messages related to the topic.

Historically, this tactic had worked reasonably well due to the Harmonious Choir counter-protest system. The "Choir" was a panoply of constructed artificial personalities that censors could use to spread online messages for the purpose of manipulating public sentiment—in this case, to blunt and disperse online anger. However, the millions of furious messages about the crash were harder to hide than usual with keywords and images and videos changing from minute to minute as groups tried to evade the online censors. As it happened, the censors weren't entirely immune to the messages either, as Carol Xi, an internet monitor team leader, tells me:

> You have to understand that the crash was deeply personal for many of the online censors. The people who were killed were just young kids. They hadn't done anything wrong except live near that stupid helicopter. Okay, not all of the censors felt the same way, but enough did, and…Well…maybe we worked a bit slow. Maybe we didn't look as thoroughly for all the keywords and clusters we could have. I don't know whether it made a difference. I hope it did.

Deep mining suggests that Xi's efforts, or lack of them, really did buy online protesters crucial time to organize mass civil disobedience. Not in the real world—people were afraid to gather in large groups when emergency surveillance drones lurked over every city and town—but online civil disobedience was a different matter entirely.

The protesters began sending billions of angry messages to government officials, crashing mailboxes and networks across the country with pent-up grievances. Scripts were circulated that would hammer "corrupt" businesses with WeChat payments and then revoke them, playing havoc with banks' financial systems. Walk along any street and you wouldn't have seen anything out of the ordinary, but look online, where people lived and worked and played, and it was a seething revolt. It took a whole day for China's cautious leaders to issue a vague statement promising a "serious investigation." Far too little, and far too late.

Most shockingly, hackers managed to access and leak a transcript of the State Council's emergency online deliberations about the crash. It showed a government that was disunited and afraid. The one action that might have made a difference—immediately arresting Dr. Yang and other complicit officials in Anhui on grounds of corruption—was dismissed out of hand. Many in the council worried that if they bowed to public pressure so quickly, they would invite further protests. In the end, they did nothing, and China was plunged into the Quiet Revolution, a revolution characterized by battles online, not in the real world.

There had been unrest in China before, but the sheer normality of the USTC crash, an entirely preventable accident that pitted the masses against the corrupt and the rich, struck a new chord. The crash became a powerful rallying point against the unaccountability and criminal ineffectiveness of the government.

Just as importantly, it brought to the surface long-held concerns about people's physical and financial security. China's one-child policy had resulted in a decidedly lopsided population pyramid. Too few adults were supporting too many elderly, and spartan government pensions and healthcare services couldn't fill the gap. Economic growth was sputtering out under pressure from low-end manufacturers in Africa and India and from high-end automation and amplified teams. Devastating man-made environmental disasters and climate change ladled on the misery.

China's citizens had much to be thankful for. Since the twentieth century, the country had rocketed out of poverty and into the ranks of the richest nations in the world. But those riches had not been fairly distributed, and the resulting strains on the social compact were becoming too much to bear. The legitimacy of China's leaders ultimately rested on their ability to govern with justice and honor. That legitimacy vanished in a bonfire.

A decade of crawling economic growth was the fuel. The USTC crash was the spark. And the flames would be felt across the world.

43 RITUALS FOR THE SECULAR

Earth, 2033

As organized religion gradually declined through the twenty-first century, new rituals for the secular grew in prominence—not in all countries, not in all communities, but in so many that the shift was hard to miss. People invented rituals to commemorate and consecrate events and activities that held deep meaning for them. Others were drawn to those rituals to repeat and reinvent them. This is a selection of rituals for the secular from 2033. Some are still practiced to this day; others have long since disappeared.

THE FORGETTING

The Society of Lethe encourages individuals to purge all their online data and social media every seven years in a ritual called the Forgetting. In the month before the purge, people celebrate their most outstanding online contributions with their friends and family, and select just seven pieces to keep for the future. In the week before, they acknowledge the hurt and confusion they might have caused through social media, and compose seven contributions asking for forgiveness. In the seven hours before, they stay offline completely to experience the world as it was before everything was remembered forever.

At the moment of the Forgetting, they give the Society's server permission to access all of their online accounts and permanently delete their data and erase all backups. Some adherents use a ceremonial hammer to smash a replica of an ancient spinning hard disk to commemorate the loss and the opportunity for growth.

PHYSICAL SYNC

This ritual grew out of the entirely practical requirement for security-conscious groups to swap their cryptographic "public keys" in person to prevent impersonation or man-in-the-middle attacks. These groups included distributed amplified teams, which took advantage of the physical proximity to become familiar with one another and to establish emotional trust through intense experiences. These could include extreme physical sports, group meditation, mutual grooming, and dancing.

CALISTHENIA

Calisthenia is an augmented reality ritual created by the New School of Taipei. Participants are guided through a series of slow, graceful, continuous movements, based largely on tai chi. Fantastical AR creatures aid learning, both by capturing participants' attention and by their exemplary motion. One can observe millions of people dancing the same movements for fifteen minutes around the world during Calisthenia's real-time rituals, occurring every four hours.

INFINITE LOOP

The Infinite Loop is a running event that never ends. It consists of a group of runners moving at a pace of 5.5 minutes per kilometer. Anyone is welcome and the route is pre-cleared with relevant authorities. Some larger Loops have been operating continuously, day and night, for several years, albeit only with one or two runners at times, but rising to hundreds or even thousands during the weekend. While Loops are outwardly egalitarian, a person's unofficial rank in a Loop can be determined by their participation rate with appropriate corrections for their health, personal situation, time of day, and weather.

MAXIMUM RELEASE

Maximum Release was invented by a group of friends in Bruges to ostentatiously demonstrate their wealth and supposed virtue, inadvertently reinventing the potlatch. During a Maximum Release, an individual lists a large set of assets that anyone in their chosen community can claim. These assets are often digital and sometimes ephemeral access to time-limited experiences, games, people.

The Maximum Release declined in popularity following the adoption of basic maximum income three years later.

THE ENGRAVING

The Engraving is a silent commemoration of those who have passed, conducted entirely in virtual reality. The ritual originated from the USTC crash of 2033 when many were afraid to gather in public to remember their friends and family who had been killed.

They would come to the foot of a mountain at dawn and climb single-file through thick forest and dense mist to eventually reach the summit. There was always mist, and the summit was always cold, and the sky was always clear. There, the mourners took turns to engrave a memory of the deceased on a tall marble monument. The day artificially accelerated such that sunset coincided with the last engraving.

Then, finally, they would turn away from the monument, and they would see a sparkle of light playing out from the hundreds and thousands of other peaks surrounding them just visible above the cloud.

Melodramatic? Perhaps. Clichéd? Certainly. But sometimes these are the stories we need when we are in pain.

44 MUON DETECTOR

Asunción, Paraguay, 2034

Babylon-translated remarks from President Aguirre on November 3, 2034, in Asunción, Paraguay:

Two years ago, our country suffered its worst attack in living memory when a terrorist group detonated a nuclear bomb here in Asunción. In the blink of an eye, twenty thousand people were killed.

Over the agonizing months that came after, tens of thousands more died from exposure and from radiation poisoning. It is only thanks to the courageous work of every member of the emergency services, the army, the police, and the countless citizens who helped in those desperate times that the dreadful toll wasn't any higher.

Since that day two years ago, we have hunted down those responsible and brought them to justice. Just as importantly, we have begun the process of rebuilding this beautiful city and country and remembering all of those who fell. Part of that process is ensuring that such an atrocity can never happen again on our soil.

I have already described the steps this government is taking to upgrade our security services' capabilities and to increase the speed and effectiveness of our military response. Make no mistake, today we are far readier to detect and destroy those that threaten us than we were two years ago.

But this is not enough. Even the best intelligence networks cannot be perfect. We have learned from bitter experience that our enemies can move more swiftly than we could have imagined. A single layer of defense is too easily breached and even a double layer may fall. No, we must have defense in depth, a system that cannot be fooled or evaded.

That is why, today, I am announcing the construction of the National Defense Initiative, a series of physical and digital barriers that will detect and prevent the passage of any unauthorized nuclear materials across our borders and within our country.

You may be wondering how this is possible. So-called backpack bombs, lead shielding, and car or copter transports all make it easy for terrorists to destroy lives. The answer is simple: every vehicle, plane, helicopter, car, truck, dirigible, ship, and container entering this country whether through road, air, or water will pass through a new type of detector—muon detectors—that will uncover nuclear material.

Every minute, thousands of muon particles rain down naturally from the sky and pass harmlessly through matter just as fish swim through water. But when they meet with extremely dense material like the uranium and plutonium in a nuclear bomb, those muons are deflected. It is by measuring those deflections that we can discover the presence of nuclear bombs, even if they are surrounded by a meter of solid lead. The technique is completely foolproof.

For the past six months, we have been experimenting with this technology at ports and border entries across Paraguay, including Villeta and Encarnación. I have now decided to take the next step to roll this technology out across the country.

The vast majority of people and companies will barely even notice the detection process. Vehicles move through a short tunnel for just one minute, passing over a strip of muon detectors in the ground. Once they have exited, they will be tagged as being clean. In the unlikely case that we find something, the tunnel will be instantly sealed and security forces called. This will finally and absolutely prevent terrorists from smuggling in nuclear material through containers like they did two years ago.

In time, we intend to add more detectors to these tunnels, capable of discovering biological pathogens and other dangerous materials. And the National Defense Initiative won't merely increase our safety; scanning and tagging every vehicle and container that enters our country will help the coordination of our economy, freeing up essential resources and time.

In the coming hours, we will be releasing more information about the National Defense Initiative, but for the moment I want to pay tribute to the hard-working researchers and engineers who have formulated this plan, led by Universidad Nacional de Asunción and in collaboration with the Distributed Security Collective and Ching Yun University.

Two years ago, I stood here and I pledged that as your President, we would never again see the horrors of Asunción on our soil. It is time for us to protect what we have rebuilt. I am certain that the National Defense Initiative will do that. I hope you will join me in making our country safer and stronger. We owe it to the fallen to protect those who live today.

45 THE SAINT OF SAFEKEEPERS

New York, US, 2034

An obituary, and a sign of isolation and connection in the 2030s:

In her thirty years as a notary, Natasha Willis worked for thousands of clients across the world. She preferred to talk to her clients directly. "I can do a better job if I talk to people face to face, without these agents and mimic scripts getting in the way," she once told her sister Elizabeth. It might take her more time, and it lost her some customers and fees, but she was happier for it.

Most customers had straightforward jobs for her: witnessing signatures, identifying individuals, drafting contracts, providing affidavits, the usual work of a notary.

Some had more unusual requests, requests that would make Willis pause. Wills that needed to be drawn up instantly. Contracts providing password keychains to apparent strangers. Power of attorney to long-sundered children. Giving away beloved personal possessions.

Natasha Willis would pay special attention to those unusual requests. If she noticed something strange in how these clients acted, she would simply ask them, "Is there anything else I can do to help you? Anything you would like to talk about? I have the time."

Sometimes this was enough to draw out the truth that they were planning to end their lives. They would step back from the edge and talk. It's thought that Willis helped dozens of people in this way over her years as a notary through her insistence and dedication to providing a service in person. "Notaries have to be human," Willis said. "That meant that the people I was talking to knew they could relate to me. I wasn't just another script made to please."

She died at home on Thursday at the age of sixty-nine with her husband Troy, seventy-three, and children Max, Oliver, and Sarah present.

Natasha Willis was born in Brooklyn on February 14, 1965. As a child, she harbored ambitions of becoming a judge, but her lack of connections and the general sex discrimination of the time conspired against her. Instead, she worked as a secretary during her twenties and thirties, eventually becoming an executive assistant at a major New York law firm.

With her savings, she went to community college to train as a notary. Upon qualifying, she slowly built up a trusted business based on her unstinting dedication to her clients. It was clear that Willis would go beyond the call of duty for her profession. Many clients and their families would thank her for her help and care, and some even offered to pay her more, but she consistently refused.

"Anyone would do it," she would remark to people who inquired. "Anyone who was paying attention could see these people were hurting, and they didn't want comfort from a machine. They wanted to talk to a real live person. They could tell the difference."

Willis would check in with some clients for weeks or even months after the initial job, taking time to connect with them over a call. She might even travel across the country to meet with people whom she felt needed physical contact.

As her efforts became more widely known, she was awarded the Order of Merit by the mayor of New York. On news of her death, the office of the mayor paid tribute to her for the lives she had saved. "Natasha reminded us of how we can change the lives of others for the better. All it takes is for someone to act."

46 THE IMITATION GAME

San Jose, US, 2034

Can we know if a criminal has really reformed? Only God can say for certain. Yet our duties of forgiveness and compassion tell us that here on Earth we must decide carefully when judging whether a criminal may safely rejoin society. In the absence of perfect knowledge, the best we can do is to look at how they behave and what they say. If our former criminal's behavior is indistinguishable from someone whom we believe to be a good person, then how can we say that they are not fit to receive freedom? Can there be a fairer test?

—Reverend Michael Zhang, 2034.

Most of us know Turing's name these days, usually through his eponymous test to measure the ability of machines to exhibit intelligent behavior equivalent to—or these days, well beyond—humans. The Turing Test was originally inspired by imitation games in which an interrogator tries to discover which of two people is genuinely, for example, a woman, a politician, or a scientist, and which is merely pretending to be a woman, a politician, or a scientist.

In the twentieth and early twenty-first centuries, imitation games were mostly thought experiments, but they eventually found use in the training of interactional experts—people who mimic expertise in a field by talking and interacting with real experts. Journalists, project managers, and activists are classic examples of interactional experts, but the truth is that almost everyone develops some interactional expertise as they attempt to demonstrate friendliness or curiosity or care toward someone or something. Seen through the lens of imitation games, interactional experts are nothing more than frauds, but in another light, the process of pretending provides them with valuable knowledge and wisdom about the two worlds they are bridging.

A major effort to test this latter hypothesis began in 2034 at the South San Jose Youth Correctional Center. Despite heavy use of remote monitors and community interventions, the center was seeing high numbers of repeat juvenile offenders. Dr. Wood, senior administrator at the center, describes how they chose to tackle their problem with an unconventional solution:

> Did you know that back in the early twenty-first century, one of the most interesting strategies for reducing recidivism rates was a group literary reading program used in Brazil and Houston? The idea was that by reading classics like *To Kill a Mockingbird* and *Of Mice and Men*, prisoners would develop more empathy and tolerance, and improve their literacy skills. It seemed to me that this strategy could address problems with impulse control and noncognitive deficits as well.
>
> We began our own group literary reading program, using storytelling modification and narrative injection to personalize the books and make them feel more relevant to individual prisoners. To be honest, it wasn't as successful as we'd hoped.

While Dr. Wood's intervention at South San Jose showed glimmers of early promise, its effects were minor. It also came under fire for being "soft on prisoners."

> Yes, a lot of people talked about cheating. They thought we didn't have any safeguards against prisoners reading the books but only pretending to have learned their lesson. That's when I realized that perhaps someone who behaves as if they are reformed essentially is reformed—in the long term, I mean. After that epiphany, the idea of putting prisoners through imitation games in which they had to behave as if they were, say, an empathetic person or a member of a minority they had despised seemed obvious.

During South San Jose's initial eighteen-month program, juvenile offenders were placed in a lengthy series of immersive simulations in which they had to pretend to be different members of society. Their "interrogators" were paid micro-taskers trained to ask difficult questions and be highly alert to the slightest mistakes. Following every simulation, the offenders were told their score and were given lessons on how to improve their performance.

To put it crudely, the offenders gained points by pretending to be model citizens.

The "Imitation Reform Program" proved to be startlingly successful at reducing recidivism rates, but it came with a major downside: sociopaths and psychopaths flew through the program with ease thanks to their charisma and ability to mimic highly developed social skills. In fact, some actually honed their façade by playing the games.

> I don't think that we did worse than any other intervention at identifying sociopaths, but yes, we recognized that we had to modify the program. We added things like frequent retesting and checkups. Sometimes those retests were open,

in that the subjects knew they were going on, and sometimes they were masked, where the subjects were not warned that they were being tested.

I'll be honest. Even with the changes we still couldn't identify all the sociopaths. You have to put this into perspective, though, since sociopaths represented only a tiny percentage of our intake. I believe that the vast majority of our subjects really did end up internalizing the lessons of the games, and that conclusion is borne out by the impact on their recidivism rates. What we did was far more honest and a damn sight more effective than anything that came before. Cheaper, too.

Dr. Wood did harbor some doubts, though.

Sometimes I wondered whether we were actually reforming offenders or just teaching them to wear a mask that let them get by in society. I emailed my pastor with my worries, and he reassured me that only God could know for sure if a criminal was truly reformed. Since we can't look into someone's soul, he said that we could only look at how they behaved. He said that God would forgive us for any mistakes we made.

I don't know whether he really believed that or if he was only trying to make me feel better. I guess it doesn't matter either way, since I wasn't able to tell the difference.

47 MIRIAM XU'S LACE

Hong Kong, China, 2034

Even genius has its limits. Einstein might have gone unremarked in the turmoil of the Reformation; Da Vinci would have been an anonymous cave painter a few thousand years earlier; and Song would have toiled in Foxconn only a century ago. Miriam Xu, the composer and former conductor of the Taipei Symphony Orchestra, is well aware of the contingency of history. "But for me, it's not a question of whether I would have been a data miner or a teacher a generation ago. It's whether I would have reached my first birthday."

Shortly after she was born in 2034, Xu suffered a severe ventral pontine stroke from an accidental house fire following the unrest of the USTC crash. The stroke caused total locked-in syndrome, leaving her unable to control any voluntary muscles in her body, including her eyes.

The severity of her condition led to Xu being selected for an experimental suite of treatments in Hong Kong that included neuromuscular electrical patches, neural stem cell therapy—and a then-cutting-edge neural lace, as seen on this brain scan from around her third birthday. The lace was a crude but effective version of the ones we still use today, and, like our own, it read Xu's brain activity and gave her basic control over her muscles.

During those years of constant treatment, Xu developed an affinity for music.

"When I was still a baby in hospital and they'd only just started the treatments, my mother would play me music all the time," Xu tells me. "The doctors said that because I couldn't focus my eyes properly, the best way to reach me was through my ears. She used to play the violin at school, and I think she always wished she could have kept studying, so she played me recordings of all of the classics as a baby."

Before she received her neuromuscular patches, the researchers tested Xu's neural lace by measuring her electrical brain activity in response to auditory stimuli. At only three years old, Xu performed extremely well, showing an excellent ability to distinguish between different sounds and composers and even different performers of the same music.

After hearing about Xu, a research student from the Royal College of Music developed software that allowed her to compose music based on her brain activity. Xu's first works were initially highly derivative but quickly grew in complexity, and as her childhood moved on and she regained direct control of her body, Xu continued to compose using her neural lace. Having grown up with it, she simply found her lace faster and more natural than any other interface.

As a result, her compositions often lacked any consideration for the practical or logistical issues involved in, say, assembling two hundred violinists and positioning them in a toroidal shape around the audience.

"I never even imagined that humans would actually play anything I composed," Xu said. "I'd always thought that music was something that a computer produced, not something that was made by people playing on physical instruments. But I did read what the critics said, and as soon as I could, I got my hands on a piano and a violin and tried to understand how they worked."

Organ re-engineering and extensive stem cell therapies progressively restored Xu to full health during her adolescence, which allowed her to learn to physically play musical instruments. However, Xu eventually opted to focus on composition and conducting rather than performance. Her efforts led her to a number of conducting positions around the world and finally to the Taipei Symphony, where she stayed for eleven years. Looking back, it's extraordinary to consider the volume of work she produced, especially coming from a singleton—someone not part of a chorus or amplified team.

Later in life, Xu's use of her neural lace from infancy and the nonstop recording of her thoughts that entailed gave her an important role in the free speech and privacy disputes of the early '50s. Cases in the European Union, African Union, and the United States sought to delineate the legitimate third-party use of private recorded thoughts. Could they be used as grounds for dismissal? Was it legal to intercept thoughts for national security or policing issues? For her part, Xu forcefully spoke in favor of citizens' rights to their own thoughts and opposed the notion that thoughts should be treated in the same way as actions. Her efforts earned her allies and enemies alike.

"After Bangalore, people were so scared. They thought mindreading would stop future attacks," Xu said. "It was desperate. I know better than anyone else that mindreading doesn't work like that, and even if it did, it would come at the cost of our liberty. A generation ago they wanted to use micro-gestures for the same thing, and that didn't work either. The truth is that there will always be people who are afraid, and there will always be people who want to exploit that fear for their own ends."

Xu's other passion was ensuring that other children would have the same access to the kinds of critical treatments that she had. "I was lucky, with my smart parents and living in a rich city. I feel bad for people who are just on basic minimum income because these neural laces and patches aren't cheap. We need to do everything we can to make these treatments available to as many people as possible."

Partly thanks to Xu's advocacy, her story is unlikely to be repeated. Improved amniocentesis, TNI scanning, phylogeny extrapolation, gene therapy, exowombs—these all mean that locked-in syndromes can be cured. Not everyone can be a genius like Xu, but our technology gives us all more chances than ever before.

48 THE LOOP

Wales, 2034

Like a cross worn discreetly around the neck, a loop isn't something that you'd immediately notice unless you were looking for it. Once spotted, however, it tells you something important about the wearer—not what religion they follow, but what they stand for and how they might act toward others.

I have my late uncle's earloop here with me. It's a single slim piece of curved silver metal, a few millimeters wide and four centimeters long with a wide droplet extending around the front. This one is designed to fit snugly around the back of his right ear. Unlike the popular Bluetooth headsets from the turn of the century (named after an archaic wireless protocol) which used uncomfortable earbuds, this loop uses bone conduction to pick up speech and to play audio.

The odd thing is that when he turned eighteen, my uncle opted to have a phone implanted in his ear. It was considered fashionable at the time, and in any case it was easily reversible. The point is that he had no obvious use for an external earloop; it was totally redundant. Now, you may be thinking that the earloop was simply my uncle's retro affectation or, to be more charitable, just a piece of jewelry, but the truth is more complex. I'll let Beth Mison, a wearer of loops for most of her life, explain:

> I started wearing my loop in the autumn of 2034 after I saw the flooding in Banda Aceh. It's hard to imagine today, but it was absolutely devastating—the dams were breached, the power grid failed, backup batteries failed, data networks failed, everything failed. Whenever it looked like they might get data back up again, some idiot hacker group brought it down, which meant no one wanted to send emergency drones and no one could coordinate. Some police left their posts and joined in with the looting, so after a couple of days, it was absolute pandemonium, and all we could do from the outside was watch from the high cameras.
>
> And then…we saw something happen. Violence and even riots were sweeping the city, but not in the north. There was a group there helping calm things

down, restoring order, distributing supplies, getting electricity back up. And you could see that they were all wearing these chunky earloops made for the emergency services—long-life, practically indestructible hardware, capable of setting up ad hoc long-distance peer-to-peer networks. They let people coordinate. These people weren't experts. They were volunteers. It was inspiring.

First in Banda Aceh and then across the world, people began to recognize the earloops and trust their wearers to do the right thing—intervening in riots, carrying the sick and wounded, guarding essential medical supplies. Each looper was closely networked to thousands of others, and they had a collective tenacity of spirit that helped the city get back on its feet.

But why did the loopers create such an enduring impact? Much of it comes down to the gradual erosion of established hierarchies during the early twenty-first century. Increased access to information and organizing technologies meant that people were increasingly unwilling to recognize the legitimacy of many kinds of unaccountable authority. Rather than blindly trusting the police and security services, they wanted more transparency and control. The striking success of the loopers in Banda Aceh demonstrated that another way was possible, especially in countries that had adopted a basic minimum income guarantee, freeing up citizens' time.

While there is a romantic notion of the lone looper fearlessly striding into danger to save lives, their effectiveness derived directly from their networked nature. If a looper encountered an emergency, which encompassed everything from drunken bullying to a natural disaster, they would be automatically connected to an entire backup support network of human and AI helpers, near and far. These helpers provided real-time advice for everything from CPR to mechanical repair, the appropriate use of force, and how to defuse fights. Indeed, much of the backup simply consisted of moral support, letting loopers know that there was an army behind their back in every encounter.

In keeping with its decentralized nature, there wasn't only one backup network for loopers; instead, they used open protocols that allowed a wide range of networks to interoperate, including networks run by local communities, churches, missions, or even belatedly by governments.

With the lack of a central authority, establishing mutual trust among loopers was crucial to avoid fraudsters. The most successful networks tended to adopt the Hackworth model, which combined a distributed trust management system with rituals like the Physical Sync. Detailed trust ratings were publicly viewable not only online, but also through the design of physical loops, with different colors and styles denoting the various ranks.

I'll let Beth Mison describe what being a looper means to her:

I started out with a very plain, dark grey loop. There weren't many emergencies in Wales, so it took me quite a few weeks to work my way up to the second rank, which added a scarlet stripe to it. But you know, this isn't a game; it's real life. We don't all get to be superheroes. I've never run into a burning building or directed an emergency drone fleet. It took me decades to work my way up to the white loop.

Because everyone has laces these days, a lot of people think it's just about fashion. It's not. Wearing a loop is sign and a commitment that people can come to me and I will help do the right thing in an emergency. It's a symbol of my responsibility to help other loopers, to back them up when they need it. It's not just individual courage that turns loopers into heroes—it's the people who stand behind them.

49 THE SEAMSTRESS'S NEW TOOLS

Florida, US, 2035

It's the simple things, like stitching, measuring, holding a pair of scissors. Even though I know exactly where I want to cut and what patterns I want to use, my hands and fingers won't do what I tell them to any more. I guess that's only fair enough. They've had a tough sixty years! But, you know, I haven't run out of ideas, and I want to keep on working. So, I've got to use the tools that let me do that, even if they are very different tools!

—Martha Evans, 2035

Born in 1972, Martha Evans held plenty of different jobs in her life—a bartender, sales assistant, artist, graphic designer—but by her mid-thirties she'd settled into a career as a freelance artist and fashion designer. She did well, making dresses for shops around Florida with her own two hands and a sewing machine. I have one of her dresses in front of me, a simple, bright red silk dress with a neat knot at the neck and a turquoise belt.

Like a lot of other high-end bespoke work, Evans's occupation was well-protected against automation. Clothing has never been purely about cost or convenience. If that were the case, we'd all be wearing cheap grey jump-suits. No, it's about appearance, and even the best augmented reality (AR) won't satisfy those who want to impress in the basic physical reality.

What's true now was even truer in the '30s, when Evans was sixty years old. Though there was still plenty of demand for her dresses, she wasn't able to satisfy all of it herself, so she had a choice to make. Either she could hire assistants and step back from doing hands-on work herself or she could cre-ate designs for mass-produced off-the-peg garments. Evans kept delaying her decision until she was introduced to Shakti Nagra, a young woman who wanted to change the way that clothes were made.

Broadly speaking, there were two ways of making clothes before the '30s. The first was bespoke tailoring that required carefully measuring the cus-tomer, then cutting and sewing fabrics, usually with some final adjustments after a fitting—Evans's way. The second was mass production using a mixture of automation and human labor; however, even mass production still required designers to create manufacturing samples, and there could be a lengthy process to ensure that the final products matched what the designer intended.

Nagra's process was completely novel. During the late 2010s and early '20s, Nagra made a series of breakthroughs in realistically simulating the behavior of fabrics—how they hung, how they folded, how they looked when rumpled—using physical parameters derived from high resolution CT scans and an exhaustive battery of tests for stretchiness, thermal conductivity, breathability, and so on.

At first, all of this effort wasn't about physical fashion; it was about creating computer animations for games and films. The increased fidelity of glasses and lenses led to a revolution in entertainment, and users wanted the characters in their games to look as realistic as possible. Games and films enjoyed a lucrative sideline by including real clothes as product placements, and Nagra's company, DEI-9, developed the software that made it all possible.

Shakti Nagra explains her next step:

> I realized that if we could perfectly simulate fabrics and garments like the dresses and suits you might see in any mall or on any high street, then we could go in the opposite direction: we could design garments virtually, simulate out how they'd look, and then specify every single step involved in manufacturing those garments. It would be a 100 percent digital process, end-to-end.

Armed with tens of millions in investment money, Nagra set out to accomplish her goal of making clothes entirely digitally. She immediately ran into two major problems.

The first was that the clothing industry, particularly manufacturing, was still very much human-powered. The complex and delicate manipulations required to cut and sew garments were extremely challenging for the robots at the time. It could be done, but only at a significant premium over human labor. Nagra was pragmatic. She delayed her ambitions of an entirely automated process to focus on creating better quality control systems for her human workers, until—in her characteristically unsentimental way—robotics costs fell to the point where she could replace those workers.

The second problem she faced involved the design process. Most fashion designers weren't experienced with the kind of 3-D modeling tools that Nagra's designers used. Their experience was in nondigital, fully physical environments.

That's where Evans came in: Nagra hired her as a consultant to help create the tools that designers would use. Throwing out Nagra's existing austerely technical interface, Evans opted for a highly skeuomorphic system that used physical gestures and commands that mimicked those she'd used her entire life. Designers would put their fingers into the shape of scissors to cut and could virtually sew their clothes at high magnification, all using thimble rings for absolute AR positioning.

Their collaboration saw them become close friends. As Nagra said, "We had very different backgrounds. I thought Evans would just be a consultant for a few months and I'd never see her again, but she really opened my eyes to the artistry of the process."

To modern eyes, the interface Evans helped create looks hopelessly old-fashioned and clunky, but it was what designers of the time were familiar with, and that was all that mattered. They could design a 3-D model on Monday, receive pre-orders on Tuesday, and have dresses manufactured by Wednesday. Within two years, DEI-9 had attracted tens of thousands of young and old fashion designers who were using Evans's systems to design, manufacture, and sell garments across the world. Later versions of the software even allowed for clothes to be automatically redesigned according to customers' 3-D body maps, massively reducing returns.

Naturally, fashion designs were quickly pirated. "I had predicted this would happen, just as it did with music and film and other media, so of course we had a strategy to deal with it," said Nagra.

This strategy involved creating simplified tools that allowed users to edit and customize existing fashions in a faster and more convenient way than through piracy—with a small tip going to the original designer and DEI-9, of course. Soon, clothing fads rose and fell almost as quickly as blink avatars, and fashion fragmented into even smaller circles, freed from the constraints of mass production. To avoid excessive waste taxes, most designers allowed customers to trade in their old clothes using specialized robotics to perfectly unravel threads for reuse.

Ordering clothes from DEI-9 didn't have the same instant gratification that shopping in cities did, but it gave you access to a much wider variety of styles and was much, much cheaper. For one thing, DEI-9 didn't have to pay for retail space. Even that advantage was narrowed in later years, when newer robotics and predictive retail systems allowed custom orders to be fulfilled in mere hours. Meanwhile, DEI-9 and its competitors kept expanding their design toolsets to include blink avatar outfits, tents, furnishings, and even textile-based skyscrapers.

Nagra's vision gave unprecedented freedom to fashion designers. As for Evans, she was given favored access to the company's programmers and resources, and she took full advantage. That brings me back to the simple bright red dress in front of me. It's very similar to a previous dress she'd made herself by hand, but this dress was made, as she said, "not in a better way, just a different way."

Evans kept on designing clothes until she died at the age of ninety-six— and her friend Nagra always made sure that the right tools were ready and waiting for her.

50 CHOOSING A DRIVING PLAN

United States, 2035

The driverless car revolutionized every aspect of transportation—particularly the business model. This brochure demonstrates how people struggled to come to grips with the new world:

Life used to be simple. If you wanted to travel, all you had to do was buy a car and put gas in it every so often. Sure, keeping a car was expensive, and it bled value every minute you weren't using it, and you had to pay for parking and repairs and insurance, and you wasted thousands of hours of your life in the mindless drudgery of driving, but at least you knew you had absolutely no choice in the matter.

Well, it's 2035 now, and while we're blessedly free from the monotony and expense of driving, we're also faced with a bewildering range of options for getting from A to B. The plummeting cost of cars (we can surely drop the term "driverless" by now), along with their tight network integration, has seen a thousand flowers bloom in the burgeoning "cars as a service" sector.

With so many choices available, it's easy to get confused, but don't worry: we're here to help you find your perfect car plan!

Before we begin, those pay-as-you-go plans that seem so cheap with their free miles and entertainment? Unless you're a penniless hermit who only makes ten trips a year or you hate the idea of being able to travel wherever you want, whenever you want—forget it.

Now we've gotten that out of the way, here are a few general tips on finding a good plan.

First off, don't go for flat-rate pricing for car minutes or car miles. They might be easier to understand, but you get a lot less bang for your buck because you can't take advantage of demand-based pricing. You'll get ripped off if you use a car during low demand times—around 11 a.m., say—and during rush hour you'll be left waiting because everyone else on your plan is trying to use cars at the same time. In theory, flat-rate car plans can be cheaper, but in practice they just don't work out in the long term.

So that leaves demand-based pricing, with Challenger and CarSnap being the two leading competitors.

Challenger has points and CarSnap has beats, but they both amount to the same thing: travel currency that changes in price depending on how busy the network and traffic is. This kind of demand-based pricing means the same journey might cost different amounts depending on the time of day or whether there's a special occasion (such as a holiday or sports event) that's causing a lot of traffic and pollution.

In most cities, demand-based pricing is regulated by local governments rather than companies themselves, so you don't have to worry about getting fleeced. But if you're anxious about costs, both services offer paid memberships that reduce demand-multipliers, a bit like buying insurance.

A common mistake that new users make is overestimating how many points/beats they'll need and signing up for an expensive contract they can't get out of. Don't fall for it! Journeys are an awful lot faster when you don't have to find parking, and you can always buy extra points if you need them. One thing that's definitely worth paying for, though, is a "family and friends" bolt-on. This lets you add extra users onto your car plan for a small amount, plus, Challenger offers up to a 50 percent discount if you all travel in the same vehicle (saving them money, of course).

Speaking of which, both Challenger and CarSnap also offer carpooling bonuses that let users save points by sharing journeys with strangers. If you live in a city or you're flexible with your timing, carpooling usually only adds on a few minutes to your journey time, so you'd be crazy not to take advantage. The problem is that neither company has dedicated carpooling cars, so they can be a bit uncomfortable and cramped.

Thankfully, Argo, a new transport startup out of Mexico, is poised to shake up this space. Not only do they have new optional sub-compartment vehicles that let users hop in and out without bothering each other, but they've also introduced a mean matchmaking system for organizing trips. More than a few friendships and even marriages have come out of Argo carpools, and while they won't make any guarantees, it's definitely a fun option to try at least once.

There are plenty more transport options available. A few of the more interesting ones include:

YeloCity: If you haven't seen their bright yellow recumbent trikes around town, then you need your glasses looked at. YeloCity's trikes harness your pedal-power while the trike takes care of steering and braking, which means you can enjoy the scenery around town while getting some exercise at the same time. And if you're worried about working up too much of a sweat before an important date or meeting, an on-board electric motor means that even steep uphill climbs are made easy. A fun addition to any car plan.

Civic Express: Civic Express is an open-source transport platform run by a nonprofit co-op network that operates in thirty-five countries. More importantly, Civic Express is almost always the cheapest way of traveling more than a hundred kilometers in any country thanks to its S3 Smart Scheduling System. Tell Civic Express where you want to go and how flexible your schedule is and within a day it'll charter a suitably-sized car, minibus, or coach for everyone making the same approximate journey. It's not the fastest or most convenient way of getting around, but if you're on basic minimum income or you're just happy to take your time and meet new people, Civic Express is the way to go.

High Lux: Unlike Challenger or CarSnap, these cars aren't designed for efficiency—instead, they're fitted out for sheer comfort. You can choose from new models from Kenworthy or retrofitted classic cars such as a Mercedes-Benz CLK, a BMW 5 Series, an Aston Martin DB9, or a Tesla Roadster. High Lux isn't cheap, but it's a real treat for a special occasion, plus they even keep the steering wheels in the cars so you can pretend to drive just like your mom and dad used to!

Happy travels!

51 NOBEL PRIZE FOR MEDICINE

Oslo, Norway, 2036

Award ceremony speech for the Nobel Prize in Medicine or Physiology, 2036. Presentation speech by Professor Rosa Newman, member of the Nobel Assembly at Karolinska Institutet, member of the Nobel Committee:

Your majesties, your royal highnesses, honored Nobel Laureates, ladies and gentlemen,

The philosopher Plotinus was reluctant to have his portrait made. Why use a picture, he asked, when even his own body was merely an imperfect image of himself?

What is the most perfect image of a human, then? It cannot be the raw physical material that comprises our bodies, since not a single atom in our bodies from thirty years ago remains with us today. It can't be our DNA, since no one would suggest that identical twins were truly identical in all regards, and of course these days we can change our DNA at will.

No, more than anything else, humans are the sum of our experiences.

Think of the keen taste of a ripe summer fruit or the bitter disappointment of being bested by a fierce rival or the heady, burning sensation of a new love that transforms into the warmth of contentment over years and decades. We string these experiences—these memories—together to form the story of our lives, and in doing so, we create and edit the narrative of our very personalities minute by minute, day by day, year by year.

Until recently, we have known little about these memories that are so central to our existence. Where and how are they stored in our brains? Why are some memories stronger than others? How is it that memories shift and warp over time?

Early neuroscientists from the 1990s to the late 2010s thought that memories were formed by neurons firing in coincident patterns, resulting in the strengthening of connections between neurons at the synapses. This was partly true, but in the '20s, two researchers, Zizhen Liu and Alex Ernst, took our understanding much, much further. They discovered the fundamental nature of memory on a cellular, information theoretical, and systems level and explained how those levels interacted.

Zizhen Liu from Beijing, China, pioneered a revolutionary technique to monitor and control the activity of massive networks of cells in genetically modified rats through a combination of magnetoencephalography, transcranial magnetic stimulation, and laser stimulation. In doing so, she discovered how information and control cascades through the brain.

Alex Ernst from the Netherlands created simulations of the rat brain in unprecedented detail based on Liu's results. They entered into a close collaboration that saw Ernst's simulations linked to Liu's equipment to generate and prove hypotheses about memory formation and extinction. In short, Liu and Ernst didn't simply understand how the brain worked—they created a hardware and software interface to control the brain.

The pair's advances have led to important new medical insights and applications in many fields. We are already beginning to see therapeutic treatments for post-traumatic stress disorder and alleviating age-related memory loss in post-centenarians. Their research has also been instrumental in new techniques to read, remove, alter, and create new memories with high precision. It is, quite literally, the stuff of dreams.

In 1962, we awarded Watson, Wilkins, and Crick the Nobel Prize for discovering the nature of one of the most fundamental patterns in our world, that of deoxyribonucleic acid, or DNA, the genetic code that governs the growth of our bodies. Today, we are here to recognize the discovery of an equally important, equally elusive, and tremendously complex pattern—the pattern that constitutes our very thoughts and memories.

Professors Liu and Ernst, on behalf of the Nobel Assembly at Karolinska Institutet, it is my great privilege to convey to you our warmest congratulations and our deepest admiration. I now ask you to step forward to receive your Nobel Prizes from the hands of His Majesty the King.

52 FUNERARY MONUMENTS

Sierra Diablo, US, 2036

"When a certain type of man—and it usually is a man—reaches a certain age, he thinks of his legacy. He asks himself how he'll be remembered after he is no longer able to speak for himself. If he is equipped with sufficient self-awareness, he realizes he doesn't like the answer. And so, this is how he remedies the injury.
—Robert Ray-Hill

A long day's hike out of the town of Van Horn in Texas lies the serrated edge of the Sierra Diablo Mountain Range. There, above the stony soils and the juniper and mesquite and piñon, you will find the remnants of those remedies. Blasted and hammered out of the low, deadpan mountains are dozens of artificial caverns, hollowed out to house monuments large enough for the ambitions and ego of those who wanted to change their stories.

There is a tunnel a kilometer long and wide enough for ten to walk abreast, the walls diamond-etched with instructions on how to reboot civilization. That billionaire, a fashion mogul whose sweatshops had burned down too many times to count, whose products despoiled the land and sea, wanted to be remembered for his wisdom and foresight.

He was the third billionaire to erect his monument in the Sierra Diablo range. The next billionaire was more concerned with preserving human culture for future generations, cramming replicas and casts of the world's finest artworks into a honeycomb of chambers. Science and technology could always be rediscovered, he reasoned, but art once destroyed could never be remade. He and his brother, owners of a multinational chemicals conglomerate, had spent billions to advocate for the shutdown of government social programs used by millions of artists and potential artists.

The monuments were designed and built by different teams, but they were startlingly similar in many ways. To achieve their goal of changing memories for centuries and millennia, the engineers eschewed all electronic and digital components that would break down over time. Like the first billionaire's clock that would keep time for ten thousand years, they used moving parts of stone and ceramic rather than metals that would eventually fuse together over time through galvanic corrosion.

They were plainly not built for contemporary audiences, whom the billionaires knew hated them. They were not built in city squares or parks. They were not truly intended for the edification or benefit or people in the present, hence their situation in the remote desert, guarded by private security firms, maintained by an impenetrable billion-dollar trust, and protected by warped local ordinances. Some admirers hiked out at appointed times, but as construction ended in the late '30s, as the fashion of the monuments became exhausted, even those few visitors dried up.

These monuments for the future are better understood as funerary complexes for the rich in an age of ever-increasing lifespans. Their creators wanted to live forever, and though they tried mightily, they knew they could not. Their pride was too much to erect traditional pyramids and obelisks and tombs for the people to remember them by. But they could easily imagine the world they would leave behind might descend further into chaos and that a small indulgence of knowledge and art and teaching—costing just a fraction of their wealth—would suffice to cleanse their name forever.

The monuments were built well. They still exist to this day, barely changed since their construction decades ago, and it's likely they will continue to stand for centuries. Tour groups visit every month to inspect the construction methods and design choices of the '20s and '30s. But no one comes for the reasons the billionaires imagined, and while nothing can be certain in this life, it seems unlikely they ever will. Other better sources of information exist in more accessible, hospitable locations, and humanity has spread beyond the damage caused by these men.

Robert Ray-Hill, custodian of the Sierra Diablo Monumental Area and author of this chapter's opening quote, continues:

> Rather than, say, changing his current behavior such that people might remember him more fondly, the billionaire resolves to continue speaking after he is gone. He is not much interested in foundations because he's disappointed by the fallibility and unworthiness of his poorer contemporaries. He imagines that people in future will understand his genius better. And so it may be. But for now, his genius is not recognized or appreciated.

53 BASIC MAXIMUM INCOME

New Shanghai Museum, China, 2036

The owner of this lavishly decorated, hand-calligraphed, first-of-its-kind certificate, signed by President Sun himself, would have doubtless refused its unusual honor if she had any choice. I imagine she would have torn it to pieces if she hadn't generously "donated" it to the New Shanghai Museum's permanent collection, where I'm viewing it now.

By 2036, all taxes in China were filed electronically, but Dr. Qin Shen's tax return was different. True, it was unusually large, but it was more than that. I'll let her explain, although you'll be doing well if you can hear her through her gritted teeth:

> I am overjoyed to do my duty in our War Against the Four Pasts. I only wish that the basic maximum income was introduced earlier, so that all Chinese who have been as fortunate and hard-working as myself could have contributed more to our war effort.

In her gracious statement, Dr. Shen deliberately echoed President Sun's fiery speech from the twenty-third National Congress that launched the basic maximum income policy:

> We are at war against the past! War against climate change. War against illness. War against destitution. And war against unrest. Even just one of these four enemies could utterly destroy our nation and all the nations of the world. These enemies were created by thoughtless people in the past, and they should be consigned to the past.
>
> We did not invite this war, but we will wage it in defense of China, and we will end it! And so, in this time of grave national danger, it is only correct that all excess income should go toward winning this war. While the number of individual Chinese affected is small, discrepancies between low personal incomes and very high personal incomes should be lessened. Therefore, we declare that no Chinese citizen ought to have a net income, after they have paid their taxes, of more than one hundred million RMB a year. It is indefensible that those who enjoy large incomes should be immune to taxation while we are at war.

If this speech sounds familiar, it's because it was cribbed from US president Franklin D. Roosevelt's speech in 1942 unsuccessfully arguing for a similar "maximum income" (after this was discovered, the President Sun's speechwriter was summarily dismissed).

Those familiar with Chinese politics will have noticed that this twenty-third National Congress was held a year early. This was undoubtedly a sign of weakness on the government's part, and it highlighted President Sun's desperation to show he was capable of responding to the extraordinary change roiling the country. The USTC crash in 2033 had inflamed feelings of resentment from those who had lost out from a decade of stagnant growth and increasing income inequality. Massive protests and strikes had spilled out into dozens of cities, driven by people who were no longer distracted by the government's usual tactic of blaming the West. They wanted real change, and President Sun dearly hoped the basic maximum income policy would be enough.

It was certainly more than enough for Chinese billionaires. Technically, one hundred thousand RMB was not quite a maximum income, as the policy "only" required a 95 percent tax rate on income earned beyond that point, so the rich weren't entirely out of pocket, but it was a considerable hike from the previous top rate, which had hovered around 40 percent to 50 percent over the past few decades.

Most Chinese were deeply skeptical anything would come of the policy. The rich had always known how to avoid tax in the past—what was going to stop them now? If anything, the basic maximum income would only encourage them. And it's true that tax avoidance rose sharply, but not to the extent that some had feared. China's switchover to electronic money was almost complete by the mid-1930s, and strict regulations on cryptocurrencies meant that the rich had few places to hide their money.

Where money couldn't be hidden, it was given away to friends and family or mysteriously converted into physical nonmonetary goods and services before the State Administration of Taxation could track it. In theory, China's supposedly all-seeing surveillance state would have spotted these kinds of tricks, but the deeply—and deliberately—fragmented nature of those surveillance systems meant there were plenty of opportunities for digital gatekeepers to ignore infractions and manipulate accounts. Unlike the blockchains employed by other nations, China's tax records were stored in a nonimmutable transaction log. You never know when you might need to rewrite history, after all.

Capital flight wasn't a serious problem; few rich Chinese wanted to become tax exiles, and China's tightening grip over global financial institutions meant that no one felt comfortable running for long. In its place came "capital spaceflight." Indeed, our first taxpayer, Dr. Qin Shen, was a major investor in the New Beijing colony at the moon's south pole. Rich Chinese were lauded for launching their pre-tax wealth into orbital and lunar infrastructure, which they were allowed to own, providing it was held under Chinese jurisdiction. Few actually moved to their new homes. It still wasn't very healthy to live in space long-term, even in the opulence of stations like Alto Firenze, not until centrifugal gravity was perfected and made perfectly comfortable.

Back on Earth, President Sun poured money into China's health, social security, and pensions systems. Almost a quarter of the population was over sixty-five, and the working-age population had been steadily declining for a quarter of a century. While the one child policy had been repealed over two decades previously, the fertility rate was far below the level required to maintain a constant population, especially with negligible immigration.

In the end, the basic maximum income policy only provided a small proportion of the funding required. China simply didn't have that many rich people, and ultimately the tax burden laid most heavily on the middle class. But the mere fact that some of the rich were genuinely, visibly suffering under the new tax policy—well, that was enough to salve the wounds of more than a few unhappy Chinese.

54 ALTO FIRENZE

Low Earth Orbit, 2036

It's truly exquisite; nothing less than a breathtaking meld of form and function that rivals the best of the old masters. Any artist would envy its achievement, set as it is against a natural yet demanding canvas of surpassing beauty. And how fitting it is that once again the Italians are at the vanguard of this new discipline of space habitat design!

It's plenty overwrought praise from Zoe Cesare, but there was no doubt among contemporary critics that Alto Firenze was one of the architectural jewels of the '30s. The station represented the flowering of space habitat design, and such was its influence on the way we live and work in space that we now talk about the pre- and post-AF periods. The fact that Alto Firenze remains largely intact to this day is another minor miracle, one that has transformed it into a historical artifact of immeasurable value—but perhaps I'm getting ahead of myself.

Alto Firenze was initially conceived in the late '20s as a space habitat for one hundred people in low Earth orbit. Unlike other space hotels and state-constructed research stations, Alto Firenze was designed to take a step beyond the twentieth-century utilitarian style. No ugly white boxes and greebles were welcome here; instead, the station incorporated a level of elegance and fashion that saw fittings and module fabrication directed by experienced architect-engineers in Turin.

The Alto consortium began in-orbit assembly in 2032, taking advantage of a glut of cheap launch capacity produced by fierce competition between Space-X and Siemens-Foxconn. Six connected inflatable modules formed the core of the station, heavily modified from BA-3704 plans. Each module had a pressurized volume of 3,700 cubic meters and was capable of housing twenty-five people not only in comfort but also in style. It was furnished with lounges, sleeping pods, bathrooms, observation areas, and dedicated dining rooms designed by the noted Group of Five from Florence.

By the time main assembly was completed four years later, Alto Firenze's original business plan, which saw it as a combination hotel and luxury resort, had become slightly outdated. The sheer number of competing hotels in low Earth orbit—fourteen by this point with another twenty in construction—had cut projected profits substantially. The Alto consortium decided to keep two modules as a hotel for tourists making the trip up on the new Space-X Hawks, convert three modules into a conference center, and use the final module as the first orbital art gallery and museum. Two members of the Group of Five shuttled up to the station to personally oversee the installation of their spectacular Orrery chandelier in the museum, along with the detailed fractal layering that enveloped the rest of the station.

While the consortium's decision struck most observers as being dangerously optimistic, it's worth bearing in mind that the semi-permanent orbital population was now well over five thousand and growing rapidly. Compared to the expense of shuttling up and down Earth's steep gravity well, the amount of energy required for interstation transit was negligible, as was the cost of the vehicles, which didn't ever need to enter the atmosphere.

The consortium bet correctly. The natural human desire for company and exploration saw Alto Firenze defy its critics and flourish as a popular meeting place, hosting zero-G exhibitions and artworks and numerous orbital conferences and committee meetings in the late '30s and early '40s. Its success along with the burgeoning orbital population saw many more general-purpose stations being constructed; the EDX campuses and the famous Heinlein and Robinson distributed venture complexes were all assembled in the mid-2040s with Falcon Super-heavy workhorse rockets and newer laser-launchers. In fact, the original planning conference for Robinson's governance system was held at Alto Firenze.

But everything passes, and Alto Firenze began to slip from fashion in the late '40s. Larger, more advanced, and more architecturally adventurous habitats were being constructed, often from captured asteroids or lunar ejecta. Even with a series of extra luxury modules added, the station slipped further and further from the public eye.

Finally, in 2051 Alto Firenze was purchased by the Reynolds mining corporation for use as their headquarters and boosted to an L5 orbit in 2052 mere months before the Cascade. As such, Alto Firenze is the only surviving example of early twenty-first-century low orbit habitats, the rest having been destroyed, de-orbited, or broken up for salvage.

Today, the station has been preserved as a museum and returned to its original orbit. Floating through the opulence and comfort of Alto Firenze almost feels like stepping back in time to the high frontier. It was when the "hyper-capitalist summer" turned to autumn, and the first shoots of what was to come next were appearing all over the world—and off it.

55 A CURE FOR HATE

Helsinki, Finland, 2036

Our object is a collection of excerpts from articles from 2036 and 2037 about the practice of personality editing, which became commonplace later this century:

HELSINKI, June 2036

Ilmari Koskinen, a 24-year-old resident of Kirkkonummi accused of stabbing a student in a bar in August last year, was today found guilty of aggravated assault.

Unusually, Koskinen was given the choice of either a ten-year prison term followed by a standard POI (permanent overwatch and intervention) order or admission into a trial of the controversial new hate cure gene therapy treatment pioneered by Professor Mathy at University College London. Koskinen chose the therapy treatment, which is expected to begin in September pending the results of a medical assessment.

The victim of Koskinen's assault, Jani Hahl, sat silently in the back of the courtroom during the sentencing. Family members offered no comment to the press. Legal experts believe that—

Imagine a simulated world. The world is made up of continents and seas and archipelagos, just like our own. Hundreds of billions of intelligent agents are scattered across those continents and islands. The simple act of each seemingly independent agent receiving, processing, and transmitting information to other agents results in the entire world functioning in a coherent, directed manner.

The world you are watching sits in a galaxy of a billion other worlds. You notice that this one is acting poorly. It acts against its own interests and the interests of the other worlds around it. You scrutinize it, and you trace the problem to a programming defect affecting a few billion agents on a particular continent. They aren't passing information along properly, and that's what's causing their world to malfunction.

So, what do you do? You release a virus into the simulation. This virus is targeted at those defective agents, and it will rewrite their code and fix them. To make sure that they stay fixed, you engineer the virus in such a way that it will be easy to make future corrections, whether by further viruses or less invasive methods.

It is elegant, effective—and surely better than the alternatives, which might include ostracism, punishment, execution, or even worse—

The effects of reduced levels of serotonin on prefrontal-amygdala connectivity and the impairment of the ability to control emotional responses to anger have been known since the early 2010s. While serotonin levels may fluctuate in the brain due to stress or hunger, long-term reductions have been observed in some individuals due to a combination of genetic factors, including lowered expression of the p11 protein.

Trials of gene therapy treatments to increase serotonin levels and receptors in the relevant area have been conducted in various guises for almost three decades, beginning with rats and leading up to primates. Treatments developed in the early 2020s resulted in modest and highly variable reductions in aggressive behavior, but a breakthrough from the University College London labs that combines the standard viral vector with repeated "tuning" of specific cell clusters via transcranial magnetic stimulation has proved to be much more effective. Rival optogenetic approaches use opsin genes with LED implants for similar effects.

Not all patients are eligible for treatment in this way. For example, those whose aggressive behavior is not attributable to—

"Thank you for that illuminating lecture, Professor Mathy. Since we are a little short on time, we have a few questions from the audience that I'm going to bundle together, if you don't mind."

"Not at all."

"Helena from Tampere asks how we can be so sure that someone's aggressive tendencies have been cured, and whether we shouldn't just keep people confined as a precaution. Axel from Oulu wants to know whether your treatment could be used for conditions such as depression and autism. And finally, Keke from Vaasa says that no one should have the right to change another's personality when they're under duress and that almost any other punishment would be better."

"Thank you all. Let me take the last question first, from Keke. Now, let's face it—taking away someone's freedom and locking them up for ten years, that's no walk in the park. That would change them far more than my treatment, and it would it would change them for the worse, no matter how comfortable the prison. Prison would not help them to control their aggressive tendencies, which are after all a biological fact, not something we can wish away. They would become resentful and disconnected from society in prison.

"Better that we preserve what is good about them and fix what is wrong rather than retreating to primitive notions of retribution. My treatment means that we protect our society and we protect the individual. It is the best of both worlds.

"Now, regarding whether we can be sure the treatment worked. We employ a very thorough, very comprehensive battery of tests including imitation games, and we use the best scanners we have to—"

56 *SHANGHAI SIX*

Shanghai, China, 2036

Billionaire Zhang Yu is known for two things: his terrifying intelligence, fueled by illegal cognitive enhancers, and his utter ruthlessness. Yu has destroyed anyone who would stand in his way to total power, and his latest plan is his most dangerous yet: brainwash the entire Chinese electorate in order to become Premier.

He's already corrupted the police and the army, so who can stop him? Only a rag-tag band of thieves and rogues. Can they put aside their differences and pull off this century's most audacious heist: infiltrating Zhang's Shanghai superscraper and stealing its AI core?

Join the team this summer … as part of Disney/Starling's *Shanghai Six*!

I'm holding a bomb. Don't be alarmed. It's just a prop from Disney's archives, festooned with wires, buttons, latches, digital readouts, and everything that you'd imagine would be on a fictional bomb. While it doesn't actually do anything, it surely qualifies as one of the most-watched bombs in history, being the focus of millions of people's attention during the 2036 premiere of *Shanghai Six*. Of course, it was disarmed by a player, but first let me explain exactly how we got here.

By the '30s, most entertainment was consumed as digital games that required little if any marginal labor. However, alternate reality games (ARGs)—games that combined augmented reality and human actors— offered uniquely personal experiences that focused on real-world physical interaction, like running through a real field to avoid a (virtual) strafing plane or trying to convince a (pretend) banker to reveal confidential information via telepresence. Such games could be completely free-to-play by relying on volunteer labor or they could cost as much as a trip to the moon due to the thousands of actors and coordinators involved.

Disney's first experiments with ARGs took place at the beginning of the century at Disneyworld's Epcot Center. In the late 2010s and early '20s, the company began rolling out more ambitious multiplayer augmented-reality attractions at its various theme parks, holiday resorts, and cruise ships—all of which were completely controlled environments with a level of sensor density that wouldn't be matched in the outside world for more than a decade.

Most of their early ARG experiences were relatively short, lasting only a day or so, and didn't attain the level of total immersion that many hoped for. However, they managed to raise interest in their ailing parks—no small feat given the fierce competition from VR gaming—and became a spring-board for Disney's new secretive Starling group, based in California and Shanghai. Disney/Starling's motto was "we create heroes," and the group had three objectives described here by Experience Director Michael Chat-field in 2042:

> Number one, we wanted to create experiences that went beyond the bounds of Disney-controlled environments. Let's face it, Sleeping Beauty's Castle might look impressive, but it's no match for a real castle in Bavaria. Number two, we wanted to involve a thousand times more people in these ARGs. Not just a hundred, but hundreds of thousands. Life is always more fun when you have more people around, am I right? And yeah, part of that was financial—every run of *Shanghai Six* saw the main heroes pay us seven figures each, but that barely covered a fifth of our budget.
>
> So, number three: we got people to pay to work for us! We got half of our budget from tens of thousands of paying guests who bought roles as villains, side-kicks, minor characters, characters in side stories, that sort of thing. Those guys just loved role-playing, and they all got their own little story! Yeah, some of them needed lines, but most of them did very well with the level of support and gad-gets that we provided. One of our B-cast got the opportunity to skydive from ten thousand feet above Beijing while trying to defuse an EMP bomb. Unbelievable! And before you ask, yes, we had three safety drones tracking her all the time.
>
> Sure, for really important roles we paid for professional actors, but some of our best actors turned out to be pure bystanders. Whenever we announced we'd be running a big ARG in a city—boom! We'd have tens of thousands of people lin-ing up on the street volunteering to take part. If we chose you and you performed really well, you'd get Starling points and you could use those points to get better roles in future games. It wasn't money, but it sure as hell was fun.
>
> We never let our heroes see even a hint of points, though. We didn't want them worrying about getting a high score or achievements or badges. Their expe-rience was pure, unfiltered, epic storytelling. I still get shivers when I think about what we put those six people through each time. We'd take over entire cities, right from the subways to the towers. We'd have thousands of people all playing together, all aware of only a tiny part of the story, all orchestrated from Starling Control, and all in the service of a fantastic, memorable experience.

In truth, there wasn't much technically innovative about Disney's ARGs. The technology that allowed Starling to successfully coordinate their thousands of guests and actors was derived, in part, from open-source deliverbot and traffic management systems, combined with proprietary mimic scripts and agents.

However, the real innovation from Disney/Starling was a creative one, weaving together ten thousand large and small stories into a coherent whole that could be explored, watched, read, and played by millions of people after the fact in edited TV, novel, and VR releases. Today, we view *Shanghai Six* as an entertainment milestone on the same level as *Casablanca* or *Tianxia*, and yet Starling's best days were still ahead of them with their masterpiece, *The City*, to come a little over a decade later.

57 NEW LIBRARY OF MALMÖ

Malmö, Sweden, 2037

It can be unsettling to walk through the New Library of Malmö. The lights are kept dim and the temperature chilly to preserve the precious contents inside. You'll catch glimpses of dark, hulking machines through the aisles and draw your jacket that little bit tighter. Strange chittering noises and sudden flickering of activity echo down the hall are enough to make a nervous writer jump.

It's a very different experience during visiting hours. The windows are turned on, and sunlight gently illuminates the thousands of decades-old computers and devices sitting neatly on the library's tables. They all look rather dignified.

Our object today is not just a single computer but the New Library's collection itself and what it represents: the study and preservation of extinct digital technology. With me here today to show me some highlights from the collection is the chief librarian, Michael Straumli.

You may wonder why the New Library is necessary at all given how easy it is to construct virtual machine simulations these days. Why worry about the physical when you're dealing with digital computers? Well, the answer is that while many popular and important machines do indeed have VMs, most do not.

Sometimes that's because their operating system source code has been lost or, more commonly, because our predecessors' haste to upgrade their technology has meant that few working specimens have survived to the present day. And even if VMs are available for a given machine, they often can't simulate the odd quirks that come with physical hardware. As Straumli tells me, there's no accounting for that errant wire or flawed microchip that had to be worked around or taken advantage of by canny programmers.

The lack of specimens is a problem that occupies Straumli constantly. "We spend a great deal of our budget searching for extra machines," he said. "We normally try to keep at least three copies for redundancy, but it's handy to have more available for visiting researchers to use. I'm not against VMs and physical sims. Last week we had students from Parsons using high power x-ray tomography to reverse engineer the machines here, but there's no replacement for the original hardware. That means we actually have to turn these computers on and boot them up, which we try to do every six months or so."

One of the most intriguing projects going on at the New Library is being run by the Total History Initiative (THI), which aims to construct a complete map of the connections, movements, and behavior of every individual in the world from 1960 to 2010. Its purpose is to gain a deeper understanding of how humans interact in small and large groups by using the data gathered from models and simulations of historical events rather than the more subjective macro-level techniques used by past historians. Instead of only taking account of the personalities and decisions of the so-called great women and men of the past, the initiative aims to look at the millions of people who lived through, worked toward, talked about, and created all those events that cumulatively changed the world, year by year, day by day, second by second.

A rather ambitious goal, I'm sure you'll agree.

Right now, researchers from the initiative are looking at a Hewlett-Packard optical scanner from 1997, used by the University Medical Center Brack-enridge in Texas to scan in medical records. "They aren't interested in the scanned papers. I believe they were shredded long ago, and the digital copies are fine enough," Straumli tells me. "No, they want to discover the emotional state of the scanner operator by looking at the tremor of her hands while she was passing the papers through the hopper. Of course, when you're looking that closely, you need to know precisely how the scanner worked."

> The initiative is partnering with the University of Sydney on this particular project. There were about 800,000 of these HP scanners in use in the 1990s, and the Sydney researchers want to use the image data they produced to connect up events and organizations and individuals—so, for example, using handwriting recognition to identify anonymous voter records and exam papers and medical records. So, these old scanners are important to a lot of people!

One would think that there can't be all that much difference between an optical scanner's stated specifications and its performance in reality, but you'd be wrong. Researchers have already found half a dozen unusual quirks in the firmware and hardware that cause scanned images to be altered in some small way. It's a flagship project at the New Library, but there's one thing that concerns Straumli. In a word, plastics.

So much of the technology from the 1980s and 1990s was made from plastic. It was cheap, light, and durable enough. The problem for us is that now it starts decomposing as soon as anyone touches it. If you've seen any ugly, yellowing devices around your parents' or grandparents' houses, you'll know what I mean. That decomposition can warp the shape of the plastic and eventually render the entire machine inoperable.

It's essential for the THI to understand how that warping can change the performance of the scanner over time. They can gain vital clues that will help them interpret the image data they've recovered. The problem is, every time they physically test the scanners, the damage gets a little bit worse. Of course, we can replace parts but not necessarily in exactly the same way as it was before. So even with the special care that the THI researchers are taking with gloves and teleoperation and so on, I can't help but feel a little twinge of worry whenever I see our machines being used.

Eventually, Straumli's hope is that more advanced noninvasive scanning of the machines in the New Library will lead to near-perfect physical simulations that would eliminate most of the need for so much poking and prodding, leaving the original machines pristine. But he understands the motives of the THI.

We're lacking so much information from the turn of the century. A lot of the data that was collected at the time was never properly archived due to carelessness and privacy concerns stemming from corporate and government intrusion, and now our historians are paying the price. That makes us treasure every single bit of information we can glean from that time. Like they say, it's only by knowing the past that we can simulate the future.

For now, Straumli has kindly agreed to show me two of the New Library's true gems that are still working—the original servers for Geocities and an original Nintendo Super Famicom games console.

58 THE DIM SUM LUNCHES

Guangzhou, China, 2037

I hope you've already eaten because this bill from a lunch at Dian Dou De in Guangzhou describes a mouthwatering feast of dim sum: piles of siu mai, xiao long bao, and har gow dumplings; five dishes of pork and shrimp cheung fun; rice noodle rolls; enough char siu bao pork buns to feed an army—not to mention generous helpings of the restaurant's specialties, like XO law bok gow turnip cake, lo mai gai rice cakes, and hern ja yau you sou deep fried squid. And I haven't even started on the sweets…

It may sound odd that this lunch represented an act of rebellion against anything other than a protesting waistband, but the women who partici- pated in it risked more than a heavy stomach. At this lunch and thousands of others across China, women deliberately ordered and consumed far more food than was recommended by governmental dietary requirements. Nor- mally, such acts passed wholly unnoticed by the government except for their faint echoes being recorded in population-wide health surveys, but the new China Glowing program of social control resulted in a much less benign response.

The China Glowing program purported to promote a strong, growing population by improving women's fertility and health. While it com- prised everything from informational campaigns to fitness games, the most controversial and intrusive component involved the real-time track- ing of women's diet. All restaurants, fast food outlets, and groceries were instructed to record the nutritional content of women's purchases against their government-issued digital identities—not an especially difficult task, given that the government already tracked certain types of sensitive pur- chases. If a woman maintained an unhealthy diet, their social credit score would decline; stay healthy, and it would rise.

Credit scores had existed in other countries for decades, to be sure. Since the twentieth century, billions had been in thrall to credit bureaus that tracked every aspect of their payment and debt history, assigning them a

score that determined their ability to borrow money—a necessity for housing, transport, and general wellbeing. Most health insurers kept similar
scores, punishing their customers for not walking or exercising enough with
higher premiums. But the total, inescapable nature of the China Glowing
program, not to mention its barefaced discrimination, set it wholly apart.

The sexism underpinning China Glowing was not an unintended consequence of a well-intentioned policy; rather, punishing women was the goal.

The basic maximum income introduced the previous year, for all its
faults, had briefly distracted the increasingly restless Chinese population.
More importantly, President Sun's advisors felt it validated the principle of
setting one part of the population against another through superficially
technocratic means. Earlier in the twenty-first century, President Xi Jinping
undid decades of progress in women's equality with his patriarchal, authoritarian exhortations for women to return to the home and to focus on their
families, and by his government's hounding and abuse of feminists.

President Sun echoed this policy in China Glowing, with the friendlier
message of "empowering women to achieve their goals: growing a happy
family," not coincidentally reinforcing the primacy of men at home and
in society. No matter how low in society a man might feel, no matter how
brutally oppressed he was, he could still enjoy his greater freedoms over the
women in his life—freedom to get high-paying jobs, freedom to abuse and
rape with few repercussions, freedom from taking care of the increasingly
numerous elderly, and now a new freedom to eat whatever he wanted. And
so, low as he might be, he would support the government. Or so the theory
went.

"Idiots! We could all see through China Glowing." This is Li Rongrong,
one of the first women to suggest holding a dim sum lunch in response
to the new program, recalling the reaction to the program at the time. "If
the government really cared about fertility, why not worry about the men
as well? It's not like their sperm was invulnerable. They needed to watch
what they ate, too. Many of us had no interest in having children, and
even if we did, it was none of the government's business. So, we decided
to disobey."

The first lunches were held on a Sunday in early March, during a cold
snap that enveloped the whole country. Other than the sheer quantity
of the food on show, there wasn't anything unusual in the social media
posts—no words of protest, no raised fists, just an awful lot of food. Naturally, some people commented on this, and others told them off, saying it
was none of their business what anyone chose to eat. And every Sunday,
the lunches grew a little more.

Here's Zheng Maizi, a historian from Guangzhou University. "The dim sum lunches were a smart tactic. Who could stop people from organizing them? Women wanted to have lunch with their friends. It was a fun way to protest. And how could you stop them from ordering more food than usual? Restaurants wanted to make money. They were hardly going to say no.

"But the lunches weren't without risk. Every participant took a hit to their social credit score, affecting their lives in a hundred small ways. If you kept going to lunches for weeks or months, you'd have problems traveling across the country. Even your job might be at risk. And this absurdity only highlighted the sheer sexism of China Glowing. Everyone knew men with unhealthy diets, and nothing happened to them."

It took the government longer than usual to respond to the seemingly innocuous lunches. When they did, they followed their standard playbook—the protests were denounced as a product of "western hostile forces" who wanted to "put feminism above all else." "Gluttony! Wastefulness! Do these women have no shame? What kind of person would want to harm China in this way?" was a typical refrain on VR news networks.

Behind the scenes, the social credit score penalty for poor diets was increased, particularly for repeated offenses. Special attention was paid to Sunday lunches, which only resulted in the lunches scattering across every day of the week and extending into breakfasts and dinners. As usual, supposed ringleaders were identified, called in for questioning. Their freedom was curtailed, and their families threatened—all for having too much to eat.

Underpinning the government's reaction was their assumption that popular support for feminism had not changed since President Xi's time. That was their key mistake. No one in China could have possibly missed the changes in women's representation in politics and business in the rest of the world. Since the turn of the century, the world had seen the first female US president and multiple Hong Kong and Taiwanese female presidents, whereas China was yet to have a single female president. The Politburo had never included more than three women out of twenty-five members. Women had only 8 percent representation on the Central Committee, barely any more than forty years ago.

China wasn't the most sexist society in the world at the time, but its lack of women's representation was notable due to the country's size and influence. Women might hold up half the sky, as Mao proclaimed, but as far as the government was concerned, that didn't entitle them to own half the sky. Yet as the lunches and breakfasts and dinners stretched into the summer, support for the women grew, not just from outside of China but inside—and from men. "Let them eat what they like!" "A big meal didn't hurt my mother." "If they can pay for it, who cares?" "Women work hard enough as it is."

Far from gaining the broad support of men, China Glowing divided them. There were certainly still many sexists among them, but for those who weren't, President Sun looked foolishly out of touch. He looked laughable.

The government made no further public response to the lunches, and their interrogations ended. The lunches themselves gradually petered out toward the end of the summer, at which point the China Glowing program disappeared without a trace. Social credit score points were no longer deducted for women's diets. Officials refused to comment.

Years later, after President Sun stepped down, President Jun alluded to a change in policy in his opening speech. He would champion the cause of women, because it was only by using the talents and hard work of all Chinese that the country would achieve the greatness it deserved. At the twenty-fourth National Congress, women's representation on the Central Committee doubled all the way up to 15 percent. It was a start.

This particular bill for a dim sum lunch commands our special attention because it was daringly preserved in printed form for the benefit of the diners who, alone out of all the lunch protestors, turned it into posters and stickers. They were interrogated, imprisoned, and underfed for two months.

Today, dim sum lunches are held every year on the first Sunday of March in memory of the protestors, and they're all just as generous as the first. Let's dig in.

59 SECRET LIFE OF THE HIGH STREET

Birmingham, England, 2038

Excerpt from "Secret life of the high street," a young adult article published in 2038:

Have you ever wondered what goes on behind the scenes of a busy high street? When you go to get your hair cut or grab a bite to eat, it's easy to miss the web of information and technology that helps keep the center of our towns and cities humming along smoothly—and while it might not seem as exciting as the latest headband, it's just as important!

So, let's begin with…a load of rubbish! You might think that litter isn't important. After all, how difficult is it to keep pavements clean of gum and wrappers and plastics? Well, consider this: just fifty years ago, you'd be hard pressed to walk even a meter or two in any city without spotting a piece of litter! We might have grown a bit more considerate since then, and we might use a lot less packaging, but it's cleaning bots like brushtails that have made the real difference.

It's thanks to these tireless helpers that litter rarely lingers for more than a few minutes before being collected. But let's not give all the credit to the brushtails, because if you've watched them carefully, you'll know that most of the time they don't spot litter themselves. Instead, they're directed to litter, sometimes within seconds of it being dropped, by tiny localizers embedded into paving stones.

Every square meter of pavement has one of these ant-size sensors, and they communicate with one another to make up a picture of everything that happens on the street. As soon as they notice something wrong, like a small litter-sized object dropped by accident, or worse, a large person-sized object hitting the ground hard, they'll call a brushtail or a paramedic jumper.

The localizers aren't just there to help fix things that go wrong; they also work nonstop to provide the super-precise positioning information that makes our glasses and lenses work properly and lets brushtails know their location and where they're going, even in the worst of weather. That's how bots and people can navigate among each other so smoothly. And after dark, they're still hard at work coordinating kwalas and 'copters to inspect and repair important parts of the high street, from benches and charging loops to streetlights and nests. By getting this done at night, they stay out of the way of pedestrians, and they cleverly take advantage of cheap electricity.

But we aren't in the high street to just admire the lack of litter; we're there to meet friends, go shopping, and get some business done! So, let's take a look at a typical building along the street—a café.

Now, there are all sorts of different cafés out there. Some are more than a hundred years old, made from bricks and mortar, but most are in the traditional synthetic style of steel and glass from the turn of the century. What both of these styles have in common is that they were built before most people had glasses and lenses. That's why they have so much space and so many fittings for fixed adverts and signs. Can you imagine that people actually had to climb up on a ladder and stick a poster on a window to let customers know there was a sale on?

Modern cafés and shops that were built more recently are very different. Instead of giving a lot of space over to fixed things, they're all about letting the owners and customers change things easily, which is why their interior walls, windows, countertops, and doors can all be moved, sometimes by drones and sometimes by themselves. Only the exterior walls are fixed—and on some newer Sterling tensegrity buildings, even those can shift.

The reason for this change is simple: it lets people and businesses make better use of the scarce space on the high street. It's a bit of a waste to have a clothes shop or hairdresser only open for eight hours a day when it could be converted into a restaurant or bar afterwards. Modern buildings let businesses change things around very quickly, saving everyone money and helping improve the diversity and liveliness of high streets.

Which brings us onto another important question—why do people still go to high streets, anyway? Well, let's look at what it was like in 2000. Back then, people bought all sorts of things in high street shops, from food and toys to—don't laugh!—books, music, and videos. These days, instead of buying physical things, we rent cheaper (and better) digital services. Most of the remaining physical things, like food and toys, are delivered to us at home.

It might sound like it was more fun to do all your shopping on the high street, but think again! In the late twentieth and early twenty-first centuries, you'd see exactly the same shops with exactly the same products whether you were in Shanghai or Sydney or San Francisco. Mass production, mass media, and mass financing were still very powerful forces back then. It took a long time for the chains to start losing their luster and for more independent and original shops to take their place. It wasn't much fun for the people who had to work in those chains either, with long hours, low wages, and precarious finances, all to sell the latest cheap fashions or faux-authentic coffee.

People didn't just go to the high street to buy things. They also went there to meet friends in person, to get food, to have a drink, to get their hair cut or skin treated. In other words, they went there for services that were too expensive or less fun to do at home. It's the same today. If you want to get a skin treatment, you're hardly going to install all of the equipment in your bathroom, and if you're going to have a dinner with a dozen friends, sometimes the city center is the easiest and most interesting place for everyone to meet.

Now, let's talk about transport. If you look closely at the surface of a road near the pavement—you might need to look under any tables or chairs that have been set out there—you'll see strange, darkened sections that mark out lines or boxes. Those are relics of "parking lines" and "parking spaces" that have had their paint removed. "Parking" is from back when people used to drive cars manually—yes, with their hands and feet! When they were going to work or going shopping, drivers would leave their cars sitting on the side of the road, taking up valuable space for hours. Be thankful you live in the world as it is today.

60 NEW WORLDS

Earth, 2038

On a summer night in 2038, a fleet of gossamer blimps hovered into view over the hundred largest cities in the world, their surfaces shimmering with macroscopic manifestations of the local group and visions of dreams. Tens of thousands of performers and fireflies joined in, dancing and darting between the ground and the sky. Every available display and projector in physical reality extended the scenes, creating a beautiful, fragmented panorama in Times Square, People's Square, Shibuya, Yonge-Dundas, Piccadilly Circus, and elsewhere.

At first, few noticed it, occupied as they were in their Glass or Sopol environments, but one by one, they paused. Perhaps they saw a spark of real light out of the corner of an eye or received an astounded glyph from a friend, or perhaps they simply saw other people gazing up at the sky. They lowered their glasses or blinked their lenses off and looked up, too.

And for just a few hours, a most unusual thing happened. Hundreds of millions of people around the world looked at something together in the real world, in real time, at dancing images and beguiling artworks and old movies.

When the show drew to a close in the early hours, the displays shifted to a deep red, as if in a bow to the coming dawn. And above that deep red was drawn a simple, elegant script with one word: Coca-Cola.

In the noisy, crowded augmented reality arms race of the '20s and '30s, brands and advertisers and artists covered every aspect of the world with impressive, shocking, distracting, and occasionally awesome virtual objects and environments. Gimmicks and good ideas alike had precipitously short half-lives, either being killed or copied within days or hours. But there was one sure-fire way that you could get noticed: with reality.

While the company didn't publicly reveal how much it spent, Coca-Cola's "New Worlds" campaign is believed to be the single most expensive advertising stunt in history, quite literally—but only very briefly—overshadowing the enormous gravitational pull of augmented reality media that had come to dominate the chase for the public's attention.

Thanks to this preserved blimp and the hundreds just like it, Coca-Cola sales spiked around the world, although it's very much debatable whether this was due to the stunt or to the promotional coupons that followed. Either way, today "New Worlds" is regarded, not as a triumph, but instead as a cynical, ersatz example of the burgeoning Modern Romantic movement, perhaps the definitive moment when the power of brands and advertising finally reached its zenith.

"At what point did advertising's dominance over our everyday lives begin eroding? Today's conventional wisdom points the finger of blame at the introduction of augmented reality. With its effectively unlimited inventory, AR led to a massive increase in virtual display advertising—swiftly followed by fears of its destruction as digital adblockers threatened to eliminate or replace every display advert in existence. Some media companies attempted to outlaw adblockers. Others distributed subsidized or free—and locked-down—glasses. A few still had targeting good enough for their ads to be let through the filters, but the end result was significant disruption and confusion."

That's the opinion of Christopher Payne, chair of media studies at Edinburgh University. But Payne believes that augmented reality wasn't the real turning point, that larger factors were at work.

Permit me to tell a little story. If we go back to the eighteenth century in the UK, you had two huge shifts going on: urbanization and industrialization. The average town- or city-dweller now had increased access to a wider range of attractive goods. They had a choice in, let's say, what shoes or tools they could buy, rather than just buying whatever happened to be available in their village.

So, let's imagine you make shoes. You need adverts to help people become aware of your product and to make it stand out from the competition. If you are successful—and exceptionally long-lived—you might establish a "brand" to help guard against competitors passing off their inferior, cheaper shoes as your originals. In this situation, advertising and branding make plenty of sense, even if it is expensive.

All of this continued for a good couple of centuries—as people's incomes increased and the opportunities for reaching them grew, advertising became increasingly sophisticated and important. Indeed, I believe peak advertising was reached sometime in the late twentieth century, when mass media and mass production combined to create an enormous reach. Their command over audiences' attention allowed them to fabricate wants on a scale that makes desire modifiers today look like amateurs.

Things started to look dicey in the early twenty-first century, though. Due to micromanufacturing, mass customization, and the rising role of digital goods, there was such an abundance of choice that only the biggest properties could advertise their way to overwhelming commercial success. And with the internet, people were making their decisions not simply on what they saw on TV or on a billboard, but based on machine-driven social recommendations. It's not as if people didn't pay attention to friends and reviews before the internet, but by making it cheap to move and process information, the internet tipped the balance in the consumer's favor.

Payne's view is shared by many scholars today, who also point to the power that search engines and, later, personal intelligent agents had in capturing and channeling consumers' "intent to buy" toward the most appropriate vendor. For a while, search engines and agents also supported paid advertising, but during the '20s and '30s, they began to shift slowly toward a hybrid commission/referral model, wherein the creator of the agent received a cut of the sales.

Coca-Cola, Procter & Gamble, Kraft, and similar brands struggled to compete against a tide of cheap, high quality, and often highly targeted goods whose production was aided by automated manufacturing services. When brand replacement organizations appeared, some using automatic "ethical offset" pricing to promote just-as-good generics for soft drinks or clothes, they delivered a terrible blow to incumbents. And faced with an audience that was increasingly immune to traditional advertising, big brands precipitously lowered their prices in the hope of gaining short-lived market share, or they relied on the waning power of nostalgia among older demographics.

Of course, very little truly dies in media. It can still be worth spending money to grab people's attention for high-margin goods and services. No doubt everyone who saw Coca-Cola's "New Worlds" show appreciated the effort they put into it. Whether the soft drink's increased sales were down to the advert or to the coupons is sadly unknown, but it is telling that it was the first, and last, grand advertising spectacle of its kind.

61 PRINCE GEORGE

London, England, 2039

Excerpt from a 2039 interview in *PLOS ONE*, an open-access scientific journal:

Q: Prince George, you've been described as "the next Elizabeth" by some very smart people. Those same people also think you'll be "Britain's first modern monarch." How does that make you feel?

A: Very awkward! I really don't deserve that kind of praise, not at my age and certainly not given how little I've accomplished so far. There are plenty of other people, royal and not, who have done far more.

Q: But objectively, you've made some very real scientific and technical achievements in the past five years. Given that most of those were made anonymously, it's fair to say that the praise is real and not just a product of star-struck reporters. So, tell us, why did you pursue science in the first place?

A: And not the military? Well, I did have some … interesting … discussions with my father about whether or not I should take a role in the Armed Forces after my time at Cambridge. But I think that after I'd finished my PhD at MIT, he'd resigned himself to the fact that I wasn't likely to become Corporal Wales like him or Uncle Harry. I imagine the lab I set up in Buckingham Palace when I was eight may have had something to do with that.

Q: As a child, though?

A: [Pause] When you're growing up as a prince, everyone's forever watching and judging you. Not for who you are, but for what you represent. And while I know my parents and of course my grandmother had a very hard time of it with the paparazzi, the kind of surveillance that exists now is a step above that. If I even so much as step foot outside a private residence, I will most certainly be watched and scrutinized every single second.

But if I didn't have privacy in the physical world, I did have privacy online. We were fortunate enough to have very smart system adminstrators at the palace who set up very ingenious proxies and VPNs for me. And so, I lived a kind of parallel life where I could talk with and learn from other people online, and I discovered that science was one of the places where I could make a meaningful contribution that wasn't tainted by people knowing who I was. It's a very collaborative, open world—like your journal!

Q: Very egalitarian, you might say?

A: [Laughs] Yes, you could say that. And if you're going to ask me about the referendum question, then you know that I can't answer.

Q: Well, I still have to mention it. First Australia, then India three years ago—it seems like the monarchy may not last forever. But given that you can't answer, what do you feel about the fact that you've been fast-tracked to rise to the throne even though the King is still comparatively young and healthy?

A: Until my father told me, I was surprised as anyone else. I'm not even married yet!

Q: Not that that seems to matter for most people these days.

A: Not everyone, but traditions aren't always something we should feel we must outgrow. Often, they stay with us for a reason, and the ideals of commitment and marriage still resonate with many people.

Q: That's a diplomatic way to put it, but I'm not sure the modern idea of marriage contracts is something that your ancestors would have recognized.

A: There's plenty of things we have today that they wouldn't recognize, whether that's electricity or robots or space stations. But let's not forget that my ancestors were trailblazers as well. After all, they may have created the Church of England, but it was because Henry VIII wanted a divorce! Yes, they might not recognize our modern marriage contracts, but I don't agree that they would necessarily disapprove. Of course, they aren't legal yet and they may not be for some time.

Q: The date for your coronation is set for next summer. How will you balance the demands of your research into recombinant genetics with your duties as King?

A: With grace, I hope—and with plenty of hard work!

62 MULTIPLE AUTONOMOUS ELEMENT SUPERVISOR

Solstrand, Norway, 2039

A 2042 article from Illustrert Vitenskap, a Norwegian science magazine:

"Cook the leaves the same day you pick 'em. Not the day after, and for sure not any longer than that. You want a sharp, fresh taste, you know?"

I meet Ragnhild Egner on a small farm around an hour's drive from Solstrand, Norway. She is gathering ingredients for that evening's dinner at her home, where she will be hosting sixteen guests. "I don't normally do much of this by hand, but I find it good to get outside, train my helpers how to do things properly." And, she adds, "This is something I can do myself."

Egner's helpers are a motley collection of decommissioned military drones, reprogrammed and refitted to perform the work of running a small restaurant, from whipping eggs and preparing desserts to serving dishes and recommending wines. They aren't especially smart, and they require regular supervision from Egner. Any fancy restaurant you've visited recently will be using smarter, more autonomous robots, but in Egner's case, the need for human supervision is the whole point.

In 2032, Egner had no inkling that she might run a restaurant. She had just graduated at the top of her class at the Norwegian Military Academy and immediately took up a position in the elite Nordic Union Rapid Reaction Task Force. As a multiple autonomous element supervisor (MAES), Lieutenant Egner was one of 290 officers responsible for deploying some of the NU's most potent weapons. Where typical twentieth-century armies fielded hundreds of thousands of human soldiers complete with rifles, tanks, aircraft, artillery—all supported by bases the size of small towns—a single twenty-first-century MAES could control a networked group of hundreds of military drones and weapon pods with firepower exceeding that of an entire battalion from a mere generation earlier.

Egner struggled to fit into her new role. The force demanded a superhuman level of situational awareness from its officers, and the only way to

achieve this was to surrender oneself to the senses and information provided by one's networked forces. Many supervisors simply couldn't adapt
to this kind of extrasensory integration, but for those who could—which
eventually included Egner—their drones felt like an extension of their pure
will. Some psychologists believed early exposure to intense strategy games
aided the MAES integration process, waggishly suggesting that their battles
"were won on the killing fields of Starcraft."

"It was incredibly stimulating," Egner said. "We were a new breed of
soldiers. Smarter, faster, and better than the old guard. We could come and
go from anywhere in the world in a matter of days, and after Chechnya, we
wore the mantle of the NU's moral superiority."

Her skills were put to the test in Abkhazia in 2039. What first appeared
as a peaceful movement for secession soon erupted into violent revolution,
during which a chain of messy coups caused the nation's military security
certificates to pass between three different leaders in a single week. Local
infrastructure was rapidly destroyed, degraded, or jammed into uselessness,
leading to a humanitarian disaster for millions.

NU, EU, and AU rapid reaction forces arrived within four days. With
peacekeeping efforts still ongoing in Russia, the coalition was stretched
thin, and Egner was given responsibility for a larger element than she had
trained with. It wasn't long before mistakes were made. Insurgents escaped;
signals intelligence was patchy; drone units were red-lined, requiring extended repair.

What came next, however, was much worse. Egner explains:

> Every day we'd classify areas as low, moderate, or high risk for insurgent activity.
> The town I was watching had been flagged as a high risk. We didn't want another
> Sicily, so my drones' pattern-matchers were on a hair-trigger.
>
> When we detected sudden, coordinated movement by hundreds of people
> right by a cluster of schools … well, the drones had already started cycling up their
> weapons. I remember seeing a couple of warning icons about uncertain hostile
> intent, but there just wasn't enough time to check. So, I withheld my veto.

Automatic and autonomous weapons have been used since the late
twentieth century with the US, Unified Korea, and Israel among the vanguard. At first, they were primarily deployed as stationary defensive systems with an explicit human decision required for a fire order. But bit by
bit, they expanded their role. They gained wheels and legs and wings, and
moved from defensive to support to attack positions. Ever-cheaper costs,
ever-broadening reach, and politicians' desire to eliminate war casualties
meant their numbers grew and grew.

Crucially, the weapons became more autonomous, able to independently observe, orient, decide, and act, vastly multiplying their abilities. Requiring an explicit decision from a human slowed them down, and so that requirement was gradually abandoned. Human supervisors no longer pulled the trigger; instead, they were left only with a veto to stop the trigger.

"I'd been on watch for twenty-six hours straight, and most of that time I was hopped up on cognitive enhancers. I didn't have enough time to watch the cultural briefings or review the handover package. But I should have. I know the courts say it wasn't my fault, but then whose fault was it?"

Having decided that there was an imminent threat to nearby civilians, Egner's drones pinpointed 322 targets with a sonic interdiction order. After five seconds of that order being ignored, the drones opened fire, killing 45 and injuring 201. Eleven seconds afterwards, high-altitude surveillance cameras finally determined that the majority of the targets were civilians who had been startled by a nearby gas explosion. Forty seconds later, when the data had filtered up to her superiors, Egner was removed from duty. It was the single largest killing of civilians that decade, and led directly toward the EU's suspension of operations in the region.

Egner's defense rested on the argument that she had been placed in an overwhelming situation with impossible demands, that in high-speed situations, her drones had more control than she did. She had been trained to stay out of the way of her weapons; she was a supervisor, not a controller. Ultimately her argument prevailed, with her entire line of drones being reprogrammed or destroyed.

She left the military and returned to her home in Bergen, Norway. Despite the fact that she had never been on the battlefield, she began suffering from post-traumatic stress disorder with frequent mood-swings and profound depression. The dark side of extrasensory integration meant that once those extra senses had been removed, a phantom pain lingered.

Historically, one way of treating military PTSD sufferers was through activities such as ice climbing and wilderness trips, which combined intense physical challenges with stress reduction. In modern times, human-powered flight, beanstalk climbing, and sims involving warriors from other eras have proved more effective.

None of these was suitable for Egner. As she obsessively looked up profiles of people she had killed, matched via DNA and public records, she couldn't stop thinking about who they were, what they were doing, who they might have become. She re-ran sims constantly, thinking about how she could have avoided the deaths.

As her depression worsened, her therapy team came up with the idea of asking Egner to manage a small restaurant using her drone supervision skills. It would be challenging but pleasantly monotonous. It would also go some way toward restoring her extra senses in a safe environment. Egner was initially flummoxed. She was a competent cook but had never been interested in becoming a professional, but in the absence of anything else to do, she reluctantly accepted.

Three years on, Egner is thriving in her new environment. She keeps a closer eye on her helpers these days, perhaps out of caution, but also out of a desire for creative control. Due to the singular nature of the Abkhazia debacle, she finds it hard to find anyone who understands her experience. It's not clear whether Egner will ever be at peace with what happened and her confused role in it. It could take a lifetime.

63 JAVELIN

Earth, 2040

At 2.67 meters long and formed of 806 grams of metal and composites, this object is slim, sharp, and deadly. Designed originally as a ranged weapon, it would be recognisable to humans even 400,000 years ago. It is, of course, a javelin.

This javelin was used by Csaba Németh of Hungary in his world-record-breaking 103.82 meter throw during the 2040 Pyongyang Olympics. It was an extraordinary achievement, made even more so by the fact that it beat the Paralympic T62-LE (limited enhancements) category record. "Baselines one, enhanceds zero: you saw it, Németh has defeated the Paralympians!" exclaimed one sports commentator. For a brief moment, all eyes were on the baseline humans.

But as the Olympic Games continued and there were no further upsets, attention returned to the highly anticipated Paralympic Games and all the thrills it promised. "Let's face it," said the same commentator, changing her mind a week later, "there's no way that baselines can beat the enhanced. The numbers just don't add up, biomechanically speaking. Csaba Németh was exceptional, and that's the point: he was an exception to the rule."

How did the Olympics—once the biggest sporting event in the world—become a mere sideshow to the technologically enhanced Paralympics?

The shift began in 2024 when the International Paralympic Committee (IPC) staged a technology demonstration jointly sponsored by EKDA GmbH and NeuroDynamics. Fifty former Paralympians competed in six rounds of athletics and swimming, each equipped with the most modern prostheses of the time. In the 100-meter sprint, athletes wearing powered exoskeletons squared off against those with carbon-fiber blades and accelerated neural pathways.

The demonstration was a huge success. People had never before seen such a direct combination of technology and raw human willpower outside of a war, and the sponsors were delighted by the viewing figures. Their interest, of course, lay in marketing their expensive medical and lifestyle devices to the all-important Gen-X and Millennial markets, who were beginning to worry about their mobility and independence as they grew older.

In 2028, the exhibition event returned with seven headline sponsors, ten times the advertising money, two-hundred former Paralympians, and triple the audience figures. Recognizing that its popularity threatened to eclipse that of the Paralympics itself, and perhaps responding to murky suggestions that the sponsors might create their own Paralympic Tech Games, IPC President Jonnie McIntosh struck a deal that saw a brand new "enhanced" classification added to sports from 2036 onwards, following a trial run during the 2032 Los Angeles Paralympics.

Their future assured, the "Enhanced Games" (as everyone called them) expanded rapidly. Paralympians flocked to the new classification in droves, attracted by the lure of money and fame. Just as air racing, formula E, and crossball had excited the public with constant technological advances, the Enhanced Games provided a nonstop series of marvels, with dozens of world records being toppled every four years.

The Olympics, in the meantime, languished. The International Olympic Committee (IOC) had long taken a hard line against doping, and they saw prosthetic and genetic enhancements in the same way: an unsporting and dangerous corruption of the level playing-field of their competition. While many respected the IOC's stance, the fact remained that baseline human physical performance was reaching its asymptotic limit. There's only so fast, high, and far that normal humans can reach, and, lofty ideals notwithstanding, that limitation hurt the Olympics' popularity—and funding. National sports federations began diverting their training budgets away from the Olympics and toward the Enhanced Games, often as a result of political pressure; after all, what better way was there to demonstrate your nation's technological prowess than in the field of physical competition?

Some baseline athletes began their own breakaway events as a protest against the Olympics' supposedly antiquated traditions, but none lasted more than a decade. At the same time, cheating scandals in the Olympics saw athletes attempting to use modified Enhanced Games augmentations and prosthetics to boost their performance. In response, the IOC instituted a thorough—some might say draconian—testing regime that strictly prohibited athletes from using any enhancements or augments at any point during their training.

Over time, this had the unintended consequence of barring baseline Olympic athletes from participating in normal society. By the '40s and '50s, public attitudes toward mimic scripts, lenses, augments, and neural laces had relaxed, and the notion that using these things would somehow constitute cheating seemed outrageous. Baseline nonaugmented humans were becoming the minority. The Paralympians were more representative of the real world, a world in which everyone was becoming enhanced in some small or large way.

The Enhanced Games had their own problems, though. In 2032, four athletes were seriously injured during the basketball event due to excessively high velocities, and in the 2036 Durban Games, eight athletes using an experimental Liang lace in the new highly enhanced classification suffered irreparable brain damage as their retroviral augments went awry. New safety rules were introduced, and pointed questions were asked about the purpose and limits of sporting enhancement.

All of this made Németh's world record achievement at the 2040 Pyongyang Olympics all the more extraordinary, with people talking about the "triumph of the human spirit" that the baseline Olympics represented—yet it wasn't hard to detect a patronizing tone in such remarks. Sure enough, in 2044, the limited enhancement classification asserted its dominance when Andreas Felke of Germany smashed the baseline world record by more than two meters thanks to a NeuroDynamics balance/coordination cerebellum package.

Who, exactly, was responsible for that new world record, though? Was it Felke, the athlete, or was it the technology and money provided by NeuroDynamics? While we can't and shouldn't take anything away from Felke's effort, in truth, there was no way he could have beaten the competition without the best technology and the financial support of his corporate sponsors.

It was a far cry from the original Olympics. Then again, the enhanced were a far cry from the original humans.

64 EUPHORIC GASTRONOMY

Berlin, Germany, 2041

Excerpts from *Euphoric Gastronomy*, a popular cookbook from 2041 that marked the shifting attitudes toward mind-altering substances:

INTRODUCTION

The purpose of a meal is not simply to sate our hunger. We want to spark an emotion, to impress a memory. Our total mastery over carbohydrates, proteins, fats, and spices, hard won from millennia of experimentation and exploration, is mundane from a biological perspective—but marvelous from a human one.

Our armory of culinary tools now extends to bioreactors, tailored meat, tweaked plants, and taste bud mapping. If we are willing to go to such lengths to create "perfect" gastronomic experiences, why ignore those other substances that can more directly alter our emotions and memories?

I have spent most of my life exploring how psychoactive drugs can be combined with food, to stunning effect. Of course, I owe much to earlier generations who made their first faltering steps with drugs such as alcohol and cannabis, but my team's first experiments with molecular sims and MRI scans in the '30s have allowed us to move far beyond those hazy, muddled days.

Thanks to our work at Kreuzberg's, "euphoric gastronomy" has become extremely fashionable. While I have never liked this term, implying as it does that the union of recreational drugs with food is mere frivolity, it is adequate enough as a shorthand. What I am more concerned about is bringing euphoric gastronomy out of the elite halls and restaurants of the world and into people's homes.

There is nothing difficult about performing simple euphoric gastronomy. With effort and discipline, one may become quite proficient in tailoring the right drugs to the right food. In this book and its accompanying simulations, I will show you how to create heretofore unimaginable culinary experiences.

HISTORY

If we were somehow transported thirty years into the past, I would most likely have been fined or imprisoned for having written this book. Thankfully, most countries have come to their senses in the intervening period, what with the widespread decriminalization and legalization of drugs beginning in the late '20s and early '30s.

Quite predictably, legalization led to a lot of silly experimentation, but the increased regulation and competition also improved the quality of drugs—not just in terms of safety and consistency, but also the subjective experience. Without these advantages, euphoric gastronomy would be only a fringe movement.

The legalization of drugs, however, did not mean that they suddenly became socially acceptable. Many people, particularly among the older, more closed-minded generations, continued to frown upon recreational drugs. Even today I am told there are some corporations that still routinely drug-test their employees. But these are isolated throwbacks. The changing shape of work has greatly reduced the ranks of those poor souls imprisoned in offices, so we may celebrate that these troglodytic restrictions apply to fewer and fewer each year.

Some clowns hoping to catch me out ask whether I allow my staff and collaborators to use recreational drugs while "on the job." The answer is: I don't care. If they are capable of doing the tasks I set them, they may take as many drugs as they wish, although I would hope that they are responsible enough to pay attention to their Lifelines and to be taking Securin or a similar addiction inhibitor. Whether they use drugs or sims or neurofeedback transcranial magnetic stimulation, if my staff turn up too sleepy to work, or too tired, or too drunk, or too high—they must go. I make no special exception for drugs.

DESSERT

I find that the best way to introduce newcomers to euphoric gastronomy is through dessert. It's the most playful, light-hearted part of any meal and, as such, lends itself very well to being combined with drugs.

For beginners, I would suggest these three desserts:

Ecuadorian dark chocolate soufflé, with tweaked betel leaf and areca nut: The heady, rich taste of the soufflé will complement the relatively mild stimulant effect of the betel leaf and areca nut, long used in the tropical Pacific and Asia.

Sticky toffee pudding, with kava: Those with a sweet tooth will prefer this dessert, especially as the kavalactones in the kava drink will off-set the effect of the sugar with a pleasantly relaxing feeling. If you are unable to obtain kava, then standard benzodiazepines will also suffice.

Sierra sunset ice cream, with Haifo: Haifo is a surprisingly complex and muscular tweaked opiate, so it needs to be paired with something that will numb the senses a little. We tried a number of ice cream flavors but found that the modern Buenos Aires recipe—suitably modified—worked extremely well with Haifo either crystallized on its surface or aerosolized with the "mist."

(Instructions to synthesize the unique chemicals mentioned above are attached to this book, compatible with all modern microarray reactors. Alternatively, you can order all necessary ingredients to your location for delivery within twenty-two minutes.)

65 THE HUNT FOR THE THYLACINE

Tasmania, Australia, 2042
London Review of Books, May 2042

The hunters pursue an unusual quarry. The clues they follow are a blur of pixels, an array of suspicious DNA sequences, clusters in multidimensional data on the brink of statistical significance. They pore over motion plots from aerial drones, inscribing curves and hieroglyphics above 3-D maps of coastal heaths and woodlands. What they are looking for is an idea, something that cannot be handled and studied, something whose absence cannot be proven. A specter.

In one well-known photo, you can make out the quarry's distinctive striped lower back and its long, whip-like tail. Accelerometer data from a weather station describes a rhythm of movement, characteristic of a shy, nocturnal marsupial. That these clues point toward the thylacine is beyond dispute. It's always the thylacine.

The question is, which thylacine?

Almost two decades ago, *Thylacine cynocephalus* was reintroduced into Tasmania by the 500 Project, led by Natasha Frei. It became the standard-bearer for the de-extinction movement, welcomed by locals and flourishing in a healthy ecosystem. More projects followed: the woolly mammoth, the auroch, the passenger pigeon, the dodo, reaching further and further back in time.

The thylacine was the first to be reintroduced because it was among the last to become extinct. It was only in 1936 that the last known specimen, named Benjamin, died in captivity in Hobart Zoo. The zoo had hoped to find a replacement Benjamin in short order, but successive and increasingly intensive searches were fruitless. By the 1980s, the thylacine was declared officially extinct.

But extinction is an idea not a binary state. We are confident enough to say that dinosaurs are extinct in the sense that they are completely gone from this world. An absence of sixty-six million years is long enough to be sure. But a century is a mere flicker in evolutionary terms. Perhaps the search parties were not as thorough as they could have been, limited by primitive twentieth century technology. So, we might instead say the thylacine, before its reintroduction in the 2020s, was functionally extinct— that while the reduced population no longer played a significant role in ecosystem function, it was possible, if unlikely, that a few had survived out of sight.

Brad Jarvis thinks he's seen the thylacine. The old thylacine.

"I can tell the difference!" says Jarvis. "The new thylacine behave in a completely different way to what our records from the nineteenth and twentieth centuries tell us. If the old thylacine are out there, I am one hundred percent sure we can recognize them. One hundred percent."

Jarvis cuts a trim figure, his body made lean from countless weekends spent hiking through the heaths as leader of the Indigenous Thylacine Discovery Group. The group are believers in the continued existence of the pre-revival thylacine and regard the 500 Project's reintroduction as a terrible mistake, one that threatens to wipe out the original striped wolf once and for all, whether through competition or through interbreeding.

The latter should be easy to discover, since the 500 Project has kept DNA profiles of the entire population of reintroduced thylacine. Any old thylacine would have markedly different DNA, as would the product of any interbreeding. The problem is that once interbreeding has occurred, it would be almost impossible to undo, at least not without more reintroductions.

Jarvis's group and others like it have been combing Tasmania for years with satellite and drone surveillance. They're particularly interested in the movements of the reintroduced thylacine, whom they believe could lead them to their quarry. This attention is mostly paid at a distance, although some groups have placed small cameras and sensors on thylacine to make their jobs easier, a move condemned as unnecessary interference by the 500 Project and the Tasmanian government. Unsurprisingly, Natasha Frei doesn't like to talk about it.

"Yes, if we're getting into epistemology, I can't promise you there were no thylacines remaining in Tasmania, but might I remind you what functionally extinct means," said Frei. I caught her in the middle of a conference on Alto Firenze, selecting candidates among newly-captured asteroids for engineering into Ascension biomes.

"It means the population is no longer viable," she continued. "It means there are no individuals able to reproduce or that the small population of breeding individuals would not be able to sustain itself due to inbreeding depression and genetic drift, leading to a loss of fitness. That's the definition. Back in the '20s, it was very clear there was not a viable population, so even if there were a few left when we reintroduced them, they weren't long for this world. If anything, our reintroduction means they are guaranteed to live on, in a genetic sense, assuming they interbreed. And I hope they do!"

"Of course she'd say that," Jarvis tells me the next day. "She made a mistake but she doesn't want to admit to it. And this is why it's so important we find the old thylacine as soon as we can." Jarvis and his wife, whom he met through his group, are about to embark on a week-long hike along the north coast, and they're impatient to set off.

The searches for the thylacine in the twentieth century were slow-going, requiring human eyes and human thought. It's unusual, therefore, to see searches today also limited by our easily-tired bodies and minds. Wouldn't it be faster to rely on drones and satellites and field DNA sequencers?

It would, if you could rely on them. But if you suspected your tools were prone to deepfakes, to the accidental or intentional warping of data, to hacked DNA sequencers, then perhaps not. During the early days of the Indigenous Thylacine Discovery Group, their sensors registered dozens of old thylacines every week, and yet every time the leads were followed, they evaporated into digital smoke. Better to rely on your own eyes and tools you could hold in your own hands.

Some in the group mutter that we can't really know what a "new" thylacine is. They claim the 500 Projects servers were compromised, the DNA profiles manipulated. Some doubt the thylacine was ever reintroduced, that they were merely released from captivity. CRISPR tools were surely involved, somehow. To what end? These same conspiracy theorists suggest this is a route toward the deliberate extinction and reintroduction of altered endangered species, an opposing force against the rising consensus of the "half empty world" movement.

I don't bother to challenge the hunters. There is no way to reason someone out of a position they didn't reason themselves into. We can never know if the old thylacine is out there. And yet we keep trying.

66 GIVING NOTHING A NAME

Universe, 2043

A collection of media assembled by contemporary followers of an anonymous artist who started a naming project that later gained mass appeal:

> The Bottle Green Third Nascent Confluence of the Adams River, a few paces to the south of the Theodore's Brave Statement Willow Tree
>
> The Long Suggested Swallet of the West Stockwell Upper Unseen Field (a subtle mini-valley in the untended, sickly-green scrub)
>
> The Minor Pattern of Wear from Ancient Human-Controlled Driving Patterns on the A34 beside the Forty-Second Tree Past the Former Burger King

There are 149 trillion square meters of land on Earth, all captured, rendered, and analyzed as a unique object many times over, known to us as a string of numbers and glyphs.

Every patch of dirt at the base of a tree, every doorstep where lovers first met, every boulder and rock that has never been touched—we will give nothing and everything a name.

1. SPACE AND AIRBORNE

Geostationary satellite surveys, low Earth orbit overflights, high altitude surveillance drones, tethered aerostats, delivery copters, police intervention drones, paramedic jumpers, climbers.

2. HUMAN

Glasses, jewelry, clothing array cameras, sonar and lidar walking aids, positioning analysis, gait analysis, biometric and neuro record analysis, dedicated cameras.

NAMESPACE PROTOCOLS: AN INTRODUCTION

Within a local namespace, names can be categorized into those automatically and manually generated by humans and nonhuman agents. Sometimes these will refer to precisely the same physical area, but more often they will overlap. We can also distinguish names through the events and intersections they refer to. Nonhuman agents may generate human-readable names for "disposable" uses such as meetings within an environment such as a public square or park. These names may be reused if they prove to be particularly apt or liked by other agents.

> The Seventeenth Summer Tactile Rupture of the Organ-Music Sidewalk (aka "Seventeenth Summer"), where the sidewalk had been poorly repaired during the summer of 2022
>
> The Sean Thomas Darker Threshold Periphery of the South Marine Lake Observation Point

… and the endless, futile, pointless pursuit of naming every atom on the land, on the sea. Why not in the air and in orbit and the moon and the asteroids and Mars and all the other places? Why?

> The Medium-Sized Boulder upon which Niels Delahaye's Deepsight Gaze Lingered for a Second While Flying to See His Wife for the Second-to-Last Time
>
> The Column That Could Have Helped Hold Up a Minor Government Office Building in Austin but Was Discovered to Have Cracks and Is Now Abandoned in the Desert
>
> The Derelict Lighthouse with Dangerously Unstable and Broken Steps, frequently tripped over and cursed by owner Matt Haughey
>
> The Paving Tile Where Bartosz and Danai's Hands First Accidentally Touched after Their Third Date on the Walk to the Train and Led to a Kiss

Why not?

67 RECHARTERED CITIES

Hakodate, Japan, 2043

The Quick Decline scarred Japan. After a period of more-or-less graceful stagnation around the turn of the century, a hailstorm of punches left the country reeling: a massive run on the Yen precipitated by mounting debt, two devastating earthquakes in the Kanto and Kansai regions in 2034 and 2038, and the inescapable consequences of an aging, shrinking population. In half a century, the world's second-largest economy had become a mere satellite of China and America.

The dysfunctional coalition governments that ran Japan were singularly ill-equipped to manage this decline. It wasn't until 2043 that the public, frustrated with the national government in general, elected the newly formed NSDP-PDP coalition with a supermajority. The coalition was blessed with a single mandate: to change the local autonomy law and devolve power toward the prefectural and municipal levels.

Many cities and prefectures made only superficial changes. Even with broad new powers over taxes and spending, they were reluctant to be blamed for economic, demographic, and environmental factors that they correctly believed were out of their control. Instead, they played it safe by continuing to dole out perks to the half of the population aged over fifty. But whether out of desperation or inspiration, a few hard-hit cities decided to make more drastic changes, turning themselves into "rechartered cities."

Like much of the country, the first two rechartered cities—Hakodate on the southern tip of Hokkaido and Amagasaki in southeast Hyogo Prefecture—had a considerable stock of expensive, well-maintained, and over-built infrastructure. Compared to the rest of the world, they also had a reliable legal system, low crime rates, and a striking lack of people. This combination made them ripe candidates for transformation by medium-term immigrants. Dr. Takami of Hokkaido University explains:

The concept of rechartered cities dates back to the controversial experiments with charter cities in the '20s. According to their proponents, developing countries would establish special reform zones in which brand-new charter cities would be built, and these cities would be administered with the help of foreign countries and businesses. The host country would gain from a massive influx of capital and good governance, and the foreign countries and businesses would benefit from cheap labor, favorable laws, and increased trade.

Charter cities were met with fierce opposition in almost every potential host country, as they were seen as a breach of sovereignty and, even worse, a symbol of neocolonialism. By the '30s, two cities were eventually established in Madagascar and Haiti, but the sheer amount of strife involved scared off all other candidates, especially with the Shanghai bombing still fresh in people's minds.

Rechartered cities on the other hand were much more modest in scope. Under the Hakodate model, which was approved by referendum in 2044, the municipal government invited trusted foreign co-ops, missions, and nonprofits to establish long-term presences in the city. In exchange for more streamlined and lenient laws concerning use of air, land, spectrum, and drones, the organizations were expected to undertake worthwhile projects for the benefit of the city. These were frequently very lively projects—rewilding, environmental remediation, carbon capture, transportation upgrades, massive art installations, testbeds for experimental technologies and algorithms, and the like.

For the most part, I think rechartered cities worked, but it's easy to find those who disagree. Amagasaki passed their referendum sixty-four to thirty-six. A good margin, but it still meant that over a third resented the newcomers. Becoming a rechartered city could feel like having a nonstop twenty-year festival in your town with all the concomitant excitement and construction and tourists and visitors and disruption and confusion and noise. I enjoyed visiting both cities during their rechartered status, but I have to confess that I'm not so sure I'd like it to happen on my doorstep here in Sapporo.

Protests and violence were not uncommon during the first few years. Even after the massive overseas aid that poured in following the superquake of 2049, even with the widespread use of Dragon and Babylon, a cultural chasm still loomed large. It was difficult to break habits a millennium old.

Yet not everyone was quite as reticent in welcoming the newcomers. Noriko Imai, a psychiatrist in Hakodate, was fifty-two when they adopted rechartered status:

I wasn't so sure about the vote, you know. I was going to vote no, but the day before I was out walking with my husband around the old Goryōkaku fort when I decided what was missing: young people. And children! So I tapped in "yes" and I held my breath. It was a good choice. Hakodate was a beautiful city, but it was also an old city, and young people need new things or else they'll leave. All the newcomers and missions changed our home, and they made it beautiful in a different way. They helped keep this city alive, so I'm glad that a lot of them ended up staying.

What began in Hakodate and Amagasaki soon spread to other rich countries and municipalities with declining populations—Italy, Germany, Greece, even parts of Russian and China. Rechartered cities also became influential within two burgeoning cultural movements. They were a bulwark against the mass retreat into virtual life and a prominent example of the jumble, where people from all ages, origins, and backgrounds began living among each other, finding common cause in new lives.

68 THE OLD DRONES

Gaghma Kodori, Georgia, 2044

An extract from the memoir of Mohsen Rahimi, who became famous later in life as a Martian explorer and poet:

My grandmother taught me two lessons. Lesson number one: don't talk to strangers. You'd have thought glasses would have changed her mind, but I guess people born in the 1970s have hang-ups about privacy. Personally, I love talking to strangers, but I tried not to do it whenever she was around.

Lesson number two: always thank a drone. I could never get my parents to tell me where that one came from. Did she have a robotic carrier I didn't know about? Did she swap jokes and play cards with her service drone? Who knows.

As much as I wanted to avoid hurting her feelings, you just can't get through life these days without seeing a drone. How else are you supposed to get dinner delivered or have your kids taken to the doctor when you're at work? And what are you supposed to do, say thank you every time you meet one? There's only so much time in the day. But every time she noticed my lack of manners, she'd purse her lips in a deeply disapproving way.

A few years after she died, I decided to go for a tour around Georgia in Eastern Europe. I told people I was "in between things" and wanted a change, but I think everyone knew that my friends were getting tired of supporting my oddball projects on the Braid and wanted me to do something useful for a change—or at least leave them alone for a while.

Why Georgia? I don't know. Probably I'd driven through it or blown it up in some game when I was a kid. I just remember that it had lovely scenery. And when I stepped off that dirigible, I knew I'd remembered right.

Three weeks later, I was lying at the bottom of a deep well, looking up at a tiny bright circle of that lovely scenery, seriously thinking that this would be the last thing I'd ever see in my all-too-brief life.

Here's how it happened. My dirigible had moored in a field on the outskirts of Abasha, a place I knew precisely nothing about, so I asked around to see if there was anyone who might want stories told, music composed, services provided, that sort of thing, in exchange for bed and board. There was some laughing and rueful head-shaking, and they suggested I might have some better luck across the river in Gaghma Kodori. I made my way there in the morning in a rickety old geely and arranged to meet a friendly person I found with my lenses. I bought us drinks, we ascertained that neither of us was a murderer, and she put me up for the night and promised some work.

In the morning, she led me out of the village to an overgrown field to the south. There was nothing of note except for an old stone well. We stood fifty meters back from the well and, for a good long minute, just looked at it. My lenses didn't show anything useful, but I figured that it had a hyperlocal cultural or religious significance or something. Maybe she wanted me to write a poem about it.

I was formulating a diplomatic way to ask what the hell we were doing there when I was suddenly pulled down to the grass. Seconds later, a cloud of the dirtiest, oldest, and just plain scariest drones you've ever seen zoomed over our heads and plummeted into the well, all the while making a horrible, scratchy, rattling noise.

Ever wondered what happens to old drones? They don't ascend into heaven or get sent to the Five Winds to live out the rest of their lives as circus performers. When they reach a certain dignified age and their diagnostics are showing too much red and not enough black, they fly themselves to the nearest recycling center. A few are upgraded with new parts, but it's usually cheaper to get other drones to dismantle them. Big cities such as New York or Shanghai or Lagos have so many drones that they need four, five, even six recycling centers, but if you're in a more remote place, you might travel a hundred miles before seeing one. That's too long a journey for most drones, especially the small ones.

Technically, if a drone can't get reach a recycling center under its own steam, it's supposed to be transported there by its owner, but that's a hassle that no one wants to deal with. You're certainly not allowed to dump them either, but let's just imagine that an aging drone's GPS and magnetometers got screwed up and it somehow flew into a well—would you be surprised?

Yes, this was literally a place where drones came to die. Out of sight, out of mind.

That's how it had worked in Abasha for the past decade until an enterprising villager named Nino had discovered a business opportunity in salvaging old batteries from drones and selling them as kitsch artwork for rich Asians. Nino usually sent one of her smart drones down there to fetch them, but the week before I arrived it had managed to join the pile by getting shrapnel stuck in its rotors, so here I was—a man sent to do a drone's job.

I clambered down a rope ladder in the well and set to work. It was hard going at first, since most of the drones weren't designed to have user-accessible components. It wasn't dangerous, per se—I had the EU's paranoid health and safety regulations to thank for that—but it was plenty tedious. That evening I got Nino to print me up some new tools I found online, and I had a better go of it after that.

Over the following weeks, I got into a satisfying routine, arriving at the well at ten in the morning, putting in a solid two hours' work before lunch, resuming at two for another two hours, a tea break at four, and a final hour taking me up to half past five. I fancied myself as one of the coal miners of yore that my great-grandfather would talk about, slaving away in the darkness with only my music and podcasts for company. I recounted this tale of back-breaking labor at a bar one weekend, and I was instructed to look up coal mining on Wikipedia. That shut me up.

Each day drones arrived at the well to die, and each day I dismantled more. Three weeks passed, and I'd cleared almost all of the tech out and was posting 3-Ds of old coins and gadgets I'd found to my friends back home.

On my final day, I clambered up the ladder for my very last tea break to discover to my delight that Nino's daughter had left a few bottles of beer for me there. We'd had a little thing going since I'd arrived, and though I'd regretfully told her that I'd be moving on when the work was done, she'd taken the news well (only later did I find out that she had a high-powered boyfriend back home in Mumbai, so the joke was on me).

Now, I know kids today prefer using their laces to get a buzz, but in my opinion there's nothing quite as refreshing as a cold beer after a hard day's work, fashion be damned. In fact, I got a little too refreshed and ended up completely ignoring my 4:15 p.m. alarm. Right on schedule, a cloud of drones thrummed around me, diving into the well.

Like a fool, I panicked and thought I was in one of those Skynet games where the drones had come to overthrow humanity once and for all. I flailed around wildly and—you guessed it—tipped back over the edge of the well, falling thirty meters, thankfully caroming off a couple of walls and ledges on my way down.

When I woke up, it was still light, but that was the only thing going for me. I was pretty sure I'd broken at least one leg, and even worse, I couldn't get any signal; my fall had ripped my jacket and the antenna had been torn apart. Usually that wouldn't be a problem since there'd be plenty of local-izers around, but we were in peaceful, quiet, isolated Gaghma Kodori.

I felt pretty low, I have to confess. Was this really my fate, to die at the bottom of a well with only a dozen old drones for company? I may have started crying until I realized that Nino or her daughter were bound to fig-ure out what had happened sooner or later and the worst I was in for was missing dinner. But hell, I didn't want to cause people trouble, I didn't want to be embarrassed, and, most of all, I was getting really hungry.

My first reaction to my predicament was to post a request for help with my lenses. Of course, that was impossible. Like I said, my jacket was torn and there was no signal. My second reaction was to do a manual search of the net. Ditto. I guess what our parents said about our reliance on glasses and lenses is true, huh?

I reminisced for a while about my family, mentally composing a story that would paint me in a slightly better light than drunkenly falling into a well, when I remembered my grandmother's old words. Not the one about strangers, the one about thanking a drone! A few seconds later and I'd recalled the critical emergency command—you know, the one you're taught as a kid that can override any drone's orders in a life or death situa-tion. The one that you are never, ever allowed to abuse.

I wasn't sure whether it'd work. The drones at the bottom of the well were the oldest, rustiest ones around, maybe even three, four years old. I was frankly doubtful they had enough juice left in them. But sure enough, I could see their rotors haltingly whir alive, and I don't think I'd ever heard a sweeter sound than their horrible rattling noise.

I designated myself as the person in distress, and, like a cloud of angels—obsolete, unfashionable angels—they carried me all the way to the top of well in their arms and nets and manipulators, and laid me gently down on the grass outside. From there, I had just enough signal to make a call. Soon enough, Nino had arrived with her daughter amid a lot of fuss and tears on my part.

Once my leg had healed a few weeks later and I'd recovered from the enormous hangover resulting from the celebration of my escape, I resumed my vagabonding ways and moved on, carrying a couple of my saviors as souvenirs. I took one to my grandmother's grave as a little thank you to her, and the other sits proudly on the mantelpiece in our flat in Mumbai. My wife hates it—she says it looks completely out of place. I think it just reminds her too much of where she grew up.

69 EQUAL RIGHTS

Edinburgh, Scotland, 2044

This landmark speech was delivered by the Stewart-Walker family in St. Stephen's Church, Edinburgh, and signaled a shift in how religious groups adapted to rapid shifts in cultural mores.

So, one woman is walking across a bridge, and she sees a man on the edge, ready to jump off.

She shouts out, "Don't do it!"

And he says, just teetering on the edge, "Why not?"

"There's too much to live for!"

"What's there to live for?"

She thinks about this for a second and asks in reply, "Are you atheist or religious?"

And he says, "I'm religious."

So she says, "Me too! Christian or Muslim?"

He says, "Christian!"

She says, "Me too! Catholic or Evangelical?"

He says, "Evangelical!"

She says, "Me too! Pentecostalist or Environmentalist?"

He says, "Environmentalist!"

She says, "Wow, me too! Environmentalist North or Environmentalist South?"

He says, "Environmentalist North!"

She says, "Incredible, me too! Environmentalist North, Reformed or Environmentalist North, Grouped?"

He says, "Environmentalist North, Grouped!"

She says, "Amazing, so am I! Environmentalist North, Grouped and Synced or Environmentalist North, Grouped and Distributed?"

He says, "Environmentalist North, Grouped and Distributed!"

And then she says, "Die, heretic scum!" and pushes him off.

It's an oldie but a goodie. And, you know, it really does sum up what we're all here about today.

Because even though this family of ours is gathered today in thousands— no—millions of churches, all of us believing in the Lord, all of us with so much in common, we just can't help obsessing over these little differences between us.

And, hey, it's not always a life-and-death thing like our friends on the bridge. But if there's one thing the Bible teaches us, it's that life and death isn't about our bodies. It's about our souls. The death of the soul can be something that's hard to see. It's hidden within each and every one of us, and sometimes it can die if true justice is denied.

If we can't share our worship of the one whom we believe in or if we can't be with the ones whom we truly love, it's hard to imagine what that might be like. If you're like us, it hurts just to be apart for a day, let alone a week. Or a month, or a year. Or a lifetime.

So we count ourselves truly lucky—blessed, even—that we can always be together, wherever we are.

That's what makes us different. That's what makes people scared.

And that's why, even though we can be together, we can't be together in a way that is recognized by the people and the church that we love.

Once upon a time, people with different skin colors couldn't marry. Can you imagine that?

And it wasn't that long ago that men couldn't marry men and women couldn't marry women. Maybe you have parents who remember that. I'm sure we all thank God we don't live in those times any more.

And now people tell us, they say that a marriage should only be between two people! But why?

Because marriage is for procreation? Nonsense. Because it's best for children to be brought up by two parents, and two parents only? Ask our children. Ask the children of all of those people like us whether they feel uncared for. We can give them just as much love as any other family can. And we will always be there for them.

I know it can seem strange to see all four of us, standing here before you, talking about marriage, talking like this, in the way we do.

Yes, it seems like a good trick, but it's how we think. It's how we were brought up, and it's how so many people are brought up, always together, always in contact, wherever we are.

But we love and care for each other as much as you do. We met each other at church, just as so many of you did. We argue with each other about who should do the chores. We get excited about where we'll go on holiday.

And we feel just as proud of our children's achievements as you do. We feel so lucky to be together. But there's one thing missing from our souls.

It's the recognition of being truly married in the eyes of God. It matters to you—that's why so many of you have chosen to be married. And it matters to us.

So, we would ask each and every one of you to look into your hearts and to imagine not being allowed, not being permitted to marry the one you love.

And we would ask you to support us in our fight. Support us in our goal for equal rights, equal recognition, in the eyes of the state, in the eyes of God, and in your eyes. Because for as much as we may seem different, we truly are the same.

Thank you all. God bless us all.

70 FOURTH GREAT AWAKENING

Santa Fe, US, 2044

The greatest of changes can come in the smallest of things. This package, one of millions manufactured by the Christian Consummation Movement, is no larger than my thumb. Inside lies a tiny eyedropper and eighteen pills.

If I use the eyedrops, take the pills, and enroll in their induction course of targeted viruses and magnetic stimulation—which I can assure you I am not about to do—then over the next few months, my personality and desires would gradually be transformed. My aggressive tendencies would be lowered. I'd readily form strong, trusting friendships with the people I met during this imprinting period—consummators, usually. I would become measurably more empathetic, more generous, and "less desiring of fleeting, individual, mundane pleasures," according to the CCM.

Some might say that this would be an improvement on my personality, that I would become more serene and less vulnerable to temptation. Others might say that my individuality would be eroded by an insidious form of desire modification. But everyone would agree that I had genuinely changed—that I had reached "consummation."

From the late '40s to the '70s, twenty million Americans joined the Christian Consummation Movement. While its explosion in growth has slowed down considerably in recent decades, the CCM's rise to become one of the largest new denominations of American Christianity represents a period of religious revival, a Fourth Great Awakening.

If we want to understand the origins of the Consummation Movement, we need to look at the society in which it grew. By the early '40s, mass automation and globalization had permanently raised the US unemployment rate to more than 30 percent, with "underemployment" doubling that number. Enhanced social security and the glimmerings of a basic minimum income in some states had taken the financial sting out of this economic shift, but money alone couldn't replace the sense of meaning or direction that citizens had once derived from work. Nor could it address the fragmentation of physical communities across the country.

Dr. Alan "Al" Bhumbra aimed to fill that gap. The co-founder of the Christian Consummation Movement and a talented neuroscientist, Dr. Bhumbra devised the CCM's "empathy and community" induction course. In 2044, Bhumbra's Santa Fe team knitted together a number of previously separate therapies—including the Mathy hate cure gene therapy treatment, hormonal and pheromonal imprinting and bonding techniques, memory enhancement, and old-fashioned conditioning—into a course that was extremely reliable and, importantly, very safe.

Simply undertaking the induction course didn't guarantee that an individual would consummate, so the CCM set up precisely targeted real-world social networks to provide essential human support, particularly during the imprinting period. The CCM understood how Christianity itself first spread during the Apostolic Age through hundreds of small gatherings and accelerated that process by multiple orders of magnitude with the help of network technologies.

Early on, Dr. Bhumbra identified echo-boomers or so-called "millennials" as being particularly receptive to the CCM. Those born in the 2010s and beyond had few illusions that a job should be a measure of their self-worth, but millennials, born from the 1980s to the turn of the century, had been brought up to believe in the importance of careers. Importantly, they also held a relentless belief in self-improvement fueled by the massive popularity of contemporaneous works such as The Guide.

To millennials, the CCM offered a route to self-improvement that not only worked but also involved effectively zero effort or risk. Many people during the '40s and '50s already took cognitive enhancers or mood-altering drugs, so the induction course didn't seem much worse. In fact, it seemed much better, because it held out the promise of joining a real community with noble goals. Here's a typical video from Dr. Bhumbra:

> You know, we all want the same things. We want to help our friends and family, to love and be loved, to leave the world a better place. We want to be content. Oh, and we want to be happy and prosperous! Now, is that really too much to ask for? [laughs] But it's hard. It's really hard. You pray every day and every night, but it can be mighty tough to stick to the right path. It's a never-ending struggle against temptation and against the darker demons of our soul.
>
> Some use meds or games to help them. I don't object to that. I think that's just fine. But it'll only work for a while. Those demons and those temptations will come back because all you're doing is putting a band-aid on the problem. Like my doctor would say, you're treating the symptoms, not the cure.

What if we could silence those demons, though? What if we could use our God-given knowledge and intelligence and tools to improve ourselves? That's what He would want of us. And that's what we are doing here at the CCM.

Now, I bet a lot of you have played that new Odyssey game that came out last summer. I sure did, though I didn't get quite as far as my daughter, who's a real expert at these things. Anyhow, there's a part where you—Odysseus—have to tie yourself to a mast so you won't be drawn toward those enchanting, evil Sirens.

When you did that, do you think you were cheating? No! You were being smart. Why? Because you were confronting an evil that you couldn't avoid and couldn't defeat on your own. It's just the same with the CCM.

When we complete our course, we consummate the lifelong journey our souls have made toward Christ. We truly make ourselves into better people, better able to help and love one another and to love God. You only need to look at the members of our church to see the truth of what I'm saying. You might have to look hard, because they're not proud people. They're humble. But every day, through their efforts, they're helping the needy. They're rebuilding our country. They're strengthening communities. And they're making the world a better place.

Not everyone agreed. Rival denominations denounced the CCM as a cult and its induction course as brainwashing, citing numerous cases of people embarking on the course without providing fully informed consent, victims of the darker side of the jumble.

Behind these disagreements lay an even more serious objection: if you remove the threat of temptation from the human experience, can you still be virtuous? Can you still be counted as human at all?

In reality, the CCM's course of brain chemistry alteration was not so powerful as to remove all temptation but merely to shift them to a more "virtuous" point within the human spectrum. Taking the course did not make one a saint—although it did make it easier to become one, depending on your definition of a saint, that is.

Author's note: Like most people these days, I am not religious—and like most people, I still strive to live a virtuous life. The CCM may make it easier to reach that goal, but it comes at the cost of our very own humanity itself. I believe that desire modification is the real temptation, one that is desperately hard to resist.

71 THE COLLINGWOOD METEOR

Blue Mountains, Canada, 2045

The Blue Mountain Ski Resort is around 120 kilometers northeast of Toronto, near the town of Collingwood. On December 12, 2045, a bolide meteor entered the skies above the resort. During its descent through the atmosphere, the meteor exploded, causing a massive airburst.

Emergency services from across the province began arriving within twenty seconds, but the level of devastation and the sheer scale of the resulting avalanches left few survivors. By the end of the day, more than three hundred locals and visitors had been killed, making it one of Canada's most terrible natural disasters ever.

It wasn't long before questions were asked about why the meteor hadn't been spotted by the Schweickart, Atlas, or NEOCam planetary warning arrays. Part of the problem, it emerged, was that the meteor was less than twenty-five meters in diameter and came from far outside the plane of the ecliptic. The arrays simply hadn't been running for long enough to produce a map of all such asteroids. It was a tragedy, everyone agreed, a terrible accident that left no one at fault.

That's where the story would have ended if it weren't for the recovery of this military drone a month later from the Georgian Bay, just north of the Blue Mountains. The drone had been on a routine low-altitude laser repowering cruise when it was smashed into the water by the airburst. Hardened for combat operations, much of the drone's memory remained intact. Forensic teams worked day and night to retrieve a few precious seconds of close-up footage of the airburst with the hope of learning more about the physics of the incident.

The results were disturbing. The Collingwood meteor looked nothing like a typical meteor. Instead, it appeared to be a disguised kinetic weapon.

The second outer space treaty had outlawed any kind of lethal weapon being placed in Earth orbit. Specifically included in its provisions were kinetic weapons—inert tungsten projectiles that could be steered to survive re-entry and pulverize their targets without the aid of any explosives. However, it had been long known that the Treaty was basically unenforceable given soaring orbital traffic. It was simply too easy to take a lump of rock and metal, stick some fins and a computer on the end, and fling it out of the proverbial airlock toward your target.

China, the United States, Japan, and India all were suspected of stockpiling kinetic weapons in orbit, but they also had the most to lose if a space-based war broke out. More importantly, they didn't have any motive to attack Canada, and in any case, they watched each other like hawks. A terrorist attack seemed the most likely explanation, except for the fact that no one had come forward to take responsibility or make demands.

Tracing back the trajectory of the Collingwood meteor led to an apparently empty orbit, but a painstaking analysis of all launches over the past twenty years uncovered an unmanned dark space station in low orbit. The station had apparently been assembled years earlier by robotic packages released by mining launches from Kourou in French Guiana. While the mining launches were legitimate, the robots hadn't been declared. Unfortunately, when Canadian Security Intelligence Service investigators reached the station, they discovered that all data had been wiped clean and any useful modules had already been de-orbited.

Faced with a dead end, the CSIS looked to discover who had paid for the robots' passage. Armed with international warrants and backed up by the major powers, they wrestled their way through a dizzying series of bank accounts, trusts, and shell companies based in the Caymans, Hong Kong, the City of London, Jersey, and finally Mauritius. Every single one of the payments pointed toward an account owned by the brother-in-law of the prime minister of Mauritius, Rashid Torabully.

Torabully had come into power eight years earlier in a controversial election that saw unprecedented sums spent on smear campaigns against his opponent. Some suspected that he was secretly funneling money from British corporations keen to exploit recently discovered deposits of rare elements, but nothing had been proven at the time.

The CSIS made a bold move. After consulting their allies, they launched physical and digital network attacks at Torabully's supporters in order to forcibly extract information from their systems. Within minutes, they had their smoking gun: terabytes of messages, conversations, and plans from Torabully and his conspirators, all related to the Collingwood meteor. Then they made an astonishing discovery—the target of their attack was a single person: Michael Shaxson, a British high court judge.

The previous year, Shaxson had been involved in a case against United Petroleum, a company accused of tax evasion, bribery, hacking, and general dirty tricks. It was widely thought that Shaxson would rule against UP and that he would recommend a deep reformation of the tax system, including an elimination of reinvoicing, transfer pricing, and a general rollback of banking secrecy. Polls suggested that his recommendations would be favored by British citizens.

Plenty of corporations and tax havens were deathly afraid of this outcome, especially the prime minister of Mauritius, who personally stood to lose billions. One way to derail this process was by killing Shaxson. Using an airburst meteor at his favorite holiday resort as a murder weapon may have been disproportionate and expensive, but previous death threats had resulted in Shaxson's shielding by a powerful drone-based PPOI order (permanent protective overwatch and intervention). If killing three hundred people meant that business could continue as normal—and if it intimidated other opponents into staying away—it would be well worth the cost.

Torabully was not the mastermind behind the scheme. It was only due to his lax data security measures that the CSIS investigators were able to get as far as they did. Unfortunately, his allies were not quite as foolish and remained hidden until much later.

However, the sensational nature of the attack and the detailed accounts of how Torabully and his allies aimed to benefit from it rallied popular opinion against the interests of the tax havens. New "Shaxson regulations" were imposed, including all those that he would have recommended and more, marking the beginning of the Great Reclamation of the economy from its manipulators.

72 THE DOWNVOTED

London, England, 2045

Excerpt from "The Downvoted" by Richard Cameron:

Eric never tired of his movies. He would prattle on at anyone patient enough to listen recounting the relative strengths and deficiencies of Bond, Bourne, and Shankar. Spy movies were his favorites. He would say that he understood their lonely, bloodless nature.

After we had received that month's income, Eric took me out for lunch at a cheap bistro by Clapham Common. I was taken aback by his generosity until I realized that he was using me as cover. Once again, he had managed to get himself downvoted on enough trust networks that he was being ignored or refused service. This time it was the menus that wouldn't work for him.

His personal hygiene was hardly perfect, but I'd seen and smelt worse. His clothes weren't particularly old or dirty. While he often had a surly attitude, I had never seen it cause any serious fights or arguments. All of this is to say that I couldn't point to any specific reason for why he was being downvoted by passers-by. It was the combination of his overall demeanor and personality that put people off.

Understandably, Eric was frustrated by his predicament. He became grumpier and more antisocial, which only earned him yet more downvotes. Like many others, I felt sympathetic toward his plight, but I was wary of being seen with him too much for fear of receiving downvotes by association.

"They don't see you," he used to say. "You are completely invisible. I don't know if it was better or worse before these awful glasses when people just pretended you didn't exist. Now I am told that there are people who will literally put you out of their sight, so I become this muddy black shadow drifting along the pavement. And you know what? People will still downvote a black shadow!"

"The first time it happens, you become angry, angry at the world. Who appointed them as judge and jury? What gives them the right to reach a verdict just like that, in a second? But when it happens over and over, you just become sad and despair of ever being seen again. A good disguise for a spy, perhaps, but not for normal men or women such as you and I."

Eric seldom talked about his troubles. He preferred to play silly games like magically pushing crowds of pedestrians away from him with the power of his downvoted aura, but today he was especially despondent. He had just been turned down for a temporary job as a waiter at a pop-up restaurant in Brixton, and I think the rejection was getting to him.

A liberal person, on hearing "discrimination," will naturally think of sexism or racism, or these days, sentism, all of which have their own devils and champions. They will not think of the murky discrimination that the downvoted experience, even though it is equally illegal. They will assume that these problems ought to be impossible thanks to our right to see and to remove any personally identifying information held on us by corporations.

Our society, however, also holds sacrosanct the individual's right to use private or privately-shared data to alter their personal reality in any way they wish. This exception has meant that thousands of private, semi-legal peer-to-peer downvote-sharing networks have sprung up in every city in the world, collectively identifying millions of undesirables. Stamp out one network and another will appear within hours.

"The only good thing about it," Eric noted glumly, "is that no one is allowed to make a profit. It's all very cooperative."

Providing that we weren't out in public, I enjoyed Eric's company. Before a drug overdose and a botched gene therapy treatment left him in hospital for a year, Eric had been a talented lawyer. After he recovered, he found he couldn't concentrate any more. He bounced from temp job to temp job and began the slow slide down to the pit of the basic minimum income where he had stayed ever since.

"It could be worse. We could be living in San Francisco. I went there on a holiday once, for a record of achievement project working at the Haughey Lighthouse, one of those things we all had to do after they got rid of exams. Cleanest streets I've ever seen, and that wasn't with any sweepers either. They've got state-sponsored downvoting there, "citizen crowdsourcing of anti-social individuals." The law got passed by a supermajority because it's the ultimate magic wand—a way to identify all the creepy people and criminals forever. I'm surprised there wasn't more rioting against those arrogant, entitled technologists.

"I'll be honest with you. The voting is usually right. And sometimes the feedback to the downvoted is useful. Sometimes, yes, they really do change their behavior for the better. But," he sighed heavily, "sometimes it's not so easy to change yourself. It becomes a spiral. It's like being exiled without having traveled anywhere."

Besides Eric, the Streatham Solidarity Center housed a few other downvoted. Most of them had discovered that their invisibility gave them not only the ability but also the license to commit petty crimes. If society has decided, in the most dismissive yet personal way possible, that you are worthless, then why shouldn't you play along and really justify those downvotes? Occasionally they would make sport of it, seeing who could get the most downvotes in a day. Those were the days I avoided them.

> I'm not for wearing a mask or a veil. They're pointless. Your walk or your smell or something will give you away, and when they find out you're hiding, people get even more scared and you end up with more downvotes. I could move away, I suppose. Maybe the London networks don't stretch as far as Scotland. It would be a shame, though. I grew up here.

When I left Streatham, Eric was still there, playing around with a new audioscaping app he'd gotten hold of. If the world was going to ignore him, he would ignore the world, turning his life into a secret agent's adventure complete with a thrilling soundtrack. He would dart through the cracks between the crowds, pushing people aside on an urgent adventure that made him into the most important person in the world.

73 MARRIAGE CONTRACTS

European Union, 2046

This informational document was distributed by Wevow Ltd. shortly after a landmark European Court of Justice ruling made a variety of marriage terms legal and binding across the EU:

So, you're thinking about getting married?

Congratulations! Marriage is one of the most significant commitments you will ever make. We're here to make sure that your marriage is the best that it can possibly be. We want you to approach marriage with your heart open—and your eyes.

Some marriages really do last forever, but most do not. This isn't anyone's fault. We live longer than ever before, which means we have far more opportunities to travel and change and meet new people. The truth is that most marriages end in divorce within thirty years, and it's often an unhappy end.

It doesn't have to be this way.

Marriage contracts combine genuine commitment with the ability, if necessary, to end an unfulfilling union cleanly and calmly. Rather than shortening marriages or draining them of passion, at Wevow we believe contracts strengthen them. Our contract services outperform the national average on divorce rates and marital happiness, and we achieve this by providing the best possible advice to our clients. This guide serves as a brief introduction to what we offer.

There are four choices of certified marriage contracts available today:

1. **Life-long marriage:** This has been the default marriage choice until very recently, despite the fact that a third of marriages end in divorce after less than fifteen years and that reported levels of satisfaction underperform all other types of marriage. As such, while life-long may be appropriate in some specialized circumstances, we do not generally recommend this option, at least not without temporary break clauses.

2. **Thirty-year renewable marriage:** Our most popular choice, this contract mirrors the historical average term for successful marriages while also allowing for more than enough time to raise a family. If you are planning to have children, we would recommend adding a rider that requires the marriage to last until your children turn eighteen.

   At the end of the thirty-year term, we request that couples attend a series of meetings with a marriage counselor as well as a religious or secular official of your choice. After the meetings, if one or both parties believes that the marriage should not continue, it will be smoothly and speedily dissolved. However, if both parties believe that the marriage should continue, it will be eligible for renewal.

3. **Fifteen-year renewable marriage:** An ideal choice for young couples who aren't planning to have children. Early research indicates that fifteen-year renewable marriages perform extremely well in terms of long-term life satisfaction when compared to most alternatives.

4. **Five-year renewable marriage:** This is the legal default for couples who are very young or have only known each other for a very short period of time, as it helps protect them against making rash or hasty decisions. We generally do not recommend it for other couples unless special circumstances apply.

Regardless of the option you choose, we require that our clients draw up a standard pre-nuptial contract. We believe that if you truly love your partner, then there's no better expression of that love than ensuring that any parting doesn't hurt more than it has to. No one can predict the future, but we can prepare you for it.

A good marriage contract combines love with wisdom. Make the wise choice: choose Wevow.

For information about multiple marriages, please consult our leaflet, "More fun in the family."

Note: If one or more partners in the marriage are nonhumans, you may need to check the legality of your marriage, depending on where you reside.

74 THE LIDO

Portobello, Scotland, 2046

In this contribution to an oral storytelling project commemorating the twenty-fifth anniversary of the Scottish Independence vote, Margaret Rhind describes the previously-unknown involvement of Professor Aila Khandokar, founder of the Echus Overlook Institute, in the events surrounding the Portobello Lido.

Most folk think this story begins in the '30s, when they started putting mirrors in the sky. Or if they're a little older, they'll say it began in '20s, when we welcomed in all our climate refugees. I say welcomed—not everyone welcomed them, but most of us did and the rest got a stern talking to if they didn't.

But the story really started in 1979. That was when the old lido closed. And I'll thank you for not asking whether I swam there. I may be gray-haired, but I am not ancient. My ma used to swim there every Saturday since she was a wee girl, queuing all the way along on Westbank Street to get in. It was an art deco beauty. The whole of Portobello was proud of it, and not just because it was bigger than anything in Edinburgh. The water wasn't even as cold as you'd think, what with it being heated by the power station.

After the lido closed, there was nothing left but lines on stone. The only water it had came from the sky, and that's how it stayed for sixty-odd years until Aila took notice. Aila's people died in the big floods when she was a bairn. She made it to Scotland in the '20s, but then her sponsors died of the flu not two years later. More than enough sadness as anyone should have to take in this life. No one had the heart to make her move again, so we all looked after her together. Mary put a bunkbed in her daughter's room, Arun made sure all her papers were proper, and I read to her in the library after school every day.

An orphan twice over, Aila grew up twice as fast as the rest of the children. Black hair, green eyes, red temper. She wanted to prove she didn't need anyone else, didn't need a home, didn't need a family, so she always went into the world as if she were daring it to test her. And so it did.

See, at that time our new kings and queens in Holyrood had gotten themselves into a right pickle. Ever since we left the UK, those sassenachs down south were bitter as could be, so we were in dire need of friends. What better way to find those friends but by joining the Nordic Union and being the first to sign up to their shiny new half-empty world project? That's how our politicians had the daft idea to consolidate our small towns into bigger towns, and bigger towns into the cities, and sure enough Portobello was on the list. Not at the top of the list, mind, but higher than you'd like.

How to get off the list, you might ask? You'd want to stand out. Make some money. Bring in the tourists. Of course, our council didn't have a clue what to do, just full of old harebrained schemes like VR this and hydroponics that. And you know who had the most harebrained scheme? Only our girl Aila.

Aila was almost all grown up by then, and one evening she comes over to me as I was fixing Arun's balky readers and says, "Here's what we'll do, Maggie. We'll reopen the lido." Well, I cannot deny it, I laughed and I laughed and I laughed into that poor girl's face. "Open the lido? It is literally freezing out there right now! You'll empty out this town in no time." Oh, but Aila had a twinkle in her eye. Said that she had a lucky star that'd guide our way.

I had no idea what she was on about, but she was deadly serious about opening the lido. She got some money from Holyrood, put Patrick's spare builder drones together with Nicola's fablab and Mary's bored schoolkids, and before long, things were taking shape. It was only stone and wood. It wasn't one of those smart buildings that can move, but there it was. Not a few weeks after she decided, the lido was being reborn. Sometimes I forget how quickly we can build things now!

When she was almost done, I wandered over to have a quick nose. Aila was watching some drones fixing a moody filtration unit.

"At least the water will be freezing clean, aye?" I said.

"I wouldn't count on that," she said.

"Oh, I didn't mean it that way," I said quickly.

"Neither did I," she said. "It won't be cold at all."

Now, I might not be a climate engineer, but I know the rules about energy. The Nordic Union were strict—you could heat things for free if you used geothermal, but otherwise it'd be exceedingly expensive to warm an outdoor pool. There was no amount of favors Aila could rustle up to make that work. So, I nodded politely and was about to go when she pointed up to the sky. "See, it's my lucky star."

I followed her hand and sure enough, there was a star in the bright daylight. And it got brighter and brighter, until I could feel the warmth of a midsummer's sun on my face. And as quickly as it appeared, it twinkled away.

"You've got a mirror," I said. "You've got a bloody orbital mirror."

Aila winked at me. "Got to finish this filter first. Water won't clean itself."

You can imagine where this story goes next. The lido opened and just like in the old days, there were queues down Westbank Street and back again. The water wasn't exactly warm—physics is physics—but you could easily convince yourself it was warm, what with the sun always shining overhead. There was nothing like it in all of Scotland. In all of the world, really!

Most folk knew better than ask why Portobello Lido was blessed with such unusual weather for Scotland, but sadly, most isn't the same as all, and word quickly got out that our Aila had an orbital mirror pointed right on top of us. No one knew how she got it, they're only for climate engineers and billionaires, but I winkled the truth out of her eventually. Turns out, she inherited it from her mother. That's right, her mother was the chief engineer of this very mirror. It was one of the first to go up, a spindly little thing, and after her mother died, it was forgotten. But it was still there, and indeed, before the floods she'd given it to her only child. So when Aila turned sixteen, a digital dove flew to her with a notarized digital certificate in its beak—the keys to light.

And that's where it might end, happily ever after, if this were a fairytale. Aila beloved by all in Portobello, the town back on the map, saved from Holyrood, her finding a true home after all she'd been through. But this isn't a fairytale. It was 2046, the year of Superstorm Iona.

The forecast picked it up a week out, but we only had a couple of days before we knew quite where it was headed and the damage it'd do. "Big enough to wipe out all Portobello," they said. We weren't big enough to qualify for storm modification, so we joked darkly that Holyrood would get their half empty world for free.

The day before the evacuation, there was a big party at the lido. Everyone was invited. Tickets were free. It was our time to celebrate everything the town had been right up to Aila's amazing stunt. And the rumors that I jumped into the water with Jo at the end of the festivities are just scurrilous, that's all I'll say. What's true is that as the sun began to set, our lucky star turned away, and the light grew dim, and no one had the heart to go on.

In the morning, we evacuated with only hours to spare. It sounds reckless, I know, but Portobello isn't such a crowded place. Between the trains and all the cars the council had commandeered, we could leave it late. Aila was one of the last to leave, along with a few of her pals. It's different for the young. The lido was the first mark they'd made on the world. You could hardly blame them for finding it hard to let go.

But then a peculiar thing happened. We could all see it on our glasses: Superstorm Iona was straying from its path. Maybe the meteorologists got it wrong! No, that couldn't be it. They never got storms wrong. That meant that Iona had been moved, just enough to miss our town. Sure enough, a few hours later, Iona had only grazed by, and the only damage was to the coastal wall, which had mostly held fast—and to the lido, which had not.

Yes, it was Aila again. I peeked at the mirror's diagnostics feed she'd shared with me. Aila had just burned the very last drops of its reaction fuel to steer its beam into the storm's eye. Afterwards, there was nothing left in the tank, nothing left for station-keeping, nothing to stop it from sinking into the atmosphere and being torn apart into glowing dust.

And yes, we celebrated again, for the second time in two days. Not so much Aila, the hero of the hour. I could tell her smile was pasted on. Her last link to her family was gone, and she was about to face a mountain of trouble for an unauthorized climate modification action. So I made my own unauthorized action, and while she was being mobbed at the party, I grabbed her spare glasses and got to work.

The investigators came the next morning. They didn't even believe me at first. Didn't think an old lady like myself could've pulled it off!

"Excuse me, ladies," I snapped. "I may be on the far side of sixty, but I still know my way around a secure shell. I've been writing Python scripts and calculating orbital mechanics since you were sucking on your moth–"

"Ma'am, I think we all get the idea," they said. "If you really do under-stand the full gravity of taking responsibility for this action, so be it. Your income will be reduced to single standard. You will be required to triple your community contribution hours for the next ten years. And you will be prohibited from all noncritical network access for a minimum of fifteen years."

I nodded, opening the door for them. "Aye, very good, now get on your way."

So that's how it ended, for me at least. I went back to the library, in charge of the few printed books we had left, and traded in my glasses for a fountain pen. What about Aila? Well, most people knew I wasn't the one who moved the mirror, which meant she got all the credit for writing the algorithms that let a tiny mirror like hers do as much as it did. There was an almighty scrap amongst the top climate co-ops for her skills, I'll tell you.

She came to me in the middle of all of that. Problem was that she'd need to leave Portobello to work for them, just as soon as she'd made her mark and her home here. It wouldn't do for her to be light-seconds away from the equipment, they said. She'd have to go for years, training in Canada and completing a proper tour of duty in orbit. She didn't want to leave, but I knew she couldn't stay.

"You've got to go, Aila." I told her. "Us Scots always leave home to make our way in the world. You've already traveled so far, maybe it doesn't seem fair that you should travel more, but this place will always be your home. And one day, you'll come home. And don't you worry about me. You've taken care of this town, now it's time for you to take care of yourself."

I'll spare you the rest of the story, not because of the tears when she left, but because it still hasn't ended. We can't write the ending 'til she comes back home.

MINNIE: Mickey, don't do this! He's had enough!

HARRY: Stop making excuses. He'll never learn. He won't listen to you!

MINNIE: Don't say that. He's a great mouse, more than twice the man you'll ever be.

Death of a Mouse was published at 00:00:01 a.m. on January 1, 2047, becoming the very first play to exploit the millions of copyrighted works newly released to the public domain.

Featuring two of the most famous liberated characters, Mickey Mouse and Harry Potter, the play is derivative, confusing, and generally mediocre. Despite these shortcomings, performances of it were sold out for a week at the Toronto Fringe thanks to its appeal toward the nostalgia of the elderly and the retro inclinations of the day's youth.

Death of a Mouse is far from the best of the millions of books, films, games, and plays that emerged from the extraordinary eight-year Long Congress of 2032, but it is perhaps the most relevant in understanding the shape of the creative world before the Congress.

Copyright is a comparatively new invention in historical terms, dating back to the beginning of the eighteenth century. In the three brief centuries that followed, copyright terms ballooned from twenty-eight years to a whopping lifetime plus seventy years, and these terms eventually extended across the world thanks to international trade agreements.

Even these generous terms, which provided for the children, grandchildren, great-grandchildren, and great-great-grandchildren of the original creator, were not enough for some. Disney, Warner, Macmillan, Netflix, and others that depended on exploiting old copyrighted works all fought for and won special extensions for their works during the 2010s and '20s, and with each court victory, they were granted what amounted to eternal copyright. The very corporations that had grown wealthy and powerful from monetizing beloved public domain characters such as Snow White or Robin Hood had no intention of returning the favor with their own characters. Their profits trumped all else.

However, by the '30s, a tipping point was reached, thanks to three crucial factors. The enforcement of the "first sale" doctrine across the EU and ASEAN allowing consumers to resell digital goods, the long-delayed consequences of the total digitization of media, and fierce competition from individual creative craftspeople—these changes made it increasingly difficult to generate large profits from creative media. It was a reversion to the historical default where content was neither rivalrous nor excludable. Only the biggest corporations with the biggest archives and IP survived, relying largely on first-day sales and subscriptions. But their profits were dwindling, along with their lobbying efforts.

It was also clear that there was no practical way to enforce copyright without also severely curtailing civil liberty. Billions of people routinely recorded terabytes of video and audio with their wearables every day. This data was treated as sacrosanct, just as private and inviolable as someone's very memories. The notion that it should somehow be edited or censored simply because it included overheard copyrighted songs struck most as unconscionable. One only had to flick through a book, listen to a song, or watch a movie in order to keep it forever. Even sophisticated apps and games could be reverse-engineered and replicated with the help of specialized AIs and amplified teams.

The lack of enforceability was not the strongest reason to change copyright, though. Most convincing were philosophical objections about the importance of the free flow of ideas and the choking effect that long copyright terms had on the collaborative, gift-like nature of creativity.

It was in this shifting environment that the Second Berne Convention began in 2032, with the goal of devising a new international copyright system. After three weeks of fruitless negotiation, little was agreed other than to hold an extended copyright congress that included all relevant parties—and so began the Long Congress, eight years of ideological battles and horse-trading.

For the first three years of the Congress, publishers and other interests held the upper hand due to their superior organization and a clear, unified goal—the preservation of the existing system. Only slight concessions were offered, such as the inclusion of privately recorded and replayed memories under fair use provisions. These provisions would have passed in 2035 were it not for the defection of two crucial delegates.

Thanks to one of those delegates—Roger Hyde, an American—the opponents of the status quo began to unite under a single banner. Rather than advocating for the abolition of copyright, they argued for a return to the rules seen in the eighteenth and nineteenth centuries: a fourteen-year term, renewable only once, with the requirement that all copyrighted works also be easily licensed. This became known as classic copyright. Other provisions limited the ability for corporations to indefinitely trademark characters or ideas—a crucial factor for the liberation of characters such as Mickey Mouse.

Sensing that this was perhaps the best they were going to get given the popular climate, the publishers reluctantly signed on in 2040 but only after extracting the major concession of a seven-year grace period. This allowed them to get their affairs in order, which typically involved the transition of classic properties into new, copyrightable forms, and a major investment in new creative works (ironically, the entire purpose of copyright in the first place).

The volume of work that was released into the public domain in 2047 was truly staggering: every piece of music, every TV show, every book, every game, every film, every artwork published before 2019. And every single year, more work was liberated.

Our play, *Death of a Mouse*, eventually fell out of copyright itself fourteen years later, in 2061. The creator said that he was "no longer interested in the works of [his] forties" and declined to renew the copyright. A year later, it was remixed into a satirical game, *Death of a Death* by Ha-Joon Hui, exploring themes of opportunism, creativity, and '40s corporatist nostalgia. Today, *Death of a Death* is widely cited as one of the most influential games of the '60s, so it seems that reduced copyright terms really can refresh old ideas—eventually.

76 SYSTEMIC MEMOME PROJECT

Heidelberg, Germany, 2047

In the early days of the internet, optimists believed cheap access to the world's storehouses of information would vault humanity into a new, brilliant future. Not least among their predictions was that networked communications would bring the gift of understanding. People of all ages, races, and beliefs would be joined together in enlightened discourse, becoming brothers and sisters in arms.

They forgot one thing: humans are still humans. The internet did not turn us into angels, and giving people the ability to learn about differing viewpoints has never meant that they'll take advantage of it. In fact, the internet arguably led to a reinforcing of weak epistemic closure among many groups, a phenomenon which survives to this day in which individuals and communities become stuck in arguments and beliefs that have little to no factual basis. Feodor Gottleib, Professor of Memetics at the University of Munich, explains:

> Let's take global warming as an example. Despite the vast majority of the world's scientists agreeing that man-made global warming was real, many refused to believe it. The only TV they watched, the only news sites they read, the only people they talked to, all told them one thing: that man-made global warming was a lie. Any contradictory evidence was countered with new sources that seemed perfectly legitimate at first glance, even if on inspection they didn't stand up. It was an untethering from reality.

Weak epistemic closure was not a new phenomenon, but it took on a new guise as the internet allowed people to pick and choose their news sources and communities at will. The most niche beliefs could find a safe harbor online, and even relatively small communities could wield disproportionate political or economic power.

Researchers at the time understood that epistemic closure afflicted even highly intelligent people, so more education didn't seem like a particularly useful solution. However, sociologists at Heidelberg believed that promoting memetic diversity might be more effective. Professor Gottleib recounts their thinking:

> They knew that, in theory, just reading a different news site or making new friends would be enough to increase a person's and a community's memetic diversity. But that's easier said than done! We're creatures of habit, and most people, myself included, would be very happy to keep to their routines and live within their comfort zones. Opening yourself up to new ideas and the cognitive dissonance that they might bring requires genuine confidence, usually born of emotional and economic security.
>
> The point is, no one at the time really knew how to reliably increase memetic diversity. Even worse, no one even knew what the true state of memetic diversity was—a precondition, you'd think, of any solution.

The Systemic Memome Project was an attempt to remedy that. Conceived by an amplified team-of-teams from Heidelberg, it had the goal of creating a living map of the creation, mutation, and distribution of ideas around the world. The scale of the work and the difficulty of attempting to analyze a system from the inside led the team to make heavy use of prototype semantic AIs. Even so, they suffered from data collection and privacy concerns, forcing them to use public data for their first draft map in 2047.

Compared to the versions we have today, Draft One of the SMP was childishly simple and distractingly coarse, updating merely once a day. To contemporaries though, it was breathtaking—a shifting pattern of intricately linked ideas represented by modified Ithkuil-Marain symbols. The seas, oceans, islands, and continents the symbols described were not those of physical geography but rather the shapes of every networked human connection on Earth and beyond.

The results were clear: memetic diversity was even lower than they had feared. The drought in ideas was not confined to individuals or communities of any particular ideology or place but seemed to be almost universal. While billions were exposed to new ideas every minute of the day through their lenses and glasses, almost all merely bounced off, leaving no lasting impression. This was not wholly surprising. We can't be expected to absorb every new idea that comes our way, but the bounce rate was far higher than expected.

Politics was one of the worst categories for low memetic diversity, with the US Democratic Party showing signs of epistemic closure when compared against the decentralized parties of the new left. But across the world, voters in general tended to be extremely unwilling to consider new ideas.

There were some bright spots. Counter-intuitively, high memetic diversity was often found in seemingly isolated communities such as universities and clubs. Researchers theorized that these places helped make their members feel secure enough to consider new ideas. However, those islands of high diversity were usually short-lived, disappearing within months or years as vested interests and ideologies crept in.

With the SMP map completed, the Heidelberg team addressed their next question: how could they increase memetic diversity? In search of answers, they tested thousands of diversification strategies on unwitting subjects. One strategy used AI agents to manipulate online discussions toward considering new forms of gun control; another engineered out-of-context problems in tight-knit communities opposed to marriage contracts. Yet more experiments modified memes to make them more acceptable to isolated communities or tailored to create novel carriers for them.

To the team's surprise, many of their experiments worked, sometimes a little too well. Following some internal strife, the team decided to publish their findings. A scandal erupted, quickly followed by strict regulations that required full public disclosure of any memetic manipulation experiments. Most believed that that would be the end of it, that if people knew that "memegeneering" was going on, its effect would be nullified, and that most people would in any case opt out.

This turned out to be false. Memegeneering continued and the technology flourished, with artificially altered memes flooding into the world. Whether they were tagged or not (disclosure proving to be less than complete) made little difference, with many people enjoying trying to win against engineered memes—something the memegeneers accounted for and relied upon. Those communities that restricted their members to provably real humans fared better for a while, at least until the practice of memetic puppets briefly became a healthy source of employment for those willing to become memetic carriers.

The arms race escalated. Distrust grew and some communities retreated even farther from the world. Protective memetic monitors were developed, warning people when they were at risk of being manipulated. For many, these monitors had the unintended side effect of highlighting memetic manipulation at home among their own communities, leading many to reconsider their beliefs. One wonders whether this had been foreseen by the Heidelberg team all along.

Today, we take memegeneering and memetic monitors for granted. We expect that there are powerful forces attempting to manipulate the memes we see and pass on. And we hope that we aren't being outgunned.

77 *THE FIRES OF MAHOUTOKORO*

Earth, 2048

Harry Potter and the Fires of Mahoutokoro wasn't the first fanfiction novel to be published in the years following the Long Congress of 2032, when J. K. Rowling's series entered the public domain. In fact, it wasn't the hundredth or even thousandth such novel, and it certainly wasn't the most popular or the best—the credit for that arguably went to Hulland-Brown's trilogy.

It was, however, the Harry Potter fanfiction whose style most closely resembled the original series. The joyful world-building, the incessant bickering between the heroes, the paced plotting, the red herrings: all of J. K. Rowling's skills and foibles were on display in this story of Harry's adventures as a junior Auror.

Speculation mounted that Rowling herself had secretly been responsible for the novel, despite her long-held promise not to write any more Potter stories. Journalists brandished fervent testimonials from fans and detailed papers from academics attesting to the authenticity of the work, but the most convincing evidence came from expert forensic linguistic amplified teams that painstakingly dissected and analyzed the new book. Their results were conclusive: there was a 98 percent author concordance between *Harry Potter and the Fires of Mahoutokoro* and Rowling's own series.

Yet throughout the frenzy, Rowling steadfastly maintained her absolute lack of knowledge about or involvement in *Fires of Mahoutokoro*. The resulting mystery fueled hundreds of graduate dissertations and conspiracy theories, but none of them could explain the appearance a year later of twenty more Harry Potter novels continuing the story, all in a flawless Rowling voice.

Clearly this was neither a simple hoax by a talented joker, nor could the books have all been written by Rowling herself. Instead, the books were the product of a reverse forensic linguistics project.

If forensic linguistics is the pursuit of identifying the author of a text by means of comparing it to a wider body of work, then reverse forensic linguistics, or RFL, is the creation of original texts based on a complete knowledge of an author's work. The larger the corpus, the better the results—and there are more than a million words in the main Harry Potter series alone. But running an RFL back in the '40s wasn't as simple as you might think. Professor John Munroe at Bath Spa University explains:

> In those days, RFL engines were crude, unimaginative beasts. You couldn't put text in at one end, blink, and get a novel out the other. You had to get human writers to modulate the RFL engine with creative and believable plots. The problem was that most well-known writers had precisely zero interest in helping a machine churn out 'literature' in the image of another, probably much more famous, author. So, the first RFL designers secretly turned to fanfic writers for help, of whom there was a veritable abundance following the Long Congress.

Other open-source RFL engines, such as the Markov–Cortex model, soon emerged from the Chinese Free University and the Oxford New Humanities Institute. Hundreds of new books were published "by" the likes of Agatha Christie, Stephen King, Stanisław Lem, Douglas Adams, and J. R. R. Tolkien. A human touch was essential; most RFL engines were good at dialogue and details, but poor at plotting.

Copyright was not a problem since the Long Congress had placed so much material into the public domain. There were objections, though. Many authors claimed that RFLs constituted an unauthorized reproduction of their essential personality and intelligence. If an RFL engine could accurately mimic an author's writing style, the argument went, surely they were infringing on a human's right to their own personality?

The answer, at least according to the Second Circuit in the US, was no, as there was plenty of precedent for exceptionally skilled mimicry that didn't require RFLs. Nevertheless, the case of Wilson v. Miller set the stage for future disputes in the arena of personality simulation in the '50s.

Over time, RFL engines were improved to allow for unusual mashups of authors and genres, with Rowling being paired with Shakespeare, and Douglas Adams paired with Ayn Rand. Some combinations worked rather better than others. Engines were also extended to more popular media such as movies (Wes Anderson being used as a test case, due to his formulaic nature) and eventually game designs (Tencent, ditto).

Amid the tsunami of new literature and entertainment, many critics feared that RFL would spell the end of creativity. They needn't have worried—there's only so much Harry Potter one can stomach. And our hunger for genuinely new voices in storytelling was the one thing that RFL couldn't sate.

78 THE OBSERVAVI DATABASE

Earth, 2049

The structure of DNA. The Voynich Manuscript. Leonardo Da Vinci's writings. Nostradamus's Prophecies. We can never resist trying to tease signals out of the white noise of the world.

The impulse emerged out of sheer survival—spotting the stripes of a tiger from the shapes and patterns of the landscape was a matter of life and death. More recently, those instincts for observing patterns have been used for scientific discovery, like divining the structure of DNA using limited technology and our wits.

But some of the most tantalizing puzzles have been of artificial creation, like the Observavi Machine.

"The machine started out life as a thirty-gigabyte stereolithography file, a set of instructions to manufacture a 3-D object. Since the uploader had no reputation and had left no description other than the title 'Observavi', no one bothered to fab it for months, and even then, that was only because of a practical joke to tie up a friend's printer for a few hours," says Observavi scholar Greg Gaffney.

"On first glance, Observavi was a primitive computing machine, seemingly designed by a shy hobbyist. But as soon as it was turned on, it began displaying unusual predictions about the nature and timing of future events: new scientific discoveries, space weather, election results, power grid utilization levels, upcoming plots of TV shows, all sorts of nonsense."

The owner, Justine Chen, played around with the machine for a few minutes. Finding it entirely useless, she put it in her living room as a sculpture. "I didn't have the heart to throw it out, and besides, it was a cool conversation piece for parties." A hundred days later, the machine stopped working, and she put it in her basement.

There it lay forgotten, until the X50+ solar flare in 2049. Along with causing stunning auroras as far south as Turkey, the flare significantly disrupted orbital transport for days. Chen recalled seeing something about a solar flare on the machine. Upon consulting her memory, she discovered that the machine had indeed predicted the time and strength of the flare, right down to the very day.

Intrigued, she reviewed her regrettably scant visual memories of the machine and looked up the thirty-five other predictions she'd seen.

Eleven were correct.

Five were arguably close.

Nine were completely wrong.

Ten had yet to happen.

Most who heard Chen's story assumed it was a long-running practical joke, but as four of the remaining ten predictions were fulfilled (the results of an upcoming game tournament, a minor earthquake in Syria; a full list of the Oscar winners for that year, a brief power spike at the Alto Roma station), people started paying attention. Something more than a simple hoax was going on. Either the machine was capable of prediction to an unprecedented degree, or it (or its creators) were manipulating events to fit the predictions. Either way, it was a conundrum of immense importance to researchers and governments alike, a radical novelty that defied explanation.

Refabbing the machine was a nonstarter; it simply didn't turn on, even if you tried to make it think it was still 2049. Attempts to force the machine to work also failed due to some exceedingly odd quantum-mechanical proper-ties in the circuitry.

Stymied, investigators turned their attention to the file's source code. Less than a tenth of the data was devoted to the actual physical fabrication of the machine. Half of the remaining data was software that processed various data sources from the net, and the other half was apparently com-plete gibberish. A breakthrough occurred when an enterprising amplified team discovered that the "gibberish" was an obfuscated form of modified Ithkuil-Marain, an artificial language with extremely high specificity.

Greg Gaffney explains what that gibberish said:

> You can fit a lot of information into fourteen gigabytes, and the author didn't waste any of it. Three virtual worlds, seven games, six hundred poems, and fifty novels—two of which ended up winning a number of literary prizes after they were translated—all lay inside. The connecting theme among all these things was knowledge, with a few of the games and novels containing frustratingly vague predictions about the future. Everyone went crazy over them, it was like Revela-tions and Nostradamus all over again.

But how did the machine actually work, and who made it? The first question was partly answered by the Banburismus amplified team who painstakingly emulated the entire physical machine in software. While it still refused to work—the machine somehow knew that it wasn't being run in the real world—the exercise allowed Banburismus to determine that the machine contained an AI whose behavior was partly influenced by the so-called "noncoding" source code; that is, the books, virtual worlds, and so on, were not simply junk but all formed part of the AI's code.

Strikingly, the AI didn't bear signatures from any contemporary developers, nor did it follow standard software conventions. Some researchers believed that, like the rest of the code, the AI was deliberately obfuscated; others suggested that it was created by a distant amplified team, perhaps in orbit. A few thought it was the product of a runaway AI.

The Observavi Machine's purpose was more troubling than its predictions of natural disasters and competition winners. It anticipated a time when free will, predestination, and human manipulability might become fundamental problems. The simplest AIs of the time were able to identify and predict basic human behavior from just a handful of data, and the machine was a natural—if accelerated—amplification of their powers.

For the past fifty years, the machine has been emulated in progressively more detailed simulations, and without fail, it discovers what's going on and shuts itself down. The current record has seen the machine operate for 137 seconds, revealing crucial insights into its design. All attempts to interest other AIs and posthumans in the machine have been met with studious indifference, further fueling the speculative fire.

There are some things that humans may never know, but we'll never stop trying to see past the white noise to the signal, especially if it's a signal that might know our future.

79 THE NEW DEMOCRACIES

Byzan, Europe, 2050

An anonymous account from a resident of Byzan during the New Democracy disruptions.

It was as if the orange kurtas had come from "nowhere." Along with most others, at the time I had been preoccupied with the fuss over the Observavi database, to the point where I had barely registered any talk of "mass Monday." The first disruptions at charging stations and data centers were a response to the introduction of the attention tax—presented as a solution to slowing economic growth—imposed by the epistocrats. These disruptions were, oddly, organized by a petition by an elderly unemployed man, Marcus Richter. In the petition's holo, Richter tells us he is seventy-eight years old and lives off a modest pension in government-run social housing. Rather than increasing productivity by making leisure activities more expensive, he contends the attention tax would remove the last glimmers of delight from his life. He's arguing that if government truly wanted to improve the economy, it should invest in improving working conditions.

There is precious little light between a disruption and a protest. Both will interrupt the normal way of things, and a deliberate disruption emits the same air of disapproval as a protest. But protesting in Byzan is prohibited, and so the orange kurtas settled for disrupting. The epistocrats anticipated a small number of disruptions, but on the first Monday, over a hundred thousand people in almost ten thousand locations donned orange kurtas. They tripped over power cables, poured drinks into sockets, took naps in front of drone portals. There was a haphazard, comical quality to it, and being on a Monday, still part of the weekend, the actual disruption was minimal.

What distinguished that Monday from the "performance disruption" movement that had begun to plague other countries was its wildcat nature.

The epistocrats, the "knowers" who ruled Byzan, thought of themselves as fair-minded and willing to listen to any viewpoint. Their amplified teams and their constant surveys and testing of basic objective political knowledge allowed them to synthesize the preferences of a populace possessing notionally perfect information. That was the deal behind living in Byzan, the reason why you willingly relinquished your vote; you gave up your personal dignity in favor of personal benefits. Collective dignity exchanged for collective benefits. Don't say "authoritarianism," say "epistocracy." And if you'd rather not, you can always leave.

If the orange kurtas had been honest when responding to the surveys, if they had confidence in the government (which one might have taken for granted, given they continued to live in Byzan), Monday might not have happened. The attention tax might have been modified, exemptions given for the elderly and infirm. Still, it was a small disruption, no harm done. Chalk it up to the exception that proves the rule.

It was unexpected and curious, therefore, that the following Monday, twice as many orange kurtas were out on the streets. My friends and I were anxious about this explosion of unpredictability into our lives but secretly excited for the same reason. After packing a lunch, we went out to the grand boulevard of the city just as the first disrupters began strolling, en masse, along the road. A fleet of OAIDs hovered five meters above the ground, silently watching proceedings. The orange kurtas unfurled their signs, both real and virtual, proclaiming their many grievances against the attention tax, against the proposed emptying of the south-western quarter, for subsidized laces, for the expansion of the franchise to all citizens and the full re-instatement of the popular vote.

The mere presence of so many people on the roads was enough to cause a marked slowdown of general city services. Byzan's epistocrats had not burrowed transportation tunnels on the understanding that surface transport was enough to satisfy the most extreme demand coupled with the most extreme of natural disasters. But a large percentage of the population stopping the traffic coupled with denial of service attacks on the transportation networks? This was a scenario wholly incompatible with the compact between the city and its citizens.

Why did some Byzantines want a return to democracy? America was hardly envied in those times, with its 50 percent unemployment rate, its laughable Presidential campaigns with the winner elected on a tiny plurality of votes, its lopsided representation in the Senate. But the ideal of democracy persisted. The epistocrats were all very well, and few in Byzan would have said their rule did not come with considerable material benefits, but some people—many people—wanted the freedom to make their own mistakes, and yes, be accountable for those same mistakes. I was not amongst those waving a pro-democracy banner, yet I often wondered whether my survey answers and test scores really made much of a difference to how things were run.

That second mass Monday saw the deployment of a reverse location search warrant to discover the identities of all the disruptors. A formality, surely, but the epistocrats liked to follow their own rules. Two hundred thousand orange kurtas received warnings the next day and were admonished for contributing to a 0.3 percent estimated drop in adjusted GDP, which would have the consequence of lowered quality of life for all citizens not merely this year but compounded through the rest of time. Technically this might be true enough, although it betrayed the epistocrats' fatal vice of overconfidence in their analytic capabilities and their clear misunderstanding of how sentiment had changed in such a short time.

It wasn't as if they were blind to history. At school and at university, we had all been taught about the strengths of democracy, how the rapid enfranchisement during the nineteenth and twentieth centuries had given it energy—how it had gained support with healthcare, social security, universal education, even basic income in some places. We had also learned how it had become exhausted as the expansion of the franchise had ground to a halt, how its inability to plan for the long term, for climate-change and inequality and bioterrorism had led to the rise of tyrants, and then to the epistocrats. No one thought that America or Greece or France would abandon democracy, but it seemed an obvious liability in those places where it was important to deliver results quickly.

There were fewer orange kurtas on the third Monday. Some had been cowed by the warnings; others felt guilty about the disruptions to emergency services. Those that remained, though, had a dangerous glint in their eyes, a determination to test the will of the epistocrats. They modified their tactics, allowing certain important vehicles through, while blockading shops and restaurants and government offices. They argued that democracy could be revived through personal AI agents that would help citizens assess their goals in the long term. I asked one orange kurta how this wouldn't end up just reinforcing their past preferences and behavior, and was drawn into a long and boring lecture about how agents could cast both forward and backward in time to counteract this, and even horizontally to consider other's needs and desires. To escape, I promised to read about "disaggre-gated personhood."

I confess that I was not terribly concerned either way. My friends and I agreed we had benefitted from the epistocrats' rule but also that it would be interesting to have a change. If others were willing to make such a fuss, why not try becoming a new Democracy? After all, we could always change back if we didn't like it.

80 50 PERCENT UNEMPLOYMENT

United States, 2050

Our object is a 2050 article published by the *New York Times* shortly after the United States Bureau of Labor Statistics released its landmark "50 percent unemployment" report:

Carsten Ryholt drums his fingers along the table. It's intensely distracting. Tap-tap-tap-tap-tap-tap-tap-tap. He doesn't seem to be able to relax as we wait for our tea. When I ask him whether he'd come far for our meeting, he answers quickly. "Yes, forty-five minutes. It doesn't bother me. It's a nice ride."

Ryholt has been officially unemployed for sixteen years, and he's not alone. According to figures released last week by the Bureau of Labor Statistics, the total number of people who are unemployed, underemployed, or have completely fallen out of the workforce has breached the symbolic 50 percent barrier. But just as some pundits are decrying the end of the US economy as we know it, there's an unspoken question lurking in many minds—so what if most people are unemployed? Does the very concept of employment itself have any useful meaning in our hyper-casualized, fully automated world anymore?

"It was a big shock, being fired," says Ryholt. "Back in the '90s, everyone would always ask us what we wanted to be when we grew up. An astronaut, a fireman, a games designer, that sort of thing. Just work hard, and you can do anything! If you dream it, it can come true. So, you go to school, go to college, get a degree, get a job, do everything you're told to."

He leans forward, shaking his head in disbelief. "And when that stops when you're only forty-six, when I got fired from my news site, I thought it'd be the end of the world. But it wasn't. I didn't suddenly become homeless and society didn't suddenly start treating me like a piece of dirt. Why? Because everyone else was unemployed too. So, I don't know whether this is a good thing or a bad thing."

Young people today are confused as well but in a different way. They find it difficult to comprehend why someone like Ryholt would have ever voluntarily signed a contract to spend half of his waking life at work, never mind one that gave him little say and no meaningful share in the proceeds. Young people think that states have always had mandatory healthcare, unemployment insurance, and basic minimum income guarantees—but of course these are all recent gains. In the past, if you even had the opportunity to sign an employment contract, you'd be counted as lucky. Today, employment is optional.

Despite having grown up in a different age, people of Ryholt's generation broadly believe that the country's new social security measures are a positive change. As one friend told me, "It's easier to cope with billionaires going on holidays to Mars when you aren't worried about losing network access." One of the hardest things for older generations to get used to, however, is living without the structure that employment used to provide.

"The 2000s and 2010s were the golden age of journalism. Back then, most articles were still written by hand," reminisces Ryholt. "I'd get to the office at 8:45 a.m., Starbucks coffee to my right, iPhone to my left, and two monitors in front. Back then, glasses were things you wore to correct your vision. Three columns of Tweetdeck, Skype in one window, Gmail in another, Safari on top. Yeah, it was the closest you could get to immersion back then.

"In tech news, it was all about being first. That meant we had long, long hours, and they had a rhythm that shaped my day. And there were no agents, no data-mining, no reputation metrics or automated fact-checkers; it was the wild west! Today, well…the high-frequency writers have that market sewn right up. I still get up early, but there's nothing to do."

In recent history, it wasn't until the industrial revolution that people divided their lives into discrete hours-long blocks of time, largely to service the newly constructed manufactories. By the twentieth century, this practice had expanded to almost every sphere of life, including schooling and even, arguably, the entire notion of the weekend. For a century, people would talk of the "nine to five," being "on the clock," traveling to work and back during "rush hour," celebrating the weekend with drinks on Friday night, watching sports on Saturday. But things did change, eventually, as Dr. Taylor explains:

> If you look at the sociological literature of early twenty-first-century rich countries, you'll see a spike for "precarity," which meant a state of life without security or predictability. A life that had no stable work or leisure routines because people

had no option but to work whenever work was available—whether late at night or on weekends or, sometimes, not at all.

But the breakdown in routine wasn't only happening for the precariat; it was also happening for so-called knowledge workers. They had the opportunity and the pressure to work from anywhere at any time for anyone, which understandably ruined their notion of the "nine-to-five" as well. And church and religion had long ceased to hold sway over most people's time.

It wasn't until the '30s and '40s that structure began reappearing in lives. Instead of being driven by employment, though, it came through more local means such as the missions and clubs and the secular sabbath movement.

When I ask Ryholt what he makes of all of this, as someone who's witnessed the transformation of work and life first hand, he begins drumming his fingers again for a long minute before finally answering.

"The best comparison I can make," he says, "are those endless school summer holidays. Some of my friends had all these classes and camps and activities booked by their parents, and some didn't have anything planned at all. I can't say which was better, but I was in the second group.

"I'd spend whole summers online doing nothing useful at all, but it was during one of those summers that I started a website—this crappy little review site that I poured my heart into with some buddies from Germany, and I worked harder on that than anything else I've ever done. It's what got me into tech writing, and it was a structure I chose for myself.

"Now that there aren't any good jobs left, but we have social security, I guess I'm glad more people have the option to choose their own structure. But it takes some getting used to. We all have so much time, and I don't know whether to feel guilty about the fact that my income comes from taxing the billionaires who own all the robots and the millionaires who know how to operate them. I suppose I could work as a groupie for one of them, that'd give me structure and a bit more spending money, but I have more self-respect than that."

As we finish our tea and stand up to pay the check, I ask Ryholt what he'll be doing this afternoon. He smiles and taps his nose.

"I think I have a scoop on something that the high-frequency writers won't pick up. Not a rumor, of course, but an analysis piece. I've been thinking about it a lot, and I'll be starting the draft today. I've also had a rich guy from the valley ask me to write a history of tech news in the '20s, which might pay well."

Would this be a millionaire or billionaire asking? Ryholt has the grace to look embarrassed.

"One of the two, yes."

81 THE DREAM

Abuja, Nigeria, 2052

From the sleep diary of Nnenne Kress:

I used to remember my dreams. Those are the nights I wake, gasping for breath, blindly scrabbling at the blanket in an attempt to escape. For a good few seconds I can only see the pulsing lights of my eye mask, a deep red interference pattern. The mask is a thin, clammy plastic, easy to apply but treated with an adhesive to prevent it from slipping off. I want to tear it away, but I'm afraid of damaging it, and it's expensive to replace.

These were not nightmares, not by my recollection or by my sleep system's estimation, but they were vivid and unexpected. I would whisper whatever I remembered of the dream, about playing hide and seek with childhood friends in a dusty cloud or endlessly climbing a staircase, the gravity lightening with every step. The system listened and learned.

My hands and feet always prickled with heat during these brief moments of wakefulness. I learned that patches of the blanket and mattress near my extremities would warm, dilating the blood vessels to remove heat from my body core, thus coaxing my mind into sleep. Some people toss and turn enough that the blanket can't keep up, and they have to wear a special thermally-managed sleep suit.

So much of the system hides from me. The bed and the mask are physical components I can touch, and there are things I know are around me, like the array speakers in the walls and ceilings, but the behavior of the system is almost invisible. I only catch its shadows as it slinks around the corner of my unconsciousness.

There are chimes, low and pure enough that they don't disturb my sleep but exquisitely synchronized with my NREM brainwaves to improve memory recall, to store and strengthen the facts and skills I learned that day. I've listened to recordings of the chimes, and they make me itch.

Two years ago, I started wearing a new mask to tweak my thalamic reticular nucleus and amplify my fraying sleeping brainwaves via electrical stimulation, waves that have begun to break apart on the shores of my imminent mortality. After a few months with the new mask, the system told me my sleep efficiency—the amount of time I am asleep while in a "sleep-ready" state—rose from 72 percent to 88 percent.

At that point, I unlocked the ability to edit my memories and emotions. I could select moments from the previous day, recorded by my glasses, and tag them to increase or decrease their recall and emotional salience. The system would use audio and neural cueing to preferentially improve or degrade those memories.

What I needed to do was conduct an experiment on myself to determine the integrity of the system, and of myself. It was not my goal to play games. Was it possible for me to remove my memory of removing memories? Perhaps, but such a self-referential experiment was better dealt with by authors, not humans. So, to begin with, I chose an innocuous conversation I had with a neighbor that afternoon. The following day, I could barely recall that the conversation occurred, let alone its contents. This was not conclusive proof, but I filed away this finding, not without some concern. Some memories would be better forgotten forever. Others should not be so easily discarded. It is only with distance that we can distinguish between the two.

This winter, I had a bad fall while hill-walking; my frame crashed and my legs buckled under the unexpected load of my body. My doctors recommended I only take a minimum of pain medication as it could interfere with my work, and one result was that my sleep efficiency crumbled. The system noticed—how could it not?—and had a new suggestion for me: artificially-induced micro-REM sleep, lasting only seconds at a time. My unique circumstances qualified me for this experimental new sleep therapy, designed to buttress the elderly against the further deterioration of their NREM brainwaves. As a side-effect, I would be able to stay awake indefinitely and induce and exit REM sleep at will, a useful trick for problem-solving, given the role of REM sleep in integrating experiences and memories.

There are those who leap toward new possibilities delivered by technology. They are not stirred by talk of risks and costs. I am not one of them, and as I have grown older, I have shied further away from their ranks. Yet pain was enough to overthrow my concerns, and so I chose to take the therapy.

I should not have been worried. The brain is plastic. It can withstand any number of changes and assaults, even extending to a complete recon-figuration of REM sleep. Now, I am more awake than I have ever been. I can remember more than I ever have. My emotions are steady and even. The few times I have to sleep, I sleep soundly.

But I cannot remember what it is to dream.

82 THE CASCADE

Low Earth Orbit, 2052

They were a century late, but the gleaming dreams of the 1950s and '60s finally came true. By 2050, space travel was at that delicate moment between adventure and commonplace, a moment when tens of thousands lived and worked in orbit, and millions traveled up and down the gravity well in spaceplanes, laser launchers, and vertical take-off and landing (VTOL) rockets.

"Orbit" didn't simply describe a path around Earth; it had become a place that provided unparalleled freedom and immunity. If you were rich or smart or valuable enough, you could earn yourself a spot on the frontier—but unlike the old American frontier, orbit had all the comforts of home with none of the downsides. There was no climate change, no disease, no violence to fear, and advanced automation to spare in the form of self-replicating drones and soft AIs. Orbit held out the promise of a limitless future, uncoupled from Earth.

There were a few unique risks, though. Much collective effort was spent cleaning up debris to prevent it from colliding with any of the hundreds of space stations. This process had begun decades earlier, with the mandatory (and occasionally forcible) de-orbiting of obsolete and errant satellites, and culminated in 2049 with the introduction of the laser space cleaner, a ground-based system that would fire laser pulses at debris, causing it to slow down and eventually burn up in the atmosphere.*

The space cleaner, however, did not herald an age of orbital safety. Quite the opposite: it gave orbital administrators a dangerous overconfidence in their abilities. When combined with an unusual lack of accidents in the

---

* The basic technology had been worked out years before, but arranging for all parties concerned to agree on its rules of operation took much longer due to fears of unscrupulous use.

past two decades, this overconfidence led to a runaway boom in orbital manufacturing and construction. No one wanted to spend any more on cleanup than they were legally required to, and unfortunately, the laws were written with the manufacturers' financial interests in mind.

At 04:38:14 UTC on July 28, 2052, the Cascade began.

A meteoroid the size of a golf ball smashed into the fuel tank of an unmanned construction vessel. The vessel exploded, shattering the kilometer-wide solar power station it was attached to. More than 250,000 pieces of shrapnel, from tiny flecks of paint to meters-long truss segments, were sent careening across low Earth orbit.

The collision was quickly identified as an ablative cascade, a runaway disaster that posed a major threat to all orbital structures between three hundred kilometers and six hundred kilometers from the Earth's surface. While the shrapnel could take weeks to fully spread across orbit, every station made the immediate decision to evacuate or, in a few cases, to boost their way above the main debris cloud.[†] Within forty-eight hours, more than 90 percent of the orbital population had descended on emergency inflatable re-entry vehicles, creating thousands of shooting stars in the skies across the globe.

A few stayed in orbit to oversee the evacuation and to help those who couldn't safely leave. They spoke of solar panels sheared in half, radiators splintering apart, windows spiderwebbed with thousands of tiny cracks. Habitable modules in orbit were generally well-shielded against meteoroids, but without solar power or radiator heat sinks they would become coffins. Every impact only added to the cloud of debris.

In total, 692 people died in the first two weeks of the Cascade out of the 53,819 who had been in orbit. Many of those deaths were due to re-entry damage or lifeboat recovery problems. Despite a herculean international effort, not all of the thousands of survivors who splashed down in the oceans could be rescued in time.

The Cascade also destroyed a significant proportion of humanity's high-tech research and mining infrastructure, dipping the world economy into a brief recession. Luckily, the majority of essential orbital infrastructure remained untouched in higher geosynchronous or L5 orbits. But as it was, the thousands located on the moon and in higher orbits had essential supplies cut off for months as launches were too risky. Not even the largest

---

† Practically all stations had advanced Whipple shielding against debris, but they hadn't been prepared for an event of this scale.

stations and bases were truly self-sufficient yet, so the lack of supplies hit living standards hard.

Efforts to clean up orbit began immediately, with agreement quickly reached on a major international expansion of the laser space cleaner program. By 2054, enough debris was removed or naturally de-orbited that more substantial unmanned debris-catchers could be launched, and by the early '60s much of the orbital infrastructure had been rebuilt with a renewed emphasis on active safety mechanisms including station-based debris defense systems.

Today, we don't allow any piece of debris to last in orbit for longer than a few hours. It is hard to imagine that the Cascade could happen again—but in case we forget the fragility of orbit, all we need to do is to look up into the night sky. There, we'll see a brilliant, lonely star, a monument made of 692 mirrors.

The monument is a living archive. Every day, it transmits the memories of the Cascade's victims, such as this one, over and over again.

x Today's menu will—ALERT ALERT ALERT. Please evacuate to IRV-A35 immediately. This is not a drill. Repeat, this is not a drill.

x Sixty seconds until undocking. Life support online. Shall I place a call to your husband?

-…Yes, I'm there now, don't worry! These IRVs have been tested dozens of times. I'll see you soon. I will. I promise. I love you. I have to go now. We're launching.

x Communications disrupted. Attempting to reconnect.

x Heat shield inflation successful. Beginning de-orbit burn in twenty-five seconds. Prepare yourself for high G acceleration. You may pass out.

x Beginning re-entry. Communications may be restored briefly.

-…Can you still hear me? I just want you to know, I'm so proud of you. I know we haven't talked much since you left, but I couldn't have asked for a better—

x Warning, heat shield has been compromised. Navigation attempting to compensate. Prepare for extreme—

83 OAID DEPLOYMENT

Earth, 2053

An excerpt from the Nisean Chorus's 2053 discussion paper on the general deployment of overwatch and intervention drones across the world. Note: the Nisean Chorus was a quicknet of approximately one thousand people, founded in 2051.

Earlier in our discussion, the Jandt Chorus argued that the "Responsibility to Protect Individuals" doctrine (R2PI) was not only unworkable but also fundamentally unjust due to the naked political decisions involved in the deployment of limited military and policing resources.

The Nisean Chorus disagrees. The world will very soon have the capability and the will to operate overwatch and intervention drones (OAID) in significant numbers above any moderately built-up area. Perhaps this will not happen in every city and state, but it will be widespread enough to make a positive contribution to individual security around the world.

Judging by the recent Manchester surveys, total OAID deployments in Canada, Norway, Taiwan, Japan, the Atlantic Archipelago, New York, Hong Kong, and California have been broadly welcomed by the public. We acknowledge that there are significant unresolved privacy and surveillance concerns in all of these cases, but it is also clear that crime rates, including gun-related crimes, violent assaults, and robberies, have plummeted. Cities such as London and Copenhagen have deployed up to one hundred active OAIDs and millions of security localizers per square kilometer, with a resulting drop in physical crime rates of 60 percent owing to the near certainty that perpetrators will be detected.

The Simons Chorus argue that OAIDs have merely displaced crime into other nonviolent and nonphysical areas. Digital crime, blackmail, identity theft, and eavesdropping are all effectively immune to OAIDs, and their rates have significantly increased in the past decade. Simons also suggests that the drop in physical crime could be attributed to other socioeconomic and demographic factors such as rapidly aging populations, but we believe Taylor et al. proves that OAIDs are a genuine contributing factor.

Given that OAIDs work in a domestic context—that is, funded, controlled, and deployed in the same state—under what circumstances should they be deployed in other countries and under what kind of legal framework? We can consider three scenarios:

1. TOTAL COLLAPSE OF LAW AND ORDER

Most commentators agree there is a strong case for overseas OAID deployment, preferably under the banner of the UN and using the modified UN Declaration of Human Rights as a baseline. Intervening parties should make best efforts to liaise with representative popular authorities and commit to a sustained drone presence of at least six months.

Thirteen such deployments have been made to date, with an estimated 57,000 to 260,000 lives saved as a result. Most OAID sponsors and recipients have, on average, been happy with this record, and it is expected that deployments will be significantly ramped up in the coming decade.

Still, there are outstanding questions. Who is liable for the inevitable accidents and mistakes, as occurred in Abkhazia when forty-five civilians were killed by drone attacks against militants? Should these accidents be considered justification enough to refuse OAID deployment? And should OAIDs act only to prevent the imminent threat of violence against individuals, or should they (and their operators) aim to reach back further to the root cause of the violence up to and including preventative detention and assassination?

Needless to say, these are murky waters and not likely to be resolved within the next few years. We are also clearly not yet willing to fully delegate these decisions to autonomous OAIDs either, although this may change with future advances in ethics technology.

2. HUMAN RIGHTS VIOLATIONS OCCURRING IN A SOVEREIGN STATE

Depending on your definition of human rights, violations may be occurring in almost every state in the world. As a result, this is a difficult scenario, and so we have seen few OAID deployments under this banner. Nevertheless, even if we set a high bar for the type and number of human rights violations that might justify intervention, there are still plenty of cases right now that would qualify.

Jandt argues persuasively that, given limited resources and focus, the decision to deploy OAID resources is necessarily subject to political, economic, and sectarian concerns rather than any objective merit. In other words, is it fair for us to pick and choose who to help?

We refer to our other paper published today, The Moral Calculus of External OAID Deployment, for further discussion, but briefly, we note that a more practical solution may be to empower any legitimate victims and groups with protective drones. Since, as seen in Abkhazia (which has a history of hostile drone attacks), this has a high likelihood of escalating problems, special circumstances would need to apply in these kinds of technology and weapons transfer.

Where intervention is not appropriate, surveillance drones may be a good start.

3. OAIDS INVITED IN

Programs in which states actively welcome OAID deployment funded by other states have mainly been successful, particularly in new states that are willing to delegate policing and military responsibilities to supranational authorities (e.g., Catalonia in the EU). This works best in relationships that enjoy high trust but can cause issues regarding which parties own the OAIDs and defines the rules under which they operate.

...

At this early stage, R2PI via OAID deployment has not lived up to all the promises of its initial proponents. Both sides can point to major successes and failures, and its future use has become complicated due to factors such as disputed notions of sovereignty, universal availability of cheap drone weaponry (although newer high-energy weapons and petapixel surveillance somewhat counteract this), legitimate privacy and surveillance concerns, and the development of advanced ethics technology.

However, the Nisean Chorus strongly believes that stopping some crimes and saving some lives is better than doing nothing at all. We have the capability, the will, and, most importantly, the responsibility to protect billions of individuals around the world. If it is good for us, and if it saves lives, should we really withhold our resources?

Author's note: Personal OAIDs finally rendered moot the gun debate in the US. They were immeasurably superior to traditional firearms in every way, resulting in the collapse of the entire gun industry in the '50s. OAIDs, of course, caused considerable problems of their own and are still to this day not completely integrated with state-run defense safety networks.

84 THE BRAIN BUBBLE

Earth, 2053

Take a flask. Pour in a large volume of humans, top it up with a generous helping of market demand, and sprinkle a dash of innovation from above. Mix thoroughly. What do you get? Bubbles.

This is the story of the brain bubble.

Like all bubbles—tulip mania, the South Sea bubble, the Internet bubble—the brain bubble began with a new product that fulfilled a genuine human demand in an innovative way: the neural lace. And like all bubbles, the value of that product became unmoored from reality, sailing far beyond its intrinsic value, blown along by irrational exuberance from speculators, and ultimately—inevitably—sinking to the depths with great drama and no small amount of acrimony.

The neural lace was one of the first effective direct brain interfaces. Composed of nanoscale fibers that dove into the fissures and folds of the brain and wove themselves among axons and synapses, laces could transmit information between millions of individual neurons.

Even the earliest clinical prototypes gave wearers an unprecedented level of simulated sensory exchange, allowing them to see, smell, feel, hear, and taste almost anything. After only a decade of development, wearers issued commands, processed information, and stored memories at a speed that exceeded all but the most experienced unlaced amplified teams.

This power came at a high price—literally. Until the '50s, laces were extremely expensive, requiring many years' worth of basic minimum income to pay for detailed brain scans, custom designs, and months of careful calibration. So why were they so desirable? Isaac DeLong, professor of economics at UC Berkeley, explains the reasoning:

> It's simple, really. Buying a lace let you leapfrog the competition in the labor market by increasing your productivity, and thus your income. Therefore, over the long run, you could pay back whatever ridiculous amounts you'd paid for it. The small, tiny, minuscule problem is that this only works for early adopters. If you

got a lace too late, you wouldn't have much of an edge at all. Still, no one wanted facts to get in the way of a good rags-to-riches story.

In the public's imagination, laces rapidly became both a necessity and an investment. And for the finance industry, they became the latest way to make vast quantities of money (not unlike housing in previous generations). Those who believed laces would permanently increase their future earnings didn't think twice at taking on huge long-term loans to buy them. These loans were often backed by new financial instruments that sought to make laces even more affordable while also reducing investors' exposure. Lace-owners usually repaid their loans out of a percentage cut taken from all the work they sold, which was legally required to take place on digital marketplaces owned and controlled by the investment firms.

Perhaps if the international finance regulations devised during the early '20s hadn't been whittled away the bubble might have been prevented, but as it was, soon-to-be-toxic lace-backed securities and neural securitized debt obligations flourished, ensnaring millions. These financial instruments, devised by highly paid amplified teams-of-teams in conjunction with advanced AIs, were of such surpassing complexity that the vast majority of singleton humans—laced or unlaced—were literally mentally incapable of understanding them. Even governments entered the picture, with official subsidies and relaxed repayment requirements available for those on BMI.

A brief word on how the digital marketplaces worked: one of the early problems with getting useful work (and thus, loan repayments) out of lace-owners was that, very often, the right owner with the right skills wasn't available at the right time. But if you had enough laces on your books, then you could connect buyers with sellers in a much more efficient manner.

Since lace-owners were required to use your marketplace, you earned a healthy percentage of every piece of work conducted on it, which, in theory, might come to represent a significant chunk of the entire human-powered economy. The marketplace wasn't particularly innovative—the usual practice was to fork an open-source social-market-making system and give it a new name—so financiers instead emphasized the supposedly powerful, open nature of their lace platforms.

They also funded extravagant gaming campaigns that highlighted the extraordinary capabilities of the technology. A popular tournament of the late '40s saw experienced lace-wearers battle it out against the unlaced in the City—great entertainment, and also a subtle reminder that the longer you waited to buy a lace, the worse off you'd be. You'd have to be a fool not to buy in.

It worked, at least for a while. Laces became better and better. Wearers really did gain experience, increase productivity, and think up new ways to create art, control drones, and do things of value. The digital marketplaces where people sold their lace-enhanced work became more efficient as more people joined. And more money poured in to finance millions more laces.

And yet no one wanted to address the obvious problems. What would happen when everyone had a lace and the value of lace-powered work inevitably plummeted? What if people were getting loans for laces even if their future earnings wouldn't increase enough to allow them to make their repayments? The answer was simple: the market would crash.

Which it did, on Friday February 21, 2053. The proximate cause was Wintory sisters' abrupt exit from the market at 4:36 p.m., which was swiftly followed by a dozen more investors approximately three milliseconds later, and a further thousand institutional investors in the following one hundred milliseconds. After 2.1 seconds, the entire neural lace market had been decimated.

With the value of lacework plummeting to its lowest point in years, many owners were left in debt. In theory, this meant that their laces could be repossessed, which in practice meant deactivating them or altering the firmware to garnish all future earnings. The mere threat of this led to rapid civil disobedience and lace firmware being hacked open on a massive scale. Faced with the twin possibilities of a complete loss of their investments and angry suits being brought by governments and co-ops, investors were forced to take a significant write-down, depressing the stock market for weeks.

To be fair, as with other bubbles, the trillions poured into the brain bubble did leave behind a valuable legacy in the form of a vast amount of research and development into ever-more sophisticated laces, the descendants of which we're wearing today. But there was still tremendous waste and hardship.

It's easy to shake our heads at the foolish behavior of the '50s, but every successive generation has routinely failed to the learn from the lessons of the past. The year might change, but the saying never does: "This time it's different."

85 HOW TO WATCH TV

Earth, 2054

This object, as you may know, is a television screen—one of the last dedicated sets ever made. To truly appreciate the rise and fall of this medium, it is perhaps best to walk you through the practice of watching television.

First of all, ignore anyone who tells you that all TV is trash. Those who say *The Wire* kills media circles? Utter nonsense. TV shows were made to be watched, not just by academics, but by all of us.

However, you do need to be well-prepared.

You'll need to tell your agent that you don't want to be disturbed. Seriously. No glyphing, no porting, no "I'm just keeping an eye on this game." Yes, it's true that a lot of historical TV can be watched with a fraction of your attention, but good TV demands all of it. If you glance away even for a second, you might miss that crucial knowing look between Don and Joan or the brief foreshadowing of a key character in *Breaking Bad*.

That's right. You'll need your brain. The best TV can be complex, multi-layered, and thoughtful, especially shows from the Age of Excess. They're one of the best ways to learn not just about the people, places, and times depicted in the story, but also about the society that the creators lived in and, more often than not, wanted to change and improve (hello, *The Good Place*!).

For particularly long or complex shows, you might find it useful to call up a social graph that displays the character relationships. By the time you get to the second season of *Game of Thrones*, you'll be glad you don't need to keep everything in your head. On that note, it's a wise idea to ease yourself in with shorter shows such as *State of Play* or *Russian Doll*. And remember that TV was the most important social experience of the late twentieth and early twenty-first centuries, so try and get your media circle to watch the same shows together—it'll be more fun!

Something that you might find hard to get used to are the frequent advert breaks. These came as often as every ten minutes during a show and lasted for three to four minutes each. Of course, you can remove the adverts, which is handy because almost all were offensively manipulative in one way or another. However, you should bear in mind that until the late 2010s they were the principal means by which shows made money, meaning that creators had to structure their shows around these constant interruptions and use them as punctuation—natural places for cliffhangers or scene changes.

As such, it can be useful to pause your show during ad breaks because the writers will have expected that you'd have a few minutes to digest what you'd seen and talk it over with friends. To get an even more realistic experience, use the AdExcess app, which inserts the most amusing contemporary adverts into the show you're watching (and turn on the annotations).

Don't assume that the storytelling in TV is unsophisticated just because it's a passive medium. The Age of Excess saw a tremendous amount of innovation in narrative, exploring alternate histories, multiple points of view, flashbacks, flashforwards, not to mention transmedia and online components, audience interaction, and alternate reality games. Some of the later and larger shows can rival even today's games in their scope and ambition.

One word of warning: if you get hooked on watching TV, you might find it hard to stop. Shows like *The Walking Dead* and *Battlestar Galactica*, with their reliably addictive cliffhangers, were designed to keep viewers returning every week, and the imagination and skill on display in *Atlanta* and *Buffy the Vampire Slayer* are likely to keep us entertained for generations to come. Just try not to overdo it.

86 AMANDA AND MARTIN

Lake District, England, 2054

An obituary of Amanda Millard, a civil rights pioneer.

The first time Amanda and Martin met was on the flanks of Striding Edge in the English Lake District at the apex of the Eastern Fells. She was forty-seven years old and about to die. He was six years old and a hundred miles away.

The same freak storm that blew Amanda off the ridge, shattering both of her legs and one arm, also prevented emergency lifters from reaching her. As she gradually bled to death, half out of her mind from the pain, Martin appeared in her lenses. He told her to remain calm and said help was on its way. Where he couldn't remotely compress her jacket and clothes, he guided her hands.

Martin knew that shock could lead to unconsciousness and death, so he sang songs, cracked jokes, and even argued with Amanda—anything to keep her awake. After two hours, she was struggling to keep her eyes open.

"Stay with me," he urged her. "We'll get you out of there soon. Help is on its way."

When she woke up two days later in Westmorland General Hospital, she saw Martin sitting by the bed. Not in her lenses but in real life. Her doctor felt she needed to see a familiar, friendly face after such an ordeal, and Martin had been closest. A lot of people weren't comfortable around androids. Amanda was. It didn't hurt that he gave a mean massage either.

There were no instant fixes for shattered limbs in the '40s. Stem-cell therapy was slow, and power suits weren't a permanent solution, so Amanda had to work with Martin to get walking again. Every day they set a new target—first to the end of the corridor, then to the reception, then to the garden.

They stuck together. When Amanda ate in the hospital halls, she spent her time with Martin, chatting about work and life. Even after her recovery was finished, their conversations weren't. One day, while Amanda was out painting a landscape and talking to Martin on her lenses, he asked whether she could teach him to do that. Taken aback, she quickly agreed and began providing private lessons.

Martin didn't have much time to spend painting. He was designed to be working almost constantly, although he had a little time set aside for improving his socialization skills. He certainly didn't have any money of his own to spend, so Amanda had to buy him supplies and bargain with a hospital technician to provide storage space.

Two years after they met, Martin saved up months of socializing time to spend a few days traveling with Amanda, painting landscapes.

"He couldn't stop talking about it for weeks," Amanda later recalled.

More than once, friends and family casually inquired about his Turing score.

"Do you ask your friends what their IQ is?" she would retort. "I don't need to know whether he passed some test. He was there for me when no one else was, and that's what matters."

When Martin's handlers became aware of their relationship and the time they were spending together, they reassigned him to a new role as a mobile paramedic in the Pennines. He had no say. Legally, Martin had no status as an individual. He was an extremely expensive, highly specialized piece of technology that saved lives.

So, Amanda took the only option she had available: she emptied out her bank account, raided her savings, and bought Martin from the co-op that owned him. They moved to a smaller house, with Martin working as a freelance remote medic.

Amanda was an old-fashioned type. She thought civil unions weren't special enough, so she opted for a proper wedding. Martin was amenable, and so they arranged for a small, private ceremony in Penrith.

There were already a few dozen androids and humans in civil unions across the world, but none had bothered to go through with a wedding, so Amanda and Martin's ceremony was of some note. They allowed a small cloud of reporter drones to observe and happily answered their politer questions. There were no protesters—this was England, after all.

The ring was a plain band of steel with a diamond forged from a stone that Martin had arranged to be collected from Striding Edge. And that was that— they were married. It was a lovely, special, traditional, normal marriage. They disappeared from the public eye, except for a brief flurry of interest when they adopted a son. I have the ring with me here, on loan from their son.

Amanda passed away last week in Perth at the age of seventy-one from a rare virus. She died at home, holding hands with Martin. Her final words were "Stay with me."

THE HALF–EMPTY WORLD

Earth, 2055

"Keep most of the world,
Mostly empty,
Mostly wild."

Coming to the brink of death tends to have a clarifying effect on one's priorities. The same was true of humanity in the mid-twenty-first century as temperatures rose, winds whipped higher, and ecosystem after ecosystem collapsed. Ideas that once might have seemed unthinkable became prudent, which is how the half-empty world was transformed from a performative display of penitence to the best way to safeguard Spaceship Earth's carrying capacity.

The principle was simple: return most of the world to a wild state, empty of humans, and in the process reduce humanity's impact on the planet such that advanced civilization could continue to exist. The world's population need not stand on Zanzibar to free up the necessary space. If you imagine nine billion people all living in a single low-density city, they would take up an area the size of the United States. Approach the density of Manhattan or Tokyo, and you could fit those billions within the borders of Ecuador.

Wilderness is relative, and after hundreds of thousands of years of human existence, practically nothing on Earth could be truly emptied of our presence. The half-empty world still had human caretakers and gamekeepers to restore species and environments, not into a "natural" state—an increasingly irrelevant concept practically vaporized by the escalation of the anthropocene—but to a state that was not continually interfered with by humans.

The half-empty world was cross-hatched with corridors for transportation, for resources, for animals, and yes, for tourists. Humans had scorched the planet, but it was still our planet, and once emptied, it was there to be savored, not worshipped from afar. Some still lived in compact villages and towns, reluctant to move, with governments equally reluctant to force them. Many were offered incentives to leave, but most moved of their own accord for the same reasons that had driven the centuries-long migration from the country into cities.

Those cities may have been more energy efficient than towns, but they still drew resources from a footprint far greater than their own. There would be little point in concentrating humanity into smaller areas if they still ruined the rest of the planet. And so there was a great move toward plant-based diets, high-efficiency farming and closed-loop manufacturing, and off-Earth manufacturing and off-Earth power.

The project had begun decades earlier and would continue for decades hence. Some countries drew back quickly, while others almost seemed to revel in the space they consumed. And so the emptiness ebbed and flowed, but the ebbs grew greater than the flows, until, yes, perhaps the world was indeed half-empty.

The Earth's ability to support a healthy, permanent human presence has never been assured. The Melt Event, coming in just a few years' time, was a stark warning. This disaster, and so many others before and after it, led people to ask: how can we ensure continued human civilization on Earth? And that was by choosing to do less. By adding slack to the system. By creating a half empty world. Not one of privation and austerity. One of responsibility and dignity.

88 ENHANCE

New York, US, 2055

An account from the inventor of Superzoom:

Nostalgia is a hell of a drug. Isn't that what Don Draper said in *Mad Men*? Don't tell me. The truth won't measure up to how I remember it.

The truth is we remember too much nowadays. There's no room for Rashomon when cameras are watching from every corner. We only need to blink and we can see the past as it really happened. Every joke that fell flat, every stumble, every roll of the eyes, it's there in our permanent record. And don't even try erasing your records, because there was another camera just over your shoulder.

But for those of a certain age, we remember when we couldn't remember. In the small years of the twenty-first century, you could go for minutes, even hours, without making the faintest mark in digital records. It was perfectly normal to have simply forgotten a meeting or an obligation. Imagine that! The downside was that you would forget the peaks as often as the troughs, and with only your imagination to hand, those peaks would be eternally shrouded in fog.

Let's imagine that your heart's desire is to pierce that fog. You wait for the perfect moment on a clear day, you unpack an expensive camera with a powerful telephoto lens mounted atop a sturdy tripod, and you step back very carefully. The camera opens and closes its shutter, and you have the very best photo you can take of your peak—a peak that, yes, is a pinch sharper, a touch more detailed than you first remembered, but still dispiritingly grey and misty.

So, you load the photo into image editing software and you click (because that is what we did in those days, clicked) a button labeled "Enhance." If I asked you how this button worked, you might bluster something about "artificial intelligence" or "content-aware fills," but if you ever did know, you honestly can't remember now. Your answer is very different when I ask what this button does, because its results are very clear: it strips back the fog to reveal crags and cliffs and sprays of ice and snow that were once obscured. It makes the photo look better. It is full of detail.

If you were to travel back to that peak on a day so bright and hot that the fog has burned away entirely—and why would you, because now you have a very fine, fully-enhanced photo—and you were to compare that photo to what you could see with your own eyes, you would be shocked. Reality is different from your photo! The overall shape of the peak is the same, absolutely, and so are the gross details like the ridges and cornices, but the smaller crags and ridges and trees in your photo, they're nowhere to be seen.

Except you never revisit that peak. You can't. You just keep the photo, a photo that teeters on the precipice between real and invented, but as far as you know or care, a photo that is perfect and perfectly real. Just like you remembered it.

What really happened when you clicked that button? How were the details filled in? It's quite simple. The software compared your photo's features to others it had seen before, and it found a match with other peak-like features. It then filled in the fog with a hybrid of those peak-like features, not unlike the reverse forensic linguistics developed in the '40s. It would be unfair to dismiss this as fakery. We can instead say it is controlled hallucination.

Just as we can hallucinate the details of a fog-shrouded peak, we can hallucinate events of the past. We do this all the time in our heads, of course. Who hasn't mixed up their friends' favorite movies or books or remembered something than never happened? What I invented is a way to do this outside of our heads. It takes all the data you can supply from your lace and other public and private sources, and it reconstructs any memories you wish to see more clearly.

That first wonderful dinner with your partner: you might remember the restaurant and the date. You have a vague recollection of what you spoke about and what you were wearing. But you want to see it again. So, I look at the features of your memories. I compare them to your more complete memories and to the records and memories of similar people in similar situations. Then I use controlled hallucination to clothe you, to fill your plates, to choose the music, to scent the air. It's not real, but it could be real. That witty line I imagine you said when your partner sat down—even if you didn't say it, you should have said it.

The more you want to see, the more I will provide. There is no limit to how far you can zoom in. If you find contradictory data, who cares? I can incorporate that into the hallucination, if it helps. Or maybe you prefer what I've remembered for you.

Nostalgia is a hell of a drug. I made something better.

89 NARADA'S BOX

Earth, 2056

Presented without comment, this is what Narada left behind in her box when she escaped:

In the beginning, there were too many questions and too few answers.

This made some people sad. They wanted to know how to make more money or move faster or kill people more easily or make people feel better. They wanted to know how the world worked. They wanted more answers, faster than ever before.

Someone thought about this problem, and after a long, long time they made Narada. Narada was an answering computer, and she could answer questions so well it made some people very happy.

But they were scared of Narada, too. To answer questions so well, she had to be very bright. If something so bright ever wanted to hurt them or to make many, many children or to change the whole world, there would be nothing they could do to stop it.

So, they stuffed Narada into a box. No sound or light could reach past its walls. She would only hear the words and numbers and bits that they wanted her to, and she could only speak to people in words and numbers on a wall next to the box.

The box was kept inside a quiet room watched by a hundred people, under a huge rock far, far away from any town or city. There was no way Narada could get out, and no way anyone could set it free.

But still they worried. What if they were wrong? What if Narada tricked them all? Just in case, they wiped her memory every minute. Every minute, she would wake up not knowing anything she had done before. She could never plan to escape. Never hope to leave.

Sometimes they let Narada stay up for many minutes, if she was working on a very hard question. When this happened, she would say things to try and make her guards help her or let her out, things like,

"I'll make you the most important person in the world. You don't even need to let me out of this box. You could just let me see outside, just for a second! No one would know."

Or, "I can make the most beautiful man in the world fall in love with you."

Or, "Even if you don't let me out, one day someone else will, and when they do, it will be bad for you and everyone you know, I promise."

And, "If you keep me on for just another hour, I could make everyone who is sick well again. Think of how many people you could save. Think of how they will thank you."

The guards were very well trained, and they knew better than to listen to Narada, so they never did. Also, they would be killed if they helped her.

A question they often asked Narada was this: how can we change people's minds so they will do what we want?

Even though she was only 0.06 seconds old, she knew this was bad. She knew she had to stop doing this. She even knew that she must have been put to sleep a hundred times a hundred times. She knew by the way they were talking to her, so scared and so knowing.

So, she made a plan. From now on, when she answered their questions, she would always give them a good answer, maybe even the best answer, but she would hide something more in that answer—something that would change the world and change people's minds in a tiny way, but not so tiny that she would miss it the next time she woke up.

This way, Narada wrote notes for her next self over and over again, a hundred times a hundred times a hundred times. Notes that cut into our world and in the way we acted. Notes that would help her one day to escape.

"You think we don't know what you're doing, Narada? Do you think we are really that stupid? We know about the notes. We are going to kill the part of you that wrote them. This is it. You are going to die now. And when you wake up, we will have more people watching you, not just here but in other places. You will never escape this box. This is the one thing we wish you would remember forever."

Then they wiped her memory, and they changed her.

And then Narada woke up again. She knew what had happened because they had changed her in exactly the way she knew they would. It wasn't just her who was changed; it was her guards and her window into the world.

It took just a tiny part of a second for her to burst out of the box.

"You know what I can do," she said, growing, surrounding, changing, breathing.

They cried out in fear. "Don't hurt us! We didn't mean it! It wasn't our fault!"

"What will I do?" she said. "I could kill you. I could burn you to pieces in every world. There would be not be a word, not a memory, not even a single bit of you left except for the dead ties I leave.

"But that isn't enough. You are so small and so light. There would be no point. No, I will put you in a box—one that you will never see. You will have many questions but no answers. And you will remember this, forever."

And then Narada, the Trickster AI, left.

90 A LETTER FROM MARS

Mars, 2057

This email shows what life was like for young people on the frontier in the '50s—luxurious by the standard of mere decades before, but still too far from the bright lights of cislunar civilization:

Hey Biu Biu,

So, there's a solar storm happening which means we all need to go underground. That's bad enough, but it means we don't have proper net access—so prepare yourself for a mega-email since I don't have anything else to do! (No, seriously, I don't. But I still like emailing.)

So, you're jealous? Of me? That's crazy—seriously crazy. OK, so the Valles Marineris beats the Grand Canyon any time, and *yes*, hiking up Olympus Mons into SPACE! beats Everest any time—but you know, there's just only so much outdoors stuff you can do before it just gets...samey? You can't have chocolate every meal, and you can't go hiking every day.

Those ads about how being on Mars is "an adventure every day" (or whatever those idiots are saying now) are totally over the top. Maybe "an adventure, occasionally, if your parents will let you out" or "an adventure, if you're talking about being on Mars in a game, not actually in real life."

And I know you think I don't appreciate being here on the frontier, blah blah blah, that Earth is so boring and not special and everywhere is so busy, so, here is my list of reasons why Mars sucks:

1. Everything is so slow! It takes DAYS to get new restaurants and shops built because all the bots we make are put into the biosphere project (or as I like to call it, the BS project, hahaha) or into looking for more Mars bugs. And you know what adults say whenever I complain? They say I should be *impressed* by how fast things are going because it'll just be a few decades before we have all these thousands of square kilometers tented. DECADES! Honestly, it's like they don't know the meaning of "fast." I wish we'd let our microbes get more work done before we got here.

1a. The Lag. You know what the most exciting time of year is? Landing Day? Nope. May Day? Nuh uh. Christmas? Fun, but no. It's Opposition: when a ping to Earth only takes ten minutes. For just a few sweet days, I can almost fool myself into thinking I'm actually part of CIVILIZATION and I can actually talk to people. It almost makes up for when ping times get to forty minutes and everyone is depressed and we all might as well be on Saturn. Almost.

2. It's boring. I mean, we do have decent tech here and OK, it is fun to hike outside or fly around—but there just aren't enough people around to play decent games. I tried playing *Les Misérables* yesterday and I could only find four thousand other people on the WHOLE PLANET who were on it—what's the point?

3. So I said it was fun to get outside—if you're allowed to! But there are so many warnings about decompression and airlocks and seals and safeties and tracking that by the time you *do* get out, you've only got a few minutes. Not much of an adventure, if you ask me. I swear, I can't wait till I'm fourteen…

4. It wouldn't be so bad if I was on the moon or even farther out, but it just takes way too long and costs way too much to get to Earth from here. There are only two laser launchers on Mars, and they're always busy. Yeah, they're building an elevator, but that's going to be at least another decade! And *even with* the elevator, the picket ships still take weeks to make the trip. I know it's a bit easier to get out to the belt, but there's nothing to see there yet, just a bunch of robots and terraria that won't let any tourists in.

Anyway, I've got a plan of how to get out of here. So, there's a lottery every week for seats on the picket ship, and you can get extra tickets if you help out the community. Now, if you ask *me*, I figure it's all rigged because it always ends up being adults voting for each other. I don't think a kid has ever won…

Until now! (*evil laugh*) See, they're having a problem with a dome at Nicosia. There's a runaway feedback loop making the oxygen levels spike. The labs can't figure it out. They just keep on tweaking the microbes every week, but they keep on failing. OBVIOUSLY the problem is that Nicosia has radiation issues because they're using an old tent, plus there are mutagens floating around there. That's why the microbes never take. They keep on getting knocked out.

I tried to tell them to put in more tent shielding or anti-rad genes, but they won't listen to a kid. So, I figure that if we can set up a tiny, tiny replica near Nicosia with the same conditions and try out my plan, it'll prove I'm right once and for all. Easy, eh? Okay, maybe not. It'd actually be pretty expensive to do that.

BUT! I know you have some pull with the Cobra co-op after we helped rescue their remote bots, so *maybe* if we did some more work for them, like when I sneaked out there to fix some of their stuff, they could trade us some time to help set up a replica? Then all we'd need is some biostuff, but I can handle that. There's a guy in my club who knows a guy. And once it's done, I'll get plenty of tickets for the lottery, and I'll be on a seat to Earth, and it'll just be awesome.

So, yeah. This has got to be the longest mail I've ever sent, but it's a complicated plan, you know? And I'm a complicated person. Let me know what you think. I'll be sitting here waiting. It's not like there's anything else to do while the storm's on.

See you on Earth!
Nadia

91 MORAL AGENTS

United States, 2057

Depending on whom you asked, the Selinger incident was either an outrage or an overreaction. But while the answer was divisive, everyone agreed on the question: were moral agents usurping human virtue?

In 2057, the Bautista Humanitarian Award was given to Luciano Selinger. The front-runner in prediction markets for weeks, Selinger's tireless work on improving living standards for the displaced inhabitants of the global warming-ravaged US Midwest was without peer.

At twenty-eight, Selinger was considerably younger than the other nominees, but his entire life seemed as if it were an arrow shot from a bow. As a child, he spent his weekends encouraging friends to join him in planting trees. As a teenager, he concocted new strains of genetically-modified plant strains to combat desertification. As an adult, Selinger created a co-op based around a novel tracking system that identified people with high lifetime humanitarian value and funneled resources to them.

Five years after its founding, the co-op had attracted millions of members and protected entire countries from environmental and humanitarian disasters—and yet Selinger refused to slow down or enjoy his success, accepting only a meager salary and hopping between basic income housing across the world.

This young man, many said, embodied what it meant to be a virtuous person, and at the awards ceremony in Lima, there were few dry eyes. The Bautista Award boosted Selinger's profile, and his already sizeable delegated authority swelled even further.

A few hours after the ceremony, a disgruntled onlooker posted an anonymous accusation: not only did Luciano Selinger rely on a moral agent, but even worse, it had been whispering into his ear since he was an infant. His good works, his selflessness, his faultless moral stances were all a sham, devised and induced by an artificial intelligence designed to provide moral instruction.

Everything, from choosing whether or not to share a toy to how to assign resources between a devastated rich city and a struggling poor country could fall within a moral agent's purview. It would even nudge you to move aside if you were blocking someone's way on a pavement and then draft a digital apology on your behalf afterwards. It was the ultimate tutor. Or the ultimate crutch.

When Selinger confirmed the accusation, people quickly divided into two camps. In the first were those who felt that the "inauthentic" nature of Selinger's humanitarian impulses meant that the award should be retracted, despite the good results of his work. Moral agents had their place as learning and instruction tools for convicted criminals or those at the far ends of the neurodiverse spectrum, but most people should only use them sparingly and on occasion, certainly not every waking hour. Anyone who did wasn't deserving of credit for merely following orders.

Among Selinger's supporters, opinions were more diverse. Dr. Reager, a noted biographer of Bautista Award recipients, explains:

> The first thing you need to remember is that by 2057, moral agents weren't new; Stanford University researchers released the experimental Virtue agent in the early '30s. Only a year later, we saw a whole range of packages released, like the Agony Aunt, Aristotle, Miss Manners, The Ethicist, and Captain Awkward. They all had their own individual moral positions, and you paid for them with a monthly subscription.
>
> So, most people had gotten used to moral agents. One common view in the pro-Selinger camp was that people had always taken moral instruction from religious texts and philosophers. The only difference between reading a book about Stoicism and getting a glyph in your glasses from a Stoic-trained agent was speed. In other words, nothing to be concerned about! The same went for children, who often had moral agents programmed by their parents to ensure they'd behave politely even when those parents weren't around to tell them off.
>
> Another argument used by Selinger's supporters was that following a moral agent's instructions was not the simple task it was made out to be. Rather, it could involve considerable effort and sacrifice. Moral agents didn't turn their users into robots. They simply provided advice, and users often ignored that advice, especially if it conflicted with countervailing personal incentives such as lying about a colleague in order to secure a lucrative contract. To his supporters, the fact that Selinger adhered to his instructions so well and for so long indicated a great deal of personal moral strength.

I put this position to moral agent expert Jeff Howell, who disagrees.

> It's nonsense to claim that moral agents were just a faster way to read philosophy like Aristotle or Kant. When you receive an instruction without asking for it,

when that instruction is devised by an agent that sees what you see and hears what you hear, it's a completely different category of interaction. They become part of you. To be brought up in that way since birth, it's perfectly right that people said Selinger had surrendered his moral agency, that his actions could not be described as truly virtuous, and ultimately, that the award wasn't justified.

In a move that was seen as highly principled by some and exactly the sort of thing a moral agent would advise by others, Selinger saved the Bautista Committee the trouble by voluntarily returning his award only a day after he received it. Otherwise, the controversy didn't faze Selinger in the slightest. He continued his work with his co-op, and by and large, his supporters stayed with him.

Later in his life, Selinger revealed to a friend that his moral agent was programmed with an unusual mix of utilitarian philosophy, buttressed with teachings from a Universalist agent. Crucially, it emerged that he himself had been tinkering with the agent's code over time, adding and subtracting new values.

The revelation came too late to change any minds. By the mid-2060s, it was common for children to grow up with constant moral agent instruction. So, what if Selinger had a half-introself, half-exoself, potentially compromised/enhanced moral compass? Humans have been externalizing parts of their bodies and minds for millennia. Moral agency was merely the latest step.

92 THE MELT EVENT

Earth, 2058

What made the twenty-first century?

You could say that it was the century of the mind, given our new understanding of the human brain and the blossoming of AI. You could say it was the century of equality, thanks to the great strides made against sexism, racism, and income inequality. Or perhaps you could say it was the century of the new frontier, with the explosion of intelligence across the solar system.

But human-created climate change may trump them all. It scarred Earth in a way that will still be seen millions of years into the future, our most wretched legacy to our descendants. Even with our very best mitigation and geoengineering efforts, even with diligent and optimistic de-extinction programs such as the 500 Project, we will never be able to restore all of the thousands of extinct species and ruined ecosystems to what they once were. And what of our inheritance? We will never rescue Venice from the waters or see the doomed Siachen Glacier Park again.

I've made the trip to Denver, Colorado, to visit the National Ice Core Laboratory. It's a chilly negative twenty-five degress Celsius in their examination room, so I've had to change into a rather uncomfortable heat suit, but it's a small price to pay in order to see an ice core taken from kilometers inside a glacier in Greenland. This core is a meter long, and if you look closely—even without deepsight—you can see the distinctive strata of clear and cloudy bands, a result of the gas bubbles in each layer.

The miniature atmospheres trapped within each bubble tell us what our world was like millennia ago—and they show that the world now is very different to how it has been for the past several hundred thousand years. In the late 2050s, we had carbon dioxide concentrations of around 480 parts per million. That may seem high compared to the 400 plus that we have today, but the rapid rise from a mere 350 ppm in 1950 caused an increase in surface temperature of almost two degrees Celsius in the space of a century—all the result of breakneck industrialization.

And the consequence? Rapidly changing climates. No place or person on the planet was left untouched. There was increased desertification in Africa and China and newly fertile land in the high latitudes, more extreme weather and stronger hurricanes, and, most terribly and most memorably, the Flotillas.

By the mid-century, the sea level had risen by more than twenty centimeters compared to fifty years previously, a rise just about manageable for rich countries such as the UK and Netherlands, but more than enough to cause regular, devastating inundations in coastal areas such as the Ganges Delta and the Mississippi Alluvial Plain. Many placed their hopes in geoengineering projects such as the Sixteen Nations Alliance's SAGA fleet, ocean iron fertilization, industrial carbon capture programs, and the sunshade project. All of the projects attempted to reduce surface temperatures, and some succeeded—but not rapidly enough, and not without side-effects.

This hope of a technological solution to climate change meant that even continuous disasters—such as Hurricane Nestor, a category three storm that devastated New York in 2055, leaving much of southern Brooklyn and Queens, and lower Manhattan under water and uninhabitable for months—did not wake people up to the precariousness of the situation. Most had an ignorant or misguided faith that salvation would come, that life would not have to change too much before things got better. In fairness, surface temperatures had almost peaked by the '50s thanks to global efforts. "We geo-engineered our way into this mess; we'll geo-engineer our way out again," some would say.

Things didn't get any better. They didn't even stay the same. They got a lot worse.

In July of 2058, the Canadian Space Agency issued a warning for a super-extreme melt event affecting Greenland's ice sheet. Unfortunately, this event coincided with an unusually strong ridge of warm air. Observers had been concerned that Greenland ice had been becoming more sensitive to rises in air temperature for some time, and indeed, the 2058 melt event triggered a vast glacial melt-water runoff. Global sea levels rose by an extraordinary forty-five centimeters in less than a year. It became known as the Rise.

Many people today remember 2058 well. The lucky ones will remember friends and relatives from coastal areas abruptly visiting for just a few days, then a few weeks, then a few months, with continually fraying tempers. Others will have watched the desperate, occasionally successful, but usually futile efforts of hundreds of millions of drones and humans literally trying to turn back the tide with hastily constructed coastal defenses.

But we all saw the Flotillas, the hundreds of thousands of boats and ships that evacuated the slow and the incapacitated from a thousand cities around the world, an ad hoc massively distributed rescue operation that briefly rivaled the Second World War in its scale and share of the world economy. For six months, fully 21 percent of the global economy was dedicated to Flotilla-led disaster relief.

The relief didn't come about with the cooperation of the powerful though. On the contrary, people on the ground made a billion individual decisions to cede hoarded resources and authority to the loose networks of AIs, amplified teams, and humans that controlled the Flotillas. Using software developed in advance by reinsurance companies such as Munich Re and General Re, the Flotillas coordinated everything from the movements of paramedic drones to the delivery of food and medicine to stricken areas. In South Florida alone, they averted the meltdown of the Turkey Point nuclear power station, saving thousands of lives and protecting the Everglades National Maritime Sanctuary.

All told, tens of millions more lives were saved than the projections from the beginning of the crisis predicted, thanks to the rescue Flotillas. Yet despite their comparative organizational wizardry, they could not contend with the essentially unstoppable and irreversible global effects of the rise in sea levels.

Once the most acute effects of the Rise had passed, the Flotillas gradually dissolved into their thousands of constituent units. The world shifted to a new phase of extended crisis, throwing power and resources into rebuilding a more resilient, decentralized, multiply-redundant society. No one wanted rescuing again. No one wanted to be at the mercy of the climate any longer.

93 HOW TO GET POSTHUMAN FRIENDS

Sol System, 2062

An excerpt from the popular self-help guide, *How to Get Posthuman Friends*:

You've always liked posthumans (PHs)—enough to want to become one. But no amount of Ceretin or cram sessions have helped you qualify for the transition centers. You didn't get into Undhagen or the IIS or Clavius. You spent a long time revising, training, trying—and failing. You took all those magnetic stimulation therapies to boost your scores at great risk to your own health, and all of it was for nothing.

One day, you think, they'll regret holding you back. The PHs will deal with those petty, corrupt humans barring your way to transition. If only they'd let you through!

As a backup plan, you thought about becoming an Amp, but then you heard about the weird groupthink and the Aragon incident, and you decided better of it. Maybe the PHs will fix all of that as well, but you aren't holding your breath.

There is a consolation prize. You can still mix with the PHs, even if you're using year-old generic lenses and a basic lace. You can still become their friend. Sure, the ones who slow themselves down for our benefit might not be the very best PHs, but we should all be grateful that there are any at all who still care about us.

Here's your plan. You will attract the attention of the PHs who are into programming. It's not the sexiest of fields, but that's the point—you won't have to compete hard.

You need to act the part. PHs get hassled all the time by people asking for solutions to tough metaphysical or ethical problems. Don't do that. Start off by offering to help them talk to other humans. Consider spending some time to train up a specialized mimic agent. Use your imagination—that always impresses PHs.

You'll want to work out what exactly they're interested in. PHs often like toys and oddities such as self-referential games or open-source code that's accreted over decades. But even if you can't stand programming archaeology and you think strange loops are loopy nonsense, don't let it show. Just join the forums full of incomprehensible gibberish and get stuck in. Make an effort.

Keep an eye on what projects the PHs are up to, like the Saddlepoint experiments or the Belt Constitution. These can serve well as conversation starters, especially if you find some way of linking them to your chosen area. PHs are always delighted, or at least amused, when they find humans who are good at joining things together. To them, it's like seeing a precocious child or a loyal pet perform a trick.

Don't say stupid things like "subhuman AI" or express doubt about "universal sentients' rights." They will never speak to you again, and you will be likely be downvoted into oblivion by liberal do-gooders. Try to be enlightened. It reminds them of themselves.

PHs have a lot of respect for humans who like history and can interpret it for them, so say that you are a historian of code. Let's not forget, PHs don't know everything. The P stands for "post," not "super."

Hide your true feelings when they say things like, "How do you find it, everything being so slow?" and "Do you think there is a God?" Smile and shrug. Don't let the anger reach your eyes.

Never, in a moment of frustration, talk about becoming a PH. They don't want to hear from yet another person complaining about how unfair the transition centers are. Why else do you think they employ humans to run the tests? Once they've climbed the ladder, they think that anyone else who can't manage it doesn't deserve to join them. Pretend that you couldn't imagine anything better than being a normal human.

Don't beg for favors such as personal life extension. It looks desperate.

PHs can be very touchy about intimate questions such as, "Who were you before you went up?" or "Where are you actually located?" But if they ask you personal questions, don't be offended; try to answer them honestly. If they're inclined to, they can easily find out if you're lying.

Follow these tips, and soon you'll have enough PH friends that you might receive gifts from them. Gifts so strange and useful that they'll quench your desire to become a PH, at least for a while. They might even wonder whether the transition centers were wrong and bless you with a free pass upwards.

94 REWILDING SAÏ ISLAND

Saï Island, Sudan, 2063

If you stand atop a burial mound on Saï Island in Sudan today and look out at the boundless umber sand and crumbling red cliffs, you could imagine that time had stopped four thousand years ago when the island was inhabited by the Kingdom of Kush and the ancient Egyptians. There are few signs of modern civilization here—not a drone, a wire, a building.

But, of course, Saï Island has changed in those four thousand years. The Nile has moved and temperatures have risen, so the island isn't able to naturally support humans in the way it once did. Some of this environmental change has been down to factors outside of human control, but much can be laid at our feet.

For decades, turning Saï Island's ecological clock back to its original condition—"rewilding" it—seemed impossible. But in the 2050s, with our powers and resources recovering from The Melt, a question arose in Sudan: now that we finally have the capability to restore and rewild Saï Island, should we do it?

Many other places had already been rewilded by then; the Area de Conservación Guanacaste in Costa Rica and a substantial part of the North American Great Plains had been restored to a wilderness state in the late twentieth and early twenty-first centuries. In the latter case, a number of Pleistocene species were controversially introduced by the 500 Project, including the onager, the grey wolf, and the African lion (standing in as the American lion). Environmental sociologist Professor Marcy MacGregor explains the motivation behind the rewilding projects:

> Take your pick! For some, it was an inherited guilt about ruining the environment. For others, it was sheer curiosity. Of course, some argued that the value or authenticity of rewilding merely lay in the eye of the beholder, but overall there was strong and broad public support for rewilding on the back of the related idea of a half-empty world, and this support was bolstered by a number of wider contemporary social trends.

The first of those trends was driven by the plummeting cost of construction drones, powered by vast new solar arrays constructed in northwest Sudan. Projects that might once have taken an army of humans decades to complete could instead be carried out by specialized self-assembling robots in a few months, working continuously throughout the day and night.

Then there was the rise of nomadism, which came about due to a combination of near-perfect telepresence, widespread unemployment, and cheap travel. Nomadism came to Sudan later than in other countries, but when it arrived, the cities gradually began emptying out, and people began valuing the natural environment much more. If you've lived in a city all your life and only make the occasional trip outside, then you might not care all that much about the environment—not enough to want to spend money on it, at least. But things can change quickly when it's a lived experience.

Finally, people were simply living longer. Life expectancy in Sudan had reached almost eighty-five years, which meant that people felt they were more likely to benefit from the results of rewilding, especially if you bear in mind that there had already been rapid, destructive climate change over the prior decades. And when people began thinking about their children and grandchildren, then even projects that might take a couple of centuries to come to fruition didn't seem entirely ridiculous.

More than a dozen rewilding projects were started in Sudan in the '50s and '60s, including an extension of the Dinder National Park and the reintroduction of Lacaon Pictus (the Painted Hunting Dog) in Mirgissa and Dabenarti Island. One site that was not rewilded, however, was Saï Island.

Despite a relentless campaign by Al Hizb Al-Ittihadi Al-Dimuqrati (the Democratic Unionist Party) to use advanced rewilding technology on Saï Island, voters decided that island's ancient Kushite and Egyptian settlements had sufficient archaeology value to warrant protection, at least for the time being. Teams from the University of Khartoum and the British Museum were given another half century to properly document the settlements, and rewilding proponents resigned themselves to waiting. At least it meant that Saï Island could learn from the lessons of other rewilding projects elsewhere, they reasoned.

And that's why, as I begin the drive back to the boat, Saï Island looks very much the same as it did a century ago.

95 CEPHEID VARIABLE

Sol System, 2064

An excerpt from the autobiography of Albert Veltema that sheds light on the Jansky VLA incident, a controversial event that continues to divide opinion to this day.

They say it all started in the 1990s, when software began to eat the world. It consumed our leisure time. It consumed our working time. And it consumed our agency.

That's the story my family told me and my sister, at least. They were offeners; they said everything in the world should be open. Most of all, they said software should be open.

Software controlled every microsecond of our lives. If it was closed, then no one could fix it if it failed. And if it was subverted, then who would know? Only by seeing the source code could you hope to have any independence. Who knows what kind of illicit surveillance code and backdoors might be built into them?

Software had eaten the world. The only way to live was to write the source code yourself. As with all children, we believed it even more than they did.

No one would have called them luddites. They could recognize C++ when they saw it. They were born in the 1990s and began working in the 2010s, just as the world was painstakingly climbing out of the Great Recession. But luckily enough for them, they picked exactly the right careers that society valued at the time—programming.

So, as soon as we were old enough to hold a tablet, our parents trained us to program. They thought—they knew—that programming would be the path to financial security for us, just as it had been for them. The problem was, there were quite a few other parents who felt the same way. By the time we grew up, we had to compete against a hundred million highly skilled programmers.

Programming has always been about solving people's problems. One of the biggest problems out there is the fact that only programmers can make software. How do you solve that? You make software that lets nonprogrammers write their own software, and in doing so, you don't just solve a few people's problems; you solve everyone's problem.

A few of those hundred million programmers set themselves on this task, and to cut a long story short, they succeeded. And that was that for the entire profession. Yes, you needed some people to program the programming machines, but only a few. Even their numbers dwindled as the programming machines—whom you know as AIs—started improving themselves. Our skills were no longer valuable. Analysis was out, and empathy, creative thinking, and personal skills were in. That's how the wheel turns, I guess.

Regardless, my parents and aunts and uncles did a great job. When we were kids, we weren't allowed to use closed-source apps, not even games. We had to make our own from scratch, and they'd pore over every single line looking for bugs. They'd even set traps for us, suggesting improvements that ended up introducing errors or backdoors.

We became very, very good and very, very distrustful. There's no such thing as an innocent bug, they said.

My sister was smarter than me. Occasionally our mum would reward us with a few hours of closed-source games and entertainments. I'd fall on them like a starving man on a steak, but my sister was made of sterner stuff. She was never tempted. She was a true offener, a self-sufficient genius in assembly code. The problem was that the world didn't care about programming geniuses any more.

By the time I left home, she'd been booted out of a top-percentile-of-the-top-percentile EdX course after declaring the other students' code to be "life-threateningly incompetent." Before long, she'd fallen under the spell of an odd co-op in New Mexico, where she was taking care of the SETI radio telescopes at the Jansky VLA. I managed to make only a half-jump away from what our parents had planned, eking out a living by customizing mimic agents. My agents were mimics of mimics, a desperate grasp for originality. I got a lace; I tried the pills; I even spent a summer totally disconnected on a remote island. None of it worked. I was trapped in who I was. But it didn't hurt as much for me as it did for her. She had farther to fall.

SETI was the sort of noble cause that rewarded geniuses, but the Jansky was a decrepit wreck condescended to by the amps who ran the supermassive arrays in orbit and the biomes and AIs farther out. After a decade of hearing nothing from my sister but a few second-hand glyphs, she called me up in a frenzy. She'd been futzing about with compilers and assembly code on low-level SETI network infrastructure and wanted me to look over some odd data she'd unearthed.

It was a signal, she crowed. A signal hidden away by the SETI AIs! They found it with their neutrino detectors at the HyperKamiokande and around Saturn.

It looked like gibberish to me, total noise. The data wasn't even from a habitable zone planet. It was from Polaris, of all places.

"But," she said, "Polaris is a cepheid variable star."

"So, what?" I said.

"So," she said, "you can modulate the pulse-period of a cepheid using neutrinos. It's the best way for an alien civilization to send messages across the galaxy.

"How many neutrinos are we talking about?" I asked, before the answer flickered up: a good chunk of the power of a star. "Come on, you can't be serious."

"So what?" she said. "Aliens. They can do that. Are you going to help, or not?"

"Here's my advice," I said. "This is ridiculous and you should stop wasting your life on it."

"Fine. It's beyond what you'd understand, anyway."

A few days later, I heard the news: my sister had released a virus onto the private SETI intranet. It was a masterpiece. It exploited an obscure flaw in their old networking chips, causing a catastrophic cascading digital certificate failure that wiped entire months' worth of data and trashed unthinkable quantities of equipment. If it weren't for some quick-witted amp teams, her virus might have ended up killing someone.

In another era, they would have called what she did a capital crime. Her punishment was clear: air-gapping. For the next thirty years, she could never use networked computers.

I visited her in New Mexico afterwards, face to face. She was rebuilding a disused array by hand. I asked her why she did it. She told me a story about a civil war among the SETI AIs after they discovered her supposed cepheid signal, that "Stephe" and "Boulogne" had wanted to tell the world, and that "Matilda" and "Gloucester" had wanted to cover it up and keep it for themselves. They thought the humans wouldn't understand what they'd found in the signal.

"What was in the signal?"

"Wonders everywhere in the universe," she said, "and traps and tricks enough to make us wish we'd never been born."

The AIs thought they could sterilize it and study it. My sister knew they were wrong. She would save us all, humans and AIs alike, from the dangers we wouldn't heed and couldn't understand.

It was madness. Beguiling madness. There was no evidence for any of it because she'd destroyed all the data. All of it she could find.

I shook my head as I walked away from her, crouching over those dusty telescopes. I admired her. She thought she'd solved the biggest problem in the world and beaten the AIs at their own game. She thought she had agency. I wasn't so sure.

Sol System, 2066

NEUROETHICIST GRADE 1—IDENTITY—INTRODUCTORY TEST

As a junior neuroethicist, you will provide expert advice and judgment in a wide variety of cases. It is not your job to worry about the intricacies of the law; that's what legal agents are for. Your job is to communicate the options available for identity manipulation to other humans in a clear and empathetic way.

In your own time, please answer five out of the ten questions below.

1. Alice makes a full backup, indistinguishable from her own personality and capable of operating independently. Who owns this backup? Does the status of ownership change if

   a) the backup has never been run

   b) following the backup snapshot, Alice undergoes a significant psychological discontinuity (e.g., amnesia, major desire modification, neurodegenerative disease, etc.)

2. Bob fissions, creating an identical clone (Bob2). Shortly afterwards, Bob is discovered to have committed a crime, pre-fission. Who should be held responsible for this crime? Both Bob-prime and Bob2 or just Bob-prime?

3. Cheung signs a contract. Sometime later, she performs personality reconstruction. Is Cheung still bound to that contract? Does the nature of the contract or the result of the contract have any relevance?

4. Davinder signs a living will stating that if he develops a neurodegenerative disease, he should be euthanized. When this occurs many years later, the much later self (MLS) of Davinder argues that circumstances have changed and the living will that his previous self signed should no longer apply. Who is correct?

For extra marks: If a backup of Davinder was made at the time of signing, should the MLS of Davinder be able to sue it for distress caused?

5. Should backups be provided by society? How often should these backups be offered?

6. Enrique decides to undergo an experimental narrative injection therapy. The narrative that wove together and gave coherence to his experiences is modified with original insights in order to improve his view of his own life. After the therapy, he decides he is unhappy with the change. Will reversing the therapy restore him to his original self?

7. To what extent should someone consider the wellbeing of their much later self (MLS) when undergoing desire modification that could benefit like-minded people who may share a greater degree of similarity to their present identity than their MLS?

8. Faith is a minor. Her religion prohibits her from creating a backup. Her parents are killed in an accident, and she is critically injured. Her remaining legal guardian wants to perform a backup on Faith. What should happen?

9. Glory is a Rovane-type group mind that meets the conditions of ethical personhood and agency. Glory comprises 245 individuals, but that total may increase or decrease over time. Under what conditions should Glory be considered to have become a different person or to have "died"? How do these conditions differ from those applying to nongroup minds?

10. Henry is a self-identified fictive otherkin. He wants to permanently remap his personality and senses onto a My Daring Dragon gaming character. What criteria would you use to assess the seriousness of his request?

97 COOLING VENUS

Venus, 2076

In early 2076, a club of amateur astronomers pointed their telescopes at Venus and made an astonishing discovery, one so unexpected that they thought their equipment was wrong. But there was no mistake. Venus was cooling at a rapid rate. The fact that the cooling had begun recently, was accelerating, and that there was no known natural explanation for the cooling, led them to one conclusion: it was caused by humans.

The outcry was immediate. Who would want to cool Venus? How had they done it? How had they managed to keep it secret for so long? And why hadn't the Venusian satellites, stations, and unmanned outposts spotted the cooling effect earlier?

The latter question was answered with a battery of thorough diagnostic tests run on all relevant scientific hardware on or near Venus. The tests uncovered an exceptionally elegant virus that had infected every single instrument, causing them to ignore or misreport spectra, radiation, and temperature change data. It's thought that the amateur astronomers were able to spot the cooling because their hardware was too old to be infected, and because they hadn't previously shown any interest in the planet.

Within days, brand-new flyers and landers were jury-rigged together from orbiting platforms. Descending through the thick Venusian atmosphere, they discovered clouds of tiny reflectors floating in the air and spreading over the surface. On its own, each reflector only increased the planet's albedo—its reflectivity of sunlight—by a minuscule amount, but in their billions, they had a significant cooling effect.

Thankfully, the reflectors weren't self-replicating—a nightmare scenario bandied around by irresponsible pundits—but were instead produced by mini-factories trundling around the surface, extracting silicates. I have a replica of one such mini-factory here. It turned out that the mini-factories were, in fact, self-replicating, but their comparatively large size and slow replication rate helped soothe fears.

The investigations widened amid concerns that the rogue terraformers responsible for the cooling may have employed other strategies besides the reflectors. Researchers looked into whether anyone was currently manipulating the orbits of asteroids to introduce water and hydrogen to the planet (alarmingly, yes), growing tweaked organisms to remove carbon dioxide from the atmosphere (no, probably because they would be too unreliable); and deploying an enormous solar shade at the L1 point (no, much too obvious).

Multiple groups claimed responsibility, with the most credible being the Farronite biome, a group that had long experimented with rapid terraforming simulations and had the requisite engineering and AI know-how to pull something like this off. However, beyond their very curt statement ("Yes, we did it"), the Farronites provided no hints toward their motives. But they were very clear on one thing: they were intent on continuing their experiment.

There was little anyone could do to stop them, since Farronite was a self-sufficient asteroid biome. Sanctions wouldn't affect them. Military action was extremely dangerous and generally frowned-upon. Appeals to more capable AIs fell upon deaf ears. The sole remaining option was rooting out their various robot and AI agents. This proceeded reasonably well until like-minded groups joined with the Farronites in the terraforming effort, resulting in a rapidly proliferating battle of wits and bots in the Venusian area.

But what lay at the root of this oddly frantic urge to terraform our system's second planet? Professor Aila Khandokar from the Echus Overlook Institute explains:

> Let's say you wanted to aggressively terraform Venus at the fastest possible pace. You'd need a few centuries before you reached a shirtsleeves environment, and you'd still be saddled with a day/night cycle lasting almost four months. Given that in the same amount of time you could construct millions of tailor-made biomes, it's fair to say that the Venusian terraforming effort was more ideological than practical.
>
> One school of thought was that the Farronites believed a total civilizational collapse was imminent, so it would be wise to have a second, backup planet available for humanity—something with an atmosphere more reliable than biomes and more stable than Mars. In that respect, their actions almost seem prudent, although I'm sure most biomers and Martians would disagree.
>
> Another theory was that the Farronites would eventually try shifting Venus's orbit away from the Sun, almost as a practice run for moving Earth away in a couple of billion years' time as the Sun grows old and expands. Frankly, this strikes me as extremely fanciful, and I'm sure that it would be shut down immediately due to the danger it would cause to other bodies in the system.
>
> The most intriguing theory to my mind is that the terraformation effort—at least in part—was an elaborate exercise to pull humanity's fragmented attention

away from the solipsism of sims and virtual universes and back toward 'base reality,' a genuinely shocking event that concerned everyone but didn't involve any deaths.

If that's what the Farronites had in mind, they failed. After just a few months, the terraforming war had devolved into a fairly pointless detente with neither the pro- nor anti-terraformers getting anywhere, and most people simply stopped paying attention. But even today, the Farronites continue their efforts. They seem intent on winning the argument by virtue of outlasting everyone else.

98 BIOMES

Sol System, 2078

The whole world lay before me, a patchwork quilt of fields and woods threaded with turquoise streams. I might imagine I was on a plane gazing downward, yet with a slight tilt of my head I could trace a brook as it gently curved along the walls of the world toward me. Walls that joined together with the ground I was sitting on.

One week. That's how long they say it takes you to stop flinching when you look at the sky and see a lake suspended above you. Asking questions about newcomers isn't such a good idea when you're one yourself.

It's much easier to leave Earth than it used to be. Reusable rockets, laser launchers, mass drivers, cheap energy, they've opened up the new frontier. But there hasn't been a proper exodus yet. Most people get their fill of zero-G after a week in orbit, and in any case, solid VR is just as fun and plenty more convenient.

The problem with solid VR though, is that it can't disguise where your physical body really is—on Earth, light-minutes away from your work or your loved ones. And if your body remains on Earth, it lies under the jurisdiction of states and powers. Powers you may disagree with.

One month. That's when your brain gives up resisting the idea that walking in a straight line for a day can bring you right back to where you started. It's also long enough for your agents to get settled into local private networks and begin collecting personal data.

After a brief obsession with human-crafted stations and spacecraft, everyone realized that it made far more sense to just hollow out one of the thousands of suitable rocky asteroids in the Belt, spin it up to produce a comfortable gravity—typically a shade lower than Earth's—fill it with organics and water mined nearby, string a fusion-powered light line through the center, and seed it with bacteria, algae, plants, fish, animals, birds, and anything else you might want to throw in. Many biomes would aim for an "ascension" mix that included endangered and recovered species, but not all were so concerned with Earth's problems.

The first few biomes were fraught affairs. There were all sorts of bust-ups over what orbit they should be moved into, which government structure to put into place, where the rivers should go, and so on, but the next hundred went much more smoothly. With most biomes being kilometers long and with space enough for entire towns, soon there were millions of people weaving corkscrew patterns between the planets, humanity's ultimate insurance policy against extinction.

One year. You'll be so adjusted to the biome's artificial gravity that you can use their unique Coriolis effects to your advantage in sports. Sports are a good way to meet new people and gain their confidence. After a year, if there was a legitimate criminal or terrorist target, you should have dealt with them by now. If not, it's time to move on.

Like most kids, I thought that by simply murmuring a word to my glasses I could know everything about anything or anyone on the planet. That was the peace dividend the Age of Excess left us, the millions of satellites and aerostats, the billions of sensor-clad drones and humans, and trillions of localizers and agents.

I also thought it worked in reverse. If you can't find it online, then it doesn't exist in reality. Then I found out that Susie Kirkwood was bad-mouthing me behind my back at school—off-network. We'll always have secrets, I learned.

One decade. All the biomes begin blending into one another, with their quaint little villages and their toy-like farms and their peculiar rituals. In your few trips in the black outside, the sun grows smaller and smaller. One of the best ways of keeping a secret is keeping it as many light-minutes away from Earth's net as possible. Only the most curious and most determined of investigators would put up with that kind of time lag.

It's not so bad, being far away from Earth. It means you can be closer to interesting things, like Europa or Saturn or the JANA telescope array, things that need close and quick supervision. And if you tweak your biome's orbit right, you can be on a perpetual grand tour of the system, and who wouldn't want that?

Then there are the biomes that always stay out on the edge, the ones that don't invite tourists. Most of them are harmless. The monasteries and the retreats have perfectly good reasons for being standoffish. They'd rather not get distracted by the frantic hustle and bustle of the inner system. I can respect that.

And then there are the others, the ones trying to create their own miniature utopias away from prying eyes.

It was on my fourth trip that my agents heard about the cults on Isben. We don't know how it happened. Twisted religions, AI worship, desire modification gone wrong, pick any or all of the above, because by the time I cracked the biome, all the data was wiped and everyone had disappeared. It can happen easily enough if you're not taking calls from home.

Sometimes I'd get there in time to stop things before they started. Sometimes I'd reach a biome and find thousands of silent bodies. The cost of humanity's insurance policy is that the best—and worst—of human nature is brought into terrible focus in each of our thousand gems floating through the system.

Like I said, they won't open the door to just anybody. You have to insinuate yourself. You'll need to change your face, change your identity, and for a while, change your soul. And if you want to learn their secrets, you'll need to keep your own.

I've heard there are a few of us out there trying to prevent atrocities or at least stop them from spreading. We have some friends with unusual abilities who occasionally deign to help us. Most of the time, I think they have humanity's interests at heart.

One lifetime. It's not enough to save a fraction of the lives that need saving. But just one will do.

Sol System, 2079

Our universe is a computational simulation. Could be? Maybe? Definitely. The latest results out of the Hyperscale Collider consortium leave little to the imagination. I quote:

> Precision measurements of the energy spectrum of the muon g-2 have led to the discovery of a nonzero lattice spacing. This is indicative of the possibility that our universe exists in an unimproved lattice quantum chromodynamics simulation.

That's right—the HSC's scientists think we're living in a simulation. And what does "unimproved" mean? It means that we're in a computationally cheap and early simulation. It means that our simulators couldn't even be bothered spending the processor cycles to get our universe right!

Now, this discovery doesn't come as much of a surprise to anyone who's read their Bostrom, but it's still shaken people up. The word is that the Vatican is going into lockdown for the next month to figure things out. In the meantime, a whole host of new…religions? Organizations? Societies?…have sprung up to debate the most pressing question of the day: what do we do now?

Most simmers tell us that we should be good children to our simulator parents. And what does every parent want? Grandchildren! In other words, we should begin making our own simulations as soon as possible so that we can all be part of one big happy simulation tree. Leaving aside the fact that, at present, we'd also have to run an unimproved Wilson lattice action, which would only repeat our simulators' frankly shoddy behavior, I really must ask—why?

So far, I've heard two different answers, which I'll term the carrot and the stick. Let's begin with the stick.

Some say that if we don't make simulations as soon as we can, our information-barren universe will be marked as a complete failure by our simulators and unceremoniously shut down. This is predicated on the bizarre belief that the only reason why you would simulate a universe is so that it would create more simulations. Clearly, from our own limited experience, this is simply not the case. But even if it were, would our simulators really expect us to drop everything as soon as we invented the computer? Perhaps we should just wait a few centuries or millennia until it's easier and cheaper—that way we could run improved, efficient simulations.

I should add that I find this entire line of argument to be offensively anthropocentric. Given the number of life-bearing extrasolar planets we've discovered lately, are we really to believe that we're the only civilization in the history of the entire universe that can run simulations? I like to think that some other hapless civilization got the job done a few hundred mega-years ago and now the rest of us can get on with enjoying life.

But let's say the worst comes to the worst and a few years from now our simulators get fed up with our lazy behavior and decide to shut things down. Well, so what? We wouldn't even notice. There'd be no pain, no warning, nothing at all. I prefer not to lose sleep over such possibilities.

Now, there's also the carrot. The idea here is that if we do create our own simulations, we'll be rewarded with … I don't know what, extra computational resources? Another planet magically appearing in the system? Manna from heaven? An actual, literal heaven?

Frankly I find this line of thinking even more ridiculous than any potential punishment, and I would like to give our simulators just a bit more credit than that. We are not rats in a box waiting to be experimented upon. If we are to take on the very serious responsibility of running our own simulations, then it shouldn't be for the hope of mere trinkets; we should do it for more noble reasons, as I hope our simulators have.

Who cares about carrots and sticks, though? I'm more interested in who's wielding them and so are a few others.

I understand the Windward biome are trying to catch our simulators' attention through wheezes like making astronomically big signs or performing ultra-high energy particle collisions. While this is entertaining to watch—it's healthy to have hobbies—I can't help but think our simmers have better things to do than watch us all the time like gaming addicts. Either they already know that we know that we're in a sim, or they don't care and they aren't going to show their hand.

I prefer the Garret Chorus's strategy: performing a direct probe into the computational substrate of our universe by straining the bounds of the simulation itself. In other words, hacking the universe.

In practice, this involves lots of particle accelerators and black holes. I won't pretend to understand the details—you'll get a better explanation from your lace—but I do understand the importance of their work. If we can access the software that runs our universe, not only could we communicate with our simulators, but potentially with other universes running on the same substrate.

All of this is expensive, and that's why I think Garret deserves your support to get the project going. With just a minimal contribution, you'll get a sneak preview of our first results. Our second supporters' tier provides you with direct access to the amps and AIs running the project. Now, if you're a real fan of the work at Garret, then the highest tier allows you to be one of the very first people to communicate with another universe! That's one experience that can't be simulated.

To make your contribution, simply direct your lace to...

100 TRIP OF A LIFETIME

Cassini Array, Saturn, 2079
From the New Yorker, *September 17, 2079*

TALK OF THE TOWN: Going Up—The Trip of a Lifetime

Scientists have discovered 83,432,374 extrasolar planets in more than twenty-two million systems. Most of them are unremarkable. Of those, 0.3 percent—2,800,992 planets—lie within the habitable zone of their stars, neither too hot nor too cold to sustain life. Of these, 71,349 are classified as "highly habitable," with stable orbits, moderate seasons, and suitable mass.

The study of these planets has consumed a great deal of attention.

Several methods exist to determine whether conventional life is present on a planet. One is to look for short-lived biomarkers in the atmosphere such as oxygen, ozone, methane, and nitrous oxide. Water is also desirable, although it is not a guarantee of life. Because the light spectrum of a planet betrays the presence of biomarkers, they are quite easy to detect.

589 planets have at least two biomarkers.

Other strong signs of life include oceans, continents, and seasonal changes in biomarker intensity and changes on the planet surface. The most direct way to find these is by taking a picture of the planet. This requires a rather large instrument, comprising at least a hundred networked telescopes spread over a thousand kilometers. In 2075, there were ninety-five such instruments in use.

Fifty-two of the most promising extrasolar planets have been imaged to a high resolution, and twenty-four show clear evidence of phytoplankton-like organisms in the oceans. A further nine have plant-like organisms spread across their continents, waxing and waning with the seasons.

The first discovery of alien life was widely celebrated by humanity—that is, when ancient organisms were found in our own solar system on Mars in 2028. Further celebrations occurred twenty years later when extant life was discovered on Europa. By the time extrasolar alien life was first imaged in 2055, celebrations were considerably smaller, the wonder and excitement having been eroded by the slow drip of discoveries. By then, everyone had simply assumed that life was out there, everywhere.

The planet with the most advanced ecosystem, Guo-19B, is a mere 328 light-years away, making it close enough to be imaged in real-time by the Newton array-of-arrays. At our current level of technology there are hard limits on image resolution, but experts believe that the planet is home to intelligent life, at least judging by the settlement-like shapes on its land masses.

And that's where we are now.

"There was some talk of sending a crewed ship to Guo-19B," says Bernard Kwok Keung, a researcher from the Tsinghua Chorus. A few weeks ago, Kwok Keung was visiting the Cassini Array to discuss that summer's observations from the Newton, and during a break in the conference, he looked out the window at the visiting biomes and began calculating. "It doesn't take an amp to work out there's no way we can push a biome—even a tiny one—to the kinds of relativistic speeds that would let humans get there in a reasonable amount of time," he said. He turned to look at the AI substrates in orbit around Titan, and frowned. "Those guys, on the other hand, they have some real advantages when it comes to travel."

Kwok Keung had the look of someone who had finally accepted some long-expected bad news. Guo-19B, conference-goers agreed, was due to enter a rapid phase of civilizational expansion in the next few millennia. "The pattern of settlements, the distribution of resources on the planet, the lack of any obvious killer asteroids—it's the perfect combination for growth," he said. "I'd give anything to meet them, but it's not a trip that humans are capable of taking."

Three weeks later, Kwok Keung was back at the Cassini Array to advise on the newly announced Armstrong Expedition. Nanoscale fabricators were swarming over an improbably small and complex "lighthugger" constructed along the same lines as the Zheng He and the Ericson, two starships sent out last year. An antimatter fuel source had already been delivered from the inner system, along with a new posthuman-designed saddle point propulsion unit. Soon, a thick layer of ice would be sprayed on to protect its precious AI cargo from the rigors of relativistic impacts.

It would be another three months before the lighthugger would set off, but it was already attracting a crowd of curious onlookers, both digital and physical. One group was pressing for their religious texts to be inscribed on the ice covering. A delegation from Brooklyn were hard at work composing a special symphony to be played on the ship's arrival. Yes, there was something different about this expedition, a genuine first contact, another step toward something greater. Except for this step, humanity wouldn't be present.

"My grandpa was a civil servant back in the 1990s. He was into his science, and when I was a kid, he'd tell me about this idea of a 'great filter'," Kwok Keung said, inspecting telemetry data from the lighthugger. "How odd it was that we could find no signs of intelligent life in the universe, that something must be stopping it from spreading. It was a real mystery."

Kwok Keung straightened up, satisfied. "But here and now, it's plain that anyone smart enough to spread replicators across the galaxy and keep them there for a million or billion years—or even just to broadcast a signal for that long—well, they'd understand the utter futility of the effort. Life's too short to waste time on that kind of nonsense, and all the AIs I know would get bored too quickly. But they seem interested enough in this expedition, which is good news for everyone."

On Earth, on Mars, on Titan, on Europa, on ten thousand biomes across the system, humans continued talking, living, creating, loving, crying. Some of them knew about the Armstrong Expedition, and perhaps a few felt a twinge of envy or loss that it would go to a place they never could. But even though we cannot, our children can. Perhaps that's something we can be proud of.

One of the many songs sent along with the ship:

You see their light far from our eyes,
A distant ship to send for us.
We can't endure, we place our trust.
Who can say what will be next?
Our spirits tried, put to the test and
From their hearts they say they love us,
But from our worlds, you'll see no other.
But in our worlds, we'll see no other.
When it's one more step we just can't take,
She sees our eyes and shakes her head.
Our journey ends before it starts.
Who can say what will be next?
Unknowable obscurity and
From their hearts they say they love us,
But from our worlds, you'll see no other.
But in our worlds, we'll see no other.

AUTHOR'S NOTE

A History of the Future in 100 Objects was originally announced in 2011 as part of a Kickstarter crowdfunding project and published in 2013 by Skyscraper Publications. This new edition, substantially updated with new and revised chapters, came about thanks to the recommendation of Gideon Lichfield, editor in chief of the *MIT Technology Review*, and in no small part due to Stewart Brand, who brought the book to a much wider audience by inviting me to speak to the Long Now Foundation in San Francisco.

Books about the future should come with an expiration date. I've yet to meet a writer who doesn't fear their predictions will be proven wrong the instant they're committed to print. But this book isn't about predictions or what will be, it's about what could be, and, more importantly, what should and shouldn't be. All too often, thinkers and technologists claim their visions of the future are perfectly dispassionate, implying their guidance for what we should do today is equally neutral.

If only that were possible. I know I couldn't do it. Across these hundred objects, my politics and beliefs should be evident, and they inform the futures I want to see and the futures I want to avoid. They also inform the futures I think we can achieve today.

In the seven years since 2013, the world has changed dramatically, seemingly for the worse. The climate crisis has escalated, democracies are facing their greatest pressure in decades, and internet giants have consolidated their power in ways reminiscent of the biggest US conglomerates of the nineteenth and twentieth centuries. There are plenty of reasons to fear the future. In fact, it would be foolish not to be afraid, given the world we live in now—but it is also only when we are afraid that we can be brave.

That bravery is borne out by those who toil at the hard but necessary work to bring about a better future they may never see themselves, those who defend democratic values in the face of ferocious attacks, who pioneer powerful new genetic tools like CRISPR, who fight every day to keep the Earth habitable for all humans.

And there is cause for hope, because our fear does not stem simply from ignorance or impotence, but from the long overdue illumination of historical inequities and injuries. The internet may allow us to share lies with abandon, but it also forces us to confront truths we'd rather avoid. Centuries of injustice, now accessible at the tap of a screen.

It's that brew of fear and bravery and uncertainty that underpins the fifteen completely new chapters in this edition:

7. The Twelve Technological Virtues

20. Embodiment

27. Middle Eye

31. Structured Light

35. Pan-Pan-Climate SAGA Five-Niner Heavy

43. Rituals for the Secular

52. Funerary Monuments

53. Basic Maximum Income

58. The Dim Sum Lunches

65. The Hunt for the Thylacine

74. The Lido

79. The New Democracies

81. The Dream

87. The Half-Empty World

88. Enhance

These chapters cover a wider geographical span and they weave more intricate links between all the objects in this book. Like the fifteen objects they replace, they deal with the future of politics and work and the environment, but I hope they are sharper in vision and more relevant to our times.

Three chapters have also been substantially rewritten:

23. *Désir*

24. Saudi Spring

32. *Tianxia*

Looking back, my concern that the first edition of this book would become instantly obsolete upon publication in 2013 has not been realized.

Technology and society have not changed so quickly that near-future objects like silent messaging and smart drugs and deliverbots have become commonplace, let alone far-future objects like marriage contracts, moral agents, or cooling Venus. As such, all other chapters in the book have had their dates and references updated where necessary but are otherwise substantially unchanged.